the weird
sisters

the weird sisters

ELEANOR BROWN

HarperCollins*Publishers*

HarperCollins*Publishers*
77–85 Fulham Palace Road,
Hammersmith, London W6 8JB

www.harpercollins.co.uk

Published by HarperCollins*Publishers* 2011
1

A catalogue record for this book
is available from the British Library

ISBN 978 0 00 739372 5

Set in Meridien by Palimpsest Book Production Limited,
Falkirk, Stirlingshire

Printed and bound in Great Britain by
Clays Ltd, St Ives plc

Mixed Sources
Product group from well-managed
forests and other controlled sources
www.fsc.org Cert no. SW-COC-001806
© 1996 Forest Stewardship Council

FSC is a non-profit international organisation established
to promote the responsible management of the world's forests.
Products carrying the FSC label are independently certified
to assure consumers that they come from forests that are managed
to meet the social, economic and ecological needs
of present and future generations.

Find out more about HarperCollins and the environment at
www.harpercollins.co.uk/green

TO CHRIS

For springtime, for a rock-and-roll show, forever

But we only called the fire brigade, and soon the fire engine came and three tall men in helmets brought a hose into the house and Mr Prothero got out just in time before they turned it on. Nobody could have had a noisier Christmas Eve. And when the firemen turned off the hose and were standing in the wet, smoky room, Jim's Aunt, Miss Prothero, came downstairs and peered in at them. Jim and I waited, very quietly, to hear what she would say to them. She said the right thing, always. She looked at the three tall firemen in their shining helmets, standing among the smoke and cinders and dissolving snowballs, and she said, 'Would you like anything to read?'

– DYLAN THOMAS,
A Child's Christmas in Wales

I dreamt last night of the three weird sisters.

– WILLIAM SHAKESPEARE, *Macbeth*

PROLOGUE

We came home because we were failures. We wouldn't admit that, of course, not at first, not to ourselves, and certainly not to anyone else. We said we came home because our mother was ill, because we needed a break, a momentary pause before setting off for the Next Big Thing. But the truth was, we had failed, and rather than let anyone else know, we crafted careful excuses and alibis, and wrapped them around ourselves like a cloak to keep out the cold truth. The first stage: denial.

For Cordelia, the youngest, it began with the letters. They arrived the same day, though their contents were so different that she had to look back at the postmarks to see which one had been sent first. They seemed so simple, paper in her hands, vulnerable to rain, or fire, or incautious care, but she would not destroy them. These were the kind you save, folded into a memory box, to be opened years later with fingers against crackling age, heart pounding with the sick desire to be possessed by memory.

We should tell you what they said, and we will, because their contents affect everything that happened afterward, but we first have to explain how our family communicates, and to do that, we have to explain our family.

1

Oh, man.

Perhaps we had just better explain our father.

If you took a college course on Shakespeare, our father's name might be resident in some dim corner of your mind, under layers of unused telephone numbers, forgotten dreams, and the words that never seem to make it to the tip of your tongue when you need them. Our father is Dr James Andreas, professor of English literature at Barnwell College, singular focus: The Immortal Bard.

The words that might come to mind to describe our father's work are insufficient to convey to you what it is like to live with someone with such a singular preoccupation. Enthusiast, expert, obsessed – these words all thud hollow when faced with the sandstorm of Shakespeare in which we were raised. Sonnets were our nursery rhymes. The three of us were given advice and instruction in couplets; we were more likely to refer to a hated playmate as a 'fat-kidneyed rascal' than a jerk; we played under the tables at Christmas parties where phrases like 'deconstructionist philosophy' and 'patriarchal malfeasance' drifted down through the heavy tablecloths with the carols.

And this only begins to describe it.

But it is enough for our purposes.

The first letter was from Rose: precise pen on thick vellum. From *Romeo and Juliet*; Cordy knew it at once. *We met, we woo'd and made exchange of vow, I'll tell thee as we pass; but this I pray, That thou consent to marry us to-day.*

And now you will understand this was our oldest sister's way of telling us that she was getting married.

The second was from our father. He communicates almost exclusively through pages copied from *The Riverside Shakespeare*. The pages are so heavily annotated with decades of thoughts, of interpretations, that we can barely make out the lines of text he highlights. But it matters

2

not; we have been nursed and nurtured on the plays, and the slightest reminder brings the language back.

Come, let us go; and pray to all the gods/For our beloved mother in her pains. And this is how Cordy knew our mother had cancer. This is how she knew we had to come home.

ONE

Cordy had never stolen anything before. As a matter of pride, when our friends were practising their light-fingered shuffles across the shelves of Barnwell's stores in our teens, she had refused to participate, refused even to wear the cheap earrings and clumpy lipstick or listen to the shoplifted music. But here she was in this no-name desert town, facing off against the wall of pregnancy tests, knowing full well she didn't have the money to pay for one. A Wild West shootout: Cordy versus the little pink sticks at high noon.

She'd wanted to do this somewhere anonymous, in a wide-aisled store that hummed with soft, inoffensive music and belonged to a company, not a person, but those stores had long ago gotten smart, put anti-theft devices like hunch-shouldered guardians at the doors. So she was in this dusty little mom and pop drugstore, her stomach churning, cheeks bright with fire.

'Strike up the drum; cry "Courage!" and away,' she whispered to herself, and then giggled, one thin hand sneaking out to grab one of the boxes – any one, it didn't matter. They'd all tell her the thing she already knew but refused to admit.

She slipped the box into her gaping shoulder bag with

one hand, the other rooting around at the bottom for the remnants of her last, months-ago paycheck, the few loose coins buried in a grave of stale breath mints, lint, and broken pens. Along the way, she grabbed a toffee bar off the shelf and presented it to the cashier, digging for a few more pennies, her hand burning when she brushed against the box hidden in the loose depths.

Outside the store, a rush of elation. 'Too easy,' she said aloud to the empty street, her skirt whispering against the sidewalk, already gone hot and sullen in the rise of spring, her sandals so worn that she could feel the insistent warmth against her heels. The pleasure of the forbidden lasted until she had made it back to the house, ramshackle and dark, where she was staying, a few people crashed on the broken furniture in the living room, sleeping off last night's excess. She yanked open the box, tossing the instructions in the direction of the trash can, and did the deed. Huddled on the toilet in the bathroom, tile cracked and shredding beneath her feet, staring at the pink line, pale as fading newsprint, her conscience caught up with her.

'It doesn't get much lower than this, old Cordy, old sock,' she could hear Bean telling her cheerfully.

'How are you going to take care of a baby if you can't even afford a pregnancy test?' Rose harped.

Cordy brushed our imaginary voices aside and buried the evidence in the trash can. It didn't make a difference, really, she told herself. She'd been headed home anyway, wandering a circuitous loop, going where the wind or the next ride took her. This just confirmed what she'd already known – that after seven years of floating like a dandelion seed, it was time to settle down.

Settle down. She shuddered.

Those words were a bell ringing inside her. That was, after all, why she'd left. Just before exams in the spring of her junior year at Barnwell College, she'd been in the study lounge in the psychology department, lying on the industrial carpet, her arms locked as she held a textbook above her face. Two women, seniors, were talking nearby – one of them was getting married, the other going to graduate school. Cordy lowered the book to her chest, its weight pressing harder and harder against her heart as she listened to the litany of What Was to Come. Wedding favours and student loans. Mortgages and health insurance. Careers and taxes. Unable to breathe, she shoved the book onto the floor and walked out of the lounge. If that was the future, she wanted no part of it.

It was our fault, probably, the way we'd always babied her. Or maybe it was our father's fault – Cordelia had always been his favourite. He'd never said no to her, not to her breathless baby cries, not to her childhood entreaties for ballet lessons (dropped before they got to fourth position, though she did wear the tutu for an awful long time after that, so it wasn't a total waste), and not to the desperate late-night calls for cash infusions in the years she'd spent drifting around the country, accomplishing nothing in particular. She was the Cordelia to his Lear, legendary in her devotion. *He always lov'd our sister most.* But whoever's fault it was, Cordy had thus far refused to grow up, and we'd indulged that in the same way we'd indulged every other whim she'd had for nearly her entire life. After all, we could hardly blame her. We were fairly certain that if anyone made public the various and variegated ways in which being an adult sucked eggs, more people might opt out entirely.

But now? Growing up didn't seem so much like a choice any more. Cordy fumbled around through one of the bedrooms until she found a calendar, counting backwards. It was almost June now, she was fairly certain. And she'd left Oregon, the last stop on that long, strange trip,

7

in, what, February? She rubbed her knuckles on her forehead, thinking. It had been so long since things like dates mattered.

But she could trace the journey back, before she'd started feeling so empty and nauseated in the mornings, before her breasts had grown tender enough that even the material of a T-shirt seemed like it was scraping against her skin, before the endless fatigue that swept over her at the strangest times, before she'd known. Washington, California, Arizona. Her period had come in Arizona; she dimly remembered a tussle with a recalcitrant tampon dispenser in a rest stop bathroom. And then she'd gone to New Mexico, where there'd been a painter, much older, his hair painted with shocking strands of white, his skin wrinkled from the sun, his hands broad and callused. She'd paused there for a few weeks, waitressing a handful of shifts to make money for the rest of the trip home, not that it had lasted. He'd come into the restaurant to eat, all by himself, and it had been so late, and his eyes were so lonely. For a week she'd stayed with him, spending the days curled on a couch in his studio, reading and staring out over the arroyos while he painted in silence: strange, contorted swirls of colour that dripped off the canvases onto the floor. But he'd been gentle, and blessedly quiet, and after so much Sturm und Drang, she'd nearly been sad to leave. The last night, there'd been a broken condom, a hushed argument, dark dreams, and the next morning she had been gone.

Slumping on the bed, Cordy let the calendar fall from her hands. What was she supposed to do now? Go back to New Mexico and tell the painter? She doubted he'd be excited to hear the news. She wasn't exactly thrilled herself. Maybe she'd have a miscarriage. Heroines in novels were always having serendipitously timed miscarriages that saved them from having to make sticky decisions. And Cordy had always been awfully lucky.

Until now.

Cordy stepped over the piles of dirty clothes on the floor and back into the hallway. The crashers in the living room were still snoring as she tiptoed through to the kitchen, where she'd left her backpack. She'd lived here one winter – it seemed like years ago, but it couldn't have been that long, since this was the address the letters had come to. Had it been years ago? Had it really been years since she had been in one place long enough to have an address?

Gritting her teeth, Cordy began shoving things into the bag. She didn't know what to do. But that was okay. Someone would figure this out for her. Someone would take care of her. Someone always took care of her.

No problem.

Bean absolutely and positively did not believe in anything even vaguely paranormal. But for the past week or so, she'd had the strangest feeling that something bad was coming. She woke up in the morning with a hard pit in her stomach, as though she'd swallowed something malignant, growing, and the weight stayed with her all day, making her heels clack more sharply on the subway steps, her body ache after only a few minutes of running on the treadmill, jewel-toned cocktails simmer in her stomach until she left them in their glasses to sweat into water on the mahogany bars of the city's trendiest watering holes.

Nothing in her bag of tricks made the feeling go away – not seducing a hapless investment banker over the din of a club, not a punishing spin class that left her so rubbery and tired that she vomited into the toilet at the gym, not a new pair of shoes that cost as much as the rent she paid for her tiny closet of a bedroom in a shared apartment in Manhattan. As a matter of fact, that last one made the rock inside her turn into steel.

When the moment she had been dreading finally came, the managing partner of the law firm she worked at arriving at her desk and asking to see her in his office, it was almost a relief. *'If it were done, when 'tis done, then 'twere well it were done quickly,'* she quoted to herself, following his wizened steps into his office.

'Have a seat, Bianca,' he said.

In New York, everyone called her Bianca. Men, upon asking for her number in a terminally hip watering hole, would have to ask her to repeat it, and then, upon comprehension, would smile. Something about the name – and, honestly, few of them had the synapses to rub together at that point in the evening to make any sort of literary connections, so it must have been something else – made her even more attractive to them.

To us, however, she would always be Bean. And it was still the way she spoke to herself. 'Nice going, Bean,' she would say when she dropped something, and her room-mates in the city would look at her curiously. But being Bianca was a part she played well, and she wondered if part of the sickness she felt inside was knowing that performance was coming to an end. Forever.

She perched on the edge of one of the leather wing chairs in his sitting area. He sat in the other. 'We've been doing a bit of an accounting audit, you see,' he said without preamble.

Bean stared at him. The pit inside her stomach was turning into fire. She stared at him, his beetled, bushy eyebrows, his soft, wrinkled hands, and wanted to cry.

'We've found a number of . . . shall we say, anomalies in the payroll records. In your favour. I'd like to think they're errors.' He looked almost hopeful.

She said nothing.

'Can you tell me what's been happening, Bianca?'

Bean looked down at the bracelet on her wrist. She'd bought it at Tiffany months ago, and she remembered the strange seizing in her stomach as she'd handed over her credit card, the same feeling she'd gotten lately when she bought anything, from groceries to a handbag. The feeling that her luck was running out, that she couldn't go on, and maybe (most terrifying of all), maybe she didn't want to.

'They aren't errors,' Bean said, but her voice caught on the last word, so she cleared her throat and tried again, louder. 'They aren't errors.' She folded her hands in her lap.

The managing partner looked unsurprised, but disappointed. Bean wondered why they'd chosen him for this particular dirty work – he was practically emeritus, holding on to this corner office for no good reason other than to have a place to escape from his wife and while away the hours until he died. She considered trying to sleep with him, but he was looking at her with such grandfatherly concern the idea withered on the vine before she could even fully imagine it. Truthfully, she felt something that could only be described as gratitude that it was him, not one of the other partners whose desperation to push themselves to the top had made their tongues sharp as teeth, whose bellows of frustration came coursing down the hallways like a swelling tide when things dared not go their way.

'Are you well?' he asked, and the kindness in his voice made her heart twist. She bit her tongue hard, blinked back tears. She would not cry. Not in front of him, anyway. Not here. 'It's a great deal of money, Bianca. Was there some reason . . . ?' His question trailed off hopefully.

She could have lied. Maybe she should have been picturing this scene all along, planning for it. She was good

11

at the theatre of life, our Bean, she could have played any part she wanted. But lying seemed desperate and weak, and she was suddenly exhausted. She wanted nothing more than to lie down and sleep for days.

'No,' she said. She couldn't meet his eyes. 'No good reason.'

He sighed at that, a long, slow exhale that seemed to make the air move differently in the room. 'We could call the police, you know.'

Bean's eyes widened. She'd never thought about that. Why had she never thought about that? She'd known stealing from her employers was wrong, but somehow she'd never let herself think that it was actually criminal (criminal! How had it come to that?). God, she could go to jail. She saw herself in a cell, in an orange jumpsuit, stripped of her bracelet and her makeup and all the armour that living in the city required of her. She was speechless.

'But I don't think that's entirely necessary. You've done good work for us. And I know what it's like to be young in this city. And it's so unpleasant, involving the police. I'd imagine that your resignation will be enough. And, of course, you'll repay your debt.'

'Of course,' Bean said. She was still frozen, wondering how she'd managed to miscalculate so badly, wondering if she really was going to squeak out of here with nothing but a slap on the wrist, or if she'd be nabbed halfway out of the lobby, handcuffs on her wrists, her box of personal effects scattering on the marble floor while everyone looked on at the spectacle.

'It might be worthwhile for you to take a little time. Go home for a bit. You're from Kentucky, aren't you?'

'Ohio,' Bean said, and it was only a whisper.

'Right. Go back to the Buckeye State. Spend a little time. Re-evaluate your priorities.'

Bean forced back the tears that were, again, welling out of control. 'Thank you,' she said, looking up at him. He was, miraculously, smiling.

'We've all done foolish, foolish things, dear. In my experience, good people punish themselves far more than any external body can manage. And I believe you are a good person. You may have lost your way more than a little bit, but I believe you can find your way back. That's the trick. Finding your way back.'

'Sure,' Bean said, and her tongue was thick with shame. It might have been easier if he had been angry, if he'd taken her to task the way he really should have, called the police, started legal proceedings, done something that equalled the horrible way she'd betrayed their trust and pissed on everything she knew to be good and right in the service of nothing more than a lot of expensive clothes and late-night cab rides. She wanted him to yell, but his voice remained steady and quiet.

'I don't recommend you mention your employment here when you do seek another job.'

'Of course not,' Bean said. He was about to continue, but she pushed her hair back and interrupted him. 'I'm sorry. I'm so, so sorry.'

His hands were steepled in front of him. He looked at her, the way her makeup was smudging around her eyes, despite her impressive ability to hold back the tears. 'I know,' he said. 'You have fifteen minutes to get out of the building.'

Bean fled.

She took nothing from work. She cared about nothing there anyway, had never bothered to make the place her own. She went home and called a friend with a car he'd been trying to sell for junk, though even that would take nearly the last of her ill-gotten gains, and while he drove over, she packed up her clothes, and she wondered how

13

she could have spent all that money and have nothing but clothes and accessories and a long list of men she never wanted to see again to show for it, and the thought made her so ill she had to go into the bathroom and vomit until she could bring up nothing but blood and yellow bile, and she took as much money as she could from the ATM and threw everything she owned into that beater of a car and she left right then, without even so much as a fare-thee-well to the city that had given her . . . well, nothing.

Because Cordelia was the last to find out, she was the last to arrive, though we understand this was neither her intention nor her fault. It was simply her habit. Cordy, last born, came a month later than expected, lazily sweeping her way out of our mother's womb, putting a lie to the idea that labour gets shorter every time. She has been late to everything since then, and is fond of saying she will be late to her own funeral, haw haw haw.

We forgive her for her tardiness, but not for the joke.

Would we all have chosen to come back, knowing that it would be the three of us again, that all those secrets squeezed into one house would be impossible to keep? The answer is irrelevant – it was some kind of sick fate. We were destined to be sisters at birth, and apparently we were destined to be sisters now, when we thought we had put all that behind us.

While Bean and Cordy were dragging their baggage (literal and metaphorical) across the country, Rose was already safely ensconced in our childhood home. Unlike Bean and Cordy, Rose had never been away for very long. For years she had been in the habit of having dinner with our parents once or twice a week, coming home on Sundays. Someone, after all, had to keep an eye on them. They were getting older, Rose told Bean on the phone, with exactly the right amount of sighing to convey that she felt she was doing Bean and Cordy's duty as well as her own. And usually her visits to our house for Sunday dinner felt like duty, equal parts frustration and triumph as she reminded our father that he had to mow the lawn before the neighbours complained, as she bustled around the living room putting bookmarks in books left open, their spines straining under the weight, as she reminded our mother that she actually had to open the mail, not just bring it inside. It was a good thing, Rose invariably told herself when she left (with not a little satisfaction on her face) that she was here. Who knows what kind of disarray they'd fall into without her?

But moving home? At the advanced age of thirty-three? Like, for permanent, as Cordy might say?

She should have been living in the city with her fiancé, Jonathan, having recently signed her first contract as a tenured professor, waving her engagement ring around wildly whenever she came back to Barnwell just to show that she was, in fact, not just the smart one, that Bean was not the only one who could land a man, and our father was not the only professorial genius in the family. This is how it should have been. This is how it was:

ACT I

Setting: Airport interior, and Jonathan's apartment, just after winter break
Characters: Jonathan, Rose, travellers

Rose had changed positions a dozen times as the passengers on Jonathan's flight came streaming through the airport gates. She was looking for the right position for him to catch her in; the right balance of careless inattention and casual beauty, neither of which would betray how much she had missed him.

But when he finally did emerge, cresting over the gentle grade of the ramp that led from the gate, when she could see his rumpled hair bobbing above the heads of the other passengers, the graceful way his tall, reedy shoulders were bent forward as though he were walking into an insistent wind, she forgot her artifice and stood, dropping her book by her side and smoothing her clothes and her hair until he was in front of her and she was in his arms, his mouth warm against her own.

'I missed you,' she said, running her hand down his cheek, marvelling at the fact of his presence. Light stubble brushed against her palm as he moved his chin against her touch, catlike. 'Don't ever go away again.'

He laughed, tipping his head back slightly, and then dropped a kiss on her forehead, shifting his bag over his shoulder to keep it from slipping. 'I've come back,' he said.

'Yes, and you are never allowed to leave again,' Rose said. She'd think back on that later and wonder if his expression had changed, but at the time she didn't notice a thing. She picked up her book and slipped her hand into his as they headed to pick up his luggage.

'Was it that awful? Your sisters didn't come home when they got your father's letter?' He turned to face her so he was standing backwards on the escalator, his hands spread over the rails.

'No, they didn't come home, and thank heavens, because that would have been even worse. It's just been me and Mom and Dad.'

16

'Lonely?' He turned back and stepped off the escalator, holding his hand out to help her step off. Swoon-worthy, as Cordy would have said.

'Ugh. I don't want to talk about it. How was your trip?'

Jonathan had been gone for two weeks, nearly the entire break, presenting at a conference in Germany and stopping on the way back to visit friends in England. Rose had carefully crossed each passing day off in her day planner, feeling like a ridiculous schoolgirl with a crush but unable to stop herself. Ridiculous, she knew. When they had been a couple for only a few months, she'd been the one to utter the magical four-letter word first, breathless and laughing as they lay on his bed and he alternated between kissing her neck and tickling her mercilessly. She'd been thinking that this was love for weeks, but she couldn't say it first, and then the words slipped out in a rush of giddiness. She'd frozen, horrified at her own lack of control, but then he'd whispered back that he loved her, too, and her relief and happiness made her feel faint. Being without him had felt like a cruel amputation, and she reached out for his hand to remind herself that he was there, after all.

He took her hand in his and lifted it to his mouth, kissing her fingertips. 'You look lovely,' he said. 'I'd forgotten how beautiful you are.'

Rose blushed and shook her head, smoothing her clothes again with her free hand. 'I look awful. I didn't have time to change and –'

Jonathan cut her off with another kiss, this time in the centre of her palm. 'I wish you could see yourself through my eyes,' he said softly. 'My vision is better.'

She drove them back to his apartment and they hauled his suitcase inside. She hadn't been here since he'd left – he had no pets, no plants, and there was no reason for her to visit unless he was there – and the air was thick and stale. She opened the windows and turned on the fan, and they sat together on the sofa, fingers entwined, until he cleared his throat awkwardly. 'I've got a little news.'

'Good or bad?' Rose wasn't quite listening. She reached out with her free hand and stroked a wayward lock of hair behind his ear. It had gotten long – she'd have to make an appointment for him to have it cut.

'Excellent, actually. While I was in Oxford with Paul and Shari –'

'How are they, by the way?' Paul had been Jonathan's roommate in their doctoral programme, and many of Jonathan's best stories revolved around their misadventures.

'Great – sleep-deprived, you know, but head over heels with the baby, and they seem happy. I've got pictures. They'd love to meet you.'

Rose laughed. 'Not likely, unless they're considering a transatlantic flight with a newborn.'

Jonathan swallowed awkwardly. 'Well, that's the thing, love. When I was over there, Paul and I had lunch with his dean.' He paused, searching for the next words, and Rose felt her heart growing colder, a thin sheet of ice covering its surface like frost on a windowpane.

'He's very interested in my research. He wants me to join the faculty there – a lab of my own, graduate students to work with me. It's ideal. A perfect opportunity.'

Rose reached for the glass of water he'd left for her

18

on the coffee table. Her mouth was painfully dry, her throat ached. Alone again. It seemed it was Just Her Luck to have finally found her Orlando, her perfect love, only to have him leave her. Shakespeare's Rosalind had never had this kind of problem; she was too busy cross-dressing and frolicking around in forests with her servant. Rough life. Rose set the glass back on the table and slipped her other hand from his.

'So you're leaving,' she said dully, when she could push her parched lips into words again.

'I'd like to,' he said softly. He reached for her hand again, but she moved so she was facing forward, away from him, her ankles crossed primly, hands folded in her lap, as though she were waiting to be served at a particularly stuffy tea party.

'But we were supposed to get married,' she whispered.

'And we will, of course we will. I'm not saying that at all. But I'd be a fool to turn this down. You can see that, can't you?' His voice was pleading, but she turned away.

'When are you going?'

'I haven't said I am, as of yet. But I could start at the beginning of the third term, just after Easter.'

'Your contract here goes through the end of the year, doesn't it? You're just going to break your contract?'

'Rose, don't be like that. Please hear me out. I want you to come with me.'

Rose turned her head towards him and barked a short, harsh laugh. 'To England? You want me to come to England with you? You have got to be kidding, Jonathan. I have a job. I have a life here. I'm not like you. I don't get to go globe-hopping every time I get a whim.'

'That's a bit harsh, don't you think?' he asked, recoiling from the bite. Our Rose, *whose tongue more poisons than the adder's tooth*! He rubbed his hands quickly on his knees and stood up, rumpling his hair impatiently. 'It could be good for us – for both of us. For me, yes, but for you, too. You haven't got a job past next year, right?'

'Is this supposed to make me feel better?' Rose had been told this spring, in no uncertain terms, that her adjunct contract wouldn't be renewed after this year. No hard feelings, nothing personal, but they hadn't any tenure-track positions open, and it was so important to keep the department adjuncts fresh, to keep the curriculum vital, you know. Yes, Rose had thought sourly, and because you can keep milling through those brand-new PhDs and never have to give them a penny more than you think you can get away with. The thought of having to find a new job paralysed her, the thought of being without a job paralysed her, and she was highly tempted to stick her fingers in her ears and sing until the entire thing blew over.

'I don't know about better. But I'd hoped you'd be at least a little happy for me.'

She looked up at him, his eyes sad and wounded, and she crumbled a little. 'I am. I'm sorry. But it's so big . . . It's such a huge change from what we were planning.'

'We always knew we'd have to consider it, love. My position here is only temporary, you know that.'

'But I thought maybe . . .' Rose didn't want to say what she had thought. She'd just assumed that he would give up this fancy academic jet-setting and find something nearby, something where she wouldn't have to go anywhere. Where she wouldn't have to change at all. 'I'm sorry,' she said again.

'Oh, Rose, I'm sorry, too. Let's not talk about it any more. Let's just enjoy being together for a bit.'

He came over to her and put his arms around her and kissed her, and that did only a little to soothe the ache inside where her heart had been bruised. So that was it. He wouldn't stay, and she wouldn't – couldn't – go. It was ridiculous to even think about it.

His hands were in her hair, slowly pulling the pins out and letting it fall down her back the way he liked it, stroking the tresses the way she liked it, the gentle pull against her scalp so soothing. She wasn't paying attention. Bean and Cordy were sitting on her shoulders, whispering in her ears like a cartoon devil and angel. Or two devils, really. 'You could go if you wanted to, Rosie,' our youngest sister said. 'Just pick up and go. It's not so hard. I do it all the time.'

'What are you afraid of?' Bean mocked. 'Don't want to leave your glamorous life behind?'

Okay, so it wasn't a glamorous life. But it was important. She was important. We needed her. Didn't we?

Bean and Cordy didn't answer. Bean was adjusting her horns, and Cordy was chasing her own forked tail. You need me, Rose thought fiercely. They turned away.

'Hush,' Jonathan said, as though he could hear the busy spinning of Rose's thoughts, and he kissed her, and we fell off her shoulders as though we'd been physically brushed aside.

21

ACT II

Setting: Interior, the Golden Dragon, a small Chinese restaurant a few towns over, famed more for its convenience than its cuisine. Also the site of an infamous embarrassment for Bean, aged eight, in which she devoured a sweet and sour pork entrée all by herself and then regurgitated the entire thing tidily into the mouth of a fake dragon hidden behind a plant, certain it would never be found there.
Characters: Rose, Jonathan, our father, our mother.

They sat around the table, the four of them, sharing dishes and companionable chatter. Tea steamed in tiny cups, and Rose was fumbling with her chopsticks, envying Jonathan's easy grace with the infernal things.

'We have something to tell you,' our father said, clearing his throat.

Rose looked up quickly, warily. This was the sort of announcement that had preceded the game-changing births of both Bean and Cordy. Whatever the news was, it wasn't bound to be good.

Our father cleared his throat again, but it was our mother who spoke, leaping in, tearing off the conversational Band-Aid. 'I have breast cancer,' she said.

The ice in Rose's throat grew solid, and she grabbed for her still-scalding cup of tea, taking a long swallow, letting the liquid burn away the freeze inside her, leaving a bubble on her tongue she would feel every time she spoke for the next few days. There was silence. The few other diners in the restaurant kept eating, oblivious.

'Mom,' Rose finally said. 'Are you sure?'

Our mother nodded. 'It's early, you see. But I found a lump – what was it, a month ago?' She looked at our father for confirmation, the quiet ease of cooperative conversation they had developed years ago. He nodded.

'A month ago?' Rose's voice cracked. She set down her teacup, hand shaking. 'Why didn't you call me? I could have . . .' She trailed off, unsure of what she could have done. But she could have done something. She could have taken care of this. She took care of everything. How had she missed this? A month, they'd been going to doctors and having quiet conversations between themselves, and she hadn't seen it at all?

'We've been to the oncologist, and it's malignant. It doesn't look like it's spread, but it's quite large. So they're going to do a round of chemotherapy before surgery. Shrink it down a bit. And then . . .' Our mother's voice caught and trembled for a moment, as though the meaning behind the clinical words had only just become clear to her, and she swallowed and took a breath. 'And then a mastectomy. You know, just get the whole problem dealt with.' She said this as though it were something she had woken up and decided to do on a relative lark. Like going on a cruise, say, or taking up tennis.

'I'm so sorry,' Jonathan said. He reached across the table and put his hand over our mother's, squeezed. He was so elegant in his sympathy. 'What can we do?'

Rose stared wildly around the restaurant, at the gilt and red and paper placemats. This is what she would remember, she knew, not the fear in our mother's eyes, or the pounding of her own heart,

23

but how desperately tacky this place was, how cheap it looked, how the chopsticks had not broken properly when she had separated them but splintered along the centre. This is what she would remember.

But when the shock passed, it had become something, forgive her for saying it, something of a relief. Thank God, a purpose. An excuse to be needed. A reason to turn Jonathan's abandonment into something important. So the next day she broke her lease, packed up her things, and moved back home, uninvited.

It wasn't until she had been home for a while, had straightened out the little messes around the house and helped our mother through the first rounds of chemotherapy that the shame of her situation had hit her. How humiliating to be living at home again. If she told people that she had moved back to help care for our mother, of course they would nod and sigh sympathetically. But still, where was she? Living with our parents? At her age? She felt like a swimmer who had been earnestly beating back the waves only to find herself exhausted and just as far from shore as when she had begun. She was lonely and tired.

Embarrassed even by the thought of herself in this rudderless life, she flushed and stood impatiently from the window seat, where she'd been staring in irritation at our mother's wildflower garden. The garden had, in the way of wildflower gardens, grown out of control. Our mother loved it – the way it drew butterflies and fat bees, the dizzy way the purples and yellows blurred together as the stems tangled – but Rose preferred her gardens to be more obedient.

She turned to look back into the living room, one dim light behind our father's favourite sun-paled orange wing-back chair spreading shadows over the opened books that covered every surface despite her attempts to keep them orderly. Our family's vices – disorder and literature – captured in evening tableau. We were never organized readers who would see a book through to its end in any sort of logical order. We weave in and out of words like tourists on a hop-on, hop-off bus tour. Put a book down in the kitchen to go to the bathroom and you might return to find it gone, replaced by another of equal interest. We are indiscriminate. Our father, of course, limits his reading to things by, of, and about our boy Bill, but our mother brought diversity to our readings and therefore our education. It was never really a problem for any of us to read a children's biography of Amelia Earhart followed by a self-help book on alcoholism (from which no one in the family suffered), followed by Act III of *All's Well That Ends Well*, followed by a collection of Neruda sonnets. Cordy claims this is the source of her inability to focus on anything for more than a few minutes at a time, but we do not believe her. It is just our way.

And it wasn't that Rose regretted being home, exactly. Our parents' house and Barnwell in general were far more pleasant than the anonymous apartment she'd rented in Columbus – thin carpet over concrete floors, neighbours moving in and out so quickly she'd stopped bothering to learn their names – but after she filled our parents' pill cases and straightened the living room, after she had finally hired a lawn service and balanced the cheque book, after she went with our parents to our mother's chemo treatments, sitting in the waiting room because they didn't need her there, not really, they would have been fine just the two of them, her life was almost as empty as it had been before.

The tiny clock on the mantelpiece chimed ten, and Rose sighed in relief. Ten was a perfectly acceptable hour to go to bed without feeling like a complete loafer. She walked towards the stairs and then paused by the mirror, warped and pale, that had hung there since any of us could remember. Rose stared at her reflection and spoke six words none of us had ever said before.

'I wish my sisters were here.'

The fox, the ape and the humble-bee, Were still at odds, being but three.

Our father once wrote an essay on the importance of the number three in Shakespeare's work. A little bit of nothing, he said, a bagatelle, but it was always our favourite. The Father, the Son, the Holy Spirit. The Billy Goats Gruff, the Three Blind Mice, *Three Men in a Boat (To Say Nothing of the Dog)*. *King Lear* – Goneril, Regan, Cordelia. *The Merchant of Venice* – Portia, Nerissa, Jessica.

And us – Rosalind, Bianca, Cordelia.

The Weird Sisters.

We have, while trapped in the car with our father behind the wheel, been subjected to extended remixes of the history of the word 'weird' in *Macbeth* with a special encore set of Norse and Scottish Sources Shakespeare Used in Creating This Important Work. These indignities we will spare you.

But it is worth noting, especially now that 'weird' has evolved from its delicious original meaning of supernatural strangeness into something depressingly critical and pedestrian, as in, '"Don't you think Rose's outfit looks *weird*?"

Bean asked,' that Shakespeare didn't really mean the sisters were weird at all.

The word he originally used was much closer to 'wyrd', and that has an entirely different meaning. 'Wyrd' means fate. And we might argue that we are not fated to do anything, that we have chosen everything in our lives, that there is no such thing as destiny. And we would be lying.

Rose always first, Bean never first, Cordy always last. And if we don't accept it, don't see, like Shakespeare's Weird Sisters did, that we cannot fight our family and cannot fight our fates, well, whose failing is that but our own? Our destiny is in the way we were born, in the way we were raised, in the sum of the three of us.

The history of this trinity is fractious – a constantly shifting dividing line, never equal, never equitable. Two against one, or three opposed, but never all together. Upon Cordy's birth, Rose took Bean into her, two against one. And when Bean rebelled, refused any longer to play Rose's games, Rose and Cordy found each other, and Cordy became the willing follower. Two against one.

Until Rose went away and we were three apart.

And then Bean and Cordy found each other sneaking out of their respective windows onto the broad-limbed oak trees one hot summer night, and we were two against one again.

And now here we are, measuring our distance an arm's length away, staying far apart and cold. For what? To hold the others at bay? To protect ourselves?

We see stories in magazines or newspapers sometimes, or read novels, about the deep and loving relationships between sisters. Sisters are supposed to be tight and connected, sharing family history and lore, laughing over misadventures. But we are not that way. We never have been, really, because even our partnering was more for spite than for love. Who *are* these sisters who act like this, who treat each other as their best friends? We have never met them. We know plenty of sisters who get along well, certainly, but wherefore the myth?

We don't think Cordy minds, really, because she tends to take things as they come. Rose minds, certainly, because she likes things to align with her mental image. And Bean? Well, it comes and goes with Bean, as does everything with her. To forge such an unnatural friendship would just require so much *effort*.

Our estrangement is not drama-laden – we have not betrayed one another's trust, we have not stolen lovers or fought over money or property or any of the things that irreparably break families apart. The answer, for us, is much simpler.

See, we love one another. We just don't happen to like one another very much.

TWO

Summers are always the same in Barnwell – thick, listlessly humid days, darkened occasionally with rolling thunderstorms that keep lushness in the lawns and fields. We remember the heat like an uninvited guest. When we were small, it was not so bad; we ran through the sprinkler, bribed our parents into trips to the college's outdoor pool, let our hair stick to our foreheads as we cooled ourselves with homemade Popsicles. But as we grew older, it became our enemy. We sat in our bedrooms, the largest fan we could find placed inches away, beating the still air into an angry frenzy that did nothing at all to reduce the heat. Sleeping was impossible, and we would often be found wandering the house, our white nightgowns gleaming in the darkness, a trio of Lady Macbeths, driven mad by the mercury.

After we had all moved out, our parents had central air-conditioning installed, too late to save the doors from warping, or halt the omnipresent mildew that plagued books that alit anywhere for longer than a few weeks, but making living here in August at least bearable. In the winter, we were still subject to clanking, hissing radiators, liberal use of space heaters, and, in one disastrous

29

experiment on Cordy's part, the employment of an antique colonial warming pan that had obviously lost its ability to insulate the coals and keep them from burning through the sheets.

Bean arrived in the afternoon, clad in a designer suit completely inappropriate for Barnwell, sweating desperately and cursing violently. Rose heard a car pull into the driveway and, closing her book carefully around a bookmark, peered out the window. Bean hoisted herself from the front seat of a cheap white compact with a painful scrape down the driver's side. She bent over, reaching into the back seat, and Rose could see a run down the back of one unquestionably posh stocking. Bean's hair had escaped from the tight French twist she had spent countless hours in front of her bedroom mirror perfecting. She looked as though she'd slept in her clothes (which, as a matter of fact, she had, pulled over into a rest stop parking lot when she was too tired to drive any more, her legs draped over the gearshift, her suit wrinkling in the heat). Rose climbed up from the window seat in her bedroom and went downstairs.

'You look dreadful,' she said, opening the door for Bean. The heat rushed in, pressing itself against the coolness inside, leaving Rose struggling for breath.

Bean glared at her. 'Thanks,' she said. 'That makes me feel loads better.'

Instantly contrite, Rose reached out to take one of the bags our sister was lugging. 'What's wrong?'

'Nothing. I'm just hot and I've been in the car forever. Will you move?'

Rose complied, and Bean stepped into the foyer, her eyes casting around for changes in the landscape. She brushed past Rose, dropping her bag beside the staircase and heading into the kitchen. Rose followed dully, feeling underdressed, as she always did next to Bean.

30

Even after what looked like an unfortunate encounter with a herd of angry cats, Bean still looked elegant, chic. Rose looked like our mother – they both favoured loose linen skirts, wide-legged pants, batik-print tunics. Normally, Rose felt exotically comfortable, but suddenly she felt dowdy. She tugged at the back of her pants, felt the line of her staid cotton panties, and swallowed a bubble of irritation, whether at Bean or at herself, she didn't know.

When she walked into the kitchen, Bean was standing by the sink, one hand resting on the silver faucet, drinking water greedily from a jelly glass. She drained it with an exaggerated smack and leaned over to refill it, leaning on the counter. Rose saw, with some relief at the crack in Bean's bedraggled perfection, a wet spot spreading on the fabric of her red suit where she had leaned against the counter. 'What are you doing here?' Rose asked. 'Mom and Dad didn't say you were coming.'

Bean, halfway through another glass of water, raised her eyebrows over the rim. 'I didn't tell them I was coming.' And then, more to change the subject than to give any additional information, she said, 'Oh, and I heard about you. Congratulations.'

'Thanks,' Rose said, her finger flicking to her ring. Not that we didn't tell you all this months ago, Beany. Don't rush on our account. It's not like Mom might be dying or anything.

'Ah, the ring,' Bean said, seeing the movement of Rose's hand. *'I gave my love a ring and made him swear never to part with it.* Let's see.'

Rose took an awkward step forward, holding her hand out stiffly. Bean grasped our older sister's thick fingers with her own manicured talons and peered at the ring. A gleaming sapphire set in antique worked white gold. Rose had treasured the romanticism and uniqueness of

31

the ring when she and Jonathan had selected it. In front of Bean, however, she was sure it looked cheap.

'Pretty,' Bean pronounced. 'Different. It's better that way. Diamonds are so boring.' As she released Rose's hand, Rose caught a flash of Bean's pinky finger, the fake nail snapped off in a jagged edge. Rose's hand hovered uncertainly in the air for a moment before she pulled it back to rest on her thigh.

'Thanks,' Rose said. 'I like it.'

'How's Mom doing?'

'Fine. You know, as fine as you'd expect. She's nearly finished with the chemo course. This is one of her off weeks – we'll take her back next week for her next treatments. She's tired, and she doesn't eat much, but it's not as bad as it could have been.' There was more she could have said – that our mother had been so exhausted after her first treatment that she had slept for nearly three days; that a little while later the chemotherapy had torn out her hair, and Rose had found her crying on the bathroom floor, nearly bald, clumps of wet hair wrapped around her limbs like seaweed; that even after the worst had passed, it seemed the fight would never end, but Bean would understand the way things were soon enough. 'We're making it through.'

'Huh,' Bean said. She could have asked follow-up questions about our mother's health, but she was more interested in the way Rose made it sound as if she were a vital part of the whole enterprise, when our parents had survived so long as a nation of two.

Rose squared her shoulders slightly. 'We're okay here. You didn't have to come home.'

Bean sneered a little bit, reaching up and tucking her hair back into shape half-heartedly. 'Yeah, I should have guessed you wouldn't be glad to see me.'

'That's not it,' Rose said, and the defensiveness in her

voice surprised her. 'I was just thinking the other day that I wished we were all here.'

'Well, now you've got your wish,' Bean said, spreading her hands out, palms up, in a what-more-do-you-want-from-me gesture. 'Cordy's not here, is she?'

'No,' Rose said. 'I'm not even sure where she is. Dad sent a letter to the last address Mom had in her book, but you know how Cordy is.'

'Good. I can't deal with her right now anyway.'

'So how long are you staying?' Rose ventured delicately.

Bean shrugged. 'For a while. Dunno. I quit my job.'

Well, that was news. Bean had worked in the human resources department – well, Bean *was* the human resources department of a tiny law office in Manhattan, though if you met her over drinks, she just would have told you she was in law, and let you assume the best. Or the worst. *The first thing we do, let's kill all the lawyers*

'Oh,' Rose said. 'Why?'

'Why does anyone quit a job? I didn't want to work there any more.' Bean pushed herself off the counter and strode over to the door. 'I'm going upstairs to change. Where are Mom and Dad?'

'Dad's at school, and Mom went out somewhere. They'll be back later.'

'Great. Then I'm going to take a shower,' Bean said, and clopped off down the hall. The excitement over, Rose followed Bean up the bare wooden stairs and went back to her book. If we had been sisters of a different sort, Bean's reticence might have been cause for curiosity. As it was, it was simply another secret we held from each other, one of a thousand we were sure we would never share.

Our parents, more out of atrophy than intent, had not changed our bedrooms in any way since we had officially moved out. This often led to curious paths of discovery, as it preserved objects and memorabilia we did not want to have with us in our new lives, but were still valuable enough that we couldn't bear to throw them away.

Bean threw her bags on her bed – the heavy, tulle-crowned four-poster that she had swapped Cordy for years ago. Cordy now had the heavy, wrought-iron white bedstead Bean had deemed not sophisticated enough. To her, at fifteen, the heavy wood posts at the corners of this bed had seemed the height of elegance. Now it looked sad, the tulle grown dark with dust, the wood dull and unpolished, the bedspread faded where the sun had fallen, leaching out the colour. She kicked off her shoes and walked over to the window, restlessly drumming her fingers against her stomach. The taut, trembling sensation in her belly would not release, even now, even five hundred miles from the city.

Pulling the curtain across the dormer, Bean walked back towards her bed, peeling off her clothes. The torn, sticky nylons went into the wastebasket, her suit she laid out on the bed. There was a grease stain on the skirt from a hamburger she had eaten on the road. She'd have to see if Barney had managed to get itself a dry cleaner while she was gone. When she took off her jewellery, a silver bangle watch and tiny diamond earrings, the tight feeling in her stomach welled up again.

She pulled off her underwear and wrapped a towel around her chest before she walked across the hallway to the bathroom the three of us had always shared. The heavy claw-foot tub still stood there, but with a new shower curtain wrapped around it in a circle. The shampoo she had left here the last time she visited – Thanksgiving? Last summer? Longer? – sat on the windowsill, thank heavens, because she hadn't had time (or, let's face it, money) to stop at the salon before she left. She turned the water on, icy cold to take away the sticky heat of the journey, and stepped under its punishing blast, baptismal, praying for the stone inside her to slip down the drain, to disappear.

Bean hadn't thought of what she would do now. She'd been so focused on getting out of the city, sure that putting miles between that life and this one would grant her some kind of pardon. Annoyingly, this had proved untrue. In the car were boxes and boxes of clothes – for heaven's sake, what had she needed all those *clothes* for? – each one a reminder of what she had done. Thief, she thought as she scrubbed her face. *Thou art a robber, a lawbreaker, a villain.* What was left of her makeup disappeared into the soap and water, but she kept pushing the washcloth over her face, her skin going raw and red.

No plan. No past. No future. She was at home, and of course Rose had to be here, too. She who might have been voted Most Likely to Judge You Harshly. Even Cordy, flaky as she was, might have been better. But Rose. Jeez.

Bean leaned down and shut off the water. She was going to have to solve this, somehow. Find a job. One that wouldn't require a reference, of course.

If she could do that, could pay back the firm and get rid of everything she'd bought with that money, maybe she could make a fresh start. She couldn't bear the thought of going back to New York yet, but another city – San Francisco? Better weather there anyway. There she could forget. There it would all be different.

At seven o'clock, the sun was finally considering its rest, bringing relief from the heavy heat of the day. In the kitchen, Bean sat on one of the counters, her back pressed up against the yellow wall, her arm hemmed in by the cabinets on one side. She hulled strawberries, as many going into her mouth as the bowl, it seemed, her fingers sticky with juice. The heavy ceramic bowl had come from our Nana, and it made Bean miss her.

Our mother stood in front of the sink, her fingers deftly flicking over a cucumber, peeling it with a knife, a skill none of us has ever mastered without risking serious bodily injury. She is a tremendous cook, but a notoriously unreliable one. If our mother is responsible, dinner is rarely served in our house before nine, and we remember, at times when we were young, our parents awakening us to eat, nodding heads drooping towards the table, thin legs in white printed pyjamas swinging sleepily like pendulums under the chairs. Our mother is capricious, likely to be struck by a whim to prepare a four-course meal on an ordinary Wednesday, and then struck by equally strong whims to wander off in the middle of that preparation and take a soothing bath, or to pick up the book she had been reading earlier and involve herself in that world for a while until the pasta water boils away and the smoke alarm (hopefully) brings her back to reality.

Summer, however, is different, because in the midst of all these farms, there are roadside stands, fertile with the bounty of the season in Ohio: crisp, sweet, Silver Queen corn; perfectly ripe, yielding tomatoes the size of baseballs; delicately flavoured cucumbers with satisfyingly watery flesh; strawberries, blackberries, raspberries, peaches – a dizzying array of colours, lush with juice. Often, in summer, this is all we eat, a table laden with fruits and vegetables, and Rose saw as she entered the kitchen that this was the case that night. Fortunate, as this also meant dinner would be ready before the crickets came out in earnest.

Bean popped a berry in her mouth and reached out under her legs for another, the bright greens nestled on top. She twisted the huller expertly and the head popped off. Seven in one blow. 'What happened to the bookstore?'

she asked. She had noticed, on the drive in, the empty windows of the storefront, the sign that read, in angry letters, FINAL CLEARANCE!

Walking up beside our mother, Rose picked up one of the naked, pale cucumbers and began slicing it thinly, setting it in rounds on a platter beside her. We always ate the cucumbers and tomatoes the same way, pushed together in stacked ovals and drizzled with sharp balsamic vinegar and fresh-ground pepper. Rose's mouth watered at the thought.

'Oh, it's a disaster,' our mother said. 'They've gotten too big for their britches, really. Remember how they used to handle the textbooks for Barney?' We did. Barnwell, the name of both the town and the college where our father taught and therefore all three of us had matriculated, with varying degrees of success, had not had a bookstore of its own for years. The bookstore in town, nestled between a diner famous for its White Castle-esque burgers and the post office, took that honour, and during textbook sale and buyback season it was crammed with college students, looking hungry and desperate among the hand-knitted throws and souvenir Rice Krispie treats in the shape of the state (which, in Ohio, is not so far from the shape of a normal Rice Krispie treat).

'Uh-huh,' Bean said, flicking a strawberry into the bowl with a gentle *ping*.

'Well, they said they didn't want to sell the textbooks any more, accused the students of shoplifting, basically.'

'They were shoplifting,' Bean interrupted. 'Their textbooks were a total rip-off.' She remembered a friend of hers, a goateed, handsome boy with enthusiastically curly black hair, telling her the only reason he owned his winter coat was because the pockets were big enough to fit a chemistry book in.

'Textbooks are expensive everywhere,' Rose said.

37

'I'm sure not all the students were shoplifting,' our mother continued. 'In any case, I don't know what they were thinking. All those parents coming into town, wanting souvenirs, and now they are going to the booster store on campus instead for their sweatshirts and what-have-you.'

'So they closed?'

'Not at first. First they opened one of those coffee bars, which was a good idea, but Maura hadn't the slightest idea how to run one. Barnwell Beanery is still open, you know, and the competition was too much.'

'Oh, you know who runs the Beanery now?' Rose asked. 'Dan Miller. Didn't he graduate with you?'

'Yeah,' Bean said, and she blinked a few times in surprise before she shifted and hopped off the counter, carrying the small bowl of discarded strawberry greens over to the trash can. She pressed her foot on the pedal and the lid popped obediently open. 'Man, he's still living here? That's crazy.'

'Bean? Compost?' our mother said, raising her eyebrows and gesturing with the knife toward the container to the left of the trash can. Too late. Bean shook the last of the strawberry tops into the trash can. She shrugged, as though it had been out of her hands, and walked the bowl over to the sink.

'It's not so bad living here,' Rose said, stung slightly.

'Oh, stop. I'm not talking about you. We grew up here, it's different. It's not like you went to college here and then just decided to stay because it was so bucolic.'

'It is bucolic,' our mother said.

'Not everyone wants to live in a city like New York,' Rose said.

'And that's a good thing. It's crowded enough there already,' Bean said, and dropped the bowl in the sink, where it clattered enthusiastically.

'What is the city but the people?' Rose quoted.

'So you're going to go back?' our mother asked.

Bean shrugged. 'I'm not staying here, that's for sure.' The knife slipped in Rose's hand, making the tiniest nick in the fleshy pad of her thumb. She lifted it to her mouth, sucking sour salt, sweet tomato.

'You really quit your job?' Rose asked, pulling her thumb from her mouth and examining the cut.

Bean looked at her. 'Yes. Why is that so hard to believe?'

'I don't know. I guess I just thought you might have mentioned it to us or something. That you were planning to.'

'What, in our chatty once-a-week phone calls?' Bean sneered. 'I didn't realize I had to keep you apprised of my five-year plan.' She could feel the meanness welling up inside her, but was helpless to stop it. It was anger that should have been directed at herself, but for crying out loud, couldn't Rose ever leave anything alone?

'You don't have to bite my head off,' Rose said. 'I was just asking.'

'You never just ask, Rose. You just want to criticize me.'

'I'm not criticizing. Forgive me for showing a little interest.'

'Girls,' our mother said. We ignored her.

'I quit my job. I didn't want to work there any more. I was sick of New York. What more do you want? *Take thy bond, take thou thy pound of flesh.*'

'Don't get dramatic. If I were going to quit a job I wouldn't just up and do it without planning. That's all I'm saying.'

'Of course you wouldn't. But we just can't all be as perfect as you are, Rose.' Bean walked over to the refrigerator and yanked the door open, staring blindly at the contents inside. The cold air pushed the tears in her eyes away. She closed the door and turned back to face them.

'You can stay as long as you want. It's nice to have you girls home,' our mother said, as though she hadn't heard our fight, rinsing her hands and shaking them dry. The last of the sunlight drifted through the window, illuminating the lines on her face, and Bean was surprised, as she always was when she came home, by how our parents were ageing. Like the changes in the furniture, Rose hardly noticed it. It was gentle as erosion to her. To Bean, it was a seismic shift. Since we were young, our mother had gathered her hair in a large, loose bun near the crown of her head, secured with invisible bobby pins. But the chemotherapy had stolen her hair, the deep brown we'd always shared with her, and her eyes, an intense blue that had lost the genetic battle with our father's chocolate brown, looked pallid. The scarf tied around her head outlined her paling skin, her eyes looking huge and lost in her face. There were the beginnings of a wattle under her chin, yet her hands seemed frail and bony, the skin taut over sharp bones.

Bean ran her own fingers nervously under her chin, which, thankfully, was still firmly hugging her jawline. When had this happened? When had our mother gotten so old? Was it just because she was sick? Or was this happening to all of us, without our noticing?

A rush of fevered guilt swept over her and she gripped the edge of the countertop, willing herself not to faint. There was no use wondering about it – we were all getting old. And while time had been passing her by, Bean had been drowning her youth in a sea of clothes and meaningless men.

'I'm going to change,' she whispered to herself, as if the words had the power to do the hard work for her. Beside her, our mother and Rose chattered away, ignoring

40

her distress. It didn't matter. Bean had a long road to go before her vow would mean anything anyway. We all did.

'Bianca, will you help, please?' our mother asked. She was hunched over, dragging a basket of wet laundry to the back door. The house had a perfectly functional dryer, but our mother insisted, when the weather allowed, on hanging sheets and towels out to dry. We'd put our collective foot down long ago about having our clothes swinging on the line for the neighbours to see, but we hadn't won the linens battle, so we put up with slightly stiff sheets and towels.

Bean was lying on the couch, her feet hooked along the back, reading a history of World War II with one hand, staining the pages with the juice from the plum she was eating with the other. She'd been home for three days, and had done nothing but sleep and read and eat, and only the fact that our mother didn't typically keep corn chips and chocolate in the house had kept her from turning her hibernation into a fully bear-like preparation for winter.

'Oh, leave it,' Bean said. She shoved the rest of the plum in her mouth, working the flesh off the pit with her tongue as she got up, wiping her hands on her shorts. 'I'll get it,' she said, mouth full. She was barefoot and bare-legged, her shorts revealing the slight shadow of her last spray tan. There was a dribble of pale juice along the neckline of her tank top.

Our mother pushed open the back door and Bean hoisted the laundry basket up, in one motion stepping out the door and spitting the plum pit towards the garden in a graceful arc.

'Lovely,' our mother said. 'Very classy.'

'Hey, maybe you'll grow a plum bush. Or tree? Do plums grow on trees?'

'Yes, trees. Classy and lacking in horticultural education.'

Bean dropped the basket under the clotheslines, the whites inside jumping and resettling on impact. 'I can do this, Mom. You should go inside and rest.'

'All everyone wants me to do is rest,' our mother said. 'I feel like I'm on a rest cure in some Victorian novel.' She bent over and shook out a sheet with practised ease, the damp fabric bursting against the thick air.

'Sorry,' Bean said. 'I didn't know.' She knew she had missed so much of what our mother had been through, that her phone calls hadn't yielded the entire story, wouldn't have even if Bean had made them more regularly.

'Get the other end of this, will you?' our mother asked. 'It's not you, Beany, I'm sorry. I do get tired quite a lot, and it's frustrating not to be able to do all the things I'd like to do.'

'Rose and I can help.' Together Bean and our mother spread the sheet across one line and fastened it with a pair of wooden clothespins.

'You can, but that's not entirely the point. The point is that I'd like to be doing these things myself, not having you girls do things for me. Getting sick takes some getting used to.' She straightened the sheet with an impatient snap that matched her irritated tone.

Bean pulled a heavy towel from the stack of laundry, unwinding it from the lascivious position it had gotten into with a pillowcase. 'How do you really feel?'

Our mother shook her head, and her face softened. 'Not so bad right now. It goes in waves with the treatments. It'll be bad for a few days after the next round – it's worst on the third day for me, and then it'll get better. But I think I'm going to be tired for a long time, and I'm already fairly tired of being tired.'

42

'But the chemo won't be forever. And then you'll feel better.'

'No, but then there will be the surgery. And maybe more chemo. And maybe radiation. And maybe more surgery, if I decide to have the breast reconstructed. It's going to be a long road.'

Slinging another towel over the clothesline and snapping the pins around it, Bean felt the same clutching feeling she'd had when she looked at our mother in the kitchen. 'Are you scared?'

'Of course,' our mother said. Her voice was sure, but her face looked troubled and distant. Our mother took the last pillowcase from the basket and hung it, her fingers confident and practised. The sheets and towels hung around them, a cool, damp fort in the blooming heat of the day. A slight breeze shifted through, and Bean watched the shadows of the fabric move across our mother's face. 'I'm not done yet,' she said, as though she were a long way away, and then paused, shook it off. 'But I've got wonderful doctors, and I've got your father, and you girls, of course. We will make it through.'

'Whatever I can do to help,' Bean said. 'That's why I'm here.'

Our mother lifted the empty basket onto her hip and speared Bean with a sharp look. 'I appreciate it, Beany, but I don't believe for a second that you are home just to help me.'

Bean froze. 'What do you mean?'

'How many pictures of New York did you cut out of magazines and paste up all over your room? How many times did you watch *Breakfast at Tiffany's* – completely missing the point of the story, I might add? How many books about that city did you beg Mrs Landrige to order for the library?'

'Thousands, on all counts,' Bean said. She recalled, just

43

barely, the way the city had seemed like the perfect escape, the way it had glittered like a mirage in the distance. But the promise had faded until it seemed like only a memory's memory, a copy duplicated so many times it had gone pale and blurry. All she could remember now was the harsh reality of the dirty streets and the crowded subways and the ridiculous rent.

'It's not like I just met you, sweetie. Whatever made you give up that dream must have been awfully bad.' Bean made a move to speak, but our mother held up her hand. 'No, you don't have to tell me. I'm not sure, honestly, that I want to know. I'm happy you're here, and you're welcome to stay as long as you like.'

'Thanks,' Bean said, and her throat was thick with tears that our mother was, thankfully, gracious enough to turn away in time to avoid seeing. The door to the house slammed behind our mother, and Bean turned to look at the back fence, where the honeysuckle grew in thick ropes around the pickets. So many of our favourite summer memories were here in this house: chasing the Morse code of fireflies in the yard at night, eating watermelon on the wide painted concrete of the front steps, the metallic taste of water from the hose, and the delicious spread of freedom in the hours arrayed across the sunlight. Even the smell of the laundry drying on the line could take us back. But that afternoon, none of those beautiful memories could reach Bean. Our mother was dying. Bean was a criminal. Rose was a bitch. Despite any promises, life was not going to get better any time soon.

THREE

'm walking into town,' Rose announced to Bean, who was sitting in the living room, reading. The day had not yet launched into the still, stifling air that would bring real heat. Bean was leaning against the window, knees into her chest, toes curled under in the strangely feline way she had had ever since she was a little girl. She looked up from the novel she was staring at. She couldn't remember a word of it, though she had turned fifty pages since breakfast. 'Do you want to come?'

Rose watched as Bean's attention moved slowly from the book, or wherever her mind had been, back to the room. Our mother pottered around in the garden outside, a broad straw hat over the scarf covering her tender scalp, anchored with a wide, elastic band. With great, solid yanks, she pulled weeds from the earth and tossed them carelessly over her shoulder, where they landed in a pile on the brick walkway, as though they had been ordered to do precisely so. 'Do you think one of us should offer to help her?'

'I did,' Rose said flatly. 'She said she wanted to do it herself. It's ridiculous, but if she feels up to it, I suppose it's not going to hurt her.'

'How generous of you,' Bean said.

'Do you want to come or not?' Rose snapped. 'I was trying to be nice.'

Bean put the book down beside her, spine splayed wide. 'Sure. It's better than sitting here. God, is there nothing to do in this town?' She got up and walked to the door, slipping into a pair of espadrilles that perfectly matched her crisp cotton blouse and wraparound skirt. She looked like an advertisement. Rose sighed, pulled a bookmark off of one of the shelves beside the window, and inserted it in the book Bean had abandoned.

'It's not that there's nothing to do,' Rose corrected. 'It just moves slower. You have to get used to the pace. If you're going to stay.'

Bean scoffed as she moved towards the door, catching a look at herself in the heavy mirror over the hall table where we kept keys and mail and anything else that happened to need a home. She tossed her hair and it fell in sleek waves over her shoulders. Rose opened the door for her.

'Do the Mannings still live there?' Bean asked. They had passed a block in silence, listening to the faraway hum of lawn mowers and children shrieking in pleasure down by the lake. Rose looked up at the house, another of the many wide-clapboard Sears catalogue homes with their long, heavy windows and broad porches.

'She's on sabbatical, I think. Some exchange programme with a college in California. He's still here, though.' Bean looked at the empty house. A bicycle stood sentry on the sidewalk, and a watering can lay abandoned among the trampled pansies by the porch stairs.

'Oh,' Bean said, somewhat sadly. Professor Lila Manning – Mrs Dr Manning they had called her, to distinguish her from her equally academically inclined husband – had been one of her favourite professors: a small, somewhat elfin

46

woman with a charmingly gruff attitude. She had become, at one point, a sort of mentor to Bean, who had spent evenings at their house, drinking red wine and watching the sun set in the backyard as the conversation drifted like clouds. They had been a young couple, though they had seemed worlds away at the time – married, two young children, a life of stability and normalcy she had hated as much as wanted. Her heart squeezed momentarily with nostalgia, but they had grown apart as Bean became immersed in city life and The Doctors Mannings' world had filled with other students, china replicas of the ones who had come before.

The birds and insects kept up a low hum that pulsed in Bean's ears as they walked along. She had lived in the city for so long that these sounds had become foreign to her, and she felt in a way assaulted by them, the way a tourist in New York would have felt at the sirens and screeching of taxi brakes. The thought of the city made her stomach flip, and she said the first thing she could think of, too loudly, the volume pushing aside the still of the summer morning. 'So how's the wedding planning going?'

Sweat stood out against Rose's bare upper arms; Bean could see the way the drops arrayed along the pores from which they had emerged, like synchronized swimmers poised for a Busby Berkeley number. Rose shrugged. 'Okay, I guess. I don't know, I never really thought about weddings. I look at these bridal magazines, and they all say things like, "You've been dreaming of this day since you were a little girl," and I haven't. I never did.'

'Me, either. Is that odd? Do little girls really dream about their weddings and dress up like brides?'

'I have no idea. Certainly no one we know did. But then again, we're hardly a representative sample. And neither Jonathan nor I would want the kind of wedding a little girl would dream of anyway. All that foof,' Rose added dismissively.

'Foof,' Bean repeated, trying out the word, unconsciously letting it slip over the tip of her tongue. Rose shot her a doubtful glance, and they both laughed. 'Sorry, it's a funny word.'

There was a pause. Rose put her hand in her pocket, checking to make sure her wallet was still in there.

'So where will you have it?' Bean asked.

'Oh, the chapel on campus, you know. And then the reception in Harris. The college doesn't usually rent the space over holidays, but Dad got them to make an exception.' Bean nodded, remembering vaguely a concert she had attended in the Harris ballroom, during her sophomore year, she thought. The band had been some hippie-folk experience, probably one of the ones Cordy had seen recently at some mud-flung venue, and Bean had spent most of it pressed up against the back wall, drunkenly permitting some boy to fondle her. She tried to remember his name for a moment, and then mentally waved her hand, dismissing it. *O, is it all forgot? All school-days' friendship, childhood innocence?*

'So how will it work, everything? With Jonathan being in England and all?'

Rose gritted her teeth and looked over at one of the houses across the street. 'We haven't worked that all out yet exactly. The wedding's still scheduled for New Year's Eve. I didn't want to lose the deposit. So maybe I'll go over there a bit for a honeymoon, and then when he's done with his fellowship there, he'll come back.'

Bean couldn't honestly imagine anyone wanting to come back from Oxford to Barnwell, but she didn't say anything. Just hummed a few bars of 'How 'Ya Gonna Keep 'Em Down on the Farm? (After They've Seen Paree)'.

'Have you started looking for a dress yet?'

48

Rose laughed. How like Bean, to go directly for the clothes. 'No. I fear it, actually.' She tugged self-consciously at her shorts, which were threatening to ride up the insides of her pale thighs. 'I can't see myself in one of those big white monstrosities.'

'No one says you have to wear a big white dress. Wear what you want. It's not going to be a big formal wedding, right? Not black-tie or anything?'

Rose shook her head.

'Then it doesn't matter if it's not traditional.'

'I guess,' Rose said, but looked slightly confused by the idea.

They had come to the head of Main Street, and Bean stopped. 'I'll look with you. We'll go to Columbus; there won't be anything here,' Bean said. She turned to Rose for a moment and smiled, a sharp-toothed strangeness that was nonetheless kind. 'You'll be beautiful,' she said, and squeezed our older sister's sweaty palm.

Rose smiled back, a more genuine smile of surprise and pleasure, and came to a stop in front of the post office. 'Thanks.' She wanted to say more, but the moment had passed, and it wasn't in our nature to prolong sentimentality. She felt, for a moment, that she could tell Bean about how betrayed and confused she felt about Jonathan's departure, how torn she was about what she would do, that somehow Bean would under-stand, would be able to help. But then she pushed it aside. Bean couldn't help her with something like that. A dress, Bean could do. A life, no. 'I've got to go in and mail this.'

'Okay. I'm gonna walk down the street and check things out. I'll meet you in the Beanery in, like, a half hour?'

'Sure,' Rose shrugged and watched Bean walk away, her hair still bouncing back and forth, the creases in her clothes unbeaten by the heat. Rose shook her head and went inside to buy the stamp to mail a letter to Jonathan in Oxford.

The library drew Bean down the street, as it had drawn all of us over the years. Our parents had trained us to become readers, and the town's library had been the one place, other than church, that we visited every week. When we were young, we had three little red wagons that we would pull into town like a parade each Saturday morning, our mother at the head like the high-stepping grand marshal. Rose liked to go last, to keep an eye on the rest of us, particularly Cordy, who was usually in desperate need of it. Cordy would be eating a Popsicle, letting it drip along her arm, stopping to lick the sticky sweet slug trails off her skin. Or she wouldn't have stacked her books well and they would fall over the sides of the wagon, Rose picking them up like a flower girl in reverse. Or she would halt, squatting down to stare at an anthill in the cracks of a sidewalk, mesmerized by the to-ings and fro-ings until Rose poked her in the behind and made her waddle on. Bean, who liked to arrive first, would be following our mother, peppering her with questions that she answered when she found the time between social conversations along the way.

The building smelled the same – dusty and damp, and Bean stopped inside the door and inhaled. With all the money the town got from the college, she would have thought they would have changed the library, but it had remained the same. The carpet was dirty marigold, step-worn. To her right was the adult fiction, in the back, by the wall of windows looking out on a spreading willow tree and an ill-tended batch of hedges, the children's section. A woman browsed in the new fiction shelves, and two children, presumably hers, sat contentedly at the yellow plastic table in the back, studiously examining books too big for their hands. A man sat at one of the battered wooden study carrels, his head bent forward so Bean could see only the curl of his red-touched blond hair over his collar.

Mrs Landrige, the librarian who had been here in the red-wagon days, had been white-haired and stooped even then, but Bean could see her at the desk, stamping library cards with a patient hand. Bean felt a rush of sweet nostalgia for the woman who had introduced us to E. Nesbit and Edward Eager and Laura Ingalls Wilder, and she found herself desperately wanting to give the old woman a hug, not that Mrs Landrige would have trucked with that. Mrs Landrige, as a point of fact, didn't truck with much.

Bean strode over to the desk and leaned forward, her voice falling immediately to a whisper. We'd been well-trained. 'Mrs Landrige.'

The old woman's head popped up, her eyes sharp, watery blue. 'Bianca!' she said without a moment's hesitation. Her recall amazed Bean. With the way professors and their families shifted in and out of this town, she wondered how many patrons this otherwise small-town place would have had, how many cards Mrs Landrige could associate with a face. 'How lovely to see you!'

'It's good to see you, too,' Bean said honestly. 'I thought you might have retired.'

Mrs Landrige smiled. 'I'm too old *not* to work. Keeps my mind off the inevitable.' She gave a wheezy little chuckle, the red and black checked bow of her dress trembling against her chest.

Bean didn't quite know what to say, so she smiled back and cast her eyes around the room again, taking in the desk with the stacks of paper, the eroded rubber stamps leaning drunkenly against one another on the desktop.

The children in the back squabbled for a moment about a book in the centre of the table, and the man in the study carrel lifted his head for a moment, giving Bean a flash of his profile – strong cheekbones fading down into a goatee, his hairline crawling back genteelly from his forehead. Bean thought he could have been handsome. Pity about the goatee.

'Back for a visit?' Mrs Landrige asked. She had gone back to her careful work, leaving a date in the future stamped, slightly askew, in a column of its relations. 'Or to stay?'

'To stay,' Bean said, and then stammered it back in. 'I mean – I don't know how long I'll be here. I might go back to the city after . . .' After what, exactly? After our mother dies? After no one wants to throw you in jail any more? When will it be safe, Bean? 'After a while,' she finished weakly.

Mrs Landrige stopped, mid-stamp, and rested her weapon on the desk. She peered up at Bean for a moment, considering, and then gave a little nod, as though she'd decided something for herself. 'Then you'll need a library card, won't you?' she said finally, as though that solved everything (which, in our family, it nearly did). She opened a drawer with one vein-knotted hand and flicked out a stack of cards. She wrote Bean's name down on one of them in her precise, schoolroom script and handed it over with a flourish. 'It's nice to have you back, dear,' she said, and smiled, and Bean suddenly felt like crying.

She blinked hard and turned her gaze away from Mrs Landrige, lest the urge to cry, or worse, to hug her, returned. The man in the study carrel gathered his things and strode towards the desk. He wore jeans and a Superman T-shirt, and his boots were battered and faded in spots. No wedding ring, about the right age. Worth a hair flip, at least.

'All ready, Father?' Mrs Landrige asked, taking the books from the man.

'As I'll ever be,' he said.

'Have you met Father Aidan?' the librarian asked Bean, who was busy blushing a little at her idea of flirting with a priest.

'No,' Bean said, and thrust out her hand, a little too quickly. 'I'm Bianca Andreas. My father's a professor here. At Barnwell,' she added, as though the town were an academic Gotham, teeming with institutions of higher learning.

He smiled, revealing teeth that were bright white, and slightly crooked, as though his mouth were off-balance in some way. 'Charmed,' he said. 'I'm Aidan.'

'Father Aidan is the new priest at Saint Mark's,' Mrs Landrige advised Bean, neatly closing the last book and pushing the stack across the desk to him.

Well, at least he wasn't Catholic. St Mark's was our church – Episcopalian, not so progressive that it would have let our Bean actually bed the man standing in front of her (at least not with any expediency), but she wasn't going to go to hell just for thinking of it. Episcopalian priests could date, could fall in love, could marry. Maybe they could even engage in some heavy premarital petting. Bean had never really had the opportunity to consider this before.

'That's great!' Bean answered, too cheerfully. She felt stymied by her inability to engage her powers of flirtation, Puck without his love spell flowers. It was great, actually, that the church had a new Father; the last one had passed his sell-by date years ago, but had hung stubbornly on, boring the populace with his creaky Christmas services long after Bean had departed for less green pastures. But she didn't want to say that. 'My parents go there. To Saint Mark's.'

53

Aidan nodded. 'You're Dr Andreas's daughter, right? Your father read for us a few Sundays ago. He's an excellent speaker.'

This is true. Years of lecturing has created a monster of a presenter – his voice dips and swoops like a roller coaster, flashing forward at important moments like fireworks, and then retreating back, pulling his audience with him. His overgrown eyebrows wiggle, Marx-like, and he spreads his broad hands across the podium, as if he has to struggle to hold the papers down, lest his high-minded thoughts spirit them away.

'Thanks,' Bean said, though none of this is to her, or our, credit.

'How's your mother? She's got chemotherapy in a few days, doesn't she?'

Bean took a step back, surprised at the question. She'd forgotten how involved our parents were in the church – how they'd raised us to be involved in the church, too, not that it had stuck, particularly. She didn't think about God a lot. None of us did. He was just there if we needed him. Kind of like an extra tube of toothpaste under the sink.

'She's okay. She says she's tired. But that's to be expected. And, you know, now I'm here to help.' Bean was fairly pleased at putting forth this idea of herself as a latter-day (if better-dressed) Florence Nightingale to a clergyman.

'So, I'll see you for services, then?' Aidan asked, bending over to hoist his books under his arm. His hand, broad and dusted with gold hair, spread easily over the span of the covers, and Bean stared at it while she concocted an answer. She hadn't been to church in years, other than when she came home for Christmas, which hadn't been often. Our parents had wanted us to believe, but they had also taught us, outside of church, to question nearly everything. It has never made a great deal of sense that our father, a man who spends his days analysing the most finite syllables contained in one book, should so easily accept the even less believable tenets of another. And this is part of the reason why the mystery of faith has escaped all of us, and why Bean – why none of us – had ever bothered to make even a pretence of making church a regular part of our adult lives.

But it's not like she had any other pressing engagements, right?

'What the hell,' she said. 'I mean, yes.' Aidan looked at her oddly for a moment while she blushed again – twice in only a few minutes, a record – and then he smiled and said goodbye, heading out the doors into the sunshine.

'Would you like to check anything out today?' Mrs Landrige asked, settling back down into the repetitive stamp, stamp, stamp of making due date cards.

'No thank you,' Bean said. 'I have to meet my sister.'

At least we made good excuses for each other.

The next night, Rose was sitting on her bed, watching dust motes dance in the air while she dialled Jonathan's number. 'Right on time,' Jonathan said, picking up the phone an ocean away.

Rose and Jonathan had a scheduled once-a-week phone call. Not very romantic, Cordy might say.

Practical, Rose would reply.

'I miss you,' she said, sighing at the sound of his voice. She walked over and closed the door to her room. These conversations always seemed both too much and too little – how could she be sure that he wasn't doing something else while they talked? How could she be sure that he really was happy to talk to her? The distance was both amplified and removed over the wire.

'I miss you, too, love. How are you?'

'Okay. Bean's home.'

'The prodigal sister returns? It must be nice to have her around.'

Rose whuffed out a breath of annoyance. Jonathan didn't understand us. His family was huge and boisterous and loving – six siblings, now multiplied exponentially by marriages and children. Visiting his parents' house at Christmas had felt like being surrounded by a litter of overly enthusiastic puppies. 'Not really. She doesn't do much. Just lies around and reads. She's no help with Mom.'

'How long is she staying?'

'That's the funny thing. She quit her job. Moved all her stuff home. Like she's staying forever.'

'That is funny.' Jonathan and Bean had met at Thanksgiving, and had, oddly, hit it off. Rose had felt a little sick at the prospect of introducing our most femme fatale sister to him, but Bean had been perfectly appropriate, entertaining him with spot-on New York accents and cursing an amusing blue streak through card games they played 'til the wee hours of the morning. 'I'd always thought she'd be a city girl forever.'

'Me, too,' Rose said. 'I think something's wrong, actually, but she won't say anything to me. I tried to bring it up and she bit my head off.'

'Give her time. If something really is wrong, if it's enough to send her away from there forever, it's probably pretty bad.'

'But I could help,' Rose said plaintively.

Jonathan laughed. 'That's my little Miss Fix-It. Never met a problem she couldn't lick.'

'Don't tease. I'd like to help, if she'd let me. She offered to go with me to buy a wedding dress.'

'Take her up on it. You hate shopping, she loves it. Perfect.'

Rose looked out the window. Our father and Bean were

sitting on the chairs on the back porch, reading side by side. 'Am I going to need it?'

'A wedding dress? Of course you are. Unless you've got something to tell me.'

'No, it's not me. I just thought . . . I don't know, I don't feel right about this whole thing. What if you meet someone there? What if you decide you don't miss me at all? What if you don't want to come back?' Rose lay back on her bed, burying her face in the pillow, ashamed at having exposed so much of her fear, and too afraid not to ask.

'Rose.' Jonathan's voice was soft, but firm. 'You are the one I love. You. I've been waiting for you my whole life, and I'm not going to give you up now. I miss you so much, and there's nothing I want more than to make you my wife. And that's not going to change. Got it?'

'But you could decide to stay there . . .'

'Wherever I go, I'm going with you. That's the deal. And I don't get to make unilateral decisions any more. We made the decision for me to come here together, and wherever we go next, we'll make that decision together. Right?'

That wasn't an entirely fair characterization. They hadn't made it together: Rose had simply grudgingly decided not to fight his desire to go abroad. Despite her misgivings, she knew this was important to his career, and though the thought of living without him for so long made her ache when she thought about it, she knew it wasn't worth losing him over. But she hadn't exactly been in favour of it. 'Right,' she said.

'Buy the dress. Order personalized matchbooks and hire the Cleveland Symphony to play. Whatever makes you happy. But I will absolutely be there on New Year's Eve, and you had better be there, too.'

'I will,' she said with a smile, picturing his hand in hers

and pushing down the inevitable question of, if they couldn't even decide where to live, what was going to happen to them after the wedding was over, when they actually had to start forging a marriage?

Rose would be lying if she said she actually liked her job. Since she had refused to take a job out of state, she had accepted a position at Columbus University, where she was a cog in the wheel. The mathematics building was cold concrete; hallways on the outside by the windows, classrooms inside, devoid of natural light. Her students stared at her, their beer-bloated, sleep-deprived faces gone sickly under the fluorescent lights glaring and sputtering above her, punctuating her lectures with an angry hum.

She shared a tiny office with two other professors, one of whom was perennially missing, the other who had an annoying propensity for leaving his coffee mug on her desk, a habit that left miniature Venn diagrams on any papers she had the ill fortune to leave exposed. His own desk was so swollen with the detritus of years of disorganization that on the one hand she sympathized with his plight, but on the other, well. You know Rose. In these conditions she graded papers, took meetings with students prone to tears at the sight of a coordinate plane, stared blankly at the walls when she was supposed to be writing, and doodled polytopes around the circles of coffee stains on her papers. The walls were cinder blocks, the white paint yellow in the light.

Rose felt as though she had been jailed, Kafkaesque, for an unspecified crime.

In a university so large, the staff interacted little, ships in the night; she felt unmoored, washing from classroom to office to faculty parking lot. Some days the only people she spoke to were her students, and you could hardly call that an actual interaction (or, Rose might say on a particularly bad day, you could hardly call them actual people). Occasionally she met a man, an alumnus at a university function, a textbook representative, a professor at another university who came to give a lecture. Her easy power drew them to her, to the challenge of making her smile, lighting her face in candlelight. But these dates were distractions, and poor ones at that, leaving her to drift the halls like Banquo's ghost, seen and yet unseen, feared and misunderstood.

And then came Jonathan.

She walked into her office one bleak January day a year ago, and he was sitting at the desk of the Mystery Professor, his feet up casually, his lower lip stuck out as he stared at a book in his lap. Jonathan, had he been so inclined, could have been terribly handsome. But as it was, his hair was sloppily brushed, a tiny shock standing up in the back as though preparing a mutiny. The rims of his glasses were nearly as black as his hair, and the lenses wanted cleaning in a bad way. He wore a short-sleeved shirt and a tie, an ensemble that always reminds us of our father, but Jonathan's shirt was burgundy, his tie a matching shade, showing evidence of some dandy tendencies. Then again, his pants were black, his shoes, brown, evidence of the same professorial fashion sense our father possessed.

Her mind a million miles away, his presence so unexpected, Rose shrieked when she saw him, the papers in her hands jumping out of their orderly stack into a sloppy bouquet. He looked up, less startled than she, and, shockingly, laughed. He'd tell her later that the improbable sound she had made, like an asthma patient on helium, had caused his laughter, but at the moment Rose thought he was laughing at her, so she blushed sharply and stared down at her papers.

'I guess I startled you,' he said. He flipped his legs up

59

and then down to the floor. He was tall, slender. One sideburn longer than the other. 'I'm a visiting professor. I'll be here through next year.'

Still staring at her papers, Rose said, 'You must be the Mystery Professor,' then blushed harder as she realized what she had said. She shuffled the pages back together, walked towards her desk. She had to turn to get between the desks, shoved together like connecting blocks to fit in the space that had really only been designed for one. This action embarrassed her, for some reason, the wide spread of her hips near him.

Jonathan barked a laugh, pure pleasure. 'Is that what you call me?' He stood, crossed the tiny distance between their desks, extended his hand. 'I'm Jonathan Campbell. I teach chemistry, but there's no office space over there so I'm exiled here. Which is why you never see me. I've been here since September.'

'Pleased to meet you. Where are you from?' she said, and took his hand. She raised her eyes to meet his, brown to nearly black, the shadow of stubble on his face like the shadow of the leaves in the Shakespearean forest of Arden.

'I'm a bit of a wanderer. I was born in Michigan, but I've lived all over.'

'So glamorous Columbus, Ohio, is just one stop on your world tour?' Rose asked, her cheeks flushing. Was she flirting?

He chuckled. 'You could say that. Last year I was in Paris.'

'Coming here must have been a letdown.' Her heart was beating quickly and she couldn't stop smiling, stupidly, like a pre-teen. She wondered what Bean would do. Flip her hair, probably. Rose patted the conservative bun at the back of her neck awkwardly.

'Not at all. Paris was overrated. So many French people. I didn't catch your name?' he asked, coaxing.

60

'Rose Andreas,' she said.

'You teach in the math department?' he asked. Rose stared at him, tongue-tied.

'Yes,' she said, finally. 'This is my office.'

Jonathan nodded, looking thoughtfully at Rose. Oh, our Rose. Her hair up like a Gibson girl, her skin stained pretty pink from the blushing, face bare of makeup, one of those flowing outfits that hid her curves, *beauty and honour in her are so mingled* . . . but would he see it? Would he see, beneath her self-consciousness, the way she could clean that stain off his tie with only club soda and the edge of her shirt, catch spiders we would be too afraid to touch, marshal our forces to pack the car for a trip so everything fit and nothing was forgotten, pick the perfect fresh flowers to make the breakfast table seem like a celebration, hold us after a nightmare, put herself aside to make sure we were happy? Would he see why we loved her so? We held our breath.

'Would you like to go to lunch?' he asked.

He saw it.

Perhaps you never liked your name. Perhaps you took every opportunity to change it: a new school, for example, where you would test out life with some pale echo of your real name – Elizabeth to Bitsy, wouldn't that be cute? A whole new you. You tried your middle name, provided it was suitable and not embarrassing, as middle names are wont to be. Or perhaps you were one of those poor souls whose well-meaning parents, in honour of some long-dead ancestor, gave you a name no contemporary soul should have to bear. Like Evelyn or Leslie or Laurie for a boy. Or Florence or Mildred or Doris for a girl – not bad names, you understood, just woefully dated, guaranteeing years of playground torture or a feeling you were destined for a rocking chair and an old folks' home long before your time.

But what if it weren't so much a matter of having a name with unfortunately predetermined gender identification, or one you felt just didn't suit you? What if the name you were given had already been lived in, had been inhabited so well, as a matter of fact, that its very mention brings to mind its original owner, and leaves your existence little more than an afterthought?

At one of Cordy's many temp jobs, she had worked in an office with a harried secretary by the name of Elizabeth Taylor. Huddled in her cubicle, desperately pretending to be worth the twenty-five dollars an hour the company was paying to her agency (without, of course, doing any actual work), Cordy watched and listened as Elizabeth Taylor answered the phone. At least a million times a day, Cordy thought, running her fingers back and forth across the office supplies she hoarded as props in her one-woman burlesque of industry, Elizabeth Taylor said, 'Yes, really.' And every time, she said it with a smile. Cordy supposed it was at least partially due to the fact that Elizabeth Taylor had married into her name, so had only had it for fifteen years or so. Given time, we were sure, she would tire of the *National Velvet* jokes, of the comments on her enthusiasm for matrimony, and one day, Elizabeth Taylor would snap, lashing out at her husband, wishing she had never married him.

With a father like ours, and with names like ours, we had reached that state years ago.

First came Rosalind, a fair choice; probably our mother's intervention spared her from something weightier. But after that, it was all our father's doing, we are sure. Because then came the second daughter, and what can you name a second daughter but Bianca? And then the third, and if it had been anything other than Cordelia, the heavens might have shaken. Bean and Rose were grateful, true, that the *Lear* comparisons could not have been made until the troika was complete, or they might have been dubbed to match the play's older sisters, and they knew there was no way to survive being named Goneril and Regan. Not in this day and age.

We wear our names heavily. And though we have tried to escape their influence, they have seeped into us, and we find ourselves living their patterns again and again.

It's unlikely that our parents ever looked up any of our names in one of those baby name books. *The Riverside Shakespeare* had obviously been the repository of choice. Once Rose had a summer camp counsellor who, as an icebreaker, looked up the meanings of all the children's names, and Rosalind was horrified to learn her name meant, yes, 'beautiful rose', but also 'horse serpent'. *Horse serpent*? If that won't give a girl body image issues for life, we don't know what will.

But mostly the thorn in our Rose's side – Cordy again with the punny – was love. For really, the transformation of *As You Like It* comes through the love between Rosalind and Orlando. How can you live up to that? How can you possibly find a man in twenty-first-century America who would paper an entire forest with love poems to you?

Well, Rose will tell you, you can't.

And if he did, he would probably also be rather creepy.

But she can tell you this only after sixteen years – sixteen *years*! – of searching through the forest, of weeding out unsuitable suitors in some sort of romantic scavenger hunt: Emotionally unavailable? Check! Oedipus complex? Check! Stalker? Check! Inability to commit? Check! Inability NOT to commit? Check! It wasn't until long into her dating career, when a particularly callous date had taken her to a production of the offending play that Rose had realized the trap of her name. Because of course, being Rosalind meant she would always be searching for her true love, but would require such extraordinary lengths to prove it that she would never find him, at least not outside of fiction.

So she dumped the playdate and vowed to give up entirely, because it's not as though her life was unsatisfying, she promised herself, and this is of course precisely when she met Jonathan, who was not the type of man to write poems and post them all over campus, but who was the type of man to agree to do that if that's what she wanted, and she figured that wasn't too shabby.

FOUR

Even if it hadn't been summer, had been fall or spring or winter, if the campus had been alive with students and more than the skeleton crew of staff that kept the town on life support during the long, slow pull between graduation and orientation, there still wouldn't have been anything to do at night. Maybe a concert by a visiting performer, or a misguided experimental piece in the black box theater would take you through to the anemic hour of nine or so, but then what? Bean had always been a night owl, had more than once been caught by Rose reading under her sheets with a flashlight when we were children and had fully embraced the ethos of the city that never slept.

And now here she was back in Barnwell. Our parents had drifted toward sleep in stages, like a series in tableau, here doing the dishes, then sitting on the sofa reading, then their voices talking softly upstairs, and now silence. Rose had taken a long walk, and when she'd gotten back Bean had been nearly desperate enough to suggest a game of Spite & Malice, a card game we had played as children that was terrible with only two players but would have at least whiled away some time, worked her into sleep. But Rose had been grouchy and silent, so Bean had thought better of it and curled up on the sofa with a book until Rose, too, had stomped up the stairs, taking her ill will with her like Pooh's little black rain cloud.

'This would never happen in New York,' Bean told her book, a weepy novel she had discovered half-read in the pantry.

The book remained, unsurprisingly, quiet.

The whole drive home she had pictured her stay in Barnwell, imagining an ascetic, nun-like existence that would serve as spiritual penance for what she had done. She would wear drab colors and eat dry bread and her skin would take on the cinematic pallor of a glamorous invalid as she modestly turned down creature comforts. But the reality of that hair shirt was beginning to chafe already. It was Saturday night, for crying out loud. At this hour in the city, she would only just be getting ready to go out, and here she was seriously considering going to bed.

'Ridiculous,' she told the book, and shut it firmly. There was gas in the car, and she had a few tens folded in her wallet, not that she was going to be buying her own drinks. Some lonely yokel would be more than happy to take care of that for her. She slipped up the stairs and into her room, opening the closet and flipping through her clothes until she found something acceptable – not good enough for New York by half, but too good for any of the bars around here. Her makeup and hair took barely any time at all – that was one benefit of being someplace with such low standards – and then she was out the door into the night, lighting a cigarette as she eased the car out of the driveway in neutral, the lights off until she hit the street, just like old times. She was Bianca again, or nearly so, if only for the night.

Bean carried the burden of Bianca Minola's name as heavily as Rose carried Rosalind's. Rose might argue that Bianca's hardly burdened her – to be the perpetual belle of the ball, argued over by multiple suitors, beloved by her father, described, after one meeting, *'I saw her coral lips to move, And with her breath she did perfume the air; Sacred and sweet was all I saw in her . . .'* How difficult is that?

Truthfully, the three of us look almost exactly alike (we have been slightly suspicious of siblings who do not resemble one another; it seems to be, somehow, cheating), but Bean has always been the beautiful one. Okay, so she has spent far more time at the gym, beating the odd figure bestowed upon us by our parents – our mother, mostly – into submission: the Scarlett O'Hara waist and small, lifted breasts, the spread into muscular arms and broad shoulders, the ballooned hips and thighs. And Bean, too, has spent fortunes at hair salons, taking our thick but notoriously independent and undeniably dull brown hair to the best stylists. She is like a parent dragging a difficult child to stiff-necked, tweedy psychiatrists, desperate to find the one who will understand.

Even if you look at us together and see that our eyes are identical: large, cow-brown, slightly too close together; our noses the same straight, strong, broad-bridged lines; our mouths identically thin-lipped but wide, you might still say Bianca is the beautiful one. We are all our father's daughters – *Your father's image is so hit in you* – but it is Bianca who turns that face into beauty.

She pulled the car into the parking lot of a bar a few towns over, spritzing a sample bottle of perfume into her hair to blur the smoke. The door gave its aching groan when she opened it and she tilted across the gravel in her heels until she hit the sidewalk. She felt better already. A little male attention, a few shots, she'd be as good as new. She could be Mother Teresa tomorrow. As long as she wasn't too hungover.

There were bars closer, but one had boasted that it was karaoke night (um, no) and the parking lots at the others had been sadly empty. She could hear the noise from outside, classic rock on the jukebox, the smell of beer seeping over the doorsill. Bean took a breath and stepped inside.

No one turned to watch her as she walked through the door. She did a quick survey of the layout and headed to a seat toward the side of the bar where she could accurately eye her prospects. The bartender eased toward her slowly, took the towel off his shoulder, and gave a cursory wipe to the sticky wood in front of Bean. 'What can I get ya?' he asked. Bean let her eyelashes flutter as she considered the meager selection.

'A double shot of Jack and a bottle of whatever light you've got,' Bean said. She looked up at him from under spider legs of mascara, but he had already turned back to the refrigerator. He wouldn't even do in a pinch anyway, she decided, eyeing his back. A little old, his belly gone soft, his eyes rheumy and red from alcohol. She could do better.

'Five-fifty,' he said, sliding the bottle and the glass onto the counter in front of her.

She began to reach for the cash in her bag, then stopped herself and pulled out her cigarettes instead. 'I'll run a tab,' she said. He shrugged and walked away.

The jukebox howled out a tinny guitar solo as Bean drained the shot, letting the alcohol burn down her throat until it became too much to bear, and she gulped at the watery beer to cool the fire. The room blurred pleasantly, and she smiled as she turned slightly on her stool, resting a bare elbow on the sticky bar.

A group of women huddled in a booth near the back;

Bean could just see the tops of their heads bobbing as they shrieked with laughter. A post-work happy hour. She knew the feeling – the giddy relief of being furloughed from the office for the night, the flush of adolescent excitement as the talk turned to sex, the camaraderie forged in the trenches and celebrated over drinks, the feeling that, as a group, you have achieved something momentous simply by surviving the workday.

By the jukebox, a few couples had formed a makeshift dance floor in between some of the tables. Bean watched them sway for a moment, and then skipped her eyes over them.

The pool table looked promising. A group of men, early thirty-something, playing a (poor, by the looks of it) game of pool for beer money. One of them was in a suit, his tie loosened, sleeves rolled up, but the rest were in T-shirts and jeans. Thick-bodied ex-athletes with once-handsome faces, now gone swollen and sad from alcohol and disappointment. Trapped in these one-horse towns, their best days behind them, the way she'd sworn she'd never be. The way she now was.

Bean had always had a way with men. There were women prettier, and smarter, and thinner, and funnier, but Bean had something special. When she was only twelve or thirteen, she had gone to performances at Barney and had drawn the gazes of the college boys who might have been – hopefully would have been – appalled if they had known her age. And when she discovered how to sneak out of the house on Friday and Saturday nights and follow the sounds of hysteria and beer, she had learned to flirt through the haze of smoke and noise, how to kiss without making any promises, and how to reel a man across the room with only a look.

She lifted her beer to her mouth, the neck hanging

between two fingers, and shook back her hair. The one in the suit. He'd do. She signaled for another shot and tossed it back before taking her beer and her cigarettes and moving to a high table nearer to the pool players.

'Nice shot,' she observed when one of the T-shirts overshot, sending the cue ball hopping over the edge, where it rolled under her chair.

'Sorry,' he said, kneeling to recover it.

'Not at all. I like a man on his knees.' His head snapped up and he looked at her, startled, then smiled.

'That could be arranged.'

Bean didn't reply, only smiled and took a sip of her beer, wrapping her lips around the opening just so. He tossed the ball in the air, nearly missed catching it, and backed toward the table.

'As you were,' she nodded, dismissing him. The others were looking now, running their eyes over her. She crossed her legs, flipped her high heel so it hung from her toes, and lit a cigarette with a sigh. Like shooting fish in a barrel. *This is a gift that I have; simple, simple.*

A game later, the man headed to the bar and brought back another beer and shot for her. 'You up for a game?' he asked.

'Sure,' she said. 'As long as you don't mind losing.' He laughed as she hopped off the stool with a practiced toss of her hair and took the stick from him.

Bean was drunk enough that it was deliciously easy to play her part without thinking – to brush up against the guy in the suit, to lean just right against the table, to get one of them to settle that pesky tab and keep her supplied with drinks.

But then there was a rush of heat coming in the door, and a gaggle of girls piled in. Maybe they were over twenty-one, but they were definitely girls. Their hair dyed too brassy, sprayed too high, their shorts too short,

70

their makeup too thick. But they, unlike Bean, were on the right side of thirty. And they, unlike Bean, were willing to play dumb, and giggle their helpless way from the bar to the pool tables, preening and posing. The air in the room seemed thinner and the lights dimmer as Bean watched the men's heads swivel, one by one, turning away from her, showing her that they'd only been using her to pass the time until something better came along. Exactly what she'd been doing to them. A lump formed in her throat and she swallowed hard. Was she going to have to fight for this? She'd never had to fight for attention before, and now she was going to have to do it for these men who hardly seemed worth having in the first place?

'Ladies,' the man who had first approached Bean said, and his voice was a throaty purr. 'Join us?' The men around the table had gone slack-jawed and simian, beer bottles held limply in their hands, pool cues leaning against the wall and the tables as they admired the display of raw young flesh in front of them. Bean felt as though she were folding in on herself like an origami crane.

The girls looked at one another, consulting, in the way that girls of that age do, as though they are constantly arriving at a telepathic agreement before making even the slightest move. 'We don't even know how to play!' one of them squealed, and the rest burst into giggles again.

'Give me a break,' Bean said. She walked to the wall and chalked her cue, running her hand with firm, prac-ticed strokes along the wood, and then blowing gently, her lips puckered just so. The men ignored her. One of the girls gave her a pitying glance, and Bean caught her breath as she recognized the look – she'd been cocky enough to give it herself once or twice – of a woman so

71

confident in the unearned beauty of youth that she could afford to feel sorry for someone like Bean. And instead of feeling superior, Bean felt as though she were in the wrong, as though she had tried too hard, was overdressed and overage and just plain over. Any fight that had been brewing in her burst into steam, like water thrown on a fire.

'We'll teach you,' one of the men said, and Bean watched the way their chests puffed out, peacock-proud, at the thought that they could rescue these helpless women from the dangers of the vicious pool table.

There was a rustle of activity as the girls shimmied their way around, pretending that they didn't know which end of the pool cue to use, and the men sidled into place beside them, swapping partners like they were all in some complicated square dance with an absent caller until everything settled down. One of the girls bumped into Bean, pushing her up against the edge of the table. 'Should we just start over?' one of the guys asked.

Bean, who had been winning the last round with her partner, restrained the urge to whack him over the head with her pool cue. She looked to her partner to support her objection, but he looked like he was about ready to dive headfirst into the prodigious cleavage of one of the gigglers. Bean twisted her body, placed a hand on her toned hip. Nothing. She flipped her hair. No response. One of the men leaned over and whispered something in his partner's ear. She shrieked with laughter and he tilted back, draining his beer bottle, looking pleased with himself. 'Fine,' Bean said, and moved back from the table again. One of the men stepped forward and racked the balls.

She stepped back into the shadows, fumbling for her glass with one hand while she watched the show unfolding in front of her. She drained the shot, not even tasting the bitter liquid, but the buzz of the bar receded and her vision tunneled out. In the darkness by the wall, she felt as though she'd stepped off the stage straight into the audience. Because there was no doubt about it – this was really happening. She wasn't waiting in the wings for her chance to come back onstage. She'd been replaced by a group of far inferior understudies – women who were louder and dumber and uglier and tackier, but who were inarguably younger.

The alcohol had turned sour in her stomach, and she realized she had to get herself home somehow now, since clearly she wasn't going to get even the runt of that litter of men. Not tonight. And while Bean wasn't usually one to walk away from a challenge, she could see the way this would play out, and she didn't like the image of herself fighting with these silly girls over these worthless men. There was so little dignity left in her life, she didn't want to waste it on them.

Since the men had paid her tab, Bean asked the bartender to call her a cab and went and waited in the parking lot, sitting on the hood of her car and smoking cigarette after cigarette, watching people drift out of the bar as the night grew old and the hope drained slowly out of it.

What did this mean for her? What do you do when you are no longer the one worth watching? When there are women less beautiful, less intelligent, less versed in the art of the game who nonetheless can beat you at it simply because of their birth date?

The cab pulled up and Bean flicked her cigarette into the gravel. She leaned her head against the window, cool from the air-conditioning against the heat of the night. What would she do now? Who could she possibly be if she was no longer Bianca? Who would want Bean? She felt cruelly sober, probably could have even driven home, and regretted that the last of her cash was going to go to pay for this ride, and that she'd have to ask someone to drive her back to the scene of this humiliation in the morning so she could get her car. A waste. Her whole night, her whole life. Wasted.

'Get up,' Rose ordered Bean. She kicked the foot of the bed for good measure. *'Fie, you slug-a-bed.'*

'Jesus, Rose,' Bean moaned. 'It's not even seven. Shut the hell up.' A lock of hair caught on her dry lips and she shoved it out of the way before rolling over and burrowing back into her pillow.

'Mom has an appointment in Columbus at eight. We're leaving in fifteen minutes.'

'Goody. Shove off.'

Rose's nostrils flared and she put her fists on her hips, glaring down at the covers piled on top of Bean. She was clearly the one who'd turned the air-conditioning down so low last night, buried as she was under a feather duvet. In June. Out of pure meanness, Rose reached out and yanked the covers off of Bean, who howled in protest and yanked them back.

'Your mother is sick, you selfish brat. I told you last night we were going up for her next round of chemo, and you said you'd come.'

'I did?' Bean asked curiously, peering up at Rose's glowering silhouette against the sunlight. It seemed remarkably unlike her to have agreed to something like that. And frankly, she didn't remember it. Ever since the night at the bar, she'd been putting herself to sleep by drinking, and last night had gotten a little fuzzy after she'd polished off the bottle of wine she'd found in the refrigerator. Maybe she'd been in one of those happy drunk moods. Or more likely she'd agreed with whatever she assumed would make Rose shut up fastest.

74

'Yes, you did. Now if your highness would kindly get dressed, we can leave. It's not bad enough I've got to get them ready, now I've got to worry about you, too?'

'I'm up,' Bean said, tossing aside the covers and sitting up. 'I'm up.' The 'bitch' at the end of the sentence was understood.

Our parents listened to the radio the entire drive, while Rose sat in the back and seethed, and Bean marinated in the fumes of alcohol seeping out of her skin and tried not to vomit. The toothpaste had helped with her breath, but not at all with the dehydrated headache of white wine the morning after, and the minty taste on her thick tongue made her throat feel clogged.

Inside the hospital, Rose led the parade. Bean veered off toward a coffee cart, Rose yanked her back in line. Bean watched our parents walking together, the stroll of the long-partnered. Our father is an inch shorter than our mother, his hair shot through with gray, his neatly clipped beard gone respectably salt and pepper. They always walk with her arm in his, his free hand darting up a thousand times an hour to adjust his glasses, their steps matched perfectly, knowing each other's gait. But at the doors to the outpatient clinic, Rose halted and sent our parents through alone. As the doors slid open, our father turned and kissed our mother lightly below the line of the silk scarf on her forehead. She accepted the tenderness like a benediction.

'We're not going in?' Bean asked. She'd found the end of a roll of mints in her purse and popped one, only slightly linty, into her mouth. She snapped it with a firm crunch and grinned at Rose's frown.

'Only one visitor allowed. There's not enough room. We'll wait outside.'

'We can't go in? Then what the hell did we come up here for?'

'Moral support.' Rose hoisted her bag onto her shoulder and about-faced toward the seating area.

'I could have been moral support at home,' Bean grumbled quietly, but she followed along, procuring coffee on the way. 'How long does this take?' she asked, settling into the seat beside Rose.

Rose glanced at her watch. 'We'll be out of here by noon, I'd say. They have to check her blood first, and then the pharmacy has to put together the treatment, and then the chemo itself takes a few hours.' She produced a book from her bag and opened it pointedly.

'What are they going to do?'

'He reads to her, usually. You did bring a book, didn't you?'

Bean reached into her purse and pulled out a thick paperback, the covers hanging by the barest edges. Rose nodded and turned to read her own book. Inside, our mother would sit in one of the forgivingly vinyl hospital recliners while a tube dripped benevolent poison into her veins, and our father perched his reading glasses on his nose and read to her.

How can we explain what books and reading mean to our family, the gift of libraries, of pages? Even at Coop, the tiny professor-run cooperative school we'd attended, a refuge of overly intellectual families, we were different. 'What do you mean you don't watch television?' one girl had asked Bean. She was new, her parents visiting professors who passed in and out in one calendar year, their sojourn so brief Bean cannot even remember the girl's name. She remembers only the strange furrow to her brow, signifying the complete and utter incomprehension at the idea of a life without.

Except to us, it wasn't a life without. It was a life with. For Rose, a life where, after our weekly trip to the library, she cleared the top of her dresser and set out her week's

76

reading, stood them on their ends, pages fanned out, sending little puffs of text into the air. One of her friends, a little girl with sunken blue eyes and parchment skin, laid her costume jewelry out in the same way, and even then, Rose had recognized the metaphor, standing in her friend's white wicker bedroom, looking at the sparkle of paste, to her, dull by comparison. For Bean, a life where the glamour and individuality she sought was only the gentle flick of a page away. For Cordy, always slightly detached no matter how many people surrounded her, clucking for her attention, a life where she could retreat and be alone and yet transported.

In college, when it became clear people might think there were more interesting things to do than read, when it was apparent the only books appropriate for decorating one's room were textbooks, weighty and costly, worth only their end-of-the-semester resale value, we were faced with a choice. Rose, who had never paid attention to the requirements of cool, carried on reading, her one concession choosing a single room after her first year, though this was probably more due to her penchant for cleanliness than for fear of being unmasked as a reader. Bean spent afternoons in the library, having discovered the classics room, filled with huge leather armchairs and ottomans, and walls lined with books into which she could escape. Cordy, as mindless of convention as Rose, but never bearing its stigma in the same way, read every-where: walking to class, during class, on the quad while Frisbees spun above her head, in bed at night while her roommate and her friends played cards on the floor, and once by a basement window at a keg party, where just enough light from the streetlamps spilled in to allow her to turn the pages. The difference between Rose and Cordy in this respect was that Rose, upon interruption, would fix the interrupter with a baleful glare, keep the book open, and reply curtly until a break in conversation allowed her reentry into the world in which she had been basking. Cordy would close the book, or slapjack it down on its open pages, and join the fun.

In New York, Bean chose the subway because of the reading time it afforded, free of questions but not of distractions – the frotteurs, the over-the-shoulder-readers, the panhandlers, the nosy parkers with opinions going spare – though Bean rapidly learned to dispatch each one of these with ease while keeping one eye moving down the page. She remembered one of her boyfriends asking, offhandedly, how many books she read in a year. 'A few hundred,' she said.

'How do you have *time*?' he asked, gobsmacked.

She narrowed her eyes and considered the array of potential answers in front of her. Because I don't spend hours flipping through cable complaining there's nothing on? Because my entire Sunday is not eaten up with pre-game, in-game, and post-game talking heads? Because I do not spend every night drinking overpriced beer and engaging in dick-swinging contests with the other financirati? Because when I am waiting in line, at the gym, on the train, eating lunch, I am not complaining about the wait/staring into space/admiring myself in available reflective surfaces? I am *reading*!

'I don't know,' she said, shrugging.

This conversation, you will not be surprised to know, was the impetus for their breakup, given that it caused her to realize the emotion she had thought was her not liking him very much was, in fact, her not liking him at all. Because despite his money and his looks and all the good-on-paper attributes he possessed, he was not a reader, and, well, let's just say that is the sort of nonsense up with which we will not put.

*　　*　　*

It hadn't really sunk in to Bean what our mother's illness meant until the third day after the chemotherapy treatment. Everything hurt our mother. She was cold, but the blankets felt heavy and hard against her skin. The barest sliver of light coming through the curtains made her turn her head away, slicing through the delicate skin of her eyelids with scalpel-like precision. She was bored, but our reading to her made her head ache until she begged us to stop. Lonely, she would call to us to be with her, and then beg us to leave, as if our presence made it harder to breathe. She vomited and then asked for food, and then vomited again. Bean hovered uncertainly in the hallway outside our parents' room, stepping in and then out again with each changing request.

'Is it always like this?' she asked Rose, who was standing at the sink doing dishes, handing them to Bean, who dried them ineffectively with a wet cloth and then put them vaguely where they belonged.

Rose shook her head, put her lips in a thin line. A soap bubble floated up from the sink and she jabbed it with a finger, watching it pop in the sunlight. 'This is bad. I read that it gets worse throughout the treatment, but I didn't expect this.'

'I hate not being able to do anything for her. How long will it last?'

'Usually it's only a couple of days – maybe longer this time, since it's so bad. I'll have to call the doctor and ask. And then she'll be tired for a few days longer than that. She's got an appointment to get the size of the tumor rechecked, and then they'll schedule the surgery.'

We washed and dried in uneasy silence for a few minutes. Outside, the sounds of summer continued – the buzz of bees, shouts of children free from school, a sprinkler whisking in circles. It seemed wrong and harsh

79

for there to be such happiness in the world at that moment.

'Is she going to die?' Bean asked uncertainly. Her voice shook a little, and she stared hard at the plate in her hand, watching the streaks of damp disappear into the air.

Rose snapped off the faucet. 'Don't say that. Don't even say it. She's going to be fine.'

'But . . .'

'Don't.' Rose held up her hand, her fingers wrinkled and white from the water. She wouldn't meet Bean's eyes. 'We can't even think about it. It's bad luck.'

Bean said nothing. She finished drying and put the last dishes away and then disappeared into the living room.

Rose went upstairs and peeked in the door to our parents' room, looking at the dim shape of our mother lying on the bed. She was sleeping; Rose could hear the steady whisper of breath. When we were little and had nightmares, we would slip into our parents' room and beg to sleep in their bed. Our mother rarely agreed to this, usually walking us back to our own beds and giving us a kiss as protection against the darkness. Now she only shifted slightly, her mouth falling open as she slept. Rose felt the urge to crawl into bed beside her. Instead she tiptoed back down the hall and down the stairs. Bean had assumed her position on the sofa, a book held loosely between her fingers. On the floor beside her was a glass of water she'd tipped over.

An impotent fury caught in Rose's throat. 'Bean, look at what you've done.'

Bean bent her head slightly so she could see over the edge of the sofa. She lifted a hand enough to right the glass and then went back to her book.

Rose stomped into the kitchen and returned with a towel.

Kneeling, she dabbed at the water on the floor and then, less successfully, the rivulets of liquid already soaking into the edges of the rug.

'It's just water, Rose. Relax.' Bean tugged at one of her nails with her front teeth. Having the acrylics removed had exposed the weakness of the nails beneath, and they constantly folded in on themselves, tearing down to the nail bed so the edges of her fingers were always bloody and sore.

'Water causes damage, Bean.' Rose finished mopping up and pushed herself to her feet. She restrained herself from throwing the wet towel onto Bean's perfectly made-up face in order to prove her point.

Bean looked up at Rose and then waved her hand dismissively. 'Move along,' she said. She hooked one leg over the top of the sofa and went back to her book.

'You are impossible. Do you have any idea what life would be like without me here?'

'It'd be a hell of a lot quieter, that's for damn sure,' Bean said. She bit another nail, tearing the white off, and spat it into the air.

'I do everything around here. Everything.'

Bean sighed and rested her book on her chest. 'Which is precisely the way you like it. Now, do you want to talk about what's really bothering you, or would you prefer to shut the hell up and let me read?'

'What's really bothering me is the way you just come back here and take everything for granted, like we're here to serve you. You get to go out all night and no one says a word. And I'm sick of running around like Cinderella, cleaning up your messes.'

'No one's stopping you from going out, Rose. Go wherever you want. You're free and twenty-one.'

'Right. So I'll just go off to England and live with Jonathan. How's that?'

'Fine with me,' Bean shrugged. She lifted up her hair so it spread out over the arm of the sofa, like Ophelia drowned in the brook.

Rose sat down, the wet towel still clutched in her hand. 'Don't be silly. I have to be here to take care of Mom.'

'They have people for that, you know. I like to call them doctors.'

'That's not what I meant.'

'Okay. Then how's this?' Bean sat up, putting her book down beside her. Rose winced at the broken spine, the leaves of the book spread out like a bird's wings. 'How's about you stay here until Mom is through her treatment, and then you go to England and wherever else Jonathan wants to go?'

'I have a job. I can't just leave it.'

'Does Jonathan get a salary?'

'Of course.'

'Do they put him up in housing?'

'In Oxford they are, but in the next position, who knows?'

'Then you don't need to work.'

'This may shock you, Bean, but not everyone works exclusively for the money.'

'Of course they do. That's why they call it work. If we got paid just to sit around and look cute, they'd call it something else entirely.'

'I don't want to be the kind of person who doesn't work. I don't want to be a housewife. I don't want to be like . . .' Rose censored herself, but the sentence was hanging in the air and Bean pounced.

'You don't want to be like Mom? This may shock *you*, Rose, but I'm fairly certain Mom could have worked if she wanted to. It's not like Dad was keeping her in some kind of pre-suffrage dungeon. Besides, I'm not suggesting that you never work again. I'm just saying that you don't have to worry about a job right this very second. Lots of people would love to be in that position. Me, for one.'

'I don't exactly see you running right out to get a job.'

'I'm gearing up for it.'

Rose huffed and looked out the window. The afternoon was gathering into gray clouds. There was a storm coming. She pressed her hands together and then pulled at each finger, stretching the muscles, while her mind played over the future. Planning to leave after our mother was better would make it look like she didn't care, like she saw our mother's brush with death as an inconvenient delay to her own plans. What kind of daughter – what kind of person – thought like that? And what if she planned to leave and then our mother didn't get better? What if it turned out that she was sitting around, plane ticket in hand, waiting for our mother to die?

'What if she doesn't make it?'

'You just said it was bad luck to say it.'

'I know. But now I can't stop thinking about it.'

'Don't get so dramatic, Rosie. I was just saying. It's not going to happen.' Bean turned back to her book.

Rose fidgeted with her fingers nervously for another minute, until Bean put down her book and looked at her, long and hard. It wasn't like Rose to look ill at ease, and it made her a little nervous.

'What will I do? What will I do if she dies?' Rose asked, and she spoke so quietly the words seemed to disappear in midair.

Bean sighed. 'If you had a brain in your head, you'd quit your job and go to England to be with Jonathan. Do you see the theme here?'

'I couldn't.'

'Then you're out of excuses. Whatever happens with

Mom or doesn't means absolutely nothing to you in terms of your future.'

'What do you mean?'

'I mean, sister mine, that the only thing keeping you here is you.'

FIVE

In Rose's dream, she was sitting in the backseat of Jonathan's car as it moved down the highway, the trees whipping by in a blur of green. There was no front seat and no driver, and she scrabbled with her fingers, reaching desperately forward, trying to grab the steering wheel and the pedals. When she looked out the windshield at the road ahead, it was dark and blurred. The car sped faster and faster, and Rose reached forward again, her hands still falling in empty space, no matter how she twisted her body.

A clap of thunder so enormous it rattled the window-panes jerked her awake, and she sat up in bed, clasping her hand to her pounding heart. Calm, Rose, calm, she thought to herself, breathing in and out slowly, in through her nose, out through her mouth, deep yogic breaths that stilled her mind and brought her heart back from its racetrack speed.

Rose had taken yoga classes for over a year, from a gentle woman about our mother's age, with shining silver hair and a body both soft and limber, combining a grand-mother's warmth with an athlete's musculature. The instructor, Carol, seemed so at home in herself that it had made Rose feel more comfortable with her own body, which she hid in billowy T-shirts, hanging to her knees over loose-fitting sweatpants, despite the way they restricted her movements.

Our mother's ancestors were Russian, sort of, from that small area of Poland that had been annexed so many times by so many different conquerors the residents had entirely ceded their nationality and stopped bothering with any such appellations. So we were what you might call sturdy peasant stock, built for farming, for breeding, for work. Rose envied Carol's slim-hipped elegance as the instructor shifted from pose to pose, but she found, in time, the legs she had hated for so long allowed her to do much the same things. This period had coincided with the most passionate love-making she had ever had, with anyone, even Jonathan, and she wondered sometimes if she had agreed to marry him partly because of the yoga. It had made her feel beautiful, luxuriant, pliant.

But then a few months ago Carol had announced that she and her husband were retiring, to Florida of all places – and the new instructor, a bleached blonde named Heidi, who wore kitten heels with her yoga pants, terrified Rose. Heidi had come in for the first class and turned the heat up fifteen degrees, so Rose found herself red-faced and sweating, clumsy in a space where she had learned to feel so lovely. As Heidi moved around the class, correcting Rose's stances repeatedly, Rose's heart had begun to pound, and she gasped for air. Finally, she had grabbed her mat and stuffed her feet, swollen from the heat, into her flip-flops.

'Leaving, dear?' Heidi had asked, coming up beside Rose, her hands icy on Rose's fevered skin. She looked at Rose pityingly, as though she had known Rose would not be able to make it through.

Rose nodded, blinking back tears, and escaped.

She had not gone back since. She could feel the difference in her body, the tightness in her muscles where there once had been flexibility, the hitches in her heartbeats becoming more frequent, but Rose had not even considered going back to such a painful failure.

But the breathing still worked, she noticed, checking her heart with her palm once more before she pushed the sheets away, sliding her legs over the side of the bed and sitting for a moment before pushing herself away from the protesting mattress. Her knees popped, an auditory reminder of her unstoppable slide toward forty, and she moved gingerly until the muscles warmed. She padded down the hallway to the stairs. Our parents would sleep through any noise, she was fairly sure of that, but she didn't want to wake Bean, asleep next door.

She was nearly to the kitchen, guided by the light our mother always left on over the sink, when she heard the sound of the screen door slapping open, and then the rattle of the doorknob. Her heart pounding again from a shot of adrenaline, Rose leaped inside the kitchen door, peering out at the interloper. Outside, a car gunned its engine and tore into the night, the sounds nearly buried under another clap of thunder.

The light from the lamps at the foot of the front steps illuminated Cordy from behind, transforming her into a shadowy outline smelling of rain and wet grass.

'Hey, Rose,' Cordy said, stepping inside as though it were a perfectly natural thing for her to arrive home at two o'clock in the morning, and just as natural for Rose to be standing by the door to greet her. Last time we had seen Cordy, her hair was black and she wore a pleated school uniform skirt with a slew of rotating band T-shirts. Tonight her hair was back to our deep brown. She wore a white peasant top with puffed short sleeves, spattered with thick raindrops, and a swirling patchwork skirt. She held a battered duffel bag in one hand, a guitar case covered with stickers in the other, a neo-hippie sent from Central Casting.

So there it was. We were all home again, just as Rose had wished. And though she'd regret that wish frequently in the future, at least the house wasn't so still around her.

Rose sighed.

'Hello, Cordy,' Rose said. Cordy kicked the door shut, mindless of the noise, and dropped her bag and the guitar, kicking off her sandals and then stepping over them to give Rose a hug. Rose embraced our youngest sister. She could feel Cordy's shoulder blades like wings through the thin, wet cotton of her shirt. The smell of her sweat clung to Rose's nightgown when she pulled back. 'I was just about to get something to eat. Are you hungry?'

'Starving,' Cordy agreed, walking into the kitchen. One of our mother's perpetual cardigans hung over the back of the closest chair, and Cordy grabbed it, pulling it around her body for warmth. 'This rain is crazy. We could hardly see on 301.'

'Who drove you?' Rose asked.

'A friend of mine. Max. He's on his way to the Rock and Roll Hall of Fame.' The way she said this made it unclear as to whether she meant Max was headed to Cleveland to visit the Cheopsian building, or if she expected he would be inducted one day. Cordy flung open the refrigerator door, her features thin and drawn in the bluish bright of the light inside. 'So I said, you know, my sister's getting hitched, wanna drive me?'

'The wedding's not until December,' Rose said, pulling down a glass from one of the cabinets and reaching past

Cordy into the refrigerator for the milk carton. 'You're about six months too early.'

Cordy peeled back the foil from a white platter and spied a couple of ears of corn. She picked one up and began to eat it, cold. 'Do you want me to heat that up for you?' Rose asked.

'No,' Cordy said. There were bits of corn stuck between her teeth, and a piece on the edge of her mouth, and Rose fought the urge to clean it off for her. 'I was kind of tired of traveling, you know, and then Mom and everything. I thought maybe I could help.' She shrugged. 'Besides, what the hell do I have to do that's better?' She laughed, and Rose was struck by how bitter it sounded.

'It's nice to have you home,' Rose said, after a pause. 'Bean's here, too.'

'Mmm. How's she?' Cordy asked around a mouthful of corn. She ate around the ear in tiny circles – always had, though the rest of the family ate in long lines.

'Don't know, really. We haven't talked much. She looks good. As always.'

'Weird, huh?' Cordy finished the ear of corn and held it delicately between two fingers as she walked it over to the compost basket and dropped it in. 'How we're all home together now?' She came over to the table and sat down, putting one foot on the edge of her chair and hugging her leg close to her like a teddy bear, a comfort object. There was a tear in one of the patches of her skirt.

'Weird,' Rose agreed.

'I heard Jonathan is in England? That stinks.' Cordy picked corn from between her teeth, examining each kernel before sucking it off the tip of her finger. Rose grabbed her hand and stopped her. Cordy ran her tongue along her teeth and then grinned. 'Got it all anyway.'

89

Her fingernails were filthy, Rose saw, and her hair had a greasy sheen to it. 'How's Mom, anyway?'

Rose stopped herself from rolling her eyes. Anyway. As though it were an afterthought. How nice to be Cordy, to assume that everything would always turn out just fine, to let everyone else watch out for the danger. 'Doing okay. They're doing chemotherapy to try to shrink the tumor before they operate. She had a treatment a couple of days ago, so she's only just getting over that. She'll be pretty tired, so no drama, okay?'

Cordy considered this for a moment. 'Cool,' she said finally. 'Well, I'm ready for bed. How about you?'

Rose shook her head. Typical Cordy. Not interested in anyone besides herself. Draining the last of her milk, Rose padded softly over to the counter, rinsing her glass and leaving it on the drainboard. 'I'll carry your bag,' she said.

Rose led the way, Cordy's damp army green duffel resting on her back, soaking through the light fabric of her nightgown. Cordy followed behind, the neck of her guitar case bumping cheerfully into every available object. 'Oops,' Cordy kept saying. 'Oops.'

Rose opened the door to Cordy's bedroom and walked inside. For some reason, Cordy had never redecorated the way Bean and Rose had as we grew older. The room was still the room of a child: pink and white, ribbons and bows. She had changed her own look a thousand times, but her room had always remained the same.

Cordy came inside and stepped out of her skirt, hurling herself on the bed wearing only her shirt and underwear. Her legs were hairy, and the bottoms of her feet nearly black with dirt, Rose noticed with a light sense of revulsion. 'G'night,' she said, and closed her eyes, halfway to sleep in a moment. Rose paused for a minute, wanting to tell Cordy to brush her teeth, or wash her face, or

90

some other motherly bedtime reminder. But she thought better of it.

For now, Rose would let her sleep.

'*Good night, sweet prince,*' she said finally, and closed the door on Cordy's hollowed face.

Our father and Rose had taken our mother for a follow-up to have the tumor measured, so when Bean woke up, she wandered outside to pick up the newspaper to keep her company during breakfast. The flag on the mailbox was down – our mail had always been delivered egregiously early, so she grabbed that, too, flipping through the letters as she walked back inside.

There was a thick, padded envelope from New York, addressed to her. She recognized her ex-roommate Daisy's passive-aggressive debutante scrawl.

She tore open the envelope, dropping the newspaper and the other mail on the table, and reached inside. There was a pile of envelopes, all addressed to her New York apartment. A couple of wedding invitations, two postcards inviting her to gallery openings, and then, what she'd been dreading. Bills. A dozen, at least. Credit cards, all of them maxed out, all of them with usurious interest rates.

And at the bottom of the stack, a note on Daisy's obnoxiously proper Southern belle stationery. A detailed accounting of what she owed her erstwhile roommates: rent, electricity, water. The sum at the bottom made her swallow, hard.

Bean had purposely left no forwarding address, but clearly it hadn't been beyond Daisy's limited finishing-school ken to track her down, which meant that the credit card companies wouldn't be far behind.

She'd been in the habit, for too long, of refusing to open the bills, as though not knowing the exact numbers

91

she owed would make them smaller, or, if she were really lucky, nonexistent.

This, unfortunately, hadn't turned out to be the best strategy.

Bean thought of the ugliness that these envelopes contained. She thought of the way the men in the bar had turned away from her the other night when the girls had come in. She thought of the empty days she'd spent at home so far, and all the empty ones spreading out ahead of her. She thought of the way our mother collapsed against the pillow after fighting another losing battle with her nausea, out of breath, ashen and sore, smudges of purple around her eyes. She thought of the new priest asking her if she'd be at church.

She sat down at the table and opened the first envelope slowly.

Cordy slept late, awakening only when the noises of the house and the insistent sunlight became too obvious to be believably incorporated into her dreams any longer. A near-decade of roaming had made her cautious upon opening her eyes – she had grown used to a slow awakening, testing the space, telling herself the story of how she had landed in that particular bed, in that room, at that moment. She lay in bed for a few minutes, staring at the ceiling of her childhood. The same crack curved over the door, the same fluted light fixture hung from the rippling, aged plaster. She had the corner room by our parents, under the attic, and the dormer windows in Rose's and Bean's rooms were offset here by the sharply sloping eaves that made the room seem shaded and womb-like.

Sometime during the night, she had climbed under the covers, and she emerged now, rummaging through her bag for something with a semblance of cleanliness. For months now, she had been living out of people's vans, crashing periodically in some youthfully enthusiastic group home, mixing with people who were milling around, desperately trying to find some lost Kerouacian glory.

It had sucked.

All of her clothes were dirty and smelled like a well-marinated mixture of sweat and pot. Her hair had grown long and shaggy, and she had been clean so rarely that she had begun to scratch idly at the film on her skin, leaving dull marks down her arms. When she woke in the morning, often staring at the scruffy-haired, anonymous boy-man lying beside her, the first thought that had sprung into her mind had usually been, I am too old for this crap. The people she had met had been kind, certainly, but not a natural kindness, more of a benevolence stemming from a cocktail of illicit substances and a quiet, frantic desire to be *liked*.

She was fairly certain none of them would have characterized themselves in this way. They were young enough to be fooled by the grandeur of their own plans, to be so absorbed in the intense romanticism of the lifestyle they were building, one hovel at a time, that they never cared to notice that there was nothing romantic about a case of scabies. But at the same time she couldn't help but love them for it, in the condescending way an adult can love the idiocy of a child. Because, and Cordy had recently come to face this, she had aged into an adult among children, and it was past time for her to move on. But given there was nowhere to move on to, she had simply moved back.

Accepting the fact that her bag held nothing clean at all, Cordy yanked open the bottom drawer of the antique dresser in the corner alcove, and dug out a pair of loose-fitting bell-bottom jeans and a T-shirt that might fit, thin as she had gotten. The other downside to the lifestyle she had been living was that she had been hungry much of the time. If they were at a concert, for instance, given by one of the seemingly millions of interchangeable nostalgic folk-rock bands, there would be some dirty, dreadlocked couple selling sandwiches within her meager budget, but they would be dry, tasteless things, homemade twelve-grain bread with cruelty-free alfalfa sprouts and unsalted butter. She grimaced at the thought, but her stomach rumbled traitorously. She placed her hand over her belly to quell the sound, and instead felt the beginnings of the hard lump that reminded her of why she'd finally come home.

Judging by the angle of the sun, she figured it was almost eleven in the morning, so she padded out of her room and down the hall to the bathroom, dropping an enormous pile of laundry down the chute on the way. Bean's door stood open, and she could see her back, taut and crooked forward like a beckoning finger. She held a phone to her ear, her fingers mottled white and red against the receiver, and she was crying. Cordy stopped, putting her palm lightly against the door as though she could give comfort through the walls.

'I'm not coming back,' Bean said, giving the choked gasp that is the sign of exhausted bawling. When she spoke again, her voice had lowered to a whisper. 'No, it won't,' she hissed.

Silence again. Cordy shifted slightly on her feet, goose bumps rising on her bare legs. 'I'm going to,' Bean said, and then, 'I know. I know.'

Something in our sister's tone made Cordy pull back, step away from the door. There was a secret here, a secret Cordy was not sure she wanted to know, because she could not remember the last time Bean had cried, at least not in someone else's presence. Something smelled sour and painful to her. She turned on grimy feet and walked down the hallway loudly, stepping purposefully on every aching board, making her presence known.

Cordy sat slumped at a table in the Barnwell Beanery. Nothing had changed, really. Mismatched furniture, heavy and chocolate brown, swaybacked and tired from constant use; battered wood floors crossed with the dark streaks of traffic patterns. There were Magic 8 Balls and Barrels of Monkeys on the tables, and paintings by local artists hung beseechingly on the walls. Cordy, looking pure Beanery – olive cords, a faded T-shirt, and a woven hemp bag – rested her head on her arms on one of the tables, her sandaled feet curled around the chair's legs. A glass mug sat in front of her, the tag of a tea bag resting on the lip, sending smoke signals of steam into the air. Cordy looked at it morosely.

'Hey, Cordy! I heard you were back in town!' Dan Miller sat down across from her, tossing a dirty dish towel over his shoulder. 'How you been?'

Cordy pushed herself up sleepily. She had pulled her hair into two messy braids, which she flipped over her shoulders as she turned to him. 'Miller,' she said, smiling. 'Bad news travels fast.'

He chuckled, his smile breaking his face into a dimpled glow. His hair was darker than she remembered, nearly black, and his face was stubbled with a day's growth of beard. 'It's not so bad. The bad news is that Bean is back, too.'

'Oh, man. What'd she do to you?'

'Nothing. Dicked over one of my roommates pretty bad, but I think we've all recovered from it by this point. I shouldn't be picking on your sister anyway.'

Cordy waved her hand magnanimously and picked up her drink, wrapping her fingers around the glass, warming herself despite the summer sun pouring in

through the windows, oozing its way across the floor.
'Pick away.'

'So how the heck are you? You look like crap.'

'I see your legendary charm hasn't faded,' Cordy said,
eyeing him over the rim of the glass before she set it
down again, fiddling with the string of her tea bag. 'I've
been on the road for a while. Following bands, you know.
Hanging out.'

'Wow. That's awesome. I thought most of us had gotten
too old fart for that.'

'Well, I am two years younger than you. Obviously
thirty is the cutoff point for old fartdom.'

'But you're back,' Dan observed. He reached up, tugging
at the neck of his camo green T-shirt with a broad finger.
The backs of his hands were furred with dark hair.
'Obviously old fartdom has come early for you.'

'Okay, so maybe I hit my cutoff point, too. You know it's
bad when Barnwell starts looking good by comparison.'

'Hey now,' he warned, tut-tutting a finger at her. 'Forget
not to whom you speak. I live here voluntarily.'

'Yeah, what's up with that? Aren't you from Philly or
something?'

'In a former life, yeah. And I just liked it better here.
That's not such a bad thing, is it?'

Cordy shrugged and picked up her glass, taking another
sip before she replied. 'Just unexpected, I guess. I mean,
I was reading one of the alumni magazines last night and
everyone else has joined the Peace Corps or become some
important cancer-curing researcher.'

'And here we sit. Depressing, isn't it?'

'Hey, I never graduated. I have an excuse.'

'I am a Small Business Owner,' Dan said, sitting up
straight. 'And a respectable member of the community. I
need no excuse.'

'You own this place?' Cordy looked around. As it was

summer, there were few people in here, but during the school year, like everything else around campus, it would be hopping.

'Yes, it's all mine,' he said, gesturing expansively. 'I'm the food service magnate of Barnwell. Bow to me.'

'No thanks,' Cordy said coolly, but she gave him a slight smile, turning up the corners of her lips, Chapstick-pink.

'How long are you around for?' he asked.

'Dunno. A while. My mom's sick, you know. And Rose is getting married. And I kind of got to think about what's going to come next. Save a little money.'

'Shit, that's a lot going on all at once.' His eyebrows bent together slightly, a vee of concern. 'You working?'

'Not yet.'

'Well, if you need a job, you let me know. Miller'll give you the hookup.' He patted his chest, then rubbed it. At the hollow of his throat, thick hair curled up from under his shirt. She remembered watching him play Frisbee on the quad, shirtless, and the way she had been amazed by how hairy he was. Neither repulsed nor attracted, but scientifically fascinated, curious about the texture.

'But I hate coffee. I mean, drinking it. I love the smell,' Cordy said.

'So there's a start, right? And it smells awesome in here, doesn't it?' Dan asked, leaning back so far that he had to hook his booted foot around the table leg to keep from falling off as he drew an exaggerated, enormous breath.

Cordy giggled.

'The pay is crap, but you're living at home, right? So no worries. Call me.' There was a moment's pause. She'd had dozens of jobs over the years – a job didn't mean she was committing to anyone or anything. Taking a job in Barney did not mean she would owe her soul to the proverbial company store. It wouldn't mean she'd have to

97

stay forever. She wouldn't even have to stay through a shift if she didn't want to.

'Okay,' Cordy agreed, and Dan hopped out of his chair, placing his hand on her shoulder and squeezing lightly.

'Jesus,' he said, prodding at her clavicle. 'You need to gain some weight, girl. I'll send over a pastry or something.'

'Thanks,' Cordy said, reaching up to squeeze his hand in return. He walked off, whistling, and she watched him go, looking at the loose fabric of his baggy jeans. He seemed so happy, and it made her a little sad to realize how alien that emotion had become.

It could have been worse, Cordy knew. She could have been Ophelia, with all the illicit sexuality and going mad and committing suicide. She could even have been Bianca, with all the beauty *and* obedience to live up to. So being Cordelia was, she was well aware, not as bad as it could have been.

Cordelia's problem – that is, the Shakespearean Cordelia, but hang on and you'll see where we're going with this – for Cordy was that she was just so un*form*ed. Her great moment of rebellion was in refusing to swear her love to her father precisely because she loved him too much. (Though Cordy was, truth be told, always kind of pleased at the middle finger that sent – albeit indirectly – to the older sisters.) And then there she was at the end, loyal and cooperative, until she, you know, dies. Okay, so there is the part where she becomes Queen of France and leads the French forces against Evil Edmund, but (a) she loses and (b) it's not like she *wanted* to lead them. If there's any way you could be a major military leader and be totally passive about it, that'd be Cordelia for you. Everything happens *to* Cordelia; she never makes anything happen.

98

To be named after Cordelia should have invited some kind of dignity, but Cordy had never really felt it. The only thing she had absolutely inherited from her name was a gentle rage against injustice, and like Cordelia, she was hesitant to speak up about it, though Cordelia's reluctance came more from some overinflated sense of goodness and Cordy's came from . . . what? Laziness? Fear? She wasn't really sure. In her most recent incarnation she had sat in hazy, smoke-filled rooms with sagging floors and listened to people mouthing off about The Patriarchy and The Establishment, and while she agreed, felt a great weight of sadness about the terrible things she knew existed in this world, she felt powerless to change them. After all, Cordelia had been executed for doing The Right Thing, and while Cordy didn't think that was likely to happen to her, she wasn't exactly eager to test the waters.

In love, too, Cordy had always been compliant. While Rose searched, and Bean made herself available, Cordy had rarely bothered to seek anything out. Her sweet and comical nature had drawn men to her, true, but mostly she took them as they came, and did not let herself be drawn into the drama falling in love entailed. She accepted these suitors, but did not care about them, not really. She had found herself, more than once, below the body of a sweating, heaving man whispering endearments in her ear, hot breath on her skin, and wondered idly how she had *gotten* there, and what all the *fuss* was about anyway. Sex had given her a bed more often than not in the past few years, but it had never held any passion, and Cordy always felt it was more companionable than anything else.

To Cordy, life was filled with things that were simply what you did when they were required of you, like sleeping with someone in exchange for a bed, or working as a hotel maid to get money to go to the next town, or marrying the king of France and leading his troops into certain death.

Rose will tell you that Cordy, being the youngest, has always gotten away with murder, and that this is entirely unfair.

Bean will tell you that Cordy, being the youngest, has always been the favorite, and that this is entirely unfair.

Cordy will tell you that both of these things are true.

Example. New Year's Eve, Cordy is fifteen years old. Rose is with her boyfriend and his family in Connecticut. She thinks she might marry this one. (She is wrong.) Bean is out somewhere unspecified. She has told our parents that she's with Lyssie (short for Lysistrata – whenever we complain about our unfashionable names, we remember that we could have been the daughters of a classics professor), that they're going to a movie, but we know she is at a party. At this party, no one will know who our father is, or care, and the house will be dirty, with peeling wallpaper and furniture racked into slanting, exhausted postures. There will be beer and pot and mattresses in unlikely places, and long before midnight Bean and Lyssie will be wholeheartedly round the bend and in the sweaty, beer-soaked arms of some boy they will forget the next day. This adventure is possible only because Bean has always been an excellent liar, and not because our parents would ever approve of such an outing.

Cordy and her best friend had decided they wanted to go to a New Year's festival in Columbus, a party with a band, fireworks, and thousands of drunk celebrants, courtesy of the beer company sponsoring the event. Cordy has never been a big drinker, really, so we didn't think she was escaping for the alcohol, the way Bean was. But still, a fifteen-year-old girl and her barely pubescent escort loose on the streets on a night known for its debauchery?

Our parents said yes.

When Rose heard this, she was a teakettle at full steam. When, having won a prize in the state history fair, she and her friends wanted to go to Columbus for the day to compete at the next level, our mother had insisted on going along as a chaperone. 'For an *academic* event!' Rose screeched.

Our parents once grounded Bean for a week after she stole a stick of penny candy from the bookstore, sneaking it inside the arm of her winter coat. Her crime was discovered when, upon returning to the house, she refused to remove the coat, despite the enthusiasm of our radiators.

Having knocked one of the new Middle Eastern Studies professor's children off of his bicycle in order to commandeer it for herself, an act that left him with a split lip and a lifelong fear of the Andreas girls, Cordy received a stern talking-to.

'*See?*' Rose asks.

But what Rose does not so much see is that this permissiveness is also a sign of neglect. Cordy's insistence upon conception surprised our parents, who had decided Bean would be the last subatomic particle of our particular nuclear family. And they were, in many ways, worn out by the time Cordy came along. So if they allowed her to go places and do things they would never have allowed Rose or Bean to do, it would be fair to take that as a measure of preference, yes, but preference toward the older of us, not the younger.

We think, too, by the time Cordy came along, they had figured out that pretty much no matter what they did, she would turn out okay. She was cuddled and loved more, photographed more, laughed and played with more, but she was a little like a new toy in that way; as often as we adored her, we equally ignored her.

These things in concert are understandably why Cordy developed what she calls her performing monkey traits. At family dinners, preferably ones in which important college officials or visiting lecturers sit at our table, she will be the one who encourages us all to hang spoons from our noses, to test the level of the table by rolling peas across it, to stage a reading from the Berlitz travel book of important Spanish phrases such as, 'Meet me at the discotheque,' 'Do you have any coconuts?' or, most vitally, 'Please leave me alone.' And Cordy being Cordy, everyone at the table (visiting dignitaries included) will participate.

She became, unsurprisingly, the actress among us, and directed, produced, and starred in every possible vehicle at our school. Puberty left her heartbroken, because up until then the theater department had called upon her to play the child's roles in every production at Barney as well, male or female. She can still sing the lisping songs from *The Music Man*. 'If anyone is going to Broadway,' people would say after the show had ended, 'it's her.'

But going to Broadway would have required a tenacity Cordy just did not possess. We were too easy on her, yes, and when she forgot to do her chores and skipped off to the pool, or pulled us away from our own work to build a fort in the dining room, we forgave her those trespasses, and did her chores for her. We helped her with her homework, we babysat for her, we let her sit in the library at Coop and read for hours at a time, and when it finally came down to it, Cordy was sorely underprepared for the fact that her smile and her ability to get an entire room full of Shakespearean scholars to do the Macarena (true story) would not necessarily guarantee her perennial success.

102

Still, Rose would tell you Cordy always got the best Christmas presents.

Bean would tell you Cordy never lost a board game in her life, even when she did.

Cordy would tell you all these things are true.

SIX

Our father does not cook. This had always been the way. Both he and our mother would have objected to the idea of the kitchen being the wife's domain, but they clearly had no problem with it in practice. So with our mother's being out of commission, barely able to eat, let alone cook, it fell to us. Bean cobbled together a vegetable soup from the odds and ends in the refrigerator, and Rose defrosted some bread from the freezer and made a cheese plate. Cordy moped around, getting in the way.

'What are you doing?' Rose asked our father. She was finishing setting the table, and he was wrestling one of the armchairs from the living room through the door into the dining room.

'Getting a chair for your mother. She won't be able to sit in one of the wooden ones long enough to eat.'

'We'll take her a tray. Put that back.'

'Your mother wants to eat with us. *We must needs dine together.*'

And so it was.

She came downstairs under her own power, tired and delicate as bone china, but present. 'It's so wonderful to have us all home together,' she said, beaming.

'Sit down and feed, and welcome to our table,' said our father. He slipped his book onto the edge of the table, where he could pretend he wasn't reading it as we ate.

Cordy, gifted in the art of taking credit where no credit was due, brought dinner to the table with a flourish. Bean was reaching for the soup when our mother cleared her throat. 'May we say grace before we begin?' she asked. Bean's hand stole guiltily back to her lap.

'Grace!' Cordy said cheerfully. Our father grinned at her, and then reached across the table. We joined hands and bowed our heads, a ritual that struck us all as so old-fashioned and sweet that Rose got a slight case of the sniffles, and our father said grace, his voice rumbling quietly, and Bean was struck by the way that our father's evening grace always reminded her of sunset.

'Amen,' our father said.

'Ay-men!' Cordy agreed, and then proceeded to serve herself fully half of the bread and cheese.

'Hello, greedy. Leave some for the rest of us,' Bean said.

'Leave her alone,' our mother said. 'She needs to gain some weight.' Cordy choked on the hunk of bread she'd stuffed into her mouth. Oh, little did they know exactly how much weight she was going to gain. She grabbed her glass of milk and drained it without stopping, trying to cover the flush in her cheeks.

'I think she's got a tapeworm,' Bean said.

'Shut up,' Cordy said, and headed out to get more milk. We watched her walk away, her pants hanging low on her hips, her elbows sharp exclamation points through her skin. Rose considered worrying about her and then decided not to bother.

'How did the appointment go today?' Bean asked. She'd been out all afternoon to points unknown, and had come back only in time for dinner.

105

'Good, good,' our mother said. 'The tumor has shrunk quite a bit, so we've gone ahead and scheduled the surgery for week after next.'

Rose stopped, a spoonful of soup halfway to her mouth. 'That's so soon.'

'What, you want to wait until the tumor has time to grow again?' Cordy asked, returning from the kitchen, her glass refilled to the slopping point with milk. She plopped it down on the table, and liquid sloshed over the sides. Rose put down her spoon and mopped it up with her napkin, staring firmly at the table.

'Not funny, Cordy. We need to plan. We need to be ready.'

'Your mother is ready, and that's what matters. *I am prepared and full resolved.*'

Was she ready? Can you ever really be ready to bid goodbye to a part of your body? Can you be ready to kneel down before the knife and surrender control in return for nothing more than a hope for the best?

Rose's thoughts were rushing. She wasn't sure what exactly they should be planning, but surely there was something someone should do. Maybe there was an Emily Post guide to caring for the newly mastectomied.

'I'd like to talk to you about something,' our father said. He put his spoon down, dabbed his napkin at his beard, which was looking grayer than Bean remembered. 'In light of your mother's diagnosis, I feel it necessary to address the issue of your own health.'

Cordy blew bubbles into her milk. Our father took off his glasses and rubbed his eyes, typically a mid-lecture sign, but in this case he seemed to be struggling unusually hard to get the words out.

He coughed.

'*Marry, sir, 'tis an ill cook that cannot lick his own fingers: therefore he that cannot lick his fingers goes not with me,*' he said finally.

106

'Um, what?' Bean asked.

'I think what your father means is that since breast cancer may be hereditary, it's important that you do self-exams,' our mother said, patting his hand as he nodded uncomfortably.

Oh. Right. We're sure that's exactly what Shakespeare was trying to say.

Cordy nearly choked on her milk. 'Awwwwwwk-waaaard,' she sang, wiping her mouth with the back of her arm.

'Gross,' Bean said.

'It's not "gross", Bianca. It's vital,' our father said.

Rose was nodding in agreement. Well, of course she was. She put fifteen percent of each paycheck in the bank and got her oil changed every three thousand miles. But who lives like that, really? Well, besides Rose.

We had a limited history of embarrassing conversations with our father. It had traditionally been our mother's role to explain the birds and bees, menstruation and its attendant supplies, and anything else in the feminine arena. Breast self-exams definitely fell into that category, and we were a little sorry for him that he had to bring up the subject.

We ate silently for a moment and then Cordy spoke. 'Fine. I solemnly swear to feel myself up in the shower once a month.'

'Cordy!' Rose said.

'*I'll perform it to the last article,*' Cordy continued. Bean was snorting laughter across the table. 'Everyone happy? Can we talk about something less uncomfortable now?'

'It's not funny,' Rose said, but everyone else seemed mollified. She sighed into her soup. Was she the only one who saw how serious this was, that we might lose our mother, and one day, each other?

She wasn't, in fact, the only one. That night in bed,

Bean lay under her sheets, a strip of moonlight falling across her feet, and she lifted one arm above her head and probed the skin gingerly. Just in case.

Cordy, whose breasts were tender for entirely different reasons, and had taken to wandering around holding them up just to relieve the tension under her skin, gave herself a desultory grope and fell sound asleep.

Rose didn't sleep at all.

'I'm going for a run,' Bean told us. 'Anyone want to come?' She hadn't been running outside in years, but without daily visits to the gym, her body was starting to itch for activity. Or maybe it was being trapped in the house with us. Either way, after her brief period of hibernation, she was grateful to feel like herself again. When we turned her down, Rose with a brief shake of the head, Cordy with a horrified shudder, she headed out the back gate and along the trails that looped through the woods, curving in and over themselves until she came out on the end toward town behind the church.

'Bianca,' someone shouted from behind her, and she gasped, tripping slightly over a root. She'd been running numbers in her head, calculating to the sound of her feet slapping against the dirt, figuring out how she was going to juggle all the money she owed with the kind of job she would be likely to get in Barnwell, and when she heard her name, she was ridiculously sure it was some creditor chasing her down. She regained her balance and turned around to see Father Aidan.

He was kneeling by the back gate of the vicarage, a word that made it sound like it should have been a small, crumbling stone cottage with a thatched roof, but was really a perfectly ordinary clapboard house whose only distinguishing feature was its proximity to the church itself (which was also not crumbling stone, as it well

should have been, but brick, and not crumbling at all).
Father Cooke had always encouraged the vines – honeysuckle, blackberry, clematis – to crawl their way up and
around, covering the wooden fence until it was only white
apostrophes among thick greenery. The sunlight shafted
through Aidan's hair, catching gold and red.

'Hey, Bianca!' he called again, waving at her with one
arm and shielding his eyes from the sunlight with the
other.

She approached him slowly, like a wary cat, pulling
her ponytail tight and wiping the sweat from her face.
Bean does not like to be caught unprepared for any
meeting with a man, pastor or no.

'How are you?' he asked as she came to the fence. He
placed his hands on his thighs and pushed himself up
with the slight, slow edge Rose knew well – the caution
born of newly awakening cracks in one's joints.

'Good, good. Just out for a run.' Thanks for that,
Señorita Obvious.

He pulled off his gloves and ran his hand through his
hair. His hairline curved back in two swoops at his temples.
Bean had always shunned, on principle, men who were
losing their hair, but she caught herself admiring him.
Maybe she'd been too hasty at the library. He wasn't bad-
looking at all. She cleared her throat and adjusted her
ponytail again. 'How's the garden?'

'I'm beginning to wish that they had taught gardening
in seminary, it's true. I'm not exactly qualified for this.
But being a country mouse isn't so bad.'

She put her hands on the fence and leaned forward
flirtatiously. Old habits die hard. 'I'm a little surprised
you'd have accepted the offer to come to Barnwell to
begin with. It's not like this is a hip and happening
assignment.'

Aidan shrugged, slapping his gloves lightly against his

thigh, and leaned up against the fence himself. 'Man proposes, God disposes,' he said. 'I go where I am sent.'

'That's an awfully Zen way to look at it.'

'What about you? Missing the big city already?'

Bean suppressed a grimace. 'Not exactly. It was time to get out of there for a while.'

'So you'll be sticking around? Good. I do like it here, but we really could use some younger blood at Saint Mark's. You haven't forgotten that you promised to come to services?'

Bean flushed. 'No. It's just been . . . well, you know.'

'I promise it's more fun than a poke in the eye with a sharp stick,' he said with a smile. Man, he really was cute. Bean's mind wandered for a moment. She could be Mrs Moore, couldn't she? Virtuous wife of a virtuous pastor? Live in the vicarage? Bake cookies or whatever it was the vicar's wife did?

'I'll be there this Sunday,' she said. 'With bells on.'

'We've got our own bells,' he said. 'But it would definitely be nice to see you.'

He seemed about to say something else, when a caterwaul came from the front of the house.

'Father!' a woman's voice called sharply. 'Father Aidan!'

'Duty calls,' Aidan said, but he didn't seem put off by the interruption, which made Bean feel slightly put off.

'Dr Crandall,' Bean said. 'I'd recognize that voice anywhere. She used to yell at us all the time for trampling through her garden when we were playing hide-and-seek.'

'You really shouldn't trample people's gardens,' Aidan said, mock stern. His eyebrows were light, drawn together over his piercing eyes. 'Ten Hail Marys for that one.'

Bean rolled her eyes. 'I'm not Catholic,' she said. 'And, just in case this slipped your attention, neither are you.'

110

'Excellent point,' he said. 'I'll have to look it up in my Catholic to Episcopalian penance converter.'

'Father Aidan!' Dr Crandall howled again.

'I'm in the back,' Aidan called, and then turned back to Bean. 'So I'll see you later,' he said. 'My apologies.'

'No need to apologize. You're allowed to do your job. There are middle-aged ladies in the town that need a little spiritual tending.'

'We all need a little spiritual tending,' Aidan said. 'It was nice to see you, Bianca.'

'Likewise, Aidan,' she said, and his name on her tongue was chocolate-warm. She turned and began to jog gently back up the path she had come from, hoping the days away from the gym had not left her with more jiggle than was feminine. She allowed herself one quick glance over her shoulder as the path faded into the woods, but he had disappeared. She turned back, her ponytail whipping her cheek lightly, bitter.

She ran a little harder now that it didn't matter who saw her. Men in bars moved closer as they were drawn in, touched her as often as possible. How do you rate a conversation with a priest on a sunny weekday morning over a fence? Not the same game.

And what was she doing evaluating this conversation anyway, as though he were target practice? He hadn't really been flirting with her, had he? Except why else would he take the time to talk to her?

Maybe he could tell. Maybe priests had some kind of sin radar that beeped to tell them when someone had been naughty and needed spanking. Metaphorically, of course.

Did that mean he could see through her? She clenched her teeth and ran harder, as though the dirt turning up behind her heels could obscure everything she wanted to hide.

*   *   *

111

When Bean returned, sweat-laden and exhausted, we were in the living room, reading. Cordy had her slightly less grubby feet resting on our father's knee, the rest of her sprawled over the couch as she pillaged some post-modern tome she had discovered beside the refrigerator. Rose lounged in the window seat, her legs brought up under her, a novel pressed awkwardly up against the window glass, turning the pages with one hand as the other busily twined a loose strand of hair.

'Be quiet,' Rose said, looking up, though Bean had made hardly a sound. 'Mom's resting.'

Bean made exaggerated tippy-toe motions, placing her finger over her lips. Cordy giggled. Rose huffed and went back to her book.

'Hello, Bianca,' our father said, intoning, as he often does, like a preacher in a pulpit. 'Did you have a pleasant run?'

Bean shrugged, sat down in an ancient wing chair and stretched her legs, wide and muscular underneath her brief shorts. 'It was okay. I'm getting out of shape. No health club.'

'They stumble that run fast,' our father said, peering over his bifocals. He held his book in one hand, the other resting on his belly, pushing agreeably at the buttons on his shirt. Cordy dropped her book down so it rested on her nose, and spoke.

'What about the gym at Barney, Dad?' Her words were dulled by the pages of the book. 'Couldn't Bean go there?'

'Well are you welcome to the open air,' he said cryptically, and returned to his book.

Cordy shoved him with her foot. 'Dad-*dy,*' she whined.

'All right, Cordelia, I will look into it. Okay?' He replaced her foot on his knee, turned back to his book, and, in an instant, had disappeared back into the pages. Ever like this, a moment here, a moment gone into the land of print and text, and woe to her who tried to pull him back out. You could be calling for a half hour and he'd never notice.

'You're tracking grass all over the floor,' Rose said. She held her book open with her thumb.

Bean lifted one shoe, then the other, admiring the grass clippings decorating the bottom of her shoes like green tinsel. Then she looked pointedly at the floor, which was, while not exactly squalorous, not exactly clean, either. 'I can't see how it makes a difference,' she said, one well-plucked eyebrow raised.

Cordy watched us, eyes flicking back and forth, watching the Ping-Pong match. 'Why don't you take off your shoes and make her happy?' Cordy asked, ever the peacemaker. 'What's the big deal?'

Bean considered that for a moment and then slipped off her sneakers, flexing her toes wide within her white socks. She made an exaggerated seated bow. '*I willingly obey your command,*' she said.

'Thank you,' Rose replied, clipped. She turned back to her book, but we could see her heart wasn't in it. Sometimes she didn't know where it came from – she didn't mean to be so harsh, only to help keep us in line. She wanted to apologize for her sharpness, but something in her heaved up and cut off the words.

'What's wrong, Rosie-Posie?' Cordy asked, pulling herself up on the sofa and adopting Rose's posture: knees bent, feet resting at her bottom. It was so like her, to call Rose something that our oldest sister would not have tolerated from anyone else. Cordy, the darling, the favorite.

'Nothing,' Rose sighed, still staring into her book.

'*Methinks the lady doth protest too much,*' our father murmured, turning a page in his book. Rose looked at him, surprised he was paying attention.

'Okay, fine. Something's wrong, and I don't want to

talk about it,' Rose snapped, somewhat unceremoniously, and went back to her book.

'Where'd you go running?' Cordy asked, smoothly changing the subject.

'Oh, you know. Down by the creek, and then through town the back way.'

'By Saint Mark's, right?' Cordy asked, a rhetorical exercise. She knew exactly where the path led. Its course had been our escape on Sunday mornings when we were younger. We'd tear off our tights and shoes, leaving them dangling like octopuses in our mother's hands, and sprint off, a study in contrast between our pretty little girl dresses and bare, dirty feet. By the time we got home, our dresses might be stained with blackberry juice, or smeared with grass stains, but they were never torn, never beyond the mildest of repairs. We weren't that foolish. And we became adept with stain removers from a young age, because our mother wasn't about to put up with dealing with cleaning them herself.

'Yeah.' Bean shrugged carelessly.

'There's a new priest, you know,' our father said, peering over his glasses at Bean. 'Young man. Handsome. But more Benedick than Claudio, so it's all right.'

'As long as he's not more Don John than Benedick,' Cordy said, curling her dirty toes.

'He's nice. I met him at the library the other day, and he was out in the garden today,' Bean said.

'Oooh,' Cordy said, leaning her book against her chest, now fully invested in the conversation. 'Making friends with the locals. So is he cute?'

'You don't trust my assessment?' our father asked, turning another page in his book.

'Of course I do,' Cordy soothed. 'But I want to know if *Bean* thinks he's cute. It's a totally different thing.'

'Sure,' Bean said. 'I guess. But he's the vicar.'

'Oh, please. He's not *dead*,' Cordy replied, and then, butterfly-minded, poked our father with her heel and changed the subject. 'What happened to Father Cooke?'

'Put him out to pasture,' our father said. *'And toil'd with works of war, retired himself to* Arizona.'

'How sad,' Cordy said wistfully.

'There's nothing sad about it,' Rose interjected. 'The man's retired, playing golf in Arizona. What's sad about that?'

'Nothing, I suppose. But in a way it is sad that he doesn't have a congregation or anything anymore, you know? Wouldn't that be hard for him?'

'I imagine it's a relief. Listening to other people's problems day in and day out for years? Having to work every weekend?' Rose smiled at her own sacrilege.

'And never getting invited anywhere except if people want a vicar handy. All the pretty ladies and not a drop to drink,' Bean added. We all recoiled at the thought of the ancient Father Cooke and any romantic exploits in which he might have been involved. 'Or not,' she said.

'Father Aidan writes excellent sermons,' Rose said, turning the tide of the conversation back. 'I don't think it's entirely appropriate to be talking about whether he's cute or not.'

'Rose, relax. We're not going to buy him a hooker,' Bean said. 'We're just talking.'

'Besides, church is way more fun when the vicar is cute,' Cordy said.

'How would you know? We only ever had Father Cooke,' Bean said.

'I have an imagination,' Cordy said indignantly. 'Besides, it's not like Saint Mark's is the only church I ever went to.'

'And in your vast ecclesiastical survey, were there lots of hot reverends?'

'Enough,' Cordy said mysteriously, and went back to reading.

Bean picked up her shoes and went upstairs to shower, leaving a trail of grass on the carpet. Rose looked after her thoughtfully. She never had been able to tell how much of Bean's boy-craziness was real, and how much of it was artifice, like her makeup and perfectly coordinated outfits. Because she certainly couldn't be setting her cap for Father Aidan, could she?

Because Bean? Dating our minister? That was the most ridiculous idea Rose had ever heard.

SEVEN

The best part of being in a relationship, for Rose, was that Jonathan was the first person she saw when she woke up, and the last before she fell asleep. This love had a nice symmetry to it, and she found it insulating; the gentle rhythm of morning chores and evening relaxation with him closed a gentle circle for her, cocooned her from the world.

But his departure had ruined the safety of their communion for her. You have to understand, our parents had raised us as good feminists, we are aware of the whole woman/man/fish/bicycle equation, but Rose was different. Rose needed security, stasis, and she had grown used to Jonathan as part of that so quickly. Some days she felt torn inside because he wasn't there, as though it were the fact of his absence, rather than his absence itself, that offended her so. It was curious to us, who had so long enjoyed the benefits of Rose's strength, had leaned on her for everything from ensuring our socks matched to keeping the secret of exactly how late we snuck out of the house to providing a sweet shoulder to cry on when things went horribly wrong, that Rose would need her own rock. But that was why he loved her better than we did – we loved her so much for her strength that we could never let her be weak, and he loved both parts of her equally.

Some nights, Rose ignored their scheduled call and set her alarm for the wee small hours, slipping it under her pillow so she wouldn't wake anyone else. When the beeping jarred her from whatever pale sleep she had tempted her body into, she got up and padded downstairs, the ghost of Hamlet's father in the darkest of midnights, to call Jonathan, dialing the extended series of numbers and listening to the strange double buzz of the transatlantic ring.

He didn't usually head into the lab until nine or so, and if she timed it right, she could catch him as he lingered over his coffee, a tradition she respected him for maintaining in the face of all that infernal tea-drinking. Rose found the time difference extremely inconvenient – if he called before he went to bed, or when he got home, it was the middle of her day, her mind occupied with the thousand things she came up with to keep herself busy during the long, slow stretch of summer. The darkness of early morning made the conversations magical, sealed on either side by sleep, her tone low and hushed, both of them still in the cradle of home before the violation of the world penetrated the steady pace of their souls.

''Allo,' he said, in the ridiculous Cockney imitation he reserved (she hoped) for answering the phone when he knew it was her.

'Good morning,' she whispered, smiling at the warmth that spread through her, unbidden, when she heard his voice.

'How's my favorite midnight caller?' Jonathan asked. He had sent pictures of his tiny student rooms, the kitchen with its funny half-sized refrigerator, the dining table against the wall of the living room, the bedroom only a nook, an afterthought between the bathroom and the back of the worn sofa. She liked to picture him there, the dull English sun pouring its syrupy way across the carpet, catching the glints of gold in his eyelashes. 'Couldn't sleep?'

'Never can,' Rose said. 'How's the weather?'

'Gray with a chance of charcoal,' he said. 'What's it like there? Disgustingly humid?'

'As ever.'

'Have you thought at all about coming over here?'

'For a visit?'

He paused. 'Sure. For starters.'

'Jonathan, I can't move to England.'

There was silence across the lines. She could picture him pinching the bridge of his nose, a gesture of frustration she had always found curiously familiar until she realized our father had the same habit. Hello, Freud. 'Okay. Fine. Not to stay, then. Just for a visit. When can you come?'

'Oh, I don't know. Mom's surgery is coming up.'

'That's great news.'

Rose furrowed her brow. 'I don't see how.'

'It's great news that the tumor has shrunk enough that they can operate. Not great that it all has to happen in the first place. So after the surgery, maybe you could come over for a while. A few weeks?'

'Weeks?' Rose squeaked. Her mind was instantly filled with the potential disasters we could wreak without her around to take us firmly in hand. 'I don't know about weeks.'

'Why not? If Cordy and Bean are going to be around, and you don't have to be back until the end of August . . .'

'I'll think about it,' Rose said doubtfully. If all went well, our mother could be up and around within three weeks. But if it didn't go well? And even if it did, who

119

would go grocery shopping and pay the bills and schedule our mother's doctors' appointments and the dozens of other things we would need to do to care for her while she recovered?

We would, we whispered to her. And we'd be just fine.

'Okay,' Jonathan said, resigned.

'I miss you,' she whispered, suddenly, passionately.

He laughed, warm and low, surprised by her uncharacteristically free expression. 'I miss you, too. You're lovely to let me go do this.'

Rose shrugged, the phone brushing against her shoulder. 'What would I do? Say you couldn't go? That you had to stay here with me and my crazy sisters?'

'They've been upgraded to crazy already? I would have thought the reunion would have lasted a few more days.'

This, unexpectedly, made her feel guilty. 'It's just . . . they're the same, you know? I think Bean's trying to pick up Father Aidan.'

This time Jonathan's laugh was loud and delighted. 'That's a riot. Well, at least it'll give those biddies in the vestry something to argue about besides who gets to make up the collection plate schedule.'

'You don't think it's . . . inappropriate?'

'Father Aidan can take care of himself. And Bean only does it for the attention, you know that.'

'Of course I know it. That's what drives me crazy. And Cordy? My parents will support her forever while she figures out what she wants to do. I don't know why she can't just settle down.'

'She's the baby,' Jonathan said, as though that explained everything.

Rose thought of Lear, of the way he had kept Cordelia as his own, staving off the threats of old age with his tenuous connection to her youth. 'You're so lucky you and your siblings get along,' she sighed. She already knew that if she and Jonathan had children, they would have only one. None of this cruel bait and switch our parents had pulled on her, setting her up to be the One and then going and having two more.

'Ah, but I never got to boss anyone around,' he teased. 'Where would you be without all those years of acting as general?'

'I'd probably have a less intense antacid habit.'

'Let it go,' Jonathan said. 'It's not your responsibility to take care of them anymore. Let them take care of themselves. People can change.'

After she hung up, she sat on the floor in the kitchen, the linoleum cool against her bare calves where the night-gown had ridden up, and listened to the quiet hum of the house asleep – the purr of the refrigerator as it cycled, the air conditioner kicking on and off, keeping the temperature steady, the occasional aged creak of wood settling. Was it true, what he said? Could people change? Or would we remain this way, forever and ever? Would Bean always be chasing one man or another, Cordy eternally chasing some shadow of a person she might never become, and Rose herself chasing some shadow of the way things were Supposed to Be? There were days, yes, when Rose felt as though she had been on this earth forever, since the dino-saurs at least, but she knew she was young. It seemed so early to have signed her whole life away, but it seemed so exhausting to change anything.

Here is the good thing about being the oldest: control.

Here's the bad thing about being the oldest: control.

When Bean arrived, something in three-year-old Rose's mind clicked, and she knew that if her coveted role of only star in the Andreas sky had been wrested from her, then she at least would have the glory of playing the director. Chips would fall not where they may, but where she said they would. It was still Rose's world, Bean was just living in it.

When Cordy turned six, Rose finally deemed her old enough to take a speaking part in the frequent plays we performed for our parents. Cordy took the part of the loyal (and mute) maidservant, the one-lined extra, the spear-carrier in all of our sheet-curtained productions in the basement, until Rose decreed that she had enough maturity to play, finally, the part that would make us complete, the three witches in the Scottish play.

Though we weren't technically in a theater, and therefore it wasn't bad luck to say the name – *Macbeth, Macbeth, Macbeth*, there, we've said it – Rose still insisted we call it 'the Scottish play'. We clad ourselves in cast-off clothes from the dress-up box, mostly old dresses from our grandmothers. We sent Bean on a mission to the neighbors' houses to find witch hats from Halloween costumes gone-by, which she produced admirably, and we pressed Mustardseed, our long-suffering cat-cum-Globe-extra into service as a familiar (Bean insisted; she figured the lack of a cat in the original play was Shakespeare's problem, not hers).

Musical accompaniment was provided courtesy of the plastic record player that had belonged to all of us and therefore rested, as things ultimately did, in Cordy's accounts. We had a scratched LP of Halloween sound effects that bumped and groaned along behind our lines, the regular sheets hung up as curtains for the stage, and Rose had secured a lobster pot from our mother large enough to boil Cordy in (and don't think the thought hadn't crossed our minds on more than one occasion).

So there was the première, with our parents seated in the dingy love-seat that hid an exceptionally squeaky pull-out bed, holding the two-of-a-kind original programs (created in Rose's perfect penmanship, *bien sûr*) with

'The Weird Sisters'—the witches of *Macbeth* – written in her hand, and a little cauldron (no more than a black bubble at the bottom) drawn by Cordy, who had thrown a whale of a temper tantrum until we allowed her to help. Rose bit her lip as she watched Cordy's careful scrawl, sure it had destroyed the program, but she had learned that you must give in to the talent if the show is going to go on at all.

The curtain opened, the gas fireplace crackling coldly behind us, and we began, our own carefully cribbed scripts set in front of us as we stirred the giant pot full of air.

'Speak the speech, I pray you, trippingly on the tongue!' our father cried out before we could speak, and he and our mother applauded wildly. Rose hushed him, breaking character in frustration before turning back to the long wooden spoon we had liberated from the jar above the stove.

Rose had neatly excised all the extraneous characters, which made it an extremely abbreviated production. We had, at one point, dispatched Cordy to our mother to request a brother, as he would have been enormously helpful, but our mother said it was not likely, and in any case it would take an awfully long time even if it were to happen, so we settled for the abridged version.

Rose kept the first witch's part for herself, being as it was the one with the monologues, and first to speak, besides, and Bean played her part with a great deal of hair-flipping, which she had seen on a television show during a sleepover at a friend's house, and Cordy got lost repeatedly, until Rose hissed at her in frustration to keep her finger on the lines. Cordy found this no help at all, and it resulted primarily in her shouting out the lines she *did* know, so it sounded a bit like this: *'The weird sisters, HAND IN HAND! / Posters of the sea and LAND! / Thus do go about, about; / Thrice to thine, AND THRICE TO MINE! / And thrice again to make UP NINE! / Peace! The charm's wound up.'* Cordy was big on rhyming.

When we finished, Rose was nearly in tears, frustrated with the way her great dramatic vision had failed to align with reality. 'That wasn't right at all!' she cried, and would have commenced to pointing fingers, had our parents not stepped in to console her. Bean and Cordy couldn't have cared less, as Bean was still practicing her curtsy from the curtain call, and Cordy was chasing Mustardseed around, attempting to complete his costume with her witch's hat, which he (not surprisingly) wanted no part of.

'Your play needs no excuse,' our father said. 'I found it lovely. It covers all the important parts without any of the major characters. Brilliant adaptation.' He kissed Rose's slightly hat-haired head.

'I agree,' our mother said. 'I always thought the three witches were the best part of the play anyway.'

'Of course,' our father said. 'It was convenient of us to have you three so we could have our very own Weird Sisters.' He gave our mother a wink over Rose's head.

'But Cordy did it wrong!' Rose objected again.

'No, she just did it differently,' our mother soothed. 'But it doesn't matter, because aren't the best plays the ones that are different?'

Well, no. Not always. We saw one production of *Much Ado* set in a USO in World War I, and that was quite good. But then there was an infamous naked *Midsummer*, and the reverse-race *Othello*, and those were both awful.

But Rose learned an important lesson: people don't always do what you tell them to do. In the interests of fairness, though, we must remind you of the other side of this. Rose is the only one who can get us out the door on time when we have theater tickets or are trying to get to church services. When our mother left pans of carrots boiling away to charred messes on the stove, Rose made

124

us peanut butter and jelly sandwiches, cutting them neatly into sailboats for Cordy. When she got her driver's license, she drove Bean to the nearest mall (which isn't really near at all) almost every weekend night, and didn't even tell on her the time she met those boys with the Trans Am and came home with vodka on her breath and vomit down the front of her blouse. And she helped Cordy sew her graduation dress even though she thought it looked hideous, and she was the professor in the math department whose course evaluations from her students always began, 'I always thought math was boring until I met Dr Andreas . . .' and as much as she hates us for taking away her throne, she has never ever pushed us off of it.

And she would be none of those things if she weren't the firstborn.

We had sent Bean to the store – Rose was helping our father move furniture in the bedroom for our mother's impending confinement, and Cordy was too unreliable to be trusted. Even with a list she would wander aimlessly through the aisles and come home with a mysterious assortment of products: a bag of sugar-encrusted gumdrops, an apple corer wide as a cupped hand, an unloved, dented box of flavorless crackers that would sit, ignored, in the pantry until they crumbled to paste. Whatever we had sent her for in the first place would be mysteriously absent.

A list clutched in her hand, the ink gone sweaty and the paper soft from the heat, Bean strolled through Barnwell Market. We hated the occasional necessary evil of the supermarket outside town: its painfully bright, wide aisles, the cold industrial-tiled floor, the incessant chirp of the cashiers' scanners twining with the music in an unsettling sound-scape. We far preferred this tiny store a block from the Beanery, with the dusty shelves holding home-made jams from the farms on Route 31, local produce

125

teetering dangerously in piles outside the store, and Mr or Mrs Williston waiting patiently behind the counter to ring up our purchases on a cash register that shook agreeably with each press of a key.

Bean filled a tired bushel basket, the bottom bowed with use, with the items on her list, and headed toward the front, stopping short at the sound of her name.

'Bianca Andreas,' a man's voice said, and she turned, surprised. She had brushed right past Mr Dr Manning, who was standing behind her, wearing a long-sleeved white T-shirt and blue nylon running shorts. He seemed older than she remembered, though it had been less than a decade; his blond hair going silver in the dim light, the tiny creases at the corner of his eyes deeper, his bare legs indecently muscled.

'Mister Doctor!' she said, the old name coming naturally to her.

He laughed, a deep, warm sound that purred along Bean's spine. 'Oh, come now. Call me Edward. You passed the Mister Doctor stage the moment you walked across the quad in your cap and gown. What are you doing back in the cornfields? I thought you'd abandoned us all for your big-city dreams.'

'*We are such stuff as dreams are made on,*' Bean sighed, with a coquettish little shrug that pushed the light cotton of her shirt down in a deep vee. She was rewarded when his eyes followed the line of her cleavage and then darted back up to her face. Perhaps she hadn't lost her touch after all. Take that, bar boys.

'*And our little life is rounded with a sleep,*' he said in agreement. 'Still queen of the Shakespearean retort, I see.'

'It's in my blood, sadly. How are you? I hear Mrs Doctor is off in sunny California.'

'With the offspring. I'm back to lonely bachelorhood,' he said, and we swear to you he winked.

126

Perhaps if Bean had been a stronger person . . . perhaps if it hadn't been so cold when she lay alone with her regrets in bed at night . . . perhaps if one of the only eligible bachelors in town hadn't been a priest, even of the non-celibate variety . . . perhaps if all those things had been true, she wouldn't have done what she did next.

But she did.

Bean stepped forward slightly, turning her foot out, red-carpet ready, and tilted her head so her hair fell across her face just so. 'What a pity,' she said. 'And nothing at all to keep you busy all summer long.'

'Oh, I'm teaching the summer workshops, but it's hardly the same. A handful of students, a handful of hours, and then the thrill of a Barnwell summer evening in an empty house.'

'It certainly hasn't gotten any more exciting since I left,' Bean said, her eyes darting over him, taking his measure, toying with the possibility. He'd always been handsome, more movie star than any professor had a right to be, but she'd never looked at him as a man, really, only as Dr Manning's husband, as the father of the children who played in the waning sunlight of the evenings she spent with them. And those children were nearly grown now, weren't they? And she was so far away, in both memory and fact. And he was very much here, going soft around the middle, but still broad-shouldered and strong, a toothpaste-commercial smile, and so focused on Bean that her breath seemed to catch in her throat.

'I fear Barnwell in particular would suffer in comparison to New York. You must come over for dinner and tell me all about it. Well, dinner such as it is,' he said, gesturing with the can of soup in his hand.

'Don't be ridiculous. You've always been an incredible cook. Surely you can do better than that on my account,' Bean said.

'Ah, but I recall your being a tremendously picky eater,' he said. It's true – his gift for culinary invention had rarely pleased her, and she had often replaced his offerings – cold butternut squash soup, buffalo medallions in a wine reduction – with glasses of wine and plates of salad. 'But I'll be happy to challenge myself for you.'

'I'll drop by, then. Maybe the day after tomorrow?'

'Seven,' he agreed, and it was done without either of them noticing it, or even paying attention to the fact that their bodies were nearly touching, her breast by his arm, her hip along his, a most indecent pose rarely seen in the Market.

'Should I bring the wine?'

'Please don't. You've always had horrible taste in wines.'

'I was nineteen,' Bean shot back, recalling the night she'd arrived at the Mannings' with a bottle of wine she'd liberated from a roommate's bookshelf, a sour, watery affair that they'd poured into the garden after one sip. She pushed down the memory of Lila, his wife who had invited her to all those dinners, given Bean knowledge and attention and warmth and asked for nothing in return, except the understood expectation not to try to seduce her husband.

'Neither age nor beauty excuses bad wine. Just bring yourself,' he said. 'That's all we need,' and Bean swayed away charmingly, a trail of tension stretching between them like vibrating wire.

O, let the heavens give him defence against the elements, for I have lost us him on a dangerous sea.

Oh, poor Bean.

EIGHT

Our family has always communicated its deepest feelings through the words of a man who has been dead for almost four hundred years. But on the subject of cancer (here comes Cordy's wording), he is silent as the grave. The word 'cancer' appears only once in all of Shakespeare's works, and it is not a reference to the disease, but comes in *Troilus and Cressida* in the same stanza as the classical names of Ajax, Achilles, and Jupiter. So we found ourselves mostly at a loss for words to describe what was happening to our mother.

We don't know how she found the lump, which Bean thinks is clear evidence that our father found it while they were having sex, but it doesn't matter, really. There was a lump, and they had been to the doctor, first in Barnwell, and then in Columbus, and there had been a biopsy. And the word 'malignant' had entered our family's vernacular.

The morning of our mother's surgery, we all got up without Rose having to wake us. How long had it been since all of us had piled into the car like this? Long enough for us to realize that though we had found the backseat uncomfortable when we were younger, it was nothing compared to how dreadfully inconvenient it was for three fully grown adults. Barnwell was small enough that we always walked, even in the winter, and regardless of the weather, and we were unused to such close quarters with each other anyway.

Rose and Cordy stood by the door for a moment and stared at each other expectantly, until Cordy rolled her eyes and climbed into the middle. 'The hump,' we had called it when we were younger, because whoever sat there had to contend with the bump where her legs should go.

'I haven't been the smallest for a long time,' Cordy complained as we squeezed her in on either side.

'You're still the youngest,' Bean said, flicking Cordy's bare leg with her fingertip. Rose noticed Bean had cleaned and trimmed her nails, and repainted them shell pink. The effect was both sad and a relief, and Rose felt the unfamiliar urge to hug her, to let Bean know that she didn't have to try so hard anymore.

'Didn't that stop meaning something about the time we could legally buy alcohol?' Cordy asked.

'Let's leave this town; for they are hare-brain'd slaves,' our father said, settling himself into the driver's seat and looking at Cordy in the rearview mirror.

'O-KAY,' Cordy said loudly, and pushed out with her knees so both Rose and Bean had to squeeze back to defend their space.

'Quit it,' they both whined. Cordy smiled angelically. She looked better. Her skin had lost the yellowish pallor it had gained on the catch-as-catch-can diet she had consumed in her stint as an American malcontent, and her hair looked shiny, bound in a thick braid that fell down her back. She had even gained some weight, Rose noticed, though she could still feel a sharp elbow digging into her ribs. That, however, was more malice than malnutrition.

130

'Isn't it nice to have our girls home?' our mother asked our father, batting her eyelashes at him in false adoration.

'How sharper than a serpent's tooth it is to have a thankless child,' our father replied, and pulled out of the driveway. No one had yet mentioned where we were going.

When we were growing up, we took a trip each summer, driving somewhere in our old, wide-bodied station wagon with its painfully sticky vinyl seats that left angry red tattoos on our bare thighs below our shorts. Our parents traded driving duties, steering us down roads that split pastures in two, through tunnels blooming into mountainous vistas, along coastal roads where the only thing between us and our Maker was a thin, low after-thought of a guardrail. We alternated arguing in the backseat with reading, coloring, and playing our father's infamous sonnet round-robins, in which we passed around a sonnet, each of us composing a line until we had an entire poem that, at the end, usually bore absolutely no resemblance to the initial topic.

The game did, however, make us uniquely good at extemporaneous iambic pentameter, not that this is a skill that benefits one much in any world other than our father's.

In this way, we saw Fourth of July fireworks in Maine, were terrorized by bears in Yosemite (Bean's fault – she had left the marshmallows out of the bear bag), had our photo taken by Mount Rushmore, sweltered through an unseasonably early hurricane in Florida, and had our tongues burned off by tamales in Austin.

When we look back on it now, it seems odd that we did not do things more fitting to our family's named interests. These trips, many of which could have been summed up by a bumper sticker bearing the name of some self-referential tourist attraction like South of the

Border or Wall Drug, seemed, if you will forgive the obviousness of it, so *American*. When we stayed at a motel with a pool and made friends with the other children shrieking around its concrete deck, half the time they might as well have been speaking another language. We didn't know their television shows, the songs they sang from the radio. We didn't know junk food, or fast food, and the only handheld game we had in the car was Etch A Sketch. We faked it well, of course, and it didn't matter because we would never see these children again, headed as they were to California, to Arkansas, to Virginia, places far from us. But we would be untruthful if we didn't admit it made us feel a little strange.

So, yes, it might be more expected for us to have summered regularly in Stratford, or London, or Padua, or anywhere in Europe with some vague Shakespearean connection, really. But we think our father genuinely enjoyed these forays into Americana. For all his high-minded ignorance about its ways, he found the lives of everyone else all around him, outside our little Barnwell-shaped academic bubble, fascinating. He marked these trips on a mental checklist he carried, some way of bringing himself – and us – into the mainstream, if only for a few weeks.

On this roadtrip to our mother's date with breastiny (™ Cordy), we had all brought books, of course, no one in our family would ever think of being without reading material, but Rose and our mother were the only ones reading. Our father was driving, holding the steering wheel loosely in his right hand while his left stroked his beard obsessively. He did this so often we sometimes wondered if he would wear tracks in it where his fingers moved. Bean was staring out the window, balancing Edward and her conscience on a mysterious set of mental scales, and Cordy was talking to our father about some avant-garde production of *The Merchant of Venice* that she had seen at a fringe festival somewhere.

'And then there was this whole thing about how the boxes Portia's suitors are trying to unlock are, like, symbolic of her *virginity*, so she kept grabbing her crotch while she was talking.'

'That's not exactly a new theory,' our father interjected. 'It's not a difficult leap of imagination to make. The word is actually "casket", and there's the connection to the death of her father because of the word choice, but they are really just boxes.'

'But did she have to *fondle* herself onstage?' Cordy asked.

'No, I suppose that's a bit much.'

'Oh, but you haven't heard the worst part yet,' Cordy said. She had clasped her hands in her lap, leaning slightly forward, her chin resting on the shoulder of our mother's seat, the earnest family dog. Bean raised one finger and dragged it carefully, metronome-like, back and forth along the window, ticking away the miles in her mind.

'Do tell,' our father said. He delights in precisely this kind of thing. In the same way Mount Rushmore was, to him, glorious in its baseness, he revels in the dreadfulness of various interpretations of Shakespeare. This meant that throughout our childhood, much of the live theater we saw was just that: dreadful interpretations of Shakespeare, including, memorably, that one all-nude production of *A Midsummer Night's Dream,* which (after Bottom – in full ass-head regalia – sported an erection upon being fondled by Titania) gave us nightmares for a week. The benefit, besides being able to quote liberally from nearly every play, was that we all became quite good at critiquing theater. And at sleeping upright.

'Well,' Cordy began, stretching the word out like salt-water taffy, relishing the moment. 'The Prince of Morocco, you know?' Our father nodded. 'The guy playing him was, like, Rastafarian? And he had fake *dreadlocks*. And an *accent.*'

She sat back, having dropped her bombshell.

Our father chuckled. *'Mislike me not for my complexion, mon,'* he said, in a clumsy patois.

'Da-ad,' Bean moaned, stopping the ticking of her finger and rolling her eyes.

'No, it was totally like that!' Cordy said, turning to Bean and then back to our father. 'Dad, you should have been there. I thought I was going to pee myself, I was laughing so hard.'

'What were they trying to do, do you think, Cordelia?' our father mused. This was, of course, the nut. Even a bad production had some value, something to be learned from it, even if it functioned as no more than a cautionary tale. 'Do you have any idea of the zeitgeist? Their aim?'

Cordy shrugged, bored now. 'I don't think there was one. I think it was a bunch of unemployed actors who think they're deep or whatever. Depressing.' She folded her hands back in her lap as though at prayer.

Our mother looked up from her book. 'It's the next exit,' she said, and the car became strangely still. Cordy opened her book and started to read.

Another family might have made preparations. Another mother might have cooked casseroles in Corningware and frozen them, labeled with instructions. Another trio of daughters might have embroidered a hospital gown, written a song in her honor, brought along massage oils and aromatherapy candles to ease her transition. For all Rose's talk, we brought only us. Unsure of what to ask, uncomfortable with the illness of a woman who had nursed us through all of ours, armed with only the books we were reading, and not entirely undamaged and unbruised ourselves. Our mother was inches away from

134

us, but we hardly knew how she was feeling – scared? Sad? Resigned?

At the hospital they wouldn't let us go any farther than the front lobby, so we kissed her goodbye there. Rose hugged her awkwardly, patting her back as though she were a casual acquaintance. Bean kissed her cheek and then squeezed her upper arms. 'I love you, Mom,' she said. Cordy was the only one who gave herself fully into it, hurling herself into our mother's arms and pressing her tightly. When she finally pulled away, our mother was crying, but only lightly, and Cordy looked weepy and a little dazed. 'I love you,' we all called as she and our father walked away. He wore, as he always did, a short-sleeved dress shirt and brown pants, which were too short, and revealed a splash of his black nylon socks as he and our mother disappeared down the antiseptic hallway.

'Tragic,' Bean said, shaking her head as they turned the corner. Our mother held her purse in her arms like a child, and our father's hand rested on her back.

'It's terrible,' Cordy agreed, still sniffling. Rose plucked a tissue from her heavy leather purse and handed it to our sister.

'I mean his fashion sense,' Bean said.

'Jesus, Bean. Have some compassion. She's going into surgery,' Rose said, shocked. Cordy started crying again.

'It doesn't mean what he's wearing isn't tragic,' Bean said, but the fight wasn't in her.

'Excuse me.' A voice came behind us, and we turned to see an employee standing behind us with a large wheeled cart, laden with supplies, linens.

'Sorry,' we said, and darted out of the way. Rose led us to the lobby, where the sun had only just begun to burn in through the atrium, the glass panels divided by heavy wood. Cordy fingered one of the plants, unable to tell whether it was plastic or real. Unyielding chairs in varying shades of blue clustered together in tiny squares. Bean and Cordy sprawled out on two rows, feet toward each other, and Rose sat primly on a single cushion. Upstairs as they prepared our mother for surgery, we imagined our parents praying, bending their foreheads together and whispering in an intimate expression of their love and their faith. We could summon neither.

Cordy and Bean pulled out their books and opened them, disappearing behind the pages. Rose sat for a long time, staring at nothing in particular, and then opened her book as well. That was it, apparently. We weren't going to talk about it, we weren't going to share any feelings or discuss any arrangements, not going to bond in any kind of movie montage moment where emotional music swelled as we hugged and wept for our mother's loss and our own fear. Instead, we were going to wrap ourselves in cloaks woven from self-pity and victimhood, refusing to admit that we might be able to help each other if we'd only open up. Instead, we'd do what we always did, the only thing we'd ever been dependably stellar at: we'd read.

Our father came to get us just before five, the air in the lobby grown stiff and warm with the glare of the afternoon sun. Bean and Rose were asleep, laid out uncomfortably, and Cordy had turned upside down, her head hanging off the edge of the cushions, her feet propped up on one of the cubicle-like walls dividing the cavernous room into smaller portions. She held the book awkwardly in front of her face, page turning a two-handed effort.

'Harpier cries, 'Tis time, 'tis time,' our father announced loudly. Cordy raised her book, her face gone red from suspension, as Rose started awake with a loud gasp. Bean continued to snore contentedly until Cordy flipped herself right side up, kicking Bean as she moved. Bean started, blinked sleepily.

We processed upstairs in silence, Birnam Wood to Dunsinane, our father's shoes squeaking officiously on the wheel-worn floors. Cordy trailed her fingers along the wide blue lines spreading along the walls. When we reached our mother's room, our father paused, turned to face us. 'I just want to warn you. She doesn't look good.'

We nodded in acceptance and filed in after him, lined up along the wall as though preparing to be captured in a group mug shot. Everything was white. The walls, the sheets, the curtain separating our mother's bed from the empty bed and the window beyond, her skin, her lips even. Colorless, ash white, cracked. The fluorescent light sputtered, angry bee, above her head. Bean bit her nails. Rose cried. Our mother looked so tiny, so drained, her bare head skeletally naked against the pillow, the normal blooms in her cheeks faded to paper.

Our father sat down on the far side of the bed, the sheets folding around the curve of his body. He took our mother's hand, stroked it gently. Bean, avoiding looking at our mother's face, noticed again how old our mother's hands were becoming, the knuckles going broad and bony, the skin traced with sparrow tracks and loose flesh around the backs. Her eyes fluttered open and she looked at our father, her eyes watery mud, pupils wide. A table stood against the wall, a cup of ice collapsing into an exhausted pool of water, a straw, a pitcher, a tiny fluted cup of apple juice, the foil peeled back. Rose busied herself by moving these items around in a Three-card Monte.

Cordy sat down on the other side of the bed, and the combined pressure made our mother's legs, wide and sturdy, stand out in relief beneath the tight-pulled sheet. After a moment's hesitation, she took our mother's other hand and copied our father's movements, stroking along

137

the bony knuckles Bean had just been eyeing. 'Hi, Mommy,' she said, and our mother turned her head slowly toward her.

'Hi, honey,' she said, her voice a dry, leafy whisper. She turned her head again, a stiff doll's rotation, and smiled at Bean and Rose. 'Hi. How are you?'

Bean grinned. 'We're great. But we're not in the hospital. How are you?' She tugged at the bottom of her jacket, cropped red linen above a long denim skirt. Trust Bean to be perfectly turned out in a crisis.

Cordy continued to stroke our mother's hand as though coaxing something from within her.

Our mother smiled. 'Tired,' she said, turning back to Cordy.

'I know, Mommy,' Cordy said. 'Why don't you sleep? We'll be right here.'

She turned to our father like a child looking for permission. He nodded, picked up her hand and kissed it, his beard brushing against her skin. Rose watched them, thinking she had never seen him look at her so lovingly, and her heart gave a soft pang for Jonathan. Our mother's eyes closed and we watched her breathe.

When visiting hours ended, we left our father snoring happily in the empty bed in our mother's room and drove home, Bean behind the wheel, Rose in the passenger seat, gripping the dashboard in horror every time we changed lanes, Cordy poking her head between the seats, still the family dog. It was strange, being just the three of us, and we spent most of the drive home arguing about what to eat for dinner. Cordy claimed vegetarianism (mostly to make things more difficult, we surmised), Bean fretted about the imaginary half pound she had gained since returning to a diet consisting of more than tapas and martinis, and Rose had been dreaming all day about mashed potatoes with butter, which fit Cordy's requirements, but not Bean's. We finally ended up banging around in the kitchen, knocking into each other as we created our own culinary adventures, and ate in a silence interrupted only occasionally by unpleasant conversation about our mother and what we should do to prepare the house for her return.

After dinner, Bean climbed out her window and sat on the roof, smoking and staring up at the stars. In New York she had never noticed their absence, but here she could see them clearly, constellations and the punctuation marks in between, the creamy swirl of the Milky Way, pushing through the thick summer darkness like the lights at the Coop prom so long ago. The sounds were strange, too; no horns, no sirens, no shouting, no electric hum, just the urgent calls of the crickets and a few early owls.

'Can I join you?' Cordy asked, sticking her head out the window and peering awkwardly up at Bean.

'Of course,' Bean said, and scooted over. Cordy climbed out, legs first, and clambered along the gentle slope of roof beside the dormer. The slate had worn down to a smooth flow where we lay in silence together.

'She looked awful,' Cordy said finally. An owl hooted its mournful agreement from one of the trees at the bottom of the backyard. 'I didn't think she'd look so bad.'

Bean shrugged, exhaled a plume of smoke that hung in the thick air for a moment, and then dissipated. 'I think she's going to look pretty crappy for a while if she has to do chemo again.'

'Yeah,' Cordy said. 'I know. It was just weird to see her that way. You know. Weak.' Bean knew. We all knew. The sturdy peasant stock we all resented was what made our mother seem formidable. She wasn't, of course, she was subject to the same flights of fancy as all of us, maybe more, and we had all seen her cry. She wasn't one of those iron women who would have been able to raise a dozen kids during the Potato Famine and still make it to Mass every Sunday. But she had always *looked* like one of those women. 'Do you think we'll get it?'

'Guar-an-teed,' Bean said in a slow drawl. 'No point in even quitting smoking. The boobs are going to get me first.'

'Rationalize all you want,' Rose said, poking her head out the window and climbing clumsily out to join us. 'It's still a nasty habit.'

'Life's a nasty habit,' Bean replied, nonchalant. Cordy elbowed her and she moved over, and Rose sandwiched in on the other end. We lay in a neat row, staring up at the sky together.

Once, long ago, our parents had gone out to a faculty dinner and left the three of us alone. Rose, sixteen; Bean, thirteen; Cordy still trailing along at ten. It was a cool night, it must have been late fall, and Bean had just bought a 45 of a pop song that had enchanted her completely, one of those one-hit wonders with a synth-pop backbeat and an infectious chorus.

We did the dishes together and then Bean put on the record, opened the front door wide, and danced on the porch below the yellow light, moths beating anxiously against its warmth. By the end, she had pulled Rose up from the porch swing, and they danced together, breathless and wild, sweating in the chill air. 'Again!' Bean cried, and Cordy scampered inside to place the needle back at the beginning, her corduroys whisking above her bare feet. We played it again and again and Cordy stood at the door and watched us dancing together, running back and forth each time the song wound to a close, and finally we pulled her out with us and the three of us whirled and spun until we knew all the words and were breathless as much from singing along as from dancing. *They dance! they are mad women!*

140

Bean cried, grasping Rose's hands and spinning her into dizzy oblivion. And then we climbed up on this roof and looked for falling stars together until Cordy fell asleep and nearly slid off.

Being on the roof again made us think of that night, but now we were older, if not wiser. 'I'm going to get a job,' Cordy announced.

'So you're staying,' Rose said.

'Yar. Is that a problem?' Cordy turned, her braid snagging on a loose tile, and she tilted up to set herself free before lying back down, looking at Rose's profile.

'Of course not. It's just, you know, odd, having you both back here.'

'Not as odd as it is being here,' Bean interjected. 'I thought I was well shot of this town. I hate this place.'

'Funny,' Cordy mused. 'It always had such nice things to say about you.'

'It feels alien. Like I'd gotten really used to being the only child and now I'm not,' Rose continued, as though we hadn't spoken.

'You haven't been an only child since the day I was born,' Bean said sharply. 'Just because we're not here doesn't mean we don't exist.'

'I know. It just kind of feels like that. You know, because I see Mom and Dad all the time . . . Oh, never mind. You wouldn't understand.'

'Yeah, because it's bullshit,' Bean said. She sat up, balanced her cigarette on her thumb, and used her index finger to flick it into the air. The tiny projectile shot out in a fireworks arc, leaving a trail of sparks as it fell toward the garden. We sat in silence again, the still air humming, bustling with summer life. Bullshit, sure, yet we all knew what she meant. We have all had the experience of being the only one in the house with our parents and there is something special, something different about it. Neither

141

Bean nor Cordy ever would have been so callous as to call themselves the only child, but we knew what Rose meant. Competition for attention came only intermittently, in phone calls from Cordy, desperate for a Western Union injection, or from Bean, a call from a taxicab on the way to a party, or, when Rose was off getting her PhD, careful letters on her elegant stationery, written painstakingly in her excellent Palmerian hand. These interruptions were more aberrations than the norm, and when they were over, they were forgotten, and the one at home could resume her post as most favored nation.

Bean lay back again, her hands behind her head. 'What's your job, Cordy?'

'Working at the Beanery. Dan Miller said he'd hire me if I wanted to work.'

'If you'd finish your degree, you could get a far better job than service. Actually, you should apply for a job at the college. Then you'd get free tuition,' Rose suggested.

'Don't I get free tuition anyway, because of Daddy?' As the baby, Cordy was the only one who put the diminutive suffixes on our parental appellations. It was, at this age, a little annoying, but we put up with it.

'You're twenty-seven. I think that benefit ran out a few years ago,' Bean said, not unkindly.

'Well, whatever. I don't care about the degree. I just want to be happy.'

'Is working in a coffee shop going to make you happy?'

'It's a perfectly noble profession.'

'I didn't say it wasn't noble. Rose is the one who thinks it's beneath you. I'm just saying that if your major life goal is happiness, make sure what you're doing is going to make you happy.'

'I didn't say it was beneath her. I just said she could do more.'

142

'Same difference,' Bean shrugged. Rose gave a long sigh, indicating that she disagreed but would not fight it. We are all gifted with communicating great depths of emotion through the semaphores of our sighs.

'I wish we had some pot,' Cordy said sadly.

'Ask your new boss,' Bean said. 'He had all the good shit in college.'

'I think he's gone respectable,' Rose said.

'Alas the heavy day,' Cordy intoned deeply, and we all giggled. 'What about you, Bean?' she asked, turning her head the other way now, and noting how much Bean looked like Rose from the side. And herself the same, she supposed. No one would ever not know we are sisters.

'What about me? I don't have any pot, either.'

'No, I mean are you going to get a job? Stay awhile?'

Bean lifted her hands and rubbed her eyes hard, the way that leaves starbursts and darkness when you open them again 'I guess so. For a while at least. I want to be around to help with Mom.'

'So you're not going back to New York?' Rose asked.

Silence huddled around us. The owl hooted again, from a different tree this time. Or a different owl, similarly melancholy. When Bean finally spoke, we could hear the dryness as her lips parted. 'Not right away. No. Maybe not for a while.'

'What happened, Bean?' Cordy asked, and her voice was as gentle as her fingers had been on our mother's hand. She watched a single tear roll down Bean's cheek, moonlight-paled, but didn't move to touch her. Bean let it trickle back toward her ear, and when she spoke, her voice didn't waver.

'I don't want to talk about it,' she said. We could see that her face was taut from holding in emotion. She looked old, Cordy thought, but she never would have said it aloud. 'But yeah. I'm going to be here for a while. I'm going to get a job, too.' Bean sat up and lit another cigarette, and Rose didn't even complain when she had to fan the smoke away from her face. Something in Bean's tone was weak and unfamiliar, and slightly unsettling to us, who had grown used to the prickly pear of her nature.

'You could get a job at the college,' Cordy suggested. 'You're an alumnus. Alumnae?'

'Alumna,' Rose said.

'Hell, it's bad enough I'm living here again,' Bean said, and her sharp edge returned, slicker than a knife blade. 'I'm not going to go back and work there, too. It'd make me feel like a failure.'

We sat for a moment, no one pointing out that we were all failures, whether we allowed ourselves to feel it or not. Rose, least comfortable with that idea, finally slapped her hands on her legs, brushing away invisible dust. 'I'm going to bed. Anybody need me to wake you up tomorrow?'

'Me,' Cordy and Bean both said.

When Rose had climbed inside, Bean finished her cigarette and stared into the quiet night. The full trees blocked our view of the town, but she knew somewhere in the sleeping darkness lay sin and salvation, both equally tempting. But the path of sin was so comforting, so well tread, so easy to slip down into quiet numbness.

'Seen the Very Reverend lately?' Cordy asked, as though she were reading Bean's thoughts.

Bean exhaled, shook her head.

'Too bad. He's cute.'

The words lingered on Bean's lip a moment, hesitating, before she spit them out. 'I'm going to have dinner with Dr Manning tomorrow.'

'Oh, really? That's cool. You haven't seen her in ages.'

'Not her. Him. She's in California or something.'

'Oh,' Cordy said. Did she know what Bean had meant?

Did she know the way that he had been drawn to the curve of Bean's lip, her breast, the quiet sadness that could be lost in a rustle of sheets?

But even if she knew, Cordy would not criticize. Who was she to judge our Bean and all that lay hidden inside her, when she carried her own secrets, warm and sweet in their pain?

Bean rubbed her forehead and then flicked her cigarette over the roof in the same trail as the first. Her mouth was dry and bitter from the smoke. 'Could you live here forever, Cordy?'

Our sister considered for a moment, toying with the loose end of a braid, rubbing her fingers up and down the exhausted split ends. 'It's no different from anyplace else,' she said finally. 'Just on a smaller scale.'

'Much smaller,' Bean said. She pulled her knees up to her chest and laid her cheek against her knee. 'Sometimes I feel like I can't breathe here.'

Cordy hesitated for a moment, and then reached over and gently ran the back of her hand along Bean's bare arm.

'That's not Barnwell,' Cordy said. 'That's you.'

NINE

It might seem callous that when we drove into Columbus the next morning, we went dress shopping instead of going to the hospital. We didn't desert our parents entirely, of course, because we arrived at the hospital by eleven, but we didn't go there immediately to commence with the gnashing of teeth and rending of garments.

Instead, there was trying on of garments at a discount bridal store with toothy saleswomen who cooed over us until Rose was sweating uncomfortably in stiff satin and Bean was nearly snarling. Cordy, her wide-legged jeans trailing into threads at the bottom, sat curled in a chair, shaking her head sadly at each meringued concoction.

'I look ridiculous,' Rose sighed at her umpteenth attempt in a stiff white dress. The store was quiet, which was good, because if Rose had had to contend with the chirping and pecking of a million happy mothers and twentysomething brides, she might have become homicidal. The dress was relatively simple, and pretty, with a fitted Empire bodice sealed with a dainty bow, flowing out into a chiffon skirt, but inside it Rose just looked tired and miserable. She made a face at herself in the mirror. 'Ridiculous,' Rose repeated. 'Mutton dressed as lamb.'

146

'Puh-leez,' Bean groaned, giving the long skirt a sharp yank to make it fall properly. 'Thirty-three is hardly mutton. I swear nobody who's anybody gets married anymore until they're at least thirty anyway.'

Rose pouted at herself in the mirror, smoothing back her hair. Cordy picked at her nails. 'Fine. I'm not mutton. But I still look foolish.'

'Because you're insisting on this stupid tradition,' Bean said. One of the saleswomen she had chased away fluttered by, ready to alight and push for a sale, but Bean bared her teeth, and the woman scatted just as quickly as she had come. 'Come on, Rose, we can do so much better, I swear, if you'll just let me do some picking. Somewhere that doesn't look like a marshmallow factory.'

Rose lifted the layers of skirt and let them float back down along her thighs, like Daisy deflating in Tom Buchanan's presence. 'But I don't want to look weird,' she groaned. 'I want to look like a bride.'

Cordy finally stood from her chair, having successfully torn her nails into ragged shreds. 'Nobody's going to mistake you for anything else at your wedding. But the big white dress just isn't for you, Rosie. Why don't you let Bean pick something out? She's a way better dresser than you or me.'

Rose looked at Cordy, who wore a ragged black tank top and jeans settled low on her hips, leaving a stretch of belly poking out. Back in the dressing room hung Rose's own clothes, a pair of olive walking shorts that left her legs sticking out like white, stumpy sausages, and a loose white shirt that made her look wide and unkempt. She had worn them for the ease of donning and doffing, but now she regretted it. Bean would have dressed up, and made sure to remain clean and perfect through the experience. *The very train of her worst-wearing gown / Was better worth than all my father's lands.*

In the center of the dressing room, in front of the wide span of mirrors that sent Rose's image spinning back at her, square, heavy, plain, sat a wooden box brides could climb on to admire the spread of a train, the detail of a hem. Rose thumped down on it sadly and buried her face in her hands. A moment passed in silence before we realized she was crying.

'Oh, Rosie,' Cordy said, and climbed toward our sister on her knees. She put her hands on Rose's knees and shook them gently. 'What's wrong?'

Rose cried.

Bean stood apart, wrapping a veil around her hand, tulle scraping against her fingers.

'Rosie-Posie,' Cordy said again, looking sweetly up at our sister's face. When Rose pulled her hands away, her eyes were red and streaks of tears mapped across her cheeks.

'I'm supposed to be beautiful,' she said, and sniffed. 'For one day, I'm supposed to be beautiful.'

'But you are,' Cordy said. 'You'll be the most beautiful bride we've ever seen.' And bless her heart, Cordy really meant it.

Rose turned to look at herself in the mirrors, bare arms swelling out of too-tight sleeves, her face gone red with the effort of sadness. It was, we'll admit, even Cordy might admit, not her best moment.

'No, no, I am as ugly as a bear; for beasts that meet me run away for fear,' Rose said, and set herself off again. Cordy lifted a hand to Rose's face, and Rose batted it away. 'Don't patronize me with your hippie crap,' she said sharply, and Cordy pulled away, stung.

Bean shook the veil off her arm and marched over to Rose's side, hands on her hips. Her heels sank into the soft carpet, and she wobbled slightly. 'Rosalind,' she said, and she pulled our sister's full name out like a warning. 'Don't be an ass.'

'Bean,' Cordy cautioned, but her softness was cut by the sword of Bean's voice.

'You look like shit because the dresses are shit,' Bean said.

Rose's head drooped like a thirsty flower, and a fat teardrop landed on the satin. Bean reached down and yanked Rose up by the hand.

'Be serious,' Bean said. 'Is this really what you want to look like?' She flicked an angry finger at a cheerfully juvenile bow on Rose's sleeve. 'This is kindergarten crap.'

'I want to look like a bride,' Rose said. 'I'm supposed to look like a bride.'

'Is this seriously about the dress?' Bean asked. 'Because this is a whole lot of drama over an overpriced pile of cheap fabric.' She picked up the price tag under Rose's arm and shook her head.

'It's not the dress,' Rose said, flopping down onto the box again. 'It's everything. Everything's just' – she flailed her arms – 'out of control.'

'You don't have to get married,' Cordy said. Seeing Rose in that white dress had made her feel uncomfortable and sad. She didn't know if it was the idea of the wedding, or the marriage, or the dress itself. She had not even the slightest urge to see herself up on that platform. Ever.

Rose and Bean looked at her as though she were a noxious substance we had just stepped in. This was a look best performed as a duet, and Cordy cringed, just as she had the million times we had delivered it in concert before. How was it possible, all these years and experiences later, that no one could wound us like the others?

'Well, you don't,' Cordy said sulkily. She retreated into a shell of frayed hems and sloppy hair.

'Hi, Cordy,' Bean said. 'Not helping.' She turned to Rose, took her hands, lifted her up. 'Take off the damn marshmallow and let's go see Mom. We'll go somewhere else and find you a dress that doesn't want to eat Manhattan.'

'If you make me look weird, I swear I'll disown you,' Rose said. Her hands felt slippery and warm inside Bean's cool fingers.

Bean rolled her eyes. 'What a tragedy that would be.' She stripped Rose out of the gown with deft, impatient fingers, and shooed her back into the curtained dressing room.

When Rose was in second grade at the local public school, one of the professors at Barney had an idea. Why, given the amount of pedagogical talent and intellectual creativity at the college, did they all send their children to such traditional schools?

A consortium of professors bought one of the old mansions near the campus, wide wraparound porch, spreading green lawn, three floors and a basement smelling of dirt and broken jars of jam. They moved furniture into some of the rooms, but left others empty, so footsteps echoed emptily against the walls. The kitchen was filled with lab equipment, the bedrooms with groaning bookshelves, and the parlor and sitting room were pressed into service as a tiny auditorium. And with this completely haphazard preparation, the Barnwell Cooperative School was born.

For Rose, who had loved every minute she had spent at what she called her *real* school, Coop, as it came to be known, was a complete culture shock. She had loved everything the professors had so denigrated – the uniformity of the desks, the tidy, old-fashioned cloakroom, the inflexible, predictable schedule, the tight single-file lines on the way to the cafeteria.

Coop had no such things. We held classes, certainly,

but they tended to take place on the whim of the professors who taught them; one week Monday might begin with biology, followed immediately by theater and then sculpture, and the next week Monday might have no classes at all. The idea behind the school was that the students would be captains of their own academic destiny, mastering all subjects through their pursuit of their interests, guided and informed by the great academic minds of the Barnwell faculty. Such a system wasn't an entirely new idea, but decades passed before Coop's philosophy was given a name: unschooling (which all of us found particularly objectionable).

Rose also blames this haphazard educational system for our flightiness, but we wouldn't have had it any other way. When the other students at college talked about locker combinations, visits to the principal's office, and Scantron forms, Cordy would mentally drift back to Coop, remembering the large brown armchair in the upper guest room she had claimed as her own, the hours she had spent there, reading Shakespeare, or Austen, or Marx, writing papers on Derrida or Pascal or Curie, or simply staring at the ceiling and wondering.

During what was, in essence, Bean's senior year – though nobody bothered with such formality, we just said we went to Coop and that was enough – she decided we needed to have a prom. She took the idea to what served as the board, who, as always, encouraged her to do it, but in the traditional Coop spirit. Which meant, of course, that the prom would include everyone, from wee babe to angsty adolescent.

We worked for months under Bean's direction to make it happen. (Well, Rose had started college by then, and was doing her level best to pretend not to know us, as Bean was already making noise at some of the keg parties on campus, and Cordy was liable to be found wandering

151

around the college's black box theater, clad in something strange like pink leg warmers and combat boots, so Rose wasn't too interested in helping, but the rest of us were all in.) While the kids at the high school a few towns over danced in a gymnasium, high heels clicking over the basketball court, abandoned tables along the foul lines and a weary cover band imported from Columbus to play 'Stairway to Heaven', we had our own celebration.

It turned out more like a low-budget family wedding. We held it in Coop's backyard, a ceiling of stars created with criss-crossing Christmas lights tied to the cottonwoods and red maples, a faux parquet dance floor crushing the patchy grass beneath. The Christian brothers acted as DJs, shuffling carefully cued tapes and records with surprising mastery, and punching each other good-naturedly when boredom set in.

On the wide porch, the elementary-school-aged children, ostensibly in charge of refreshments, scrambled back and forth (more often over one another than around, more often dismantling than helping). A few of them – Carrie Obertz, clad in a lemon-yellow pile of chiffon she had once worn as a flower girl dress, adding to the general nuptial air of the proceedings; Michael Taylor, who discarded his clip-on tie, leaving it dangling over the edge of the punch bowl, adding a dapper and unique touch to Professor Shapiro's crystal; and Hannah and Henry Holtz, who now run the best, albeit only, chocolatier in Barnwell – were of actual use, until, around nine o'clock, they collapsed into small, fluffy heaps on the patio furniture like tiny wilted flowers.

Coop being the kind of place it was, Barnwell being the kind of place it was, and the student body consisting of the children of disaffected, geeky ex-hippies, most of the twelve- to eighteen-year-olds didn't come in traditional prom style. Cordy arrived in our mother's wedding dress

(an oh-so-sixties Empire-waisted minidress of a disturb-
ingly quilt-like fabric), and danced with every available
man, including Dr Ambrose, a Cretaceous relic in the
mathematics department, and Henry Holtz, whose head
came approximately to Cordy's hip, but who presented
her with a lovely hydrangea blossom that she tucked into
her bra strap, leaving a trail of impossibly blue petals
wherever she walked for the rest of the evening. Bean's
best friend Lyssie came in a pair with Benjamin Marcus,
she in a Heidi-esque dirndl, he in a saggy pair of lederhosen,
but they redeemed their shall-we-say-unorthodox attire
by spending the entire evening together in a slow, sweet
clinch in one corner of the dance floor, no matter the
tempo of the Christian brothers' selections.

Bean was really the only one who wouldn't have
seemed out of place at an actual prom. Her dress, which
would have looked ridiculous on anybody but her, was
silver lamé with a sweetheart neckline and a wide,
flouncing skirt straight out of Tara, if Scarlett O'Hara had
been partial to silver lamé. Her date, one Nick Marchese,
wore a stiff, rented tuxedo with a silver lamé bow tie and
cummerbund. They would have made *Seventeen* proud.

Even Rose came by, standing on the corner halfway
between the kids on the dance floor and the unneeded
chaperones, perched like fat chickens on the edge of the
porch. And though Rose is not prone to saying things like
this, she will indeed tell you that night held magic: the way
the paper lanterns we had made, decorated with Chinese
characters someone had been studying, swayed in the
breeze, the way the false stars of the light strings twinkled
below the real stars, giving the impression that she could
have reached up and held the light of a thousand years ago
in her hands. She stood for a while, watching Cordy's serious,
studious waltz with Dr Ambrose, Bean and Nick's stiff-
armed rocking, and, most wistfully, Lyssie and Benjamin's

chastely impassioned repetitive circle. When Bean and Nick turned again, she caught Rose's eye, and they paused for a moment. And then Rose smiled at Bean, showing in that simple expression how proud she was of the way we had transformed that undernourished scrap of yard into something so beautiful, and Bean smiled back, and then Rose disappeared into the darkness, leaving behind the enchantment for her cruelly cinder-blocked dormitory.

When we got to the hospital, our father was sitting in one of the chairs, reading a wide-spined tome, while our mother poked suspiciously at a tray of food. She looked sallow and tired, the blush we so love in her cheeks still absent.

'Ah, it is my *dog-hearted daughters*,' our father said, barely looking up from his book. His clothes were rumpled, stray hairs crawled up his cheeks from his beard.

'*A decrepit father takes delight to see his active child do deeds of youth*,' Cordy shot back.

'That's a sonnet,' our father retorted.

'No one ever said sonnets didn't count,' Cordy said.

'Ignore him,' our mother said, and her voice sounded reedy and thin. 'Come give me a kiss.'

'*Then come kiss me, sweet and twenty*,' Cordy singsonged. 'Is that better, Daddy?'

Our father humphed again and went back to his book. We went over to our mother's bed and gave her kisses. Rose hugged her tightly, and our mother squeaked at the pressure. Bean gave her a whisk of a kiss, like a broom sweeping clean, and Cordy climbed into bed on her good side and curled up in the crook of our mother's arm, cat-like.

'How was traffic? You're here late,' our mother said, shifting gently, leaning back against the pillows, white as her skin.

'Bean drove,' Cordy said. 'We got here lickety-split.'

'We went dress shopping for Rose,' Bean said, leaning up against the wall, her legs crossed, fashion-model.

'Find anything?' Our mother reached up to scratch her scalp, which had begun to itch as her hair grew back in, and winced at the stretch of the skin under her arm.

'I'll do it,' Cordy said, and sat up, rummaging in the thick wool satchel hanging across her shoulder until she produced a mangy-looking, soft-bristled brush, and sat beside our mother in the bed, stroking the brush over the wisps that were appearing along the shocking bare skin of her scalp. We sat in silence for a moment, wondering at the sight, the contrast between the thick spill of hair we remembered, the way it fell, dark wood, over her shoulders when she loosened it, and the sparse fur that was her hair now. When we were little, we loved to watch our mother brush her hair, the long, luxuriant strokes bringing forth the shine, and then the quick, efficient movements as she twisted it into a bun. Cordy's hands looked thick and inept in comparison, our mother's head as delicate as an unopened bloom.

'No,' Rose said. The fact that other mothers might have been more eager, flipping through bridal magazines, begging to come along or even organizing the trip them- selves, did not go without notice. But this was not our mother. She was not the kind of woman to raise her daughters to read bridal magazines, and therefore, of course, would not read them herself. 'Everything looked hideous on me.'

'That's because everything was hideous,' Bean said.

'It's a hideous culture,' our mother said as Cordy finished brushing the light fuzz of our mother's hair. Cordy had propped her up awkwardly, the pillows pressed into the small of her back, and when her gown gaped across her clavicle, we could see the spread of gauze across her skin,

155

and the trail of clear tubing draining the wound. 'Why would you want something like that anyway, Rose?'

Rose's cheeks burned with angry shame, and she fumbled for the right words, pushing her lips into silent protestations.

'It's her wedding, Mother,' Bean jumped in. 'Besides, it's not like she can wear your wedding dress. Cordy ruined it.'

'I did not,' Cordy objected. She dropped the brush back into the unexplored caverns of her bag, and our mother relaxed into her pillows again, Cordy curled beside her like a question mark.

'You spilled punch all over it at the prom.'

'I had it cleaned, dumb butt,' Cordy said. 'You can't even tell. Rose could wear it if she wanted to.'

Rose did not reply, but we all knew our mother's swinging sixties minidress would be about as flattering on her as any of the hysterical poufs of fabric we had suffered through that morning. In any case, the subject had been changed, Cordy had been blamed, which was the way it ought to be, and at least nominal peace had been restored.

'Out, out, out,' a nurse shooed us, as she walked into the room, her crepe-soled shoes squeaking insistently against the floors. We outed, scooting around the portable toilet the nurse had rolled in with her. Standing in the hallway, Cordy went back to shredding her cuticles until Bean batted her hand away from her mouth. Cordy stuck out her tongue at Bean, and Rose shot them both a disapproving glance.

'When's she coming home?' Rose asked our father, changing the focus from our disobedient sister.

Our father cleared his throat, stroked his beard with the hand not holding his place in his book. *'Tomorrow, I know not whether God will have it so,'* he said, as though he

156

were lecturing to a particularly erudite class of undergraduates, which we suppose we are, in a way. 'The hospital is sending a nurse to let us know what to do.' He looked somewhat confused by the idea, as though he were not sure what would possess them to do such a thing. Bean looked relieved. She was wearing high heels like railroad spikes, and elegantly loose trousers draped in a cunning camouflage over the Andreas family thighs. This was not a woman any of us could see acting as home health aide, least of all Bean herself.

'You should come home with us tonight, Daddy,' Bean said. 'You look a mess.'

Our father shrugged. 'Your mother and I haven't spent a night apart since we were married, and I'm not about to start now. I'll clean up in the bathroom.'

True, that. Our parents had married impossibly young, our father a fresh-faced master's candidate, our mother a recent graduate, and possibly already pregnant (scandalous!). Our favorite photo of them shows them recessing down the aisle, the guests at the ceremony fashionably turned out in a blur of bobbing hats and elbow patches. Our father walks slightly ahead of our mother, whose veil trails out behind her in an invisible wind. He is smiling as though he has just won the jackpot. She is smiling as though she has discovered a secret.

In any case, even the night Rose was born, back in the days when men were not typically present in the delivery room, let alone acting as paramedical assistants in cutting the cord, and babies were dutifully welcomed into the world with a hearty slap on the rump to elicit an (unsurprisingly) objectioned reaction, our father slept in a chair much like the one we had found him in today, having insisted Rose's bassinet be brought into the room. With one hand extended to clutch the plastic edge of the container, he slept happily through both mid-night feedings.

157

There is much made in the psychological literature of the effects of divorce on children, particularly as it comes to their own marriages, lo those many years later. We have always wondered why there is not more research done on the children of happy marriages. Our parents' love is not some grand passion, there are no swoons of lust, no ball gowns and tuxedos, but here is the truth: they have not spent a night apart since the day they married.

How can we ever hope to find a love to live up to that?

TEN

'Cordy, come on!' Bean hollered from the foot of the stairs.

'I'm coming!' Cordy shouted back. We were headed to a medical supply store to pick up some things the nurse had arranged for but that they had refused to deliver all the way to deepest, darkest Barnwell – a seat for our mother for the shower, a special camisole that wouldn't press the drain into her skin, a pillow to allow her to sleep without moving too much, some kind of hand exerciser to help her recover the full range of motion in her arm.

In her room, Cordy was frantically digging through her clothes, trying to find a shirt that fit. Her breasts had been tender for a long time, but in the past week it seemed they had grown enormously, and June was busting out all over. Her hippie skirts were doing the trick on the bottom half, but the little T-shirts and tank tops she was accustomed to wearing made her look like a stripper. She had snuck one of Bean's sports bras out of the laundry, its compression making the change at least slightly less noticeable.

'Cordeeeeeeeeeeeeeeeeeeccceeeeeeeelia!' Bean shouted again.

'I am coming!' Cordy howled, stubbing her toe on the edge of the bed as she leaped over a pile of shoes she'd abandoned in the middle of the floor. 'Dammit.' She finally found one of Rose's loose tops, also liberated from the laundry room, and yanked it over her head. She shoved her feet into two sandals from the pile, fairly certain they belonged to the same pair, and clomped down the stairs.

'Nice outfit,' Bean said. 'Good that you took the time to put it together.'

Cordy looked down. The top was batik, the skirt patchwork. She looked like she'd rolled in a bin of fabric remainders. 'W.E.' she said.

'We?'

'What. Ever. Let's go.' She hopped down the last two steps and grabbed her bag. How much longer was she going to be able to get away with forgiving elastic waistbands and pilfering clothes from our laundry piles? It was a good thing she'd given up the indie rock look – the miniskirts and baby tees would have given her away already. She'd have to buy new clothes soon. Maternity clothes.

And she'd have to tell us.

She sat in the passenger seat biting at her ragged cuticles as Bean drove, singing tunelessly along with the radio. It was all happening too fast. She'd already gained weight, back in our parents' house where food was plentiful and actually tasted good, and her nausea was abating slowly. Time was ticking away. Maternity clothes were just the beginning – there needed to be doctor's appointments and baby clothes and all those things meant money.

She was going to have to take Dan up on his offer of a job. But how much would that pay? And what if our parents kicked her out when she told them?

She could tell Rose first. Rose would come up with

some kind of plan. Except Rose was even touchier than usual. Cordy tugged at a scrap of skin at the edge of her nail with her hands and it started to bleed.

It might not be too late to have an abortion. The fog around her head cleared for a moment. The father – if you could call him that – wouldn't care. He didn't even know. And our family wouldn't care if they didn't know, either.

But she cared. She didn't want to but she did.

Putting a hand on her stomach, she pushed against the tiny swell. We knew what the church had to say about abortion – we knew what it had to say about a lot of things, but that had never stopped us before. Cordy would be hard-pressed to say that it was anything to do with our faith that was giving her pause.

She looked over at Bean, whose eyes were hidden behind designer sunglasses, still singing along with the radio, wandering in and out of pitch as though she were embroidering around the notes. Bean would have an abortion, no doubt. Probably already had had one. Rose would have the baby.

But what would she do?

She pictured herself with an infant, a toddler, a pre-teen, a teenager. Impossible. Hadn't she just been a teenager herself? Wasn't she still? Reaching out, she flipped the air-conditioning vent up so the cold air blew into her eyes, making her squint against the pressure.

She couldn't make this kind of decision. She never had – people always made decisions for her, or the wind took her where it would and she made the best of it. She'd make an appointment with the doctor and she'd think about it then. Not now.

When they got back from the store, where Cordy had plopped herself into a wheelchair with pink bicycle streamers coming off the handlebars and been little to no help at all to Bean in checking items off the list, they walked inside to a quiet house.

'Helloooooooo?' Cordy called, dropping the bags and shower seat Bean had harassed her into carrying in from the car. 'Where is everyone?'

'Upstairs,' Rose called. 'Come up, please.'

Bean and Cordy went upstairs into our parents' bedroom. Our mother was lying in the bed, her eyes closed. Our father sat beside her, holding her hand. Rose was leaning against the fireplace, her eyes closed.

'What's wrong?' Bean asked. She and Cordy sat on the hope chest where we stored extra blankets.

'The results from the lymph node biopsy came back,' Rose said. 'They were positive.'

'Meaning what?' Cordy asked.

'Nothing good,' Bean said. She'd found a book on breast cancer at the library, and had read it, but the medical terms had jumbled in her mind and she found herself unable to follow the complicated flow charts of combinations and treatment options.

'It means the cancer has spread to the lymph nodes under her arm. They'll have to do radiation and maybe more chemo.'

'Shit,' Bean said.

'No doubt,' Cordy agreed.

No one seemed to have anything else to add to that pithy pair of statements. We'd convinced ourselves that after the surgery it would all be okay, problem solved, and we could move on.

'It could be worse,' our father said. 'It's stage IIIC. Treatable, provided everything goes well. *And what remains will hardly stop the mouth of present dues: the future comes apace; what shall defend the interim?*'

'Daddy,' Cordy groaned. 'Speak English.'

'We'll just have to deal with it,' our mother said softly,

162

opening her eyes, which looked bright against the white of her skin. 'We knew there was the possibility that things could be worse. And your father's right – it's treatable. The doctor said since the tumor responded so well to the chemotherapy, it's likely it will respond equally well to radiation and maybe another round of chemotherapy.'

Another round. As if she were buying drinks. Bean pictured our mother sitting at a bar, offering chemo cocktails on the house.

'Well, we got all the things the nurse suggested,' Bean said, clearing the image from her mind.

'Bring them up,' Rose ordered. 'We'll get things set up in here.' The nurse had suggested that we move our mother downstairs during her convalescence, but our mother was horrified by the thought of turning the dining room into her bedroom for the duration, and flat-out refused, despite the nurse's perfectly reasonable arguments. So we had resigned ourselves to schlepping ourselves, our mother's things, and, if need be, our mother, up and down the stairs for the next few months.

Bean and Cordy trudged downstairs and brought everything up, and we settled ourselves into a rhythm of work and fussing, bumping into each other until our mother complained about the noise and we scattered like seeds into our own rooms to bury ourselves in all the things we didn't want to talk about at all.

Bean's hands were cold as her heels clicked up the sidewalk to the Mannings' front door. The evening wrapped, warm and humid, around her, the silk of her camisole pressing against her heated skin, but her fingers were chilled and shaking.

'Bianca,' Dr Manning said as he opened the door to her knock. He was wearing a dress shirt, the sleeves rolled neatly up, the fabric's deep blue echoing in his eyes. 'You look beautiful, as always.'

'Edward,' she said, and proffered her cheek for a kiss. His lips were warm and dry and almost familiar, and he lingered a moment longer than technically appropriate, inhaling the scent of her.

'Come into the kitchen,' he said. 'Dinner's almost ready.'

Bean slipped off her shoes by the front door – barefoot, he was only a few inches taller than she – and followed him. The kitchen had been remodeled since she had been here last, with expensive appliances that gleamed, self-satisfied, in the dim light. Bean might have asked about it, but doing so would have brought reality dangerously close to the fantasy, would have entailed mentions of Lila and the children, and Bean knew better than to spoil the moment. Leaning on the edge of the marble-topped island in the center of the room, she watched Edward's hands as he deftly opened a bottle of wine and poured her a glass, the liquid settling joyfully into the bowl.

'Let's have a toast,' Edward said, filling and then raising his own glass. 'To old friendships, rekindled.'

'To the future,' Bean said.

Same as the past.

There had only been one married man on Bean's too-long list, an attorney at the firm where she worked, too old to not yet be partner, tired and beaten down and welcoming of the wonder of this young beauty who brought pageantry and drama to his staid life. They made love on his desk, Bean laid bare on open files, a cold paperweight against her arm. They rented obscenely expensive hotel rooms for only a few hours. He bought her jewelry, plied her with lavish dinners, whispered lyrics from old power ballads in her ears. In his Walter Mitty dreams, he was powerful and dominant, and Bean let him believe that, let him be magnanimous at the expense of her own strength. But it wasn't any of that which bothered her. It was the family pictures she turned her back on when she lay on his desk, the handmade card she found in his pocket while he showered in their room at the Plaza, lost in steam and floral soap. It was the way that when he moved above her she could picture him kissing his wife goodbye in the morning, pushing his children on the swings, living the life that she was pulling him away from.

It appeared, after all, that Bean had some standards.

But then here she was again, watching a very married man, married, frankly, to a woman who had done nothing but good for her, make her a very fancy meal. Pickings were, after all, rather slim. But, oh, it was so nice to be so obviously wanted. So nice to worry about her hair and her makeup instead of money and her awful prospects. So nice not to be turned away from for someone younger, prettier.

There was a picture of Lila and their youngest child, who'd been only a baby when Bean graduated, on the refrigerator, nestled together against a backdrop of snow. Lila's eyes, bright and blue, crinkled at the edges, above cold-pinked cheeks. Bean closed her eyes for a moment and sent out a silent apology. For these gifts we are about to receive, may the Lord make us truly sorry.

'How are we so lucky to be graced with your presence again?' Edward asked. He held his wineglass in one hand and deftly worked a wooden spoon in a skillet on the stove.

Bean sidled around the edge of the island so she was closer to him, the picture behind her. Her heart beat faster, her hand slipped against the stem of her glass as she set it down. 'It's so noisy in the city,' she said. 'I thought it was about time for a little piece of quiet.'

Edward nodded. 'Then you're in the right place. I can't

remember the last time I had to complain about the volume in Barney.'

'You're obviously not spending a lot of time at the keg parties,' Bean said. She rested her hand against the countertop and turned, pushing her hips toward him, calculatedly making herself available.

'My interest in partying with college kids died shortly after bell-bottoms abandoned us. I think there's an evolutionary limit on how long drinking warm beer can hold your interest.'

Bean stepped closer again. 'But all those nubile young coeds? Come on, don't you find it the least bit tempting?' Oh, it was so easy for her, every move planned for maximum effect, every phrase calculated to raise the temperature. The thrill of the chase still excited her; though she knew its inevitable conclusion, though she could predict every breath along the way, there was pleasure in its incredible power to dull everything but the two people in this room. If only those silly boys at the bar knew what they were missing.

'Children,' Edward said dismissively.

'I was one of those children once,' Bean pouted.

'But you're not now, are you?' he asked. 'You're a woman.' His fingers still wrapped around the bowl of his glass, he brushed the back of his hand over her collarbone, his eyes locked with hers.

And Bean, if she had ever been planning to fight, surrendered.

Cordy's first shift at the Beanery was quiet, as it would be in the summer. If you have never been in a college town in the summer, it is hard to explain. It's a small town with a lot of large, empty buildings, and people knocking around between them like lost billiard balls. During the year it explodes, but in the summer there is nothing but time stretching thick and slow.

166

So it was just Cordy and her trainer, a junior at Barnwell who had stayed over the summer because his girlfriend had a work-study job on campus. To be honest, he could have run the Beanery just fine on his own. But he patiently walked her around and showed her the menu, and allowed her to inhale the rich scent of the coffee he made, and then banished her to the sandwich counter. Not that it felt like a banishment, she thought, the slick crust of the bread against her freshly washed hands as she spread egg salad between the slices, sneaking in some chopped dill to sharpen the quiet thickness of the eggs and the rich bread. She tucked the halves of the sandwich into a foam clamshell, closing it with a satisfying squeak, and handed it to the customer, who left, nudging the door open with his hip. When she had finished, she swept the stray crumbs into the well at the edge of the counter.

'It's good you're starting now,' Ian told her. 'Because during the year, it's crazy like woah.'

Cordy nodded. This seemed to be stating the obvious. Would she be here during the year? She wiped her hands on her apron, delicately festooned with edgings of powdered sugar from the lemon bars she had been slicing, and tried to imagine herself, her belly swollen and full, standing in front of piles of college students, their cheeks fresh from winter cold, the air swirling with the smell of stubbed-out cigarettes and the sound of books slamming down on tables and counters.

The bell at the front jingled. 'Look sharp,' Ian said, motioning with his spiky hair toward the door. 'It's the ladies who lunch.' A series of maternal chortles swept in with a rush of humid air, and a gaggle of college employees, mostly department secretaries enjoying the quiet laze of summer, came up to the counter.

'Cordelia? Is that you?' Cordy turned, self-consciously

167

adjusting the chopsticks holding her hair back in a spiky knot. The leader of the pack, as it were, Georgia O'Connell, was smiling at her expectantly. Mrs O'Connell had worked as the secretary of the English department for as long as Cordy could remember. When we were little, our mother had taken us on walks to meet our father for lunch in the student union, and Mrs O'Connell had let us each have a piece of candy from the omnipresent jar on her desk – butterscotch, or sometimes root-beer-flavored drops that released a sickly syrup when we bit into them.

'Mrs O!' Cordy said, and leaned across the counter for a hug, which left a smear of powdered sugar on the woman's clean pink shirt, like frost on raspberries. 'What are you doing here?'

'Working, can't you tell?' Her face curved into rich wrinkles that pushed together as she smiled. 'More to the point, what are you doing here?'

Ah, the sixty-four-thousand-dollar question, that. Cordy shrugged, cast a winsome smile at Mrs O. 'You know, my mom and everything.'

'Of course.' Mrs O's smile fell away, and she nodded seriously. 'How is she?'

'Okay, I guess. Still on the pain medication, so she's kind of out of it. But we're thinking we could sell some of it aftermarket, you know, make a few bucks off of the deal.'

Mrs O was not amused. 'What can we do for you?'

'We're okay. You know Rose is living at home for a while, and Bean's back, too. So there's lots of hands.'

'All of you together again. Your parents must be thrilled. Your father misses you and Bianca terribly, you know. Always talking about what you're up to. Can't stop him, really.'

'Ugh. How embarrassing. On behalf of myself and my sisters, I apologize.'

'That's what it's like when you have children. Wait

168

until one of you has children. Then he really won't be able to stop crowing.'

'Bite your tongue,' Cordy said, flushing.

'He says you've been traveling a great deal. How lovely to get to see the world.'

The world? She'd hardly seen the world. 'Yes.'

'I'll admit I'm surprised that you're back. I always thought we'd see you end up in the theater. You were always so lovely in the plays.'

'Me?' Cordy laughed. 'No. I don't think I had it in me.'

'Well, you certainly had me fooled. I thought I'd be getting autographed *Playbill*s from New York all the time by now. Do you remember Kalah Justin? She was around your year, wasn't she?'

'Sure.'

'Well, she's had a few plays produced in New York. Maybe you should call her, dear.'

The thought of calling Kalah Justin, who had smoked French cigarettes and worn sunglasses indoors for every class Cordy had with her, was about the least appealing thing she could imagine. Cordy elected to change the subject. 'What can I get for you?'

Mrs O looked a little surprised by Cordy's sudden businesslike attitude. 'Oh, yes. Well. It's lovely to have you working here. I'll have to come in and see you all the time now. I'd like a chicken salad sandwich, please, and a cup of the soup.' Cordy rang up all the women's lunches and then began to work, setting the meals on trays, which Ian capped off with drinks and delivered to the tables. She heard the hen clucks of the women as they ate their lunches, and busied herself cleaning underneath the coffee machines. On breaks, she wandered back into the remnants of the kitchen that had been here when the space had, even beyond our memories, been a restaurant. Now it was a labyrinth of boxes – cups and napkins and

169

straws and the interminably squeaky foam clamshells she had been wrestling with all morning. She walked around the rows meditatively, dragging her fingers along the dusty surfaces.

So this is what she had come to. The quiet silence of Barnwell again. An unscratchable itch surfaced inside her, like a phantom limb. When would she get to leave? Where could she go next? And then a gentle tug on the string of her mental balloon. She couldn't go anywhere, not anymore. There had been a before, and now there would be an after.

Nearly two hours later, Cordy felt like she had cleaned every possible surface when Dan came in. He and Ian exchanged one of those high-chinned nods of greeting only men of a certain age seem to be able to master, and Ian shucked his apron, disappearing into the back.

'Cordeeeeeelia,' he greeted her. 'How's it going?'

'I'm ready to chew my leg off from boredom, but other than that, it's good.'

Dan barked a short laugh. 'Enjoy it now, baby. It never gets this quiet during the school year. In case you've forgotten. It's nonstop busy.'

'Like woah,' Cordy agreed, straight-faced.

Dan laughed. Cordy, as always, had pegged her target perfectly. 'Mock if you must, but he makes a great cup of coffee. I'm going to be so bummed when he graduates. So what's Ian kept you busy with?'

'Ringing. Making sandwiches. I think I've cleaned everything like seven times.'

'You can bring a book with you, you know. You do still read, don't you?'

'Have you *met* my father?'

'On occasion. But I've also met Bean. I don't think she cracked a book the whole year I lived on her floor.'

'Ah, this is Bean's clever conceit. She graduated magna,

did you know that? But she never let anyone see her study. Ruins the party girl image.'

'She had me fooled.'

Dan had opened the cash register and was stacking the bills all going in the same direction.

'That is a sign of serious psychosis,' she said.

Dan laughed again, and Cordy smiled. 'You're hired. I'm so glad to find someone who actually wants to make a sandwich without figuring out how to poison someone with it. You haven't poisoned anyone, have you?'

'Not yet. But it's still early.' Cordy fluttered her eyelashes endearingly.

'Then I'd better send you home. Come in tomorrow around this time, and I'll show you around a little more.'

'You want me to leave now? Won't you be alone?'

'Oh, and the rush is going to kill me,' Dan said, looking around the Beanery. A couple was sitting in a pair of chairs by the window, leaning over the tiny table between them, and a student lounged by the chess table, head lolling sleepily over the barely turned pages of Rilke in his hand. Probably just for show anyway. 'G'wan. You must be bored stiff.'

Folding the damp towel, she dropped it onto the edge of the sparkling sink. It should have been sparkling – she'd gone after it with baking soda and lemon juice earlier. 'I'm usually working as a waitress on a dude ranch this time of year. It's out-of-control busy – so, yeah, this is a little weird.'

'Miss it?'

Cordy, untying her apron, stopped to think. She thought of the hot, wide-horizoned days and the cold, star-studded nights. She thought of being free to go anywhere and do anything, and owing and owning nothing. She thought of drugs and dizzy youth and eternal hunger, and the people she had kissed and left, promises she had made and broken.

171

'No,' she said, and it was impossible for us to tell if she was lying or not.

Cordy poured herself a cup of lemonade and flipped her apron over her shoulder as she left. The heat of the afternoon, slowly burning itself into evening, felt clammy against her chilled arms. She walked slowly, letting the humidity soften her skin. A few cars hushed past on the streets. Maura, the bookstore's owner, poked her head out of the front door, waving at Cordy, who waved back half-heartedly, not crossing over. Maura disappeared back behind the FINAL CLEARANCE banner, which Cordy was beginning to think was all a ruse, since there was nothing FINAL about a CLEARANCE that lasted this long. The postmistress tooted her horn as she drove by, turning off Main and then disappearing into the alley behind the Beanery, and Cordy waved again.

So was this it, then? Was this her after? Kalah Justin was in New York becoming a star, and Cordy was in Barnwell becoming a barista. If only she'd finished college. If only she'd come home years ago when the shine started to fade, instead of grimly holding on, hoping it would get better. If only . . .

'Too late,' Cordy said to no one in particular.

ELEVEN

'Have you ever thought about the word "no"?' Bean asked. She dropped her bag on the table by the door and kicked off her shoes. Across the room, Cordy was sitting cross-legged in an armchair, a book in her lap.

'Not really, but I'd be happy to do so if it would make you happy,' Cordy said.

'I have heard the word "no" fifty thousand times today. I went to every place in town and beyond looking for a job. Nobody's hiring.'

'Well, duh. It's totally the wrong season.'

'Yeah, it's also totally the wrong town.' Bean flopped down on the sofa and stretched her feet out. 'Anyway, you got a job.'

'I think that was out of pity.'

Bean snorted. 'I'd take a pity job at this point.'

'Bianca, can you please move off the couch?' Rose was rounding the corner, holding our mother's good arm. Bean hopped up.

'Whoa. It lives!' Cordy said.

'Thank you, dear,' our mother said. 'Your bedside

173

manner is absolutely wonderful. I think you should go into medicine.'

'No prob,' Cordy said. She went back to her book. Bean walked over and helped Rose bring our mother to the sofa, settling her into a nest of pillows. She looked better; her skin touched again with pink, the whites of her eyes not so faded. She hadn't been able to shower since the surgery, but they'd given her a sponge bath before she left the hospital, and she smelled pleasantly of sun-dried laundry and lotion. If we didn't look at her torso, we could pretend that it hadn't happened at all, that she was suffering from nothing more than a pesky summer cold.

Rose took a quilt from the back of the sofa and draped it over our mother's legs, covering up the lurid pink toenail polish Cordy had inexpertly applied in a bid to make herself useful during hospital visiting hours.

Bean stood back and admired their work. *'The barge she sat in, like a burnish'd throne; burn'd on the water: the poop was beaten gold . . .'* she began.

'Poop,' Cordy said. 'Ha ha ha.'

'You're out of control,' Bean said.

'Thank you for the Cleopatra reference, Bianca. I'll elect to take it as a compliment,' our mother said. Rose bent over and lifted a small bulb from beside our mother's leg and rested it on her lap.

'You can't sit on that, Mom. It won't drain right.' She eyed the setup critically, and then walked into the kitchen.

'That's the surgical drain?' Bean asked. 'I thought it would be bigger. Like a hot water bottle.'

Cordy put down her book and squinted across the room. 'Dude, that is nasty.'

'Again, darling, thank you,' our mother said. 'I do hope that if you ever get ill we can all return the favor and make you feel similarly attractive.'

174

'Oh, Mommy,' Cordy said, clambering out of the chair and crawling across the floor to the sofa, where she butted her head against our mother's hand, like a cat. 'I'm just kidding around.'

'I know, love,' our mother said, petting Cordy's hair. 'Now what's this about a job, Bianca?'

'Nothing. No job. Nobody wants to hire ye olde Beanster.' Bean sat down in the chair Cordy had vacated and rubbed her feet.

'Did you try the college?' our mother asked.

'Aye. No luck, unless I want to work in the electrical department, which I would totally do, but I think would be a bad idea for everyone involved, seeing as I don't know anything about electrical wiring.'

'Good call,' Cordy said, tapping her nose with her index finger.

'Did you really go everywhere?' Rose asked. She was returning from the kitchen with a glass of water, which she put neatly on a coaster beside our mother.

Bean narrowed her eyes at Rose. 'Yes, Rose, I really did go everywhere. The past two days I have inquired into the fields of beauty, fertilizer, accounting, food service, and everything in between.'

'Fertilizer,' Cordy mused. 'That sounds interesting.'

'Don't bother. They're not hiring,' Bean said, and Cordy shrugged.

'If you're really serious, if you really get out there and pound the pavement, I'm sure you'll come up with something,' Rose said.

Bean's mouth dropped open. 'Are you kidding me? You don't have any idea what I've been doing.'

'Girls, girls,' our mother said ineffectually. Bean was so mad she looked like a cartoon figure with smoke coming out of her ears. Rose retreated slightly. 'Bianca, something will come up.'

175

'And in the meantime, you've got no expenses, right?' Rose asked.

'Right,' Bean said, staring at the floor.

Rose frowned. She'd intended for that to be helpful, but Bean's expression was just as foul. She tried again. 'If you need help, like, making up a budget or something . . .' She trailed off.

'That's nice, Rosie,' Cordy jumped in sweetly before Bean could lash out. 'That's really nice.'

Bean exhaled through her nose. It wasn't Rose's fault. She didn't know. She didn't know that Bean could feel the debt on her shoulders like weight, that Daisy had now sent two letters, the second even more insistent, demanding that Bean pay what she owed them, that there was a passel of attorneys out there who could have her in jail as easily as take a breath . . .

No, Rose didn't know. And Bean couldn't tell her, even though she wanted to. When she woke up in the morning, the first thought she had was of money. When she got dressed, she calculated how much each piece of clothing had cost. She passed by stores and shoved her hands in her pockets, now sickened by the thought of spending anything at all. She dreamed of the faces of her debtors, angry and screaming, and she woke with tears dried on her face and a feeling of helplessness lying on her like a shroud. The back of her neck felt hot, and she wondered what would happen if she did spill her secret, open her mouth and let the pain go. The idea of relief was so tempting, so close.

But the idea of shame was worse. And the thought of what Rose might think of her if she told . . . she couldn't face that.

Our mother was right. Something would turn up. Something had to turn up. Soon. The alternative was unthinkable.

*   *   *

Rose walked into town to the pharmacy to pick up our mother's prescription. We'd asked Cordy to get it on the way home from work the day before, but she had, shockingly, forgotten. After Rose paid, she wandered the aisles, not wanting to go back out into the heat, letting the cold air chill the sweat on her skin as her eyes tripped over the shelves.

'Dr Andreas?'

Rose looked up from the battery display. She still started a little when someone called her by our father's name, even though she had earned her own PhD and therefore the title.

'Oh, Dr Kelly!' Rose said, and walked over to the woman standing by the door. Dr Kelly had been Rose's favorite math professor in college, and was now the head of the math department. 'It's so nice to see you. How have you been?'

'Excellent. We just got back from a lovely cruise in Greece with the family.'

'Greece. Wow. Grandchildren and everything?'

'Grandchildren and everything. Carl and I were celebrating our fortieth anniversary, and we thought it would be nice to have everyone along.'

'It sounds wonderful. Greece is supposed to be gorgeous.'

'It is. You and Jonathan must go someday. Maybe for your honeymoon?'

'Maybe.'

'How's your mother?'

'Mixed. She's recovering okay from the surgery, but they found cancer in some of the lymph nodes they removed, so she's in for some radiation and maybe another course of chemotherapy.'

'I am sorry,' Dr Kelly said. 'What can we do to help?'

'She'd like some company, I'm sure. Other than us, that is.'

'I'll give a call and see how she's feeling someday, then.

177

The thing is, Rose, I was actually thinking about giving you a call.'

'Oh?' Rose asked. She shifted, crossed her arms. The prescription bag crinkled under her arm.

'I'm retiring after this year. Carl's been retired for a while, as you know, and he'd like to move. Be closer to the family.'

A little spark of hope lit up inside Rose, and her heart beat faster. This could be the answer to her prayers. She'd always wanted a job at Barney, and now that her current university wasn't going to renew her contract, the timing was perfect.

'So we'll have a tenure-track position open. One of the current faculty will move up to department head. Are you still interested?'

'Are you kidding? Of course I'm interested.'

'I thought maybe with Jonathan abroad, you might be joining him.'

'In England?' Rose laughed. 'No, you know me. I'm a homebody. I'd be thrilled to join the Barnwell faculty.'

Dr Kelly tilted her head slightly, looking at Rose, who was beaming so brightly she could have lit up the whole store. 'Then you'd better start getting your application packet together. We'll announce the opening in the fall. And Rose, I wouldn't go repeating this, but your name was the first one to come up when we began to discuss candidates. I'm fairly sure the job would be yours if you want it.'

'Oh, thank you, Dr Kelly!' Rose said. She hugged her tightly, surprising even herself, and ran out the door. 'Come by anytime,' she called over her back.

She ran nearly all the way home. When we were little, Bean liked to have fashion shows, Cordy liked tea parties, and Rose liked to play school – she always got to be the teacher, of course. But it was never an elementary school classroom where she saw herself when Bean and Cordy would cooperate long enough to play. It was always one of the classrooms at Barnwell. When our father took us to work with him, she'd wander into one of the empty rooms and sketch on the board, delivering a lecture to an imaginary class until some actual college student came along and burst her bubble.

And now it was happening. She ran inside, dropping the pharmacy bag in the kitchen, and bounded up the stairs to her room. She called Jonathan, but there was no answer, and he didn't have a machine. Where was he? She was bursting to tell him – it was the answer to all their problems. He could finish his year in England and then come back and get a job at Barney or one of the city universities. And then she wouldn't have to leave. Nothing would have to change.

Impatient, she called again, but it wasn't even five minutes later and there was still no answer.

More irritated than deflated, Rose checked in on our mother, who was sleeping, and our father, who was working in his study and didn't even hear her greeting. Cordy was at work, and Bean was out looking for a job again. What was the use of having wonderful news if there was no one to tell it to?

She reached for the phone to call Jonathan again, and then dropped her hand to her side. And then she realized, what if he wasn't excited for her?

Odds were that he wouldn't be. He'd said the first time they met that he was a wanderer, and he'd proven that by wandering off when the first opportunity presented itself. And Rose wasn't a wanderer at all. Jonathan probably would be better off with someone like Cordy, whose feet tapped impatiently when she was in any place for more than a week, it seemed.

This thought made her irrationally jealous, and she nearly laughed at herself.

179

She'd just have to make him see how perfect it was. Explain it carefully, show him how much sense it made to settle down here when his time at Oxford was done. How important it was that they be close to our parents, and only a brief plane ride from his. It made such good sense, and Jonathan was so logical. He'd see it her way. Of course he would. He had to.

TWELVE

Sunday morning, thunderheads loomed above, thick and rich with rain. Cordy had been up before us all making pancake batter with blueberries purloined from the neighbor's bushes, their delicate bodies splitting against the wooden spoon, staining the batter with violent violet. Lately she had been a culinary one-woman band, serving up symphonies of simple, delicious food. Even Bean could not resist, but she limited herself to two pancakes, with only the delicate veil of a sneer touching her lips as she watched Cordy, her arms still stick-thin, but her skin blooming pink again, devour an enormous stack until her chin was sticky with syrup.

Our mother ate with us, though she could barely finish one serving, and mostly drank water, complaining of heartburn. After breakfast, without discussion we changed and headed to church together, as we had done every Sunday morning of our childhood. Whenever we came home, our parents just assumed we would join them at church, probably assumed that we were all going regularly even when we weren't at home. And because it was important to them, because though their faith never came out in bombast or brimstone, it was just as much a part of who they were as the books they read, we always agreed.

Our father and our mother went in the car – she was still too weak to walk even as far as St Mark's – but the three of us headed down the path we'd walked a million times, the trail that curved through the silent woods behind the church and spilled out again between the houses of our street. When the path narrowed, we walked in a line, Rose at the head, small puffs of dust bursting from her heels each time she put one comfortable sandal in front of the other. Bean followed behind, her cardigan, ready to preserve the modesty of her haltered vintage dress, swinging from the tips of her fingers, the skirt brushing against her knees. And last, of course, came Cordy, humming to herself and dragging a stick along the bushes lining the inside of the path.

'Who owns this?' Cordy asked, her voice breaking the still of the air.

'The town,' Rose called over her shoulder. A tiny curl had escaped from her taut bun and bounced cheerfully as she strode. Bean watched our older sister's clunky steps, her hips wide and heavy, weighing her down, and tightened the muscles in her own calves.

In the heart of the woods, the buzz of insects grew quieter, muffled by the waxy green of the leaves. Bean paused to hear the symphony above them. Cordy, staring at the tip of her stick bouncing along the bushes, nearly bowled her over. 'What?'

'The birds. I never hear birds like this in New York.' Oddly, she'd gotten used to it. When she was little, she would wake up and lie in bed, listening to the conversations of the wrens outside, the flutter of angry wings as the blue jays strutted into each other's territory. We had built a house for robins in the yard, and Bean remembered being lifted up, leaving the sharp, thick grass beneath her feet and pushing up the top of the birdhouse to see two tiny eggs, deep as Mexican turquoise, resting in the nest inside. They had seemed impossibly bright inside the darkness of the box, and Bean had been filled with an ache to touch them, but when she had reached her hand inside, our mother had pulled her away. Not until the birds had been born and shrieked in hungry, wet-feathered anger every day did our mother pull the shells from the nest, presenting them to us in the palm of her hand like a precious gift. Bean had put them on her dresser, stroking them gently every night, memorizing the delicate variations in color until she knew the fragments better than she knew her own face.

'When birds do sing, hey ding a ding, ding,' Cordy sang, somewhat tunelessly, which couldn't be helped, for, lack of musical talent aside, the music for Shakespeare's songs had long fallen by the wayside, though our father was always interested in contemporary efforts to reconstruct the tunes.

Ahead on the path, Rose had stopped and was waiting, a hand resting imperiously on her hip. 'We're going to be late,' she said.

Bean was still staring up, sightless, like those baby robins in the nest. The shadows of the sunlight slipping between the trees cast a spiderweb on her face. She turned to look at Rose, but her eyes held no recognition, only a vacant freeze.

'I got fired,' she said.

No one said anything, but Cordy stopped poking at the ground with the stick, and Rose's hand dropped off her hip.

'They fired me.'

'What did you do?' Rose asked, and then wished she could take back the question. It sounded sharp. *Whose tongue outvenoms all the worms of Nile.* But Bean didn't seem to notice.

183

Keeping it inside had been easier. Her stomach had held a heavy, leaden ache she knew to be the weight of the secret, but it was easily reduced to a dull roar, muffled into submission with the simple distractions of daydreams and job-hunting. Speaking it aloud made it impossible for her to ignore. Running from New York had given her distance, made it seem like someone else's life, someone else's disaster, but to say it here, in these woods?

'What simple thief brags of his own attaint?' Bean asked. We stood still. We waited. Finally, she turned again to Rose, and her eyes looked clear and direct this time, bright with tears. 'I fucked up,' she said. 'I stole. From my job. I stole money. I stole so much fucking money.'

Her shoulders shook as she began to cry, pained, keening wails, ululations of grief and shame. Mascara ran thick trails down her cheeks, wiping away the subtle glow of health that makeup had put there, leaving dark shadows beneath her eyes and pale lines along her mouth, pulled down and aching in grief.

Cordy moved first, dropping her stick and pulling Bean into her arms, her fingernails, still stained with blueberry juice, stroking quietly along our sister's back, tracking the lines of the fabric. Rose came forward tentatively, questions on her lips, but Cordy shook her head, and when Bean dropped her forehead to Cordy's shoulder, Rose reached out, delicate, as though to touch a feral cat, and stroked Bean's hair softly.

She told us, then, the whole story. Yes, she'd been naïve, not understanding fully how much it would cost to live in New York. But that wasn't what had made her do it. It was everything Bean needed to play her part effectively: the shoes, the clothes, the makeup, the drinks at bars and clubs where a bottle of water alone ran nearly ten dollars. One of her roommates, a bitter-faced young woman named Stella, worked for a publication house that owned a

184

number of women's magazines, and would scour the beauty closet for the complex range of grooming products that turned Bean into Bianca. And she learned how to get invited to sample sales, and to make friends or sleep with people in PR, who had all the best collections (she attributed her *pièce de résistance,* a fabulous crocodile handbag even A-list celebrities hadn't been able to get ahold of for months, to a particularly adventurous romp in a limousine on the way home from a completely forgettable book launch party). But it still wasn't cheap.

You might forgive Bean for what she did if some kind of desperate need – rent, food, protection payments to the Mafia – had inspired the first embezzlement. But it wasn't like that. Let's be honest. It was too many nights out at too many nightclubs, too many drinks bought for herself on a slow night when no man offered to buy for her, too many (and one was too many, really) pairs of shoes that cost more than a semester's worth of textbooks at Barney. But she was sitting at her desk doing the payroll. The firm was small enough that she wrote the checks out by hand and took them to one of the partners for signature, and she realized, though the thought had never crossed her mind before, that it would be so easy to add a little extra to her own. The partner never looked at them, he just signed them, and she would just do it once. Just to recoup some of the exorbitant overdraft charges she had accumulated. And she would pay it back.

And since it didn't go missing once, and there was a sample sale at a handbag warehouse where she knew some people and could get in and get first shot at some of the current season's bags, she did it again. And then a delicious Hollywood star had taken over the lead in some revival on Broadway, and Stella was absolutely dying to go, so Bean took her for her birthday. And there was a completely swish winter coat on sale, and she really couldn't wear her old winter coat; not in this city. And on. And on.

This is not to say Bean didn't feel guilty. She did. Every time she deposited her check at the bank, thanking her stars the firm hadn't gotten around to direct deposit, she expected the teller to look at her, to see her burning cheeks and the lies in her eyes and call her out for what she was. A thief. But it was so easy to forget in the simple pleasure of spending, of treating her girlfriends to a night out. Until the next time payday came around and her bank account was empty and she had to do it again.

It wasn't pure selfishness either; she gave as generously to others as she did to herself. The one thing she never did was travel, and this is part of the ugly truth as to why Bean came home so rarely. She knew the one day she was out was the day she'd be discovered, and so she was there, day in and day out, and she felt a little sick about the way people in the firm complimented her on her excellent work ethic, on the way she showed up even when she was burning with fever, brushing it off as enthusiastically applied makeup, and she grew to hate herself for it, but she couldn't stop.

Now, if you are a psychologist, you might say something about how Bean hated her job, and might even have hated New York, and this was all her way of getting the hell out of it all without having to do any of the heavy lifting herself.

And you might well be right.

She had not told us everything, of course, not nearly. She hadn't told us how she'd been hiding the sick, dark feeling inside by burying it in dangerous fantasy. She hadn't told us about Edward and the way she'd betrayed Lila. She had told us none of this.

Sisters keep secrets.

Because sisters' secrets are swords.

186

But at that moment, we were thinking not of what Bean had done wrong, but how she could make it better. 'It'll be okay, Bean,' Rose said softly, her words as gentle as her fingers on our sister's head. 'We'll make it okay.'

Rose was waiting with a towel when our mother stepped out of the shower. She genteelly averted her eyes, but the angry red incision, hatched with dark thread, persisted in her mind. The empty space where her breast had been looked odder than a missing limb, Rose thought. More like a face without features, the absent nipple a missing mouth. Our mother winced as she lifted her arm for the towel, and Rose handed it to her, let our mother pat herself dry and then drape it carefully across her chest, ignoring the water pooling on the floor. She still could not raise her arm enough to fold a towel around herself or to tie the scarves that she wore to cover her head. The fabric had a tendency to loosen into sloppiness until one of us was annoyed enough to rewrap it for her. Rose stepped behind our mother and turned off the tap in the tub, which was still dripping. Our mother reached out with her good arm and wiped away the steam on the mirror.

'Do you want help?' Rose asked.

'No thank you, honey,' our mother said. She was staring at her reflection.

'I'll be in the bedroom. I'll help you with your exercises and we can put on new bandages.'

'Goody.'

Rose slipped outside the door, pulling it shut behind her, and as she moved, she saw our mother let the towel slip down to reveal her cockeyed chest, and place a bare hand across the emptiness of her skin.

It must be so strange, Rose thought. We had never made much trade in our breasts, small as they were on all of us, but to lose one? Or both? And our mother's

187

breasts, the ones that had fed us, against which we had cried when we were young. Oh, it was selfish of us to think it, but we missed them as well.

Sitting on our parents' bed, so high that an old-fashioned step sat at the foot to aid entry, Rose felt the comforter sink down below her as she pulled the lotion and gauze out of the bedside table. Once, when she was a teenager, she had walked into the kitchen to find our mother, her hands in soapy dishwater, our father behind her at the sink, his hands cupped over her breasts possessively. He kissed her neck, whispered something in her ear, and they laughed. Rose had retreated, embarrassed not so much by the scene but by the way her inopportune entrance had violated their privacy. Now she wondered when they made love again, would her father kiss the scar? Caress the empty space?

When it happened to her – it no longer seemed a maybe – would Jonathan?

'I feel so much better,' our mother announced, coming into the bedroom. She held the towel in front of herself again as she lay down on the bed, leaning on Rose, grimacing slightly as she shifted toward the center. 'But I'm sick of these stupid scarves. I wish my hair would grow faster.'

'We could get you hats. Or you could just not wear them at all. It'll be long enough soon that it would just look like you cut it that way,' Rose said. She pulled the towel down carefully, preserving what little modesty remained in our relationship by exposing only the wound – it was still a wound, wasn't it? Not yet a scar.

'I think it'll be a long time before it looks like anything intentional.'

'Do you miss it?' Rose stretched our mother's arm gently, moving it in the patient way the physical therapist had shown us.

'I do. I still haven't gotten used to it – every time I look in the mirror I think it's a skeleton in the reflection, not me.' Our mother took a deep, shuddering breath, and Rose saw tears in the edges of her eyes. 'Well, maybe it's for the best,' she said finally. 'It's impractical for a woman my age to have that much hair. It's like the Sphinx's riddle, isn't it? We start with short hair, grow it long, and then cut it all off again. Haven't you noticed that?'

'Noticed what?' Cordy asked, coming into the room and bouncing onto the bed enthusiastically, causing Rose to shoot her a scolding look. Cordy ignored it, rolling onto her side and propping herself up on one arm.

Our mother turned to her and smiled as Rose continued to manipulate her arm. 'That older women never have long hair.'

'I think you're still too young for the once-a-week hairdo,' Cordy said.

'You're getting flour on the bed,' Rose said. 'Are you baking again?'

Cordy peered at the spread. 'It's white. It doesn't show. And yes – I'm making challah.'

'It smells good,' our mother said.

Rose squirted some lotion into her palm and rubbed her hands together before stroking them up and down our mother's arm. She could feel the muscles beneath the gentle droop of age. Cordy sat up and held out her hand, and Rose poured lotion into her palm so we could rub her arms together.

'Now this is the life,' our mother sighed. 'If I'd known I'd get treated like this, I'd have gotten sick years ago.'

'Gallows humor,' Rose said.

'No, if this were the life, we would be cabana boys and you'd be on a beach somewhere,' Cordy said.

'I could hardly keep up with a cabana boy nowadays,' our mother said. 'I feel like all I've done for the past six

189

months is lie around. I'm going to have muscle atrophy by the time this is over.'

'We'll get you some servants to carry you around in a palanquin,' Cordy said. The phone rang, and she flopped backward into a seemingly impossible position, her pants slipping down to reveal her belly as she reached above her head for the receiver. Our mother gingerly stretched her arm up as Rose put on the new bandage.

'Hel-LO,' Cordy said. 'Hi, Jonathan! How's my favorite brother?' Rose's eyes flicked to the clock. After midnight there. Unusual. A little flicker of panic zipped through her.

Cordy paused, wiggled her eyebrows at Rose. 'We're good. Getting Mom ready for bed.' She tucked the receiver against her shoulder and helped Rose as we pulled our mother to a sitting position, grabbed the white nightgown and tossed it to Rose, who pulled it over her head. 'Uh-huh. She's better. What's up in England? Had any good tea lately?' There was a pause again, and she giggled. 'Totally. Hey, isn't it like a million o'clock there?'

Our mother gasped as Rose pushed her arm slightly too roughly into the sleeve of the nightgown. 'I'm sorry.'

'Here, let me give you to Rose before she breaks Mom's arm. See ya!' Cordy handed the phone to Rose and then tugged our mother's nightgown down over the towel before pulling it out, like a magician pulling a cloth from a table.

Leaving Cordy plumping up the endless pillows our mother could never be without, Rose stepped out into the hallway.

'Are you okay?'

Jonathan laughed. 'That's my Rose. Always looking for the disaster.'

'Stop. You know it's past your bedtime.'

'You always call me when it's the middle of the night there. Turnabout is fair play.'

190

'I'm glad you called, actually. I was trying to get you last night, but you weren't in. Can't you get an answering machine?'

'I could. But that would spoil all the fun. I was in London at that conference, remember? Presenting my paper?'

'Oh, of course,' Rose said guiltily. She'd been so excited that she'd completely forgotten he was presenting. 'How did it go?'

'It was great. I was awfully nervous, but once I started reading, it got much easier. And there were some wonderful questions afterward. Got to go to some good sessions, too. So why were you trying to call?'

Excitement swelled up in Rose and she forgot all about her careful wording. 'I've got some really exciting news.'

'Do you? I do, too. Who goes first?'

'Me,' Rose said. 'I've been jumping up and down since I heard.'

'There's a mental image.'

'Metaphorically.'

'Disappointing. So what is it, love? It's nice to hear you so happy.'

Rose went into her bedroom and closed the door, lay across the perfectly made bed. 'I ran into Dr Kelly at the pharmacy yesterday. Do you remember my telling you about her?'

'Sure. She was your favorite professor in college, right? Supervised your honors thesis? How is she?'

'Yes, that's her. She's fine. She's getting ready to retire, actually, at the end of next year.'

'Oh.' He inhaled slowly on the other end of the line, and if Rose had been in any state of mind to hear it, she would have known that her plan was about to fall apart.

'She wants me to apply, Jonathan. She says they'll take an internal candidate to be department head, and then

191

there will be a tenure-track position open. And she said it was mine if I wanted it. She actually said that. Can you imagine? A year from now, I could be teaching at Barney.'

'I thought we'd talked about looking for somewhere else after next year,' Jonathan said. His voice was cautious, probing.

'We did. But this is Barnwell, Jonathan. I've always wanted to teach there, ever since I was a little girl. Isn't it exciting? I know it sounds stupid, but it's like a dream come true.'

'Yes, I guess it is.'

'You don't sound happy.'

'I'm not *un*happy. I just . . . You've taken me a bit by surprise here. This isn't the direction I thought we were heading in.'

'No, it's not like we'd talked about it. But it's so perfect. I could be near my parents, and you'd be so close to home, too, and I know Columbus would take you back – the provost said as much, even though you broke your contract. And it's so much more affordable here than in the city. You could commute, and, well, it would just be perfect!' Rose could hear the hesitation in his voice, and she pushed through, forcing cheer into her own, as though she could inflate him with her excitement from miles away. She bit her lip and waited for his reply.

'It's funny that you're telling me this now, because the thing is . . .' He stopped, cleared his throat, laughed awkwardly. 'It's kind of ironic, really. I've been offered a visiting professorship.'

'Where?' Rose said, but her stomach was already souring. He was going to leave her. He was going to leave her alone.

'Here! It's amazing. Two years. I'd be able to finish my research. I've got these amazing doctoral candidates to work with; I know we could finish and publish in that time.

192

It's incredible, really, Rosie. You wouldn't believe the competition.'

'I didn't even know you were applying,' Rose said, and she could hear how weak she sounded, and she hated herself for it. She sat up and leaned forward on the edge of the bed, her stomach pressing into her thighs.

Jonathan's voice softened. 'I didn't want to upset you. You're upset, aren't you?'

Rose swallowed. 'No, I'm happy. Happy for you.' It was a lie and he knew it.

'But I haven't even told you, Rosie. They're moving me into an apartment, so there will be room for you, too. You can come over and we'll be Brits for two whole years.'

'In England.'

'That is the primary location,' Jonathan said. Tension thrummed behind his voice. 'Think of it, Rose. It's like a sign.'

'But we're getting married,' Rose said, and it was more of a cry, her voice cracking in the last syllable.

'And we still are,' Jonathan said. 'But it means you could come here, take a sabbatical.'

'I can't. There won't be a position open when we come back. Do you know how long I've waited for something to open up here?'

'Does it have to be Barnwell?'

'Does it have to be England?' she asked. She sounded ridiculous, whiny, childish, but she couldn't stop herself.

'Rosie,' he said, and he sounded stern. 'This is the chance of a lifetime.'

And it was. For him.

'For both of us,' he said. How well he knew her.

'You want me to come to England,' she said.

'No, you're coming to England anyway. I want us to live in England. For a little while. Rose, you know what a coup this is for my career. And you know the odds of a position opening mid-year are so small. It's perfect for me, and it's perfect for you. You can write and get some articles published, and then we'll find positions some-where else. Somewhere that sees you for the incredible researcher and teacher you are.'

Rose said nothing.

'Rose, I've got to have you with me. I miss you so much. Every day I look at those stupid dreaming spires and I wish you were here to see them, too.'

'Jonathan, I don't know,' she said. 'I mean, my mother, and the wedding, and we were going to buy a house, and I . . .' She trailed off. It was so unfair. He knew how much she'd always wanted a job at Barnwell. And a tenure-track job at that. Security. No pulling up roots every two or three years to head somewhere else only to have to do it again. No wondering where she'd be living in a few years' time, or what might happen if they couldn't find jobs at the same place.

'You can't live in Barnwell your whole life, Rose. There's so much out there you're missing. And it's missing you.'

'I don't know what you're talking about,' she said, her voice flat. Cold.

'You are so much more than that town. You're so bril-liant, and you're such an amazing teacher. You know that. And you'd only learn more if you'd spread your wings a little and try out a few other places.'

'And my mother?'

'She'll be okay. And you said it looks like Bean is sticking around. Let her keep the home fires burning for a while. You need to take care of yourself for once, Rose.'

'I don't know.'

Silence hung across the line for a moment, and then he sighed heavily. 'Look. We don't have to make any decisions right now. I know what they said, but we don't even know if you'll get the position at Barney for sure, right?'

'Right,' Rose said carefully, wondering if she was ceding some important ground just by admitting that.

'We'll think about it. And you're coming out in a while to visit, right? You can see how you feel about it then. Have you bought your ticket yet?'

'Not yet. It's been a little busy here, Jonathan.' This was not entirely untrue. But she had been procrastinating on making travel plans, a little in the same way that Bean had refused to open her bills. *We are more alike than we would ever admit.*

'I understand. Why don't you see if you can take some time and get a flight, and we'll talk about it more when you're here. Okay?'

'Okay,' she said. She suddenly felt near tears, and very, very tired. All the excitement of seeing Dr Kelly yesterday had run out of her. Jonathan wasn't going to whoop with joy about turning down this job and moving back to Barnwell with her forever and ever. And she couldn't imagine having worked her entire life, hoping that one day she'd have the opportunity to take a job here, only to turn it down.

One of them was going to have to give, or the whole thing was going to fall apart.

Bean was extraordinarily hungover, which was embarrassing enough at her age – shouldn't you leave those things behind along with consumption of alcohol through funnels? – but even worse on a Thursday morning. The sun was a cheerful irritation pushing its way through her designer sunglasses, and her stomach pushed and rolled with every step she took.

When she had walked up to the house that morning, Rose, barreling down the porch steps, had nearly knocked her over. 'You're just coming home? I didn't realize you were going to be out all night.'

She hadn't known she would be, truthfully. She had headed out with the intention of shaking off a little of the small-town stink and burying her troubles in alcohol. She hadn't made it far, only to Edward's house, to the front door, where he greeted her with a drink, and she returned the favor by slipping off her dress and draining the glass as he kissed his way down her neck.

'It wasn't intentional,' Bean had said to Rose, pushing her way past our sister into the kitchen. She was more than aware that the scent of cigarettes and alcohol was pushing its way through her skin, underscored by the dank, vinegar smell of sweat and desperate sex.

Rose followed her back inside. 'You smell like a brewery.'

'And yet I haven't been in one. Odd, no?' Bean filled a glass with ice and then let the tap run, the ice cubes cracking, startled by the difference in temperature.

'What if something had happened?'

'Then I'm sure one of the three other able-bodied adults in the house, if not all of you, would have handled it with alacrity.' She took a long drink of the water, forcing her stomach back down as it lurched against her ribs in protest.

Rose felt the burn of unfairness in her stomach. It wasn't right that Bean could just run around like this, while she was taking care of things. It wasn't fair.

She opened her mouth to speak, to pass judgment, but at that moment, Bean put down her empty glass and their eyes locked. Bean's hair was uncharacteristically ruffled, her eyes bloodshot and tired. She had mis-buttoned her shirt, and her hands were shaking slightly as she went to fold her arms over her chest. When had Bean last looked so exhausted, so weak?

When Rose was six and Bean three, our mother nearly ready to give birth to Cordy, we were in the kitchen playing while our mother baked. We had brought in a set of wooden blocks and were constructing a castle with wide towers and drawbridges that moved with the aid of our clumsy hands. After she put a cake in the oven, our mother wandered out into the garden, forgetting us, perhaps, absorbed as we were in our architectural fantasies. Finally the scent of chocolate bursting in the oven's heat became too much for Bean's empty stomach, and leaving Rose building the walls of an empty moat around our creation, she toddled over to the stove. With arms deliciously baby-fat, Bean reached for one of the dish towels that hung over the oven's door handle and pulled down. She blinked at the rush of damp heat that flooded out, the smell wafting into her hair and the weave of her dress. Before Rose could stop her, Bean reached inside and put her hands on the heavy glass pan, wanting to pull the richness of that scent to her.

Bean's scream was unforgettable, Rose says. But what we remember is the way Rose sprang into action – yanking Bean away from the oven and letting the door slam shut with a thick metallic rattle, then lifting her onto a stool and running cold water over her hands and arms, already blistering red and white from the stove's furious heat. We don't know how she knew what to do, how to grab a towel and fill it with ice from the plastic bin in the freezer, place Bean's arms on it. Bean, eyes wide and tears stilled by Rose's efficiency, but mouth still working thick sobs, watching it all, the way our sister had saved her from herself. And then Rose running for our mother, whose own reaction was slowed by the weight of her belly and the way her mind was so often far from us.

Looking at Bean's face now, Rose could see her wounds as easily as when she had cared for her burns all those

197

years ago. She stilled herself and walked over to the cabinet beside the sink. She opened the door and flipped efficiently through the half-bottles of medicine until she found some aspirin. Shook two into her palm, refilled the glass on the counter, and handed both to Bean.

'Take these. And drink some water. You'll feel better if you sleep.'

Now, hours of dreamless rest and one tentative piece of toast later, Bean was sitting on one of the hopelessly outdated chairs in the library. The faded orange wool scratched against her thighs as she shifted. Bean had one leg curled under her, a bent-legged stork. Across the uncomfortably wide table lay a handful of discarded books: a few on résumés, one on the color of her parachute, and a coffee table photographic journey through the distended bellies of the third world. She had eschewed all of them in favor of a fantasy novel. Not her normal fare, but guaranteed not to make reference to anything that might evoke one of the beasts of her current craptastic situation, the way one of those modern-day tales of shoes and ex-boyfriends, or even the drama of small-town life in Ireland, might. Someone was always getting betrayed in those books, and the fact was, being a betrayer at the moment herself, she couldn't bear to think about it.

'It's about that time, Bianca,' Mrs Landrige called from the desk, where she was sitting, her hands folded neatly in front of her. The library was empty. 'Are you checking anything out?'

Bean looked up, blinking, and lifted her sunglasses up, squinting through the lights to the falling dusk outside. Another day in paradise, gone.

'Yeah,' she said, slumping forward against the table to pull the scattered books toward her.

'Yes,' Mrs Landrige corrected her, and Bean parroted the correction without thinking. That was the problem with coming home. You turned smack back into a teenager again.

Her stomach had stopped swirling and now it growled insistently as she replaced the books on the shelf before heading over to the checkout desk. 'I'm glad you came in, Bianca,' Mrs Landrige said, stamping the book efficiently and placing the card in the tray for filing. 'I hear you're looking for a job.'

'You do?' Bean asked. 'Who said that?'

'Rose. She was in the other day and she mentioned that you were having a spot of trouble finding something. Not surprising, really. Wrong time of year, even if Barnwell were a booming economy.'

'Rose told you I needed a job?' Bean asked, still stumped. 'My sister Rose?'

'What are you acting so surprised for? She is your sister. She's worried about you.'

'Worried about me,' Bean said, 'Right.'

'In any case, it's not exactly a big secret. Maura at the bookstore mentioned you'd been in to see her, and you've been in the 650s all day.' She nodded in the direction of the books Bean had just replaced. Mrs Landrige knew the Barnwell library without looking. You could ask her anything, and she'd spit out the Dewey decimal number and point a taut hand in the direction of the shelf. Puberty rites? 390, by the study carrels. *Charlotte's Web*? Juvenile literature, by the windows. Soccer? 796, to the left of the drinking fountains. When we were little, we sometimes tried to stump her, thinking of the most arcane topics we could, but we never won. Mrs Landrige was the champion of the Dewey decimal system.

'I suppose,' Bean said. 'It looks like I'll be here for a while.'

'I'm taking a leave of absence. Hip replacement surgery.' She looked up at Bean. The neck of her dress – it was

199

always a dress, she was Of That Age – framed her neck, which looked so delicate against the fabric, the taut cords and loose skin standing out against each other. Bean stroked her own skin unconsciously, sure she could already feel the loosening of her jowls, the emergence of her clavicle.

'I'm sorry. Are you okay?'

Mrs Landrige smiled. 'It's the problem with living so long, Bianca. Everything gets worn out. Makes me wonder if all these medical advances are really worth anything. But it's apparently relatively common, so I'm sure I'll be fine, albeit out of commission for a while. So I'm wondering if you would be interested in taking over for me in my absence.'

'As the librarian?'

'Certainly.'

'But I don't know anything about it. I mean, I don't have the right degree.'

Mrs Landrige, had she worn glasses, would have looked over the rims at Bean. 'Don't be ridiculous. It's the Barnwell Public Library, not the Library of Congress. You've been coming here since before you could walk, and I trust you implicitly.'

Bean nearly laughed out loud. The last people who had trusted her could have had her arrested. 'I don't know, Mrs Landrige. I don't know if I'd be any good.'

'It's hardly rocket science, dear. Be sensible. You need a job, and I need someone here. You can stay until we both get back on our feet.' She smiled at her little joke.

'Well, okay.'

'Then you'll come in tomorrow bright and early and we'll get started on a little training?' She pressed the book into Bean's hands, and Bean looked dumbly at the cover. She couldn't remember why on earth she'd chosen a book about a half-naked warrior woman with the thigh muscles of a Tour de France winner. And she couldn't figure out how she'd suddenly been anointed the successor to a Barnwell institution.

'I'll get paid, right?' she asked.

'Of course. We'll talk about all that tomorrow.' Mrs Landrige looked at Bean for a moment as though she were going to speak, and then closed her mouth. Bean turned to go. 'Bianca?'

'Yeeeees.' Bean turned. She knew that scolding tone. It was the same one Rose had used on her that morning.

But Mrs Landrige's voice was softer, almost maternal. 'Get some sleep.'

Bean flipped her sunglasses down again and headed toward the door. She walked quickly down the front steps outside, feeling the muscles in her inner thighs twinge, and she tried to shake off the memory of last night. How had she found herself in that house again? Wasn't she supposed to be making a fresh start? Confessing everything to us so she could be free?

But she hadn't confessed everything, had she? She was no cleaner than she had been when she arrived. *Drunkards, liars, and adulterers, by an enforced obedience of planetary influence.* When she had woken that morning, wrapped in the sheet, what had seemed so giddy and right in darkness looked only violent and sad in the light. A bottle of wine empty on the floor beside his crumpled, abandoned clothes. Her mascara, crusted dark under her eyes. The film in her mouth, sour and dry. His sleeping face, drawn and empty without his lust for her.

Bean turned her head, shook it. She passed a family on their way home, the mother and father, each holding a hand of the little girl between them, lifting her high in the air and swinging her for a few steps before setting her down again.

In trying to apologize and repent, she had betrayed

someone else she cared about, someone who had been nothing but good to her, who had opened her heart and her home and her family only for Bean to twist into something ugly. Again. She hadn't changed. She hadn't changed at all. Suddenly, she was filled with a hatred for herself so intense she had to dig her fingernails into her palm, letting the burn of physical pain take away the emotions, but it was too late. She was already crying.

Bean tried on identities the way she now tries on clothes. She considered entomology (Rose was better at science), acting (Cordy was a better performer), dancing (our thigh issues have been mentioned), poetry (all our work was judged against standards you can probably guess at, and obviously deemed lacking), being the first female president (Cordy was a better public speaker), modeling (thighs again), fashion design (as a family, we are decidedly lacking in artistic talent, which is also why she could not go into painting), and business (Rose had to hold Bean's money if we went into town to buy something, because Bean would either spend it on something pointless, or lose it before we rounded the corner onto Main Street).

The hardest cuts were the ones where we beat her at her own game, where she tried something only to discover Rose had done it first (not a problem) and better (problem), or for Cordy to swoop in and do it second (not a problem) and better (problem). In some ways, we think this is why Bean ended up in a lifestyle so unlike the Andreas family value system, because there was simply nothing left.

What do you do if you keep losing the game? You take your marbles and go home. Or in Bean's case, you take your marbles and go to New York, and you decide to care about things like clothes and designer martinis and how best to pick up and bed an investment banker and still make it home before the city's night life fully kicks into gear. And this makes you different, but it will not make you special.

Caught in the middle, Bean felt sometimes as though she were jumping up and down, waving her arms and shouting, 'Notice me! Notice me!,' but the only times she got the attention she wanted were when she was very, very bad. So in high school she learned to stay out late, and came home coated in the thick, sweet smell of dope, and she snuck out with boys and they teepeed trees until they were caught and brought home by the apologetic town police, and she skipped her classes in college until her professors pulled our father aside as he strolled along the paths, and she worked out until she was sick-stick-thin, and still she could have jumped up and down for a thousand years and waved her arms and not gotten enough of our parents' attention.

We could have told Bean we were screaming and waving, too, and none of us ever got what we wanted, not when it came to attention. No one does.

THIRTEEN

During the summer in Barnwell, even in August, the educator's longest Sunday, everything closes early. Without the restless hum of students to fill the businesses until decent (or indecent) hours, the locals shut down and head home before dinner. Walking around the town after six in the summer, you might expect to see tumbleweeds or hear the squeak of a saloon door, if either of those were likely to happen in a small town in Ohio. As it is, there are just blank, dark shop windows and empty streets and sidewalks.

Cordy and Dan closed the Beanery at five, though no customers had come in since three, and they had long since finished all the cleaning and restocking, and Cordy had even been reduced to scraping the gum from the underside of the tables in a desperate attempt to find something worthwhile to do. The storm that had been threatening for days finally broke, sending cascades of rain sweeping down the street in tidy sheets, pushing leaves and occasional trash along the gutters.

'You want a ride?' Dan asked, emerging from the office. Cordy had finished wiping the counters and was sitting in one of the aged brown chairs, her legs hooked over the arm, staring at the ceiling. She was fairly certain that, at one point, it had been stamped tin, but the years of careless paintwork had rendered it merely lumpy and noncommittally white. She had in her hand a yellow plastic Barrel of Monkeys that she shook periodically, like a cheap maraca.

Looking out the window at the Ark-tic flood (did we warn you about the puns or did we not?), Cordy nodded. 'That'd be nice, if it's not out of your way.'

'Nothing in Barnwell is out of the way,' Dan said. Which was patently untrue. He lived on the east end of town, past the dorms, in an apartment building only slightly too pricey for the college students. Research at the Barnwell Historical Society had informed him that it had once been given the grand name of The Theodore, though now it was more often referred to as Old Yeller, since some well-meaning landlord had decided to paint the entire exterior a rich butter yellow that gave off a near-radioactive glow in the sunlight. But still, it would take him five minutes to drive Cordy home, and then another ten to get back. An eon in Barnwell time.

'Thanks,' Cordy said, and then pointed up at the ceiling. 'You ever think about cleaning all that crap off? I bet the ceiling's really nice under there.'

'In all my imaginary spare time? Yeah, I could do that.'

'How come you don't live upstairs?' Upstairs was a wide, roomy apartment with scuffed wooden floors. Cordy vaguely remembered a beer-soaked party her freshman roommate had dragged her to. It had been loud and sticky, the hallmark of all college parties, but mostly what she remembered is how the scent of the Beanery downstairs had overwhelmed even the scent of the beer and she had felt all night as if she were covered in coffee grounds. But it hadn't bothered her. When her freshman-year room-mate had gone out of town, Cordy would make coffee in the pot just to let the smell cover the room, like the other students on the floor did with incense.

'I could. It would cut down the commute, that's for sure. But then I'd be here all the time, you know? Never getting away from work.'

Cordy shrugged, lazily pulling her legs back over the chair as Dan shut off the machines behind the counter. 'How far are you away from work anyway?'

'Good point,' he said. He pulled up the hinged counter and came out in front. 'Hey, it looks great in here,' he said. Cordy had straightened the puzzles, games, and magazines littering the tables, and swept the dust from the corners of the tired floor.

'Slow day,' she said.

'When the kids come back, you'll be wishing for this,' Dan said. He pushed in a couple of chairs and went to lock the front door, pulling down the heavy green shades. He turned toward Cordy. 'You are staying, aren't you?'

'For a while, yeah,' she said.

'Good. I've gotten used to having you around,' he said. 'You're far more interesting than the average worker.'

'That's just because I'm far *older* than your average worker.'

'That too,' he said. 'And better-looking.' He shot her a wink, his dark, thick lashes casting shadows on his cheekbones in the fading light.

Cordy narrowed her eyes at him. Was he flirting with her?

More importantly, did she mind?

They headed out the back door, leaving the darkness of the Beanery behind them, and sprinted across the parking lot to Dan's car, a silver sedan that looked suspiciously new and smelled pristine. 'Nice car,' Cordy said. She had been holding her bag over her head, though it had done little to nothing to keep her dry, and dropped it on the floor. 'Smells new.'

'It is. Selling out pays well.'

'Better than the Peace Corps, certainly. Do you still sell pot?'

Dan, one hand on the key in the ignition, turned to look at her. 'You buying?'

'Nah. Just curious.'

'No. Not anymore. If there's anything more depressing than being the old guy who still lives a mile from campus, it's the old guy who still lives a mile from campus and sells pot to students.'

'It could be worse. You could be the old guy who lives a mile from campus, sells pot, and hits on all the students.'

Easing the car out of the parking lot, Dan paused and checked for oncoming traffic. There was none. Cordy could hear the tires kicking up fountains of water as he pulled onto Main and headed west. The water sluiced down, mindless of the windshield wipers, which swished, futile against the deluge. 'That's something I definitely have no interest in. I look at them now and all I see are kids. You know? I mean, the difference between the freshmen and the seniors is big, but the difference between a senior and a thirty-year-old is like a chasm. Huge.'

'I don't know. I keep waiting to feel old, to feel like a grown-up, but I don't yet. Do you think that's the big secret adults keep from you? That you never really feel grown-up?'

'I feel grown-up. I think buying the Beanery did it to me. Maybe that's why I'm resisting buying a house. That'll be like the ultimate surrender.'

The shadows cast by the sprays of water rolled down his face as they drove. He needed a shave, Cordy saw, though his dark hair made it more noticeable. Under his full bottom lip, he was growing a tiny soul patch, an affectation that on most men just seemed, well, affected, but on him looked both sweet and dangerous.

'I guess you're right,' Cordy said, thinking of the lost twenty-somethings who had surrounded her wanderings on the road, filtering in and out of her days. After all, hadn't she given it up because she'd finally felt too old for it? 'What I mean is, I still feel like *me*. It's not like I wake up and think, I am a responsible adult. I just look in the mirror and see myself. The same stupid person I've been looking at for years.'

Without taking his eyes off the road, Dan reached over and stroked the curve of her face with the backs of his fingers. She could feel the tiny hairs, and the dryness of his skin from washing dishes. 'There's nothing stupid about you, Cordy.' He put his hand back on the wheel as he made the turn onto our street and pulled up in front of the house, stopping in front of the curb.

They turned toward each other, and Cordy knew he was going to kiss her. His eyes were dark and rich, the color swollen with desire, and something else she did not quite recognize. 'I'm glad you came back,' he said. His hand rested on her knee, and the heat seeped through her faded jeans. 'It's good to have someone to talk to.'

Cordy stared at his hand for a moment, at the way his broad palm curved over her knee, his fingers spread slightly across her thighs, and then she pulled her gaze up to meet his. The rain pounded outside, the lights at the edges of the driveways on the street only barely breaking through the cloud-soaked darkness.

When they leaned toward each other – it was mutual, don't let Cordy tell you any different – she felt her breath catch in her throat and then she exhaled as their lips met. His mouth was wide and strong and soft against hers, and that kiss felt deeper and sweeter than all the kisses she'd shared over the years.

And then she pulled back.

'I'm pregnant,' she told him.

'That was fast,' he said.

'Dan. Really. I'm pregnant,' she said, and her fingers went to her mouth, ripping at the nails. She turned away from him and stared out into the darkness.

'So . . . there's someone else?' he asked.

'No,' she said. 'There's no one.' She turned to him and flashed him a quick, soulless smile.

'Shit,' Dan said, and exhaled. He put his hands on the bottom of the wheel, and where his palm had rested on her leg felt cold and bare. 'Does your family know?'

'No,' she said. 'Not yet.'

'What are you going to do?'

'I have no clue.' She turned toward the window, which had begun to steam up, and dragged her index finger along the glass in a series of disconnected lines. 'See, this is why I'm not a grown up. Grown-ups don't make mistakes like this.'

'Grown-ups make mistakes – and I'm not saying this is a mistake – all the time. You're being too hard on yourself.'

'Too hard on myself? I'm fucking *pregnant*, Dan! I'm going to have a *baby*! I, Cordelia Beatrice Andreas, am going to be responsible for the life of another human, when it's been made more than clear to me by everyone I know that I can't even take care of my own life. Is that the biggest joke you've ever heard or what?' She could feel herself starting to cry, and tried to push it back under her anger.

Dan sighed, leaning forward slightly and shifting in his seat before leaning back again. The engine hummed, and the rain poured down, beating against the roof, clamoring for attention. 'Whatever I say, you're going to bite my head off, so I guess I should just keep my mouth shut.'

With a swipe of her hand, Cordy wiped away the streaks she had made through the condensation. 'I'm sorry,' she said without looking at him. 'It's not your fault. I'm just . . . I don't know what to do.'

'You've gotta tell them, Cordy. You've gotta tell your family.'

'I don't know. Rose would love it, of course, just another example of my being an idiot for her to point at. And Bean's got her own crap to deal with.'

'So you're just not going to tell them? Sooner or later, they're going to figure it out.'

'I know. I guess I was just hoping I could wait until . . .' She didn't finish the sentence. She didn't know when she had thought it would be the right time to let us know.

'Until when?'

'I don't know,' Cordy said. But she did. Until it was time to go. Until it's time to shake some dust and disappear. Because that's what Cordy does. Cordy leaves better than anyone we know. No heartbreaks, no recriminations, just a ghost trail in the night and she's gone.

She flipped her braid over her shoulder and looked at Dan. Tears were streaking down her face and she sniffed hard, wiping her nose with the back of her hand. 'There's just so much going on. It's not right to make them deal with this, too. My mom, you know, and my dad's like not even on this planet. I shouldn't be freaking out like this on you. I just feel like there's no one to talk to.'

'There's me,' Dan said, and at that moment he looked so sweet and generous, Cordy smiled through her tears. He reached out and took her hand and they sat like that, while the fan blew cool air against their faces, drying Cordy's tears, and the rain slackened to mist outside.

The next day, the storms had cleared, leaving humidity rising thick from the wet ground as the sun pounded down.

210

Bean and our mother were lying out on the patio chairs by the garden in the back. Clad in a bikini that showed the muscles in her thighs, Bean smoked a cigarette, sunglasses covering her eyes, fly-like, her hair pulled back away from her face. She looked ready for the Riviera. Our mother had pulled her chair back from the reaching fingers of the sun, and her legs poked, pale and vein-speckled, from her shorts. The scarf around her head was tied in a new style, the loose ends trailing over her shoulder like an echo of the tresses she had lost. She was reading a magazine of unknown provenance. We were not much for magazines, but there was always one or two lying around, usually courtesy of the five-finger discount afforded by our dentist.

'Bean! What are you doing?' Rose asked, the screen door banging behind her as she stepped onto the brick patio.

Slowly, as though she did not know what Rose was getting at, Bean lifted her cigarette to her mouth and French inhaled. Curls of smoke drifted up into the still air and hung, blue and frothy. 'I'm sunbathing,' she said.

'You're smoking around Mom,' Rose hissed. 'You want her to get lung cancer, too?' She made a move as if to grab the offending butt from Bean's hand, but Bean dropped her arm, her fingers drooping lazily over the edge of the chair's arm, and the cigarette remained between her fingers.

'I figured we'd go for the cancer trifecta. Skin, lungs, breast.'

'It's not funny,' Rose said, frustrated by Bean's obvious callousness, by our mother's unwillingness to speak up for herself. Rose waved her hand in front of her face, fanning away the smoke in a melodramatic motion. She was wearing another one of her seemingly endless supply of tunics and loose-waisted pants. The pattern made her look like an angry art teacher.

'It's fine, Rose,' our mother said. She flipped a page in the magazine. 'I'm upwind of her anyway.'

'It's not fine,' Rose insisted. Bean took a final defiant drag and crushed the cigarette in an ashtray by her feet.

'Relax, Rosie. I have to go to work anyway.' Bean stood up, gathering the jelly jar from which she had been drinking, and kissed our mother on the forehead. 'Have a nice day.' She breezed inside, smelling of coconuts and sweat and the burning sting of cigarette smoke. She'd been going to thank Rose for putting in a good word for her at the library, but the constant attacks made it hard to be grateful. We were all hoping that whatever was bugging Rose would get resolved, and soon. It was like living with an unusually bossy thirteen-year-old. Again.

With a melodramatic sigh, Rose dropped into Bean's empty chair, still warm from her body and slightly slick with suntan oil. 'It's not fair,' Rose said.

'What's not fair?' our mother asked. She leaned the magazine against her chest, where it hung, lopsided. Rose averted her eyes. Somehow, the intimate act of helping our mother bathe was not as hard as looking at the empty spot inside her clothes.

Rose pursed her lips. 'How is it that they get everything? I did everything right, and they do nothing right, and it all turns out okay for them.'

'You'd rather they be punished for their mistakes?'

Rose considered this. *Some shall be pardon'd, and some punished.* She pictured Bean stretched on the rack, charm bracelet jangling, stilettos askew as her torturers pulled her limbs farther and farther apart. For Cordy, perhaps water torture, a slow, painful dripping. Neither of these thoughts gave her any pleasure. She rather thought less of herself for having them in the first place.

'Not punished. Just . . . how come it always comes out right for them and not for me?' Rose stood up and pushed her chair back away from the heat of the sun.

'What is it that hasn't come out right for you? You have a career, a lovely fiancé. You're beautiful and bright and you've earned everything you've worked for. You have a blessed life, Rosie.'

Rose grumbled something disagreeable under her breath, and our mother reached out and put her fingers lightly on Rose's hand.

'We've always been so proud of you. Of all of you. And if your sisters have had a little more trouble finding their way, then it's nothing to be disappointed in them for. They just need a little more support than you do. You've always been so independent. Even when you were a baby, you stopped breast-feeding so much earlier than Bean and Cordy. You wanted the bottle, because you could look around while you were drinking it.' She paused for a moment, then laughed. 'I swear, you started crawling out of sheer spite because I didn't move fast enough for you.' Her hat, wide and floppy, threw a tremble of shadows across her face when she moved her head. She smiled, and Rose could see the lines traced along her eyes, her lips.

Despite the sour curdle inside her, Rose smiled. She loved to hear stories of herself as a baby. The memories made her feel warm and special, like she was the One again, instead of one of Three.

'It just doesn't seem fair,' Rose sighed. Bean had the beautiful clothes and the body to wear them, Cordy was the one everyone wanted to be around, the one whose smile seemed to cast a light on its recipient. And she was – and always would be – stodgy, dependable Rose. No one beautiful, no one special. Did she hate us, or herself? The difference had seemed so clear to her when she sat down.

213

'What's eating at you, Rosie?' our mother asked. She brushed her fingers, light as satin, across our sister's hand. Our mother's skin has always been petal-soft, as comforting as her words. We may go to our father for intellectual stimulation, but our mother is the one who soothes our souls.

'It's Jonathan,' Rose said. 'He's been offered' – offered, or taken? – ' a visiting position at Oxford. For two years.'

'You mean on top of the year he's already doing?' our mother confirmed.

Rose answered with a nod. Out in the garden, she could see the bees swerving back and forth between the flowers. She could see the dark curls and lines inside the pansies edging the path. *There's rosemary, that's for remembrance; pray, love, remember: and there is pansies. That's for thoughts.* 'He wants me to come over there. To live.'

'And?' our mother asked.

'And it means I wouldn't be able to apply for the position at Barnwell.'

'I see,' our mother said. She put the magazine back in her lap, flipped a page. 'But you don't know you'd get that job at Barnwell, right?'

'No, I guess not. They'd have to do a national search. But they'd pick me. I'm sure of it. Dr Kelly said as much.'

Our mother smiled. 'So you think you have to choose between your career and Jonathan.'

'That's exactly what he's making me do.'

'I don't think he's making you do anything. He hasn't issued an ultimatum, has he? Did he say he'd be willing to talk about it?'

'Sort of,' Rose said grudgingly. 'He wants me to come visit. He says we'll talk about it then.'

Our mother nodded thoughtfully. 'Well, you should certainly go visit the poor man. He's probably quite lonely.'

214

'He doesn't sound it.' Rose was petulant. If none of us were on her side, what were the chances that he would be?

'Don't sulk, darling. It will give you wrinkles.' Rose looked at our mother, who gave a long, tinkling laugh. 'I'm joking. So what's the worst thing that could happen if he took the position and you went over there to stay with him?'

'I'd miss the position at Barney.'

'There are other schools.'

'I wouldn't be able to get a job.'

'So Jonathan would support you for a while. It's not like you're an expensive habit to keep, Rose. You're no Bean.'

Rose closed her eyes, but the bees still buzzed red patterns against the darkness of her lids. 'What would I do there, anyway? I mean, Jonathan would be working, and I'd just be what? A housewife?'

A silence there, because of course this is exactly what our mother is. Rose thinks guiltily back to her conversation with Bean, but she cannot fight the feeling that our mother's life is less than she wants for herself. What does our mother do with her days? She reads, she cooks, she tends to her garden. To Rose, it seems such a small life. And then she berates herself for thinking this, because how is her own life so grand? Bean or Cordy, their lives have drama, at least. Not to say that Rose wants drama; she may envy the reflective glamour it adds, but she has never been able to cope with any of its inroads into her own life. And hasn't she had a good life, our mother? Hasn't she raised children, and read good books, and traveled and laughed and had a marriage lasting for, what, thirty-three years? If you look at the statistics for Barnwell, they will tell you half of the town is unemployed, but that is, practically though not technically, false. Barnwell is full of people like our mother, married to spouses who dragged them to the middle of a cornfield and set off for the academic races with no more than a kiss and a cheerful exhortation to go ahead and build a life for themselves in the middle of nothing.

'I'm sorry,' Rose said. 'I didn't mean that . . .'

'*Youth, thou bear'st thy father's face,*' our mother said unexpectedly. She is the least likely of us to quote the immortal. 'He'd go mad if he weren't busy all the time.'

'I don't mind the busy part. I just like a schedule. I like to know what's going to happen. And I don't want to become lazy.'

'I know you, Rose. You'd never allow yourself to sit still long enough to gather moss.'

'So you think I should go?' Rose asked, turning earnestly toward our mother like a sunflower in the light of approval.

'I think opportunity is knocking,' our mother said, and tapped on the metal arm of her chair for good measure. The contact made a hollow, echoing sound that to Rose sounded ominous and sour.

Before work one morning, Bean drove her car to the mechanic. She had bought it for $300 on the way out of New York – no one, after all, has a car in the city – and now it was nothing but an albatross, a reminder of her need to make an escape. When our father had made a remark about its continued presence as a blight upon the driveway (*'What ugly sights of death within mine eyes!'*), Bean had taken the hint and called the mechanic's wife, who had graciously agreed to take it off her hands. Bean knew that making the nine-hour drive back from the city had sucked whatever lifeblood remained in the engine, and to have them buy it was a gesture of goodwill, not commerce. So there it was, gone, and she had a hundred dollars in

216

a purse that had cost five times that, and she was headed to her new, glamorous life as a small-town librarian. *The ripest fruit first falls.*

But she had to admit that simply being in the library made her peaceful. There was so much to learn and yet nothing, because she knew by heart the way the light fell through each window, every pull in the carpet, the exact smell of the books that clung to her clothes at the end of the day. She felt safe. And Mrs Landrige, figure of both love and fear, had become so frail. Bean hadn't noticed the difference until they were together all day Mrs Landrige had hardly risen from her chair, and when she did, her brow furrowed at the effort and she used a cane to move slowly across the room.

With two of them there, there was little to do, so Bean was (needlessly) reading shelves, replacing or straightening the occasional volume that had been separated from its flock, when she saw Aidan come in. His hair caught her attention from the corner of her eye, but she had just enough time to brush the dust from her skirt and undo a button on her blouse before she felt the shock of his touch against her elbow. His hand felt warm and sweaty. He carried a stack of slightly rippled pages.

'Father Aidan,' she said. Her library voice had encountered her bar voice and it was low and husky, reverential. 'What are you doing here?'

'Can't get a thing done at the church. People keep coming by. It's my secret sanctuary, this place.'

'No longer such a secret, I'm afraid, now that you've told me,' Bean said. She turned so she faced him, grateful for the unnaturally close personal space allowed by their surroundings. He looked more surfer than priest, sunglasses pushed up in his hair, a loose white shirt over cargo shorts, and impossibly strong calves ending in sandals. Even the hair on his legs glinted in the sunlight, cast copper in the glow.

'There are no secrets in a small town, I guess,' he said.

Oh, if only you knew.

'But I'm glad I ran into you. Are you working?' he continued.

'Vaguely,' Bean said. 'What's up?' She leaned back against the shelves, crossing her legs at the ankle, bringing forward the curve of her hips under the slim skirt she wore. Being Bean, she had flipped through her wardrobe in search of clothing to suit her role, and, being Bean, she had found it. Her blouse was short-sleeved and ruffled, and her skirt was knee-length. She had momentarily considered glasses, but decided against them.

'I've been thinking about getting together some of the younger members of the congregation for some community service works. Twenty-somethings and young marrieds.'

'Are there that many?' Bean's impression of church, especially during the summers, was of a great deal of white hair. She stifled the next question, You want me to do *community service*?

'We've probably got fifteen to twenty, which is more than enough. They're building some Habitat for Humanity houses over in Cadbury. I figured we could go over on a weekend. Then take it from there. Maybe during the school year, we can head into the city, see if any of the churches there want to do something together.'

'That sounds great. I love that kind of thing,' Bean said. She was a liar. Bean, while a nice enough person, had never spent any sort of time considering community service. In spite of (or because of) having spent so much time in a city with so much misery all around her, she had willfully shut out the idea of doing for her fellow man until that very moment.

'Great. You want to come by and we'll kick together some names and make some calls?'

'Sure. Day after tomorrow? After I finish here?'

'That's fine. I've got to leave at six, though. I'm heading up to the city to see some friends.'

'Oh,' Bean said. Honestly, she had hoped they might do their business, and then she could suggest a glass of wine, and then they would talk. . . .

'I'll see you later, then,' he said, and disappeared into the stacks.

Bean stood upright, stretching her shoulder blades back where the books had dug into her skin. Looking casual was so much work.

She went back to straightening the shelves, flicking her finger along the uneven tops of the books. It interested her that some of the shelves were so much dustier than the others. Apparently nobody in Barnwell was big on self-help books or slow cooker recipes

Aidan puzzled her. If this were New York, she'd have been fairly sure he was stalking her, what with the running into her all the time, but here, there were a limited number of people you could run into. It was all coincidence, she was sure. Except today he'd clearly wanted to talk to her. Was he . . . interested in her?

Someone had left a few books on one of the tables, and Bean scooped them up as she passed by, looking idly at the numbers and then searching out their homes. Dating Aidan wasn't beyond the realm of possibility – he was young and single and cute, and so was she.

Her better nature leaped into her throat and she shook her head, slipping the last wayward book onto the shelf. Yes, Beany, you'd make a great partner for him. What with the embezzling and the adultery and the drinking. That's what every man wants in a wife – a vaguely alcoholic, fornicating thief.

No, he was just being nice. She'd take it as nothing more than that. Well, maybe she could drink a little less. And make sure that she looked good when she went out for a run, just in case. And Edward . . . She wasn't quite ready to give up that particular drug yet. No. It was so nice to be able to forget for a little while.

FOURTEEN

The fluorescent light flickered, idly threatening to burn out altogether. Cordy stared up at it, her eyes burning from the disco-ball sputters, and waited. 'This will be a little cold,' the nurse said, and held up a tube of gel, drizzling a thin line on Cordy's stomach as though she were topping a sundae. The sensation was, indeed, cold, though less unpleasant than a chilly stethoscope or, worse, an icy speculum. Cordy turned her head to see the monitor as the nurse pressed the wand against her skin.

Nothing for a moment, a blur of white, the pressure of the plastic against her belly, and then the nurse pushed harder, angling her hand back and forth. 'Your uterus is retroverted,' she said conversationally, and Cordy said, 'Oh,' as though she knew what that meant.

'No big deal,' the nurse said, continuing to press. 'It'll tip itself the right way by the second trimester.' She slid the wand, and then stopped, pushing again.

'Ah-ha!' she said, as though she had just located an elusive contact lens, and clicked a few mouse buttons, marking tiny plus signs on the screen. She pushed again, slid over the slickness of the gel, clicked again. 'Looks like about ten weeks,' she said.

221

Cordy peered at the screen, trying to make something out in the din of pebbled gray space. The image spread out like the cartoon beam of a flashlight, and in the centre, she could see the kidney-shaped darkness of her uterus. Inside, a white circle like a clenched fist, marked from end to end with the tiny plus signs. The body did not look so much like a baby as a tiny intruder, a gallstone or an ulcer, and Cordy stared at it curiously, wondering about its origins.

Inside her, the tiny thing turned, and Cordy could see the articulated vertebrae of its spine, the swell of a head like an alien, and in its unformed ugliness, she instantly loved it.

'Mine,' Cordy whispered to herself, her fingers reaching toward the screen. 'Mine.'

Nothing had ever been just hers before. Clothes, books, toys, jokes, once Rose's or Bean's – or worse, both – then were Cordy's. The curse of the hand-me-downs. New-to-me, not just plain new. Cordy remembers in particular a dress she had coveted, watching it go from Rose to Bean, waiting impatiently for the day it would be hers. A soft brown plaid, Peter Pan collar, puffed sleeves, skirt like a ringing bell around our knees running home from church.

She had wanted it desperately, had traced its lineage through her sisters, had counted the times they wore it, ticking away the wears until it would become hers. The fabric washed into softness, the lace at the collar pulled away from the fabric, our mother mended it. Good as new. But not new. And then, finally, the day Bean had outgrown it, cast it aside. Cordy grabbed it from the pile of clothes in the laundry room, ran to her own room, slipped it on.

It was too small. Bean had bloomed late, Cordy early,

both of them springing into their teenage bodies at the same time, and it did not fit her. The tiny pearl-sheen buttons gaped at the chest, the delicate sleeves strained when she reached her arms forward, the feminine collar choked her. Cordy ripped the dress off, stuffed it in the garbage can, mourned it bitterly for years afterward, lime on chapped lips.

But this baby, this would be hers forever. That sense of wonder kept her warm as she dressed, pulling her clothes on with a tender respect for the swell of her belly, as she floated out of the sterility of the office into the parking lot to Dan's car. He'd wanted to drive her, but she'd insisted on going alone. A thrust of nausea hit her hard, and she braced herself, one hand on the car door. Swallowing the sick rush in her mouth, she turned and leaned against the warm metal.

There would be no more leaving now. No more drifting on the jet-stream, no more picking up on a whim and skipping out on unpaid bills and unwanted lovers and unsatisfying jobs. This hand-me-down was staying. Forever.

Cordy's eyes watered, and she wiped them with her shirt cuff, blinking into the sun. The edge of the car key pressed against her skin, a reassuring pain.

But she could go, couldn't she?

She could leave right this minute, disappear into the darkness of the map, shudder into a new town, another new life. The promise of a full tank of gas and an empty future ached inside her.

No. She couldn't. Because even in that new incarnation, she would still be carrying a baby inside her. She'd never be able to disappear again.

She drove back to Barnwell, through acres of waving sheaves, green in the water-swollen summer. She walked through the empty kitchen and dropped the keys on Dan's desk in the back of the Beanery without stopping to say hello, and walked home, her hands resting on her stomach. Though it was neither physically possible nor technically true, she felt as though she had started the day with nothing to her name and ended it with something to call her own. When Dan came by after work, she was standing in the kitchen, punching down dough, and staring out the window at the sprinkler, which was spitting arcs of water into the dissolving sunlight.

Dan leaned against the counter, arms crossed, hair hobbit-thick on his arms. His voice was low, deep, and Cordy thought of the rumble a man's voice made when her head rested on his chest. 'What are you going to do?' Dan asked, leaning forward. Above his eyes, his eyebrows furrowed dark and wide.

The dough stretched warm and elastic in Cordy's hands, and she rolled it between her fingers lovingly, turning it to cover the surface with shortening, painted white around the inside of the bowl. She pushed it back to the center of the stove, placed a wet towel over the top. 'I'm going to have it,' Cordy said. 'I'm going to have a baby.'

Dan nodded, pulled his eyes from Cordy, looked at the refrigerator, where for years we had hung art projects and homemade magnets and now was a repository for expired coupons, notes from Rose that no one ever read, and one set of Shakespearean magnetic poetry, which had currently been arranged into a number of lines, including, 'Tongue tart lustily among knights,' and, 'Kate resolv'd blush footed groves hey kissed.' (Authors: our father, the former, and Bean, the latter. Thought it would be the other way around, didn't you?)

'When are you due?' he asked.

'Christmas,' she said. 'Or thereabouts. You don't think I'm a bad person, do you?' She looked up at him, eyes round and bright.

'Why would I think that?'

'I can't afford a baby,' she said. 'This wasn't really part of the plan.'

'There's a plan?' Dan asked, mock surprise. 'No one ever tells me anything. Let me have a look at this plan.' He smacked his hand, open palm, on the stove top, and the bowl shuddered agreeably.

'Don't be an ass,' Cordy said. 'I'm like one of those women they make documentaries about. A burden on the state.' She looked gloomily at her hands, still sticky with dough, and went to the sink to wash them.

'Okay, let's put the cart back behind the horse for a minute,' Dan said. 'This is not the smartest decision you could make right now. But for you, it's the right one. So you make your decision and you go with it, or you spend nine months wishing and washing back and forth over whether or not you've done someone wrong.'

'Right,' Cordy said, and her voice fell to a whisper again. She dried her hands on the dish towel and they slipped again to cover her stomach. *Mine.* Nothing had ever been hers. Nothing.

Bean had been surprised at how hard it had been to do something good. She and Aidan had brainstormed a dozen charities, but every one had been full up with volunteers for the next three months. Who knew?

When she'd finally gotten to the bottom of the list, to the house-building duty Aidan had initially suggested, she'd nearly been ready to lie and tell Aidan that they were full up, too. Working outside? In this heat?

But she was really in no position to go pissing God off any more than she was doing on a daily basis, and lying to a priest and cheating a charity out of volunteers was two strikes too close to being struck down by an avenging angel.

So she made the call, and of course they were delighted to have them. Of course.

She borrowed some of Cordy's clothes, which couldn't have gotten any grungier if she'd skipped the manual labor and rolled directly in the dirt, limited her makeup to sunscreen, mascara, and lip gloss, and headed out to the site. She was sitting on the trunk of the car, swinging her legs and whistling, when Aidan arrived with a group of the volunteers from St Mark's.

They'd all carpooled. Shit. She should have thought of that. That was what good people did.

'Bianca,' he said, shaking his head when he saw her. 'You look far too nice for this.' She looked down at her clothes, surprised, since a look in the mirror before she'd left had made her fairly sure she'd be yanked off the street to serve as an orphan understudy in a revival of *Oliver!* He tapped his fingers against the arm of her sunglasses. Her hand went protectively, covered the mother-of-pearl logo. Well, she could have gotten them on Canal Street. He didn't know.

'I'm not afraid to get dirty,' she said, the oversized lenses hiding any flicker of insecurity. Pursed her lips, shook her hair. She held up her hands, free of nail polish. 'Bring it on.'

Bean didn't know any of the other volunteers there. The people she'd known from school had grown wings and flown, just like her, albeit with less spectacular crash landings. Her friends from the loud, beer-drenched parties, the tough, cruel-mouthed girls and the menacing, heavy-handed boys, had disappeared into the ether; moving, taking jobs – real jobs that paid less every week than those sunglasses had cost – or having children, becoming grown-ups before the thought of adulthood had ever crossed her mind.

But the others in the St Mark's group were nice, were

226

kind, were welcoming. She knew some of them from the library, a young mother who came in with her children, the couple who had bought the hardware store and had donated supplies for today. Three professors, fresh-faced and newly anointed. And all of them, Bean found, were more useful than she was. We lived a life of the mind in our house, which was all well and good, but sometimes Bean wondered, back when the threat of The Bomb had hung above our heads like the Sword of Damocles, what would happen to us if the end did come? No one would need people like us. Poetry and art would be useless. We would need farmers, and carpenters, and scientists, and leaders. But not a disgraced adulteress of an office manager with a useless ability to quote Shakespeare and a budding knowledge of the Dewey decimal system.

For she could now, admittedly not with the panache of Mrs Landrige, surely, take you easily and directly to the section you wanted, occasionally home in on the exact book, pull it off the shelves and place it into your grateful hands, and then wave away your thanks carelessly. But here, put to fetching and carrying, she felt clumsy and in the way, arms spread awkwardly across plywood, rushing back and forth between the spit of the saw and the noisy sting of hammers in her ears. Soon she was sweaty and tired and she knotted her hair in on itself and wiped off the mascara sweating its way down her cheeks and tried to forget who she really was and why she was really there.

At lunch, she sat in the shade next to the young mother from the library. 'It's so nice to meet someone my age,' the woman said. Amanda.

Bean started at that. She looked at Amanda, the tiny bouquet of wrinkles beside her eyes as she smiled, the bow of a frown line between her nose and her mouth, her hair messy, her hips widening. Were they the same age? Bean had grown so used to thinking of herself as a twenty-something, just another fabulous gal about town, living some glamorous roman-à-clef-to-be. When she was little she would calculate how old she would be at the millennium, and it had seemed so ancient, so far in the future that it could not possibly be connected to the girl she was at that time. But now, here she was, past that inconceivable age, even.

She folded in on herself and ate her sandwich silently as Amanda chattered on beside her, until it was, mercifully, time to go back to toting barges and lifting bales.

At the end of the day, Bean was sore and splintered, divested fully of makeup, hair gone wild (but alluringly so, she had checked in the windows of the roofer's truck).

'How are you feeling?' Aidan asked. His hand rested on her back, Bean automatically straightened, her shoulder blades wings on her back, the same way she did whenever she saw an old woman hunchbacked with age.

'I'm beat,' Bean said, twisted her lips into a humble smile. 'But I feel good. Like after a really good kickboxing class, but better.'

Aidan laughed. 'Maybe we should consider selling it that way. Community service as physical fitness.'

'Franchises in strip malls with pictures of us holding out our enormous jeans.'

'Now that's something to aspire to,' Aidan said. A few of the St Mark's workers flitted by. Aidan greeted them, a hand on the shoulder, the other in a firm handshake. He laughed, told Amanda he'd see her in church on Sunday. Amanda lingered for a moment, possibly hoping for an audience with Bean rather than with Aidan, but then she slipped off and they were alone again. 'I'm glad you came,' Aidan said.

'Me too,' Bean said, and she half meant it. It was nice

to find forgetfulness in something other than a bottle of wine or Edward's bed.

'We can really do something with this young members group if everything is as successful as today. And you did a great job putting it together on short notice. Should we do it again in a couple of weeks?'

'How about next month?' Bean suggested. 'I think people like to have their weekends. Not me, of course, as I am now officially a spinster librarian and must stay home with my cat and drink tea.'

'Really? That seems awfully unfair.'

Bean shrugged. 'Them's the rules. It's in the manual.'

'Well, I guess we should hit the road. I've got to finish writing my sermon for tomorrow and it looks like everyone else is ready to go.'

'Ooh, Father Procrastination,' Bean said, nudging him gently as they walked toward her car.

'It's not that. I just like it to be . . . fresh out of the mental oven.'

'Piping hot homilies.'

'Exactly. And you?'

'Home,' she said, but that was a lie.

Bean herself could not define the gravitational pull that drew her to Edward's, only that it made her as sick inside as it delighted her.

'Don't say anything,' Bean said as Edward held the screen door back for her. He was smoking a cigar, the sour smell turning her stomach a little as she brushed past him. 'I've been doing good all day, and I know I look like hell.'

'So you came by to do a little evil?' he asked, holding his cigar to his mouth and waggling it before he took another puff.

'I came by to take a little shower,' she said.

'And then?' he asked teasingly.

'Meet me upstairs in ten minutes and find out,' she said.

'You are a very bad apple,' he said, gesturing up the wide stairs to the second floor, and giving her a slap on the bottom with his free hand. There was blues playing on the stereo, and the newspaper was scattered around the living room. He'd adjusted so easily to the bachelor life, it was easy to forget that every time she was here, she burned away any good she could possibly do with a measly day of community service. His wife, his children, she wronged them all just with her presence. All the sermons we'd heard growing up, all the Bible storybooks we'd read until they fell apart, it had all been for nothing. It had occurred to Bean that she was ticking her way down the Ten Commandments, violating each one in an orderly fashion until there'd be nothing left of her soul but a tiny, torn shred, fluttering in the empty darkness inside her.

She walked toward the steps and turned back to look at Edward over her shoulder. He grew less handsome every time she saw him, she thought, his teeth still white, his hair still candidate-perfect, but his face distorted by alcohol and disappointment. But when he winked at her, toasting her with the tumbler in his hand, she winked back. And when she stood under the spray, washing away the sweat and the dirt of the day, and he joined her, she ignored her better judgment and let him dizzy away the cold, uncertain world and her new place in it. This was her life, then. Good on the outside, rotten on the inside. She was a bad apple, all right. Rotten to the core.

Our father was sitting at the kitchen table, reading his *Riverside Shakespeare*. Rose came in and sat down at one of the straight-backed chairs across from him. 'Daddy,' she said, but he held up one finger, not taking his eyes from his book. This was his signal – just a moment, I'm reading.

Rose rolled her eyes. It wasn't like he didn't know the ending, whichever play he was reading.

When he finished, he placed the book facedown on the table. Rose's fingers itched to take it and mark his spot. 'I need some advice.'

'Neither a borrower nor a lender be; For loan oft loses both itself and friend, and borrowing dulls the edge of husbandry,' he said with a self-satisfied little grin. Oh, Daddy, a *Hamlet* joke. How lovely. You shouldn't have.

Rose forced an answering smile. 'Thanks. But this is about work.'

'Ah. The lure of tenure,' he said. 'What did Jonathan say?'

'He wants to stay in England. It's ridiculous. Because then two years from now we'll have to look again.'

'There are other universities. People move from college to college all the time.'

'You didn't,' Rose said accusingly.

'No,' our father admitted. 'But it was a different time. Vietnam left us with a glut of academics, and we were fortunate to find a space, especially at a school as prestigious as Barnwell. But you have options I never had. And you work in a field far less crowded than mine.'

'So you're saying I shouldn't take it.'

'I'm not saying anything other than pointing out, quite logically, my little mathematician, that there's nothing forcing you to take it.'

'But what if I can't get another job here?'

'Then you'll go somewhere else.'

'I can't leave you,' Rose said.

Our father beetled his brow. 'And why not?'

Rose faltered. 'Well, Mom. And Bean and Cordy are here now.'

'And none of these is your responsibility, Rose. No one ever asked you to care for us. I suppose it is your mother's and my failing that we have allowed you to do so for so long. It's always been your gift to care for others, but it's a gift that's come with a certain amount of sacrifice for you, whether you know it or not.'

Allowed. Rose had never thought of all the responsibility she had taken on as having been permitted by someone. It was something that she just had to do. At dinner in a near-empty Italian restaurant, Bean and Cordy playing hide-and-go-seek between the legs of deserted tables, their shrieks making the waiters jump as they carried full platters to the table where our parents ate with their friends, Rose escorting them to the entryway and keeping them occupied with crayons and a long white strip of butcher paper. At a summer department picnic, Cordy tearing off her clothes to run through a sprinkler until her diaper was heavy with water, Rose, embarrassed by Cordy's childish nudity, taking her inside to dry her off and put her back in her yellow seersucker dress, tying the bow neatly on her back. At the grocery store when our mother had forgotten to buy anything we could pack for lunch, Rose having learned where the grocery money was kept, in a jar by the sink, carefully picking out white bread and bologna so our sandwiches would look like those of every other child at the table (until we went to Coop, of course, where the kid next to us was more likely to have hummus than Campbell's in his thermos). In the living room, Rose carefully knocking the ashes out of our father's pipe as he slept peacefully in the chair. Truly, no one had ever asked her to do these things, but we had relied on her to do them, relied so heavily that it had never occurred to us how unfair to her it might be, how much she had begun to think of herself as the person who did those things.

But if she didn't do those things – if she no longer took care of us – then who would she be? Who would Bean be

232

if she dropped her beautiful mask? Who would Cordy be if she stepped up to the plate in her own life? Who would Rose be if she weren't the responsible one anymore?

'You're going over for a visit, right?'

Rose was surprised that our father had registered this fact. She'd announced her trip, written it on the family calendar in the kitchen, but she'd fully expected to have to remind everyone a dozen more times before she left. When had our father started paying attention to things?

'So you'll go and you'll see.'

'But what should I do?' Rose asked, even more lost than when they had begun.

'This above all: to thine own self be true, and it must follow, as the night the day, thou canst not then be false to any man.' He reached across the table and patted her hand and then picked up his book again.

Conversation *finis.*

Thanks, Polonius.

FIFTEEN

The night before our mother began her first week of radiation, Cordy dropped her bombshell at the dinner table. She had made bread, as she was always doing these days, and she had set it in a basket, broken grain against butter-yellow checked cloth, steam rising from the slices, scenting the air with yeast and comfort. Rose had said grace, and we were settling in to eat when she spoke.

'I'm going to have a baby,' our baby sister said.

Our father, buttering a slice of bread all at once, in strict defiance of our mother's rule to spread only a bite at a time, stopped. His hand, holding the cream-striped knife, settled against the tablecloth. 'Oh, Cordelia,' he said, and there were worlds in those words.

Bean looked up, unsurprised. She was still dressed from work, a lavender jacket over a white T-shirt, tucked into jeans she would tell you honestly had cost more than three hundred dollars. Mrs Landrige would not have approved of the denim, despite the price tag. 'Wow,' she said.

'You're kidding.' Rose, tight-lipped, brow furrowed.

'What?' our mother asked. She was humming to herself,

234

cutting a tomato into small pieces, her knife scraping against the plate.

There you have it. Our family in a nutshell.

'I'm pregnant. I'm having a baby.' Cordy said it again, as though we had not all heard her. Well, our mother had not, but that was nothing new. She was always delayed in her responses, spent most of her time picking up the threads of conversations as they spun across the table and weaving them back together herself.

So much was explained now, the weight gain, her quietness in the morning, the way Rose had noticed her stomach swelling against the waistband of her pants, her desperate urge to feed us all. And yet there were a million questions to be asked.

'Who's the father?' Rose asked, leading the charge, and Cordy looked shaken, as though she had been unprepared for this question, as though it had never occurred to her that there was a father, that people might be curious as to his whereabouts.

'I don't know,' she said, and our father flushed red, the streaks of white at his brow standing bright against his skin. 'No one who matters.'

'Goddammit, Cordelia,' our father said, and his knife clattered to his plate, a sharp sound that made our mother jump. 'You can't have a child.'

'Too late,' Bean said, and smiled to herself. 'I think the horse is out of the barn on that one.'

'Jim,' our mother said, a spill of silk over his anger.

'How are you going to support yourself? Pay bills? Feed the baby? Pay a doctor, for heaven's sake?'

'I'll manage,' Cordy said, and it was as much an oath to herself as a promise to our father. 'I've got my job, and I'll take another one if I need to.'

'And who will take care of the baby while you're working all the hours God sends?'

'We will,' our mother said, and now the silk was steel. 'We're not going to leave a child of ours alone if she needs our help.'

The look that passed over our father's face was painful to see. Had we ever seen our father cry? At his own father's funeral, yes, he crumpled and wept in the church as the priest called a litany of Pop-Pop's good works. But this expression was sadder, a thousand betrayals screaming across his face in an instant. He got up and stalked out of the kitchen, leaving his napkin on his chair as an afterthought.

'Nice going,' Bean said.

'Shut up, Bean,' Cordy said, and she looked miserable. 'Like you're not just as big a fuckup as I am.'

'Girls,' our mother said mildly. 'Language.'

'You haven't heard of birth control?' Bean asked. Cordy closed her eyes as the memory flashed across her mind. The painter, the desert, their last night on his tired futon. How long ago had that been? No more than three months. It seemed like forever.

'I've heard of it,' Cordy said.

'When are you due?' our mother asked, speared a piece of tomato delicately and chewed.

'December,' Cordy said. 'Maybe Christmas.'

'Well, this is certainly going to change your life,' our mother said.

'I know,' Cordy said, and it was impossible to tell what the tears shining in her eyes were for. 'I know.'

Later that night, we sat in the living room, pretending to read. After years living in this house with wooden floors, we had learned each other's steps. Our mother, quick and light. Our father, heavy and purposeful; Rose, heavy and hesitant. Bean, firm and sharp, and Cordy, a flat run every few steps. We listened to the steps passing above us, our mother walking across the bedroom to

236

the vanity, sitting down to put on her moisturizer. Standing again, walking across to the bathroom door, where her nightgown hung. Our father, ponderous and mournful, trodding into the bathroom, water running, plodding back to the dresser where he would empty his pockets onto the top, the coins clattering into the tiny dish where they would lie until one of us claimed them in the name of an ice-cream cone. And weaving through it all, the vibration of voices. Our father, loud and angry. Our mother, softer. Our father, angry again. Our mother, her voice raised to match his. The squeak of the bathroom door.

Bean looked up at Cordy, who was crying, silent silver tears streaking down her face, slipping – plop – off her chin and spotting the thin fabric of her T-shirt. 'Hey,' she said, and stood, walking over to our sister, who sat on the couch. Though Cordy was not any smaller than us – we were all the same height – she seemed impossibly tiny right then in the middle of the couch, her legs crossed under the book, her tank top and olive green pants ill fitting and old. Bean sat down beside her, stroked her arm. Cordy kept crying.

'Hey,' Bean said again. 'It's going to be okay. You threw him for a loop, you know?'

'I know,' Cordy said, in the crying way of hearing without believing a word of it. She wiped her nose with the inside of her wrist. Rose stood up, grabbed a box of tissues, and carried it over to her, sitting on her other side. Cordy took a tissue and blew her nose.

We sat on either side of her, our hands consoling her in a steady rhythm. 'He's just surprised,' Rose said softly. 'He's not really angry.'

'He'll come around. He's going to have a grandkid. That'll totally blow him away. And he'll help you out, he always does. He's just upset right now,' Bean said.

237

'I know,' Cordy said again. She took another tissue, wiped under her eyes. She looked up at us, our little sister, with dark circles under her eyes and streaks of tears drying on her cheeks. 'I just wish he could be a little happy for me. Just a little. I know this is stupid in a million ways, but I want this baby. And I will be a good mother.'

'Of course you will,' Rose said. 'And we will help you.'

'You'll be a great mother,' Bean said, stroking Cordy's hair. These were the supportive things to say, but we don't think anyone on that couch entirely believed them yet. *Lions make leopards tame . . . Yea, but not change his spots.* Will alone could not make Rose brave, could not make Bean honest, could not make Cordy sensible. Weren't we proof of that, this sad sisterhood, bound as much by our failures as by our hopes?

A few days after Cordy's announcement, Rose was sitting in the living room reading when she heard Bean and Cordy thumping around in Bean's room together. Jealousy rose, a smooth wave inside her, before she pushed it down again. Had she come this far only to be drawn back into the decades-old tug-of-war between the three of us? Resolutely, she put down her book and headed upstairs. She lingered for a moment, afraid we would not welcome her.

In Rose's first two weeks as a freshman at Barnwell, she had lost twelve pounds. Not intentionally, but because, confronted with the daunting task of approaching the dining hall with no knowledge of its workings and no sure friend to sit with, she chose to eat in her room instead. Day after day, she ate cereal in the morning, milk from the tiny dorm fridge her roommate had brought, careful to keep the clatter of the spoon from waking said roommate. At lunch, she skittered into the Student Union, where our father had bought us hamburgers a thousand times, and ate alone. At dinner, she strolled into town, ate in the safety of the diner or the bookstore, or snuck home, claiming she missed our mother's cooking, even when she had pulled one of her mental disappearing acts and there was no cooking of hers to be had. Not until a frothy, pretty girl with a hemp necklace and a slightly wide-eyed stare Rose would soon learn was chemically induced invited her to dinner with the other girls on the floor did she set foot in that place, and then she stepped so carefully after her savior, eating exactly what she did, placing her feet, her silverware in precisely the same place, you would have thought she was a shadow.

Before Rose had to summon up the courage to open the door, Cordy flung it wide. *'Who talks within there? ho, open the door!'* she cackled.

'Oh, we were wondering who was creeping around in the hallway like that,' Bean said, glancing over her shoulder at Rose, and then returning, disinterested, to the pile of clothing on the bed. Rose suppressed a sigh at the sight of the room. It looked not unlike Bean had opened every box and bag she had brought with her – and she had fit an impressive number into that tiny compact, like a clown car – and sprayed their contents around the room. Cordy was clomping around in a mismatched pair of stiletto heels, pants, a skirt, a long-sleeved T-shirt, and a pashmina draped around her head as though she were expecting to be picked up for a ride in a convertible. In 1952.

'I was hardly creeping,' Rose said. 'What in God's name are you doing in here?'

Cordy paused, cocked her hip and waggled a critical finger at Rose. 'Don't take the Lord's name in vain, dahling,' she said. 'It's so gauche.' She flipped the edge of the shawl back over her shoulder and pranced off in another direction.

'I'm cleaning. And Rita Hayworth here is helping. Or so she claims,' Bean said, waving her fingers at Cordy.

Rose walked over to the bed, leaning her thighs against it, and fingered some of the fabric splayed across it. 'You have a lot of clothes,' she said.

'I know.'

Questioning, Rose flipped up the sleeve of a rose-pink jacket, silk shantung. 'This one still has the tags on it.'

In the corner, Cordy retrieved a bright green leather handbag from a box and clomped back across the room, skidding slightly in her heels. Bean has always had the biggest feet of the three of us. Cordy paused halfway in her circuit, blew Rose a kiss, and then continued her runway sashay.

'I know,' Bean said again, her voice shy with regret. God, how many of these did still have their tags on? So much of it had been the will to possess, to own, to open the tiny broom cupboard of her closet and see the spoils of war bursting forth. And then there was fashion, of course, the fickle courtesan who changed her mind seemingly in the time it took to order a drink, leaving her stranded with last night's shoes or this morning's hair.

'Do you really need all of these?' Rose asked.

Bean looked up sharply, her eyes narrowing defensively.

'No, I'm not being mean. I was just wondering. Because you could take them to a consignment shop in the city. Sell them.'

Bean's hands moved quickly, folding, sorting, shaking out the lines of a suit. She paused, hands on a gray pencil skirt, a matching jacket. Bad luck. This was the suit she had worn when they had fired her; she could still remember herself tugging the hemline down to an acceptable length

240

as she sat. She tossed the piece aside, shaking her hands afterward. Did other people feel that kind of voodoo about their clothes? Certainly there were lucky socks, favorite items, but Bean felt the opposite, too, that if something bad happened when she was wearing a specific item of clothing, she would never wear it again. This certainly counted.

But if she sold them, she could be rid of that memory altogether. Or closer to it, at least.

'You'd make a crapload,' Cordy said. She hopped up on the bed, Bean's heels dropping off her feet with a clatter, and obediently lifted up her hip so Bean could pull out the clothes she was sitting on. Cordy opened the purse she had claimed and began to go through the pockets, pulling out tissues, a half-eaten roll of mints, and far too many pennies.

'Well, I owe a crapload, so it's all fair,' Bean said. She had furrowed her brow in a way she might once have tried to wipe away, already considering cosmetic surgery.

After her breakdown in the woods, when Bean had told us her story, we had stood in awe of the amount of money she owed, and the impossibility of raising it, but we had not counted on Bean's couture. Rose, who neither knew nor cared about what was in vogue in Paris this season, peeked at a label, her eyes widening. A crapload, imprecise as that measurement was, was exactly what Bean would net.

'You might even make more than you owe. You could keep what's left over,' Cordy said.

Bean and Rose looked at each other, and both shook their heads. 'I don't want the money,' Bean said, and Rose smiled – surprised, but proud.

'I just want to pay it back,' Bean said. 'This is a good idea, Rose. Thanks.'

Rose, flattered, blushed slightly.

241

'And thanks, by the way, for talking to Mrs Landrige about hiring me. That was really nice. You didn't have to.'

'I wanted to help,' Rose said. 'I still do. If you need anything.'

'Naughty, naughty, Beany,' Cordy said, her ticking finger wagging like a metronome again. She had produced a silver cigarette case from the depths of the purse and was holding it open like a locket. When she turned her hands to reveal the contents, Rose blinked.

'You carry your marijuana in that?' Rose asked, nodding at the case, smudged with careless fingerprints but clearly antique, and clearly expensive.

'Well, you have to carry it somewhere,' Bean said.

'That is so true,' Cordy said, mock-serious, as though Bean had just shared the secret of perfect happiness.

'I'd forgotten about it, actually,' Bean said, reaching out to Cordy, who had pushed the pashmina off her head, leaving her looking turtle-like inside the folds of fabric. Our baby sister sniffed one of the joints like a fine cigar.

'Obviously,' Cordy said. 'This is some stale crap.' She passed the case to Bean.

'Beggars can't be choosers,' Bean said.

We cannot believe Rose had never gotten stoned before, but she definitely was now. After all, if she ever would have been, it would have been with us, and by the time Bean and Cordy discovered pot, Rose was in college, and refused to have anything to do with us anyway. The only disappointment here was that Cordy couldn't indulge along with us. We lay on the roof, watching the clouds weave in and out of the blue. Rose rested, fully supine, her feet, broad and pale, dangling off the edge. She felt sleepy and disconnected, and the effort of keeping her eyelids open was too much, so she had let them fall shut, a heavy thud that shut out the world but still left her feeling strangely open.

'Are you going to move to England?' Bean asked Rose.

Rose's jaw felt unbelievably heavy, as though she were moving through sand, and there was a long pause before she responded. 'England is very far away,' she said, her words dreamy and smoky against the push of her lips. 'Very far away.'

'But you're the only one who hasn't been far away,' Cordy pointed out. 'You've never even lived outside of the state.'

This was true. Rose clung to Barnwell, climbing it like a vine on a trellis, tendrils reaching the top before winding their way down again.

'I think it's good to live somewhere else,' Bean said. 'It changes your perspective. I mean, it even changes the way I see Barney now.'

'I like the way I see Barney,' Rose said petulantly, and her lower lip moved into a pout, causing Cordy to giggle. 'Barney is my friend.' This made Cordy giggle even harder.

'But Jonathan's your friend, and he's going to be in England,' Bean pointed out, as though she were talking to a small child, which was precisely the effect the drug seemed to have had on Rose. 'Don't you want to be with Jonathan?'

With a tremendous, languid push, Rose sat up, her eyes still closed. She crossed her legs, yogi-style, her back stiff and straight. She had always had such good posture, which we forgot sometimes, as she hid her body under folds of fabric that made her look prematurely matronly. 'I want to be with Jonathan. I miss him,' she said, and her voice held heavy sadness. 'But I don't want to be in England.'

'You loved England when we went to Stratford,' Cordy said.

'We were on vacation,' Rose said. 'This would be living there. British people all the time.'

'With their funny accents,' Bean said supportively.

'And their weird food,' Cordy added.

'Iago said England was sweet,' Bean said, flicking ashes from her feet, her arms wound tight around her calves.

'I don't think he meant sweet – like, *sweet*!' Cordy said.

'Iago was a liar,' Rose said.

'Forget Iago,' Cordy said. 'I say we take a vote. Everyone who says Rose should move to England, raise your hands.' Bean and Cordy put their hands in the air. 'All opposed?' Rose made no response. 'The ayes have it,' she said triumphantly.

Silence fell for a moment, and then Bean reached out and put her hand gently on Rose's. 'It wouldn't be forever, you know. Maybe it's a sign or something.' Rose snorted lightly, but Bean pressed on. 'Like you were meant to do something else. You'll see when you go visit him. You'll see if it's the right thing.'

'Stop pushing me,' Rose said, her eyes snapping open, pupils hard and dark, crowding out the iris.

She knew they were right. She knew it when she woke in the morning, fresh from dreams where she was locked outside of her classroom, pounding on the door, begging to be let inside. She knew it when she sat in the window seat, staring out at the garden and wondering what was beyond the path she had so neatly trod. Rose was not one to believe in signs, or meanings beyond what she could measure and see, but she couldn't help wondering if someone was whispering something to her, and she couldn't help wondering how long she would be able to refuse to hear it.

Bean looked at our sister and sighed. Cordy leaned forward, wrapping her arms around her knees, her shoulder blades flexing like angel's wings. *'For use almost can change the stamp of nature,'* she said, and leaned her cheek against her knee, looking at Rose.

'What is in my nature that so needs changing?' Rose asked.

No one answered her.

It's a good thing that Cordy had told us she was pregnant when she did, because it was suddenly impossible to ignore, the swell of her stomach no longer attributable to the fact that she was getting actual nutrition instead of existing on noodles and bean sprouts of questionable origins. Her hair had grown thick and dull, her nails stronger, and she caught Bean looking enviously at them when she passed the salt at dinner. Before dressing, Cordy stood naked in front of the mirror, tracing a newly formed road map of shadowy veins across her expanding breasts (another thing Bean looked at enviously). She drank a glass of water every hour, it seemed, standing by the kitchen sink and gulping greedily, desperate to quench this unfamiliar new thirst, and found herself in the bathroom just as often.

Her bloom counterpointed our mother's withering. Our mother had lost a breast; Cordy's grew. Our mother's mouth was dry; Cordy drowned in liquid. Our mother's hair had disappeared, her pale skull hidden underneath an assortment of scarves that made her look curiously glamorous; Cordy's hair grew thicker. Our mother's skin, oddly, glowed; Cordy developed pimples that made her moan in grief, asking whither the much-touted complexion of pregnancy, and how it was possible she should have to deal with wrinkles and pimples at the same time.

Cordy's nausea was fleeting, leaving her hungry and creative. Our mother's was persistent and the smell of food aggravated it most. One night, Cordy had decided to make bread with orange juice instead of milk, and it had turned out so stiff and crumbly the only thing to do with it was make French toast, which she and Rose were working on in the kitchen in the morning.

'Stop!' our father cried, clattering down the stairs. Rose and Cordy, doing nothing more dangerous than dipping bread in eggs and listening to a news show on the radio, froze.

'Your mother can't take the smell,' he said. He was still in his pajamas, his hair gone slightly wild from sleep, his glasses askew. His belly poked out against the pajama shirt. Our parents have always been so formal about dressing for bed; they have never gone the route of nightshirt or sweatpants. Our father wears traditional cotton pajamas with executive stripes, our mother, night-gowns that were more than once pressed into service for various and sundry mad scenes in our theatrical productions.

'Oooookay,' Cordy said, a slice of bread still dripping thick yellow egg into the bowl. Rose sprang into action more quickly, flipping on the fan above the stove with one hand and pulling the pan off the burner with the other.

'Open the window,' Rose demanded. Cordy dropped the bread back in the batter and reached for the window. 'Wash your hands first!'

'Jeezo Pete,' Cordy said. 'Some people sure are bossy.' Our father retreated, a vision in flapping pajama bottoms. We worked in silence for a moment, fanning the invisible scent out the window. Rose took a plate of cooked slices off the counter and dumped it into the trash can. She closed the lid, then reopened it, tied the bag, and took it outside. 'So we can't eat anything with a smell?' Cordy asked.

'Cordy, the woman has cancer. You're upset because you can't have French toast?'

'Who said I was upset? I just want to make sure I understand the rules now.' She headed for the refrigerator and rummaged around, pulling out fresh berries and yogurt.

'Don't be selfish,' Rose said. Cordy paused in the act of mixing the berries into the yogurt, splashes of blue and rose in the white, and stared at our sister. Her mouth gaped open and then closed, sealing the thought inside.

'I'm sorry,' Cordy said finally.

Dan needed his car, so it was Rose who drove Cordy to her doctor's appointment. 'Cordelia Andreas, four o'clock,' Rose barked at the receptionist. The waiting room was filled with women in varying stages of pregnancy, from the long-suffering swollen-anklers to the bright-faced newbies still bothering with makeup. Cordy stood behind Rose. Her pants were too long, and the hems by her heels had gone to threads trailing on the carpet.

'License and insurance?' the receptionist countered, unfazed. We suppose if you are surrounded by hormonal women all day, even Rose is not much of a threat. Rose turned back to Cordy and held out her hand.

Now, Rose would tell you that normal people would know these things were expected, that you might even have the documents in your hand when you approach. Cordy will tell you nothing about her is normal, haw haw haw, so why start here? The other women in the office had proper handbags, sensible black, playful silver. Leather. Cordy had draped her woven bag over one shoulder like a bandolier, and she reached inside, emerging with a book, a tampon that had seen better days, an empty pack of gum, a plastic spoon (in case of a spoon emergency?), the crumpled stub from her last paycheck, and finally, a tiny case functioning as a wallet.

'She doesn't have insurance,' Rose said. 'You brought money, right?' she asked, turning to Cordy. Cordy nodded.

'Okay, she can pay when we schedule her next appointment,' the receptionist said, and bartered Cordy's driver's license for a pile of forms. Rose sailed over to a chair in the corner, Cordy trailing behind, feeling very much like the third wheel. When she sat down, Rose had already clicked her pen officiously and begun filling out the form in her tiny, precise script.

'Are you going to have the exam for me, too?' Cordy asked, more out of curiosity than sarcasm.

Rose, chastened, stopped, and then shoved the clipboard and the pen at Cordy. 'Do it yourself, then. I was just trying to help.' She reached into her own (grown-up) handbag and pulled out a book. Cordy stared hard at her and then completed the form, jamming the pen so hard against the paper that it scratched against the board underneath. The truth was, she was more than a little worried that she couldn't do it without Rose. That she couldn't do any of it without Rose – not the labor or the diaper changing or the cutting off of peanut butter and jelly sandwich crusts. The wanderlust crept up again inside her like a shooting star, a sudden, violent urge to escape disappearing into darkness again. She pushed down the afterglow and focused.

When the nurse called her name, Cordy reached for Rose's hand. 'Come with me,' she said, and her fingers slipped clammy against Rose's.

To say Rose disapproved of Cordy's decision to have this baby would be an understatement. Everything about the idea of Cordy having a baby worried her, from the fact that Rose should have been first, to the fact that she was pretty sure Cordy would flee from responsibility at the first opportunity. But then she looked at Cordy, trembling with the unknown, and she was just our baby sister again, and all she needed was someone to take care of her. 'Okay,' Rose said, and they rose and walked together, hand in hand, into the office.

SIXTEEN

When Edward emerged from the shower, Bean was curled up on the bed reading. She had long ago given up being offended by men who compulsively showered after sex. It was an excellent time to get a little reading done without anyone trying to talk to her.

Edward plucked the book from her hands, his fingers making wet prints on the pulpy pages, a bead of water skidding down the front cover. Glancing at the back cover, he scoffed and tossed it aside. 'So what have you been up to all day?'

'Working.'

Edward flopped onto the mattress, the towel loosening around his waist. The sheet had come loose during their exertions, and he slipped slightly on the silky bare mattress. Bean rescued her book just in time, folding back the corner that had bent when he dropped it. 'What do you think about the two of us getting away for a little while? A long weekend?'

'I can't. I have to work.'

He dropped his face onto his cupped hands for a moment.

'Bianca, surely that disaster of a library can survive without you for a couple of days.'

Bean whacked him fairly sharply on the head with her book, rolling over and pulling the loose sheet over her bare skin. 'I have loved that disaster of a library since I was old enough to read.'

'Fine, fine,' he said, lifting his hands in front of his face to ward off blows. 'I'm sorry.' (He wasn't.) 'Let me begin again. Fair Bianca, I long to journey to the countryside with thee for a few days. Can thy temple of learning spare thee?'

'No,' Bean said, and rolled onto her back, opening her book again. Edward slapped it away, and Bean huffed in frustration. 'What do you want?'

'I want a romantic weekend away with a gorgeous woman.'

Bean's eyes became small and mean. 'Romantic? What exactly made you think I was interested in romance?'

'Every woman is.'

'Don't be so stereotypical. There's nothing romantic about this relationship, Edward. This is a cheap affair.'

He actually had the gall to look hurt, which made Bean feel sorry for him. But only for a moment.

'Is that what you think of me?' His skin was still pink from the shower, and he looked swollen and tired.

Bean sat up and yanked the sheet tighter around herself. 'What do you expect, Edward? This is not the great love of the century. You are, if I may remind you, married to a pretty terrific woman with whom you have some pretty terrific children. This is sex.'

The hurt look stayed. Dear Lord, Bean thought. He'd had some image of himself as a dramatic hero, a scandalously talented older lover to her young(ish) ingenue, and she'd gone and shattered the dream – shattered him – by

251

being honest. She reached out to touch his arm, but his face was already turning cruel.

'You ought to be grateful for this. You're not exactly in your prime anymore, Bianca.' She touched under her chin, unconsciously testing the sag. He saw the weakness and smiled. 'It's not like you have any other offers going, do you?'

Bean flashed back to that night in the bar, the faces turning away from her when someone younger and prettier came in. But he didn't know. She tilted her head, defiant. 'Would you like to test that theory? I imagine only one of us would be sleeping alone.'

Edward bent his arm behind his head and leaned back. Normally, Bean might have curled onto his chest, felt him warm and solid beside her against the coldness inside her. But his face was arch and she felt stiff inside.

'Maybe we should end this,' he said, but she knew he was just trying to get her to come back to him, to apologize. She was suddenly tired, suddenly wanted to be home in her own bed, the sound of our breathing in the rooms around her.

She dropped the open book on her face so she was breathing cheap paper. When she exhaled, the pages hummed like a blade of grass. 'You're being overdramatic.'

And kind of an asshole.

'I don't see why it matters. If this is just a cheap affair, just sex, and you apparently have willing lovers lining up outside the door, then ending it will mean nothing to you.'

Bean squinted at Edward. With his wet hair pushed back, she could see his hairline receding. His chest was puffed out, and a tiny, self-satisfied smile played at the corners of his mouth.

No, Bean thought. His anger didn't make her sad. It made her pity him. She didn't want to be that way – bitter at getting older, living in a movie that played only in her own head, hurting anyone who dared to love her just because she was disappointed in herself. She could be better.

She distracted him the way she knew best – with a flash of bare leg against white sheets, the tumble of hair over her naked shoulders. But she couldn't help but hate herself a little bit as his mouth moved over her skin and she drifted into another night empty of goodness.

'You know, I wasn't a virgin when I married your father.'

'Mom!' Rose said. She dropped the book into her lap, surprised. She had begged us to read to her; the light hurt her eyes too much. Everyone had said that radiation would be easier than chemo, but so far it didn't seem to have been the case. Her skin burned an angry red across her chest, and the medication made her endlessly nauseated. She was constantly exhausted, a bone-deep fatigue she was hard-pressed to explain, but we saw it in the slow movements of her arms, the delayed reaction when sunlight spilled into the room and she tried to turn away, caught in the molasses of the fight inside her body.

Our mother continued, either ignoring or unaware of Rose's discomfort at this particular bit of news. 'I don't know if your father knew. We never talked about it.' She spread her fingers across the covers, the sensation of softness against her aching skin.

'Do you want me to stop reading?' Rose asked, looking for a conversational escape. Our mother turned her head slowly to look at Rose, her eyes watery with pain, exhaustion, diluting the blue another shade toward white.

'Yes,' she said. Rose reached for a bookmark and placed the book on the edge of our father's night table, perfectly aligned with the edges. They sat in silence for a moment, Rose's hands folded neatly in her lap. We looked like our father in so many ways, but Rose and our mother together reflected photographic images of each other,

253

sepia aged. The twist of their hair behind their heads, the tired lines at the corners of their eyes, the gentle slope of their shoulders, the way their mouths compressed in anger.

'It was the boyfriend I had before I met your father. Jack Weston. I loved him – not the way I love your father, you know, but I did love him.' We have seen pictures of this boy, this man who could have been our father. A camping trip in Pennsylvania, green mountains behind him, bare chest sunburned, a casual arm thrown around our mother's shoulders. She is laughing, looking away from the camera, a joke told off-screen, but he stares into the lens, his eyes green and direct, teeth crooked and white against that slightly orange tone of early color photographs.

Rose sat, still waiting for the moment to pass, hoping the meat of the story would not turn out too meaty.

Our mother's breathing was oddly thick and slow, and she paused between her sentences, summoning up the energy to continue. The light between the curtains grew heavy and yellow, sinking toward the horizon. 'I thought we would get married. He was so passionate.' Here Rose tensed, but there was no need. 'He was a dreamer. He believed in a better world. That's why we didn't get married. Not because I didn't want what he did, but because he wanted it more. He signed up for the Peace Corps, to spend a couple of years in Africa. And he wanted me to come.'

Silence again, except for the rusty flow of her breathing. Rose nearly said something, should have asked – would later regret not asking – if our mother was okay, but Rose was too distracted by our mother's sudden unburdening. Our mother's eyes traced back and forth against the crepe of her lids.

'We don't have to talk,' Rose said. She picked up the

book again, ran her thumb up and down the spine, feeling the sharp folds of the cover around the bundle of pages. 'You can tell me later.' Or never. Never's good.

'You need to hear me,' our mother said, her voice suddenly sharp. When she spoke again, it was quieter, lost in the fog of memory or pain. 'I was too scared to go abroad. I couldn't picture myself there. I was scared I'd get sick from the water. Or that I wouldn't be strong enough to do any physical work. Or that I'd be . . . homesick. Something.'

'That's okay,' Rose said. 'I'd be scared, too.'

'Oh, honey,' our mother said. She moved her hand across the covers, feeling blind, and found Rose's fingers, squeezing them tight. 'I know. That's why I'm telling you this.' There was another long pause, and Rose thought she might have fallen asleep. She spent most of the time drifting in and out of semi-sleep, the twilight of anesthesia, as the poisons duked it out inside her.

'You have to go,' she said finally. Rose looked at our mother. Her eyes were still closed, her lips gray and cracked, despite the ice cubes we brought her hour after hour. She ate hardly anything, and drank even less. 'You'll regret it forever.'

This was a previously unseen development. Had we always been so selfish, presuming our parents' lives began only when we did, and ceased, living in suspended animation, when we were outside of their orbit? Were they spinning through their days just like us, a jumble of memories, emotions, wishes, hopes, regrets?

Rose, at that moment, realized that she didn't know our mother at all.

'But I'm scared,' she said, and that admission took so much, made her deflate, feel as exhausted as our mother felt, lying in bed on a perfectly beautiful summer evening, waiting to live again.

'Do one thing every day that scares you,' our mother said. 'Eleanor Roosevelt.' She still held Rose's hand.

'You don't need me here?' Rose asked plaintively.

'Oh, Rosie, of course I love having you here. But what I need is for you to do whatever it takes to make you happy. And you're not happy now, are you?'

'Not at this particular moment, no.'

'Then go,' our mother said, and weakly stroked Rose's hand. 'Go and see what might be. Before it's too late.'

Rose felt tears at the corners of her eyes, as she watched our mother drift into sleep, exhausted by the conversation. But when Rose moved to stand and leave the room, our mother's eyes opened again.

'I'm not sorry I didn't go,' she said quietly. 'But I wish I had. I could have been a different person.'

This was a possibility that had never really occurred to Rose.

'I want you to know I think what you're doing is cosmically stupid,' Bean said to Cordy, who was doing her the kindness of driving her into the city. In the back of our parents' car sat boxes of Bean's city wardrobe, culled and wrapped like harvested sheaves of wheat, ready to be sold to the highest bidder at the consignment store she'd found.

'Thank you!' Cordy said. 'I haven't heard that recently. It's nice to be reminded that I'm maintaining my title for another year.' She flipped the turn signal, drifted into the next lane.

'I'm not done. I also think it's brave. And it's not unprecedented. You were always so good with kids. Not like me.'

'You aren't bad with kids, Bean. You just never enjoyed them very much.'

'But you did. And if you can get all the practical stuff sorted out, you'll be a great mother.'

'Thank you,' Cordy said, her voice softer-edged. 'I'm glad to hear someone supports me.'

'You know they'll support you in the end. And by "they" I mean Dad. Mom's already supportive. She's just too exhausted to care about anything right now, I think.'

'I hope so.' But Cordy's voice was glum, tremulous.

It was so hard, the way our father retreated from Cordy, hiding even more than usual in his study, behind a book, grunting in response to her overtures, drifting through the house near us, but never with us. She had gone from most favored nation to useless ally, from Cordelia to Ophelia.

'Are you going to tell them about you?' Cordy asked. Her eyes remained fixed on the road, unreadable to Bean.

'No!' Bean said, scandalized at the thought. 'Christ, can you imagine?'

'It'd take the pressure off me. I'll do it for you,' Cordy said, a weak joke that made us sick to our stomachs. Other sisters did that kind of thing, probably, but despite our petty conflicts and discomforts, we were not that kind of sisters.

'Cordy, seriously. You can't tell anyone. Ever.'

'You can't just pretend it didn't happen.'

'Pretending? You don't even know. I think about it all the time, Cord. It's the first thing I think of when I get up in the morning and it makes me so sick I just want to vomit.' It makes me so sick I have to spend the night in another woman's bed, using her husband's midlife crisis to make me forget myself.

'I know that feeling,' Cordy said, and she didn't mean just morning sickness, but Bean wasn't listening.

'I hate myself. I hate what I let myself turn into, what I let myself do. It's like the person who did all that didn't even . . . It's like someone I don't even know. Because I wasn't raised like that. I don't have some excuse, like

257

some troubled childhood with a hole I've got to fill. I just did it because I thought I needed it. I thought I deserved it. It's sick.'

'You like him, don't you?'

'What?'

'Father Aidan,' Cordy said. She looked over her shoulder, reflex despite the cardboard blocking her view, moved toward the exit off the highway into the city limits. 'You *like* him like him.'

'What the hell does that have to do with anything I was just saying?'

'Everything,' Cordy intoned.

'Look, he's hot,' Bean said. 'For a priest. But do you think a priest would have me?'

'I don't think priests are supposed to *have* anybody,' Cordy pointed out. She pulled to a stop at the light. Beside us, a man gone ragged from wear held a sign drawn on cardboard. Cordy smiled and shook her head, and he rattled his way down the exit ramp.

'I just like him. As a friend. I think he can help me.'

'Just for the record, fucking is not helping,' Cordy said.

'Shut up,' Bean replied.

'If you want him, you're going to have to break it off with Dr Manning,' Cordy said.

Bean froze. Cordy looked over at her and shook her head. 'Bean, you can't think we wouldn't notice.'

'I didn't . . . It's not . . .' Bean began, but there was nothing to say. Caught, again.

'I don't think you're a bad person, you know. You've done worse things, I'm sure. Hell, I've done worse. But that isn't seriously what you want, is it?'

'No,' Bean whispered, and her throat was thick with tears and guilt. 'I mean, when I'm with him I'm happy, but . . .' She trailed off. She wasn't, of course. Forgetting wasn't the same as being happy. Being drunk wasn't the same as forgetting, and as often as she was literally drunk when she was with him, she was just as much intoxicated by the effort of forgetting everything she had to face.

'No, you're not,' Cordy said cheerfully. 'You're obviously miserable, Bean. We're at our most miserable when we're doing it to ourselves. Sad, but true.'

'Like you're so happy,' Bean said.

'They'll have me whipped for speaking true, thou'lt have me whipped for lying; and sometimes I am whipped for holding my peace.'

'Don't martyr yourself on my account,' Bean snorted, but Cordy's words had the sting of truth.

'I never claimed to be happy. Fortunately, we're not talking about me. We're talking about you. And how you're going to break it off with him. Whether you want Aidan or not.'

'I can't,' Bean said, retreating again.

'You must,' Cordy said. It doesn't make you feel the way you want it to make you feel. It doesn't solve anything. It doesn't make anyone's life any better. It just keeps you from moving on.'

'Moving on to what?' As if there was anything in Barnwell worth moving on to.

'Whoever you're going to become,' Cordy said, as though that solved anything. 'The new Bean.' And then she said, 'New Bean,' again, because it made her giggle.

Meet the new Bean, same as the old Bean.

In New York she and her roommates had had a house-warming party, at which Daisy's boyfriend had been in attendance. As usual, Bean had drunk too much, and the next morning, easing her way back into sunlight, a cautious vampire, Daisy had confronted her in the kitchen. 'Leave Michael alone,' she threatened, the power of her words for once not undercut by the sweet sway of her Georgia accent.

'What?' Bean asked. She was off-kilter, a sailor back on land, and she had to grip the edge of the tiny table to face Daisy. The woman's face had gone so white with anger that her freckles stood out like stars.

'You were all over him last night. My boyfriend.' Daisy jabbed a finger perilously close to Bean's chest. Too exhausted and hungover to focus, Bean had stared at the doughy flesh, noting the unmanicured nails, the wide palm that had stretched the seams of the gloves in her debutante portrait.

'I didn't mean anything by it,' Bean had stuttered, searching her memory for an apology. There was a dim image, a twist of her arm around Michael's shoulder, her mouth near his ear. Her hand went to her face involuntarily. Crap.

'That's your problem, you know? Ya'll just never learned how to deal with a man when you weren't fucking him.' The profanity startled Bean, coming in such sweetly laced syllables. Daisy caught the emotion crossing over Bean's face and nodded, satisfied that her sally had hit the mark. 'Yeah, I've seen it. You slinking around those bars, coming home stinking of cigarettes and beer and who knows what else. But I'm not going to put up with it. Leave. Us. Alone.' Bean had felt so betrayed, so righteously wronged. But Daisy had known her better than she had ever wanted to know herself.

The new Bean. She wanted to laugh, but she was sure that if she did, she would cry without stopping instead. There was no new Bean. There was only the same rotten apple, hiding herself under layers of makeup, lying and stealing – money, another woman's husband. It was all the same thing. She'd sworn to change, but she hadn't. She knelt for communion in church as though she were worthy of it, she went to community service projects as if the darkness inside her wouldn't seep into the foundations of the homes they built, leaving trails of decay under coats of paint. Her stomach lurched, and she put her forehead against the window, letting the air-conditioning against the glass cool off the heat of her skin.

How much lower was she going to go? How many more lies could she tell?

Who was going to save her?

Cordy was right. She had to end it with Edward. And Aidan . . . She pictured his face in her mind, the way he touched her shoulder when they spoke, his shoulders spreading wide and strong when he worked on a house, his warm greeting when he saw her at church with our family.

It wouldn't be so bad to love Aidan, she thought. Something about his presence made her feel clean again, made her feel like someday she could be whole, pulled back from the edge, restored from damage. She wanted that feeling all the time.

Rose had been wrong before when she told Jonathan she thought Bean was after Aidan. Or maybe she'd just been prescient. Because even though Bean hadn't seriously considered him before, she was definitely thinking about it now. And as she thought of him, flipped back through her mind, he grew taller, more handsome, more perfect.

He was the one. He could save her from herself.

SEVENTEEN

Our mother was recovering from her first week of radiation. She'd been tired for so long now, we'd nearly forgotten her any other way. She didn't complain, though we knew she'd been having chest pains, and even the tiniest effort seemed to exhaust her.

Bean was working, and Rose had gone into town, leaving Cordy alone with our parents. When our father had brought our mother home, she had seemed tired, but she played a game of Scrabble with Rose, and walked in the garden, and sat down with us at dinner, though she ate hardly anything, her presence serving mostly to smooth the rumpled silence between Cordy and our father.

The next morning, Cordy awoke to the sound of our mother vomiting, and though she had lately been doing the same thing herself, this seemed worse, desperate and painful in a way hers was not, uncomfortable as it was. Cordy stumbled out of bed, her hair tangled in the loose bun she slept in, T-shirt speckled with holes, and pajama pants tied loosely at her hips, and felt her way, sleep-blind, into our parents' room.

How old were you when you first realized your

parents were human? That they were not omnipotent, that what they said did not, in fact, go, they had dreams and feelings and scars? Or have you not realized that yet? Do you still call your parents and have a one-sided conversation with them, child to parent, not adult to adult?

Cordy, we think, figured this out at the moment she saw our mother lean back against the bed, our father's arm around her shoulders, her mouth wet with saliva, her skin gone white and papery in the unforgiving arm of sun reaching through the curtains. Our father put down the silvery bowl we had all used, at some point, when in the grips of some awful intestinal trauma. The hollow clang against the bedside table made Cordy shiver with memory. Our father dabbed our mother's forehead, then her mouth, with a wet washcloth, and she smiled at him, and he smiled back, and then she closed her eyes.

'Is she okay?' Cordy asked, her voice no more than a whisper. Our father shifted on the bed, turning to see her, and she thought how he always looked surprised to see us, as though he had not known us for our entire lives. *Who goes there?*

He took off his glasses, wiped them unnecessarily with the handkerchief he kept in his pocket for these purposes – such a gentleman, our father – and replaced them, peering at Cordy as though clearer lenses might resolve the mystery of her presence. To that, we have this to say: Good lucky, Daddy-o. 'She'll be all right,' he said. 'I think it's just the medications.' He looked slightly disappointed at this news, as though the chemical chains present in the pills had let him down on a deep and personal level.

'Can I help?' Cordy asked. She stepped forward cautiously, bare foot lapping over the ridge between the wide-slatted floorboards and the edge of the rug, gone bare at the edges from wear. Beside her, fingers fluttering, birds in flight.

'Come here,' our father said, and patted the bed on the other side of our mother. She did not open her eyes, but she smiled thinly when she felt Cordy sit down.

'Hi, Mommy,' Cordy said, and our father handed her the washcloth, which she dabbed carefully along our mother's jawline, her mouth. She had always had such beautiful skin, taut and fuzzed softly like fruit, the tiniest freckles along the bridge of her nose (none of us had inherited those and how bitter we were about it), petals blooming in her cheeks. Our father stood and went to the bathroom, Cordy listening to the familiar clank of that bowl against the sink, the way it rang as he rinsed it out. 'Do you need anything?'

'No, honey, thank you. I'm just tired.' Her eyes were still closed, flicking slightly under the blue-veined tissue paper of her eyelids. 'Will you make your father some breakfast?' She paused, licked her lips. 'And then maybe you can come up here and read to me.'

'Sure,' Cordy said. She kissed our mother's forehead, gone cool and clammy, and stood up gently, careful not to move the bed. The air was cool in their room still, and she adjusted the thick white comforter before she pulled the curtains shut, blocking out the inquisitive rays playing their way, like fingers on a keyboard, across the covers. Cordy had always had this way about her, a calm willing-ness to accept what came. We had too often stolen toys from her chubby fingers before she had the motor skills or the will to fight back. But we would be dishonest if we said it did not still her to see our mother lying that way on the bed. Savasana. Corpse pose.

In the kitchen, Cordy clanked and fussed, cracking eggs, dicing vegetables for an omelet, considering the tiny bottles of spices. Rose alphabetized the jars and cans in her kitchen.

Here, they were piled against each other, drunken sailors spilling drifts of dried leaves across the bottom of the cabinet.

'She's sleeping,' our father announced gruffly, making his way into the kitchen. He must have gone out already, the paper was unfolded, a mug of coffee gone cold beside it. He lifted the front section as Cordy deftly slipped a plate onto the table, golden omelet flecked green and white with onions and peppers from the garden. 'Thank you,' he said, looking at her and then back at the plate, pondering the mystery of how the girl and the meal were connected.

'You're welcome,' Cordy said. She poured and cooked another omelet, eased it onto her plate, and joined him at the table. Our father hid behind the paper, but she heard the sounds of his silverware, the grimacing swallow as he drank his coffee, bitter and black.

As a child, Bean had developed a tremendous aversion to the sound of chewing. At the breakfast table, faced with the melodious crunching of our entire family's teeth working against their cereal, she would grow furiouser and furiouser until she stood and stomped off to eat elsewhere, in peace. Cordy had never been bothered like this. She loved the symphonic harmony of people eating, the gentle sigh of pleasure at the meeting of taste and bud, the percussive notes of cutlery.

'I really like working at the coffee shop,' she said, apropos of nothing. Our father lowered the paper, brows down, and stared at our sister. 'I was just thinking, I love all the sounds. Like the steamer, and the bell on the door, and the conversations. I can work, and I can just listen to all those sounds around me, and it's kind of comforting, you know?'

'*If music be the food of love,*' our father said, and gave a short smile. Cordy took it, a crumb. He went back to his paper. She felt tears sting in her eyes. It had never been like this. He had always listened to her stories, asked her to share her dreams, laughed the hardest at her jokes. Now it seemed he could hardly bear to hear the sound of her voice, couldn't even be civil enough for small talk.

Cordy was sure we were wrong. He wasn't going to come around. Maybe not ever.

How had she never known how good she had it until it was gone?

She finished eating in silence, the food tasteless in her mouth, and went back upstairs while our father did the dishes. She stood for a moment, watching our mother rest, the quiet rustle of her breath in and out. Is this what it would be like? Wondering always if what you were doing was right, was enough, was tender and gentle and caring enough to soothe pains and nourish hopes? A little pulse of panic fluttered around her heart at the thought of so much importance. At least here we could pick up after Cordy when she left things undone. But a baby would be hers. Hers alone.

She shifted slightly. When she heard the creak of Cordy's feet on the floor, our mother opened her eyes. 'Did he eat something?' she asked. This is our mother. The four horsemen of the Apocalypse could be bearing down hard and fast upon us, and she would want to make sure our father had eaten. So he wouldn't, you know, get hungry in the afterlife or something.

'Aye,' Cordy said. *'The duke hath dined.'* She looked at our mother more closely. 'Are you okay? You look kind of' – she waved her hand – 'funny.'

Our mother sighed. 'I'm fine. Just tired, as usual. And hungry.'

'Do you want something to eat?' Cordy turned to head back to the kitchen.

266

'No thank you, honey. Even if I could keep it down, everything tastes like metal these days. It's awful.'

'Oh.' Cordy turned back and walked toward the bed. 'You want me to read to you now?'

'That would be lovely,' our mother said.

Cordy picked up the book on our mother's bedside table. 'Tolstoy?' she asked suspiciously.

'I figured I'd have a lot of time,' our mother said, and smiled wryly. We are notorious for our efforts to read the (non-Shakespearean) classics, but are similarly notorious, with certain exceptions, for our inability (or unwillingness) to finish them.

Cordy nodded, hopping up on our father's side of the bed rather enthusiastically, and apologizing at our mother's grimace. 'You haven't started it yet?' she asked.

'No. Your father was being dreadfully bibliographic at the clinic, so we watched a movie. Something about a dog.' Cordy knew exactly what our mother meant. Occasionally our father would get in a mood, particularly while reading something complex, where he would harrumph repeatedly, and then stop at random intervals to read the quotes aloud, as if to say, 'Can you believe this malarkey?' Not that he is likely to use the word 'malarkey'.

Cordy nodded, opened the book. Our mother turned her head, her hair spilling across the pillow, and looked at her. 'My baby,' she said, smiling up at her, and Cordy touched her hand to her stomach. 'My baby,' our sister said.

Because you know our family now, you will not be surprised that when our father broke the ice, he did so with a note. And you will similarly not be surprised this was not a note written, but a photocopied page of his *Riverside*, lines gone carefully over with highlighter.

Polonius to Ophelia. Our father had once written a paper pulling apart the advice given to Laertes (*This above all: to thine own self be true* – the same lines he had quoted to Rose) and that given to Ophelia (roughly: don't sleep with Hamlet, you ninny). Now, given the way things turn out for Laertes and Ophelia, we have always figured that despite the gender inequity inherent in these two exchanges, Polonius was spot-on in both instances, and Ophelia really ought to have listened. After all, Hamlet = bat-shit crazy, and apparently it was catching.

But these words were more tender than we have admitted, and in our father's gift to Cordy, they seemed innocent and kind. *'You speak like a green girl, Unsifted in such perilous circumstance . . . Tender yourself more dearly . . . I do know, When the blood burns, how prodigal the soul lends the tongue vows: these blazes, daughter, Giving more light than heat, extinct in both, Even in their promise, as it is a-making . . .'*

Cordy gripped this paper in her hands, sitting in the shadowed alley behind the Beanery. A year ago, this would have been her cigarette break, but now was simply a moment where she leaned against the gritty sharpness of the brick wall to inhale the scent of aging garbage. Her apron was marked with incomplete handprints, as though she had recently been assaulted by a floury, three-fingered monster. She had unfolded, read, refolded it how many times now? The paper was already going soft along the creases from her sweaty palms.

Here's one of the problems with communicating in the words of a man who is not around to explain himself: it's damn hard sometimes to tell what he was talking about. Look, the sheer fact that people have banged out book after article after dramatic interpretation of this guy should tell you that despite his eloquence, he wasn't the clearest of communicators. Not that any of us would ever say this to our father, but we had certainly thought it.

Cordy knew our father thought she was making a mistake, being immature, juvenile, that this was a passing fancy. And this assumption of juvenility was largely her fault. All her life, she had reveled in the favored daughter status, had taken pleasure in being the beloved baby, and here was the other side of that double-edged sword. Who would believe her now, when she said she had decided to be a grown-up?

'Cordy!' Dan called from inside. She put her hand to her face, feeling the burn of old humiliations. Who was she kidding? Our unspoken admonitions burned around her, swirled, twisting through her hair and blurring the edges of her sight. Had she ever succeeded in anything besides drifting, which was no accomplishment in and of itself? Long ago, she had thought bravery equaled wandering, the power was in the journey. Now she knew that, for her, it took no courage to leave; strength came from returning. Strength lay in staying.

She opened the screen door leading into the kitchen – once, long ago, the Beanery had been a restaurant, and Cordy had begun to eye the industrial ovens cannily, wondering – and listened to the squeak and the slam behind her. Ahead, the tiled floor spread narrow into a hallway, and then wider behind the counter. She walked toward it like a nervous bride.

'Hey,' Dan said, and he smiled at her. Cordy, like a pup kicked too many times, relaxed. 'I've got a couple of sandwiches need making.' He nodded at a mother and daughter sitting at tables across the way. A high school student on a tour, it looked like. They sat stiffly, looking around, the mother judging, the daughter trying it on. This could be where I come on a date. This could be where my friends and I hang out after classes.

269

'Chicken salad on croissant, turkey on focaccia.' He handed her the order slip and a wink, and Cordy set to work.

When she had finished the sandwiches, split them neatly on a plate, pickle slice, potato chips, watermelon cubes arrayed in an edible bouquet, she walked them over. 'It's so small,' the mother said, her fingers fiddling absently with her straw. 'I'm not sure you could get used to being so far away from . . . everything.'

Cordy's ears snagged on this statement, and a million thoughts rushed to her mind, but she simply smiled, set the plates down. Her approval wouldn't have mattered anyway. The girl was like Bean, she could see, full of her own dreams and demands and ideas, and who wouldn't fall in love with a place like Barney anyway? The evocative wide-stoned walls of Main, the bowed original staircases of Rubin, the skylights in the Student Union, deceptively alluring during summer campus tours, threatening in the depths of winter, the spread of the Quad, soft green in the shade of the maple trees. The campus is gorgeous, and lesser girls than she have fallen for its siren song.

'You live here, right?' the mother asked, and it took Cordy a moment to realize the woman had addressed her.

'Yes. Born and raised.'

The mother raised her eyebrows and nodded slightly at her daughter, as if to say, 'You see what befalls people from a place like this?'

'Isn't it difficult, being so isolated?' the mother asked.

Cordy hesitated. She couldn't have cared less whether the girl came to Barney or not, but it seemed so unfair not to let her try it on for a little while, to stand in front of the mirror and turn this way and that, modeling the possibility of her future.

She turned toward the daughter, uncomfortable in her

270

interview clothes, a green suit that hemmed in whatever personality she had. 'It's true, Barney is a bit isolated. But you'd be amazed how the campus comes alive during the school year. There are a million things happening – the admissions office usually has a calendar they can give you to show you what a week might look like – and if you want to take advantage of it, you can.' She found herself consciously guarding her accent, watching the betraying Midwestern vowels. 'I think you'd find most people who go to college in a city are so wrapped up in the campus anyway they don't go out much. And as a college student, you'd be too poor anyway.'

The daughter gave her a grateful smile. The mother looked cold.

'And besides, we're only an hour from the city. Enjoy your lunch.' She smiled and headed back behind the counter. Dan was in his office, flipping through papers and sighing, so she set herself to work. Pushing her hip against the counter as she cleaned, she felt the crinkle of paper in her pocket and pulled out our father's note again. She knew he was not warning her away from sex – it was completely obvious it was too late for that – so from what?

The towel in her hand drew circles on the counter, cold white imitation marble traced with gray veins. She remembered herself, maybe eight? When Bean and Rose had begun to draw away from her again, when she had become a less amusing plaything as she developed a will of her own. Rose had begun her quest for her Shakespearean prince, and Bean had become involved with anything more interesting than Cordy, who was so useless she could not even be bothered to remember to finish doing her hair, and consequently ran around with one ponytail and one loose shock of hair flopping against her neck on the opposite side.

271

Finding herself abandoned like that was lonely, somewhat stunning. She threw herself into books, emulating each character she met. She read a story about a girl who read in her closet while eating chocolate-chip cookies, so she did that. She read her way through Nancy Drew and the Hardy Boys, and looked for clues everywhere she went, noting them down in her *Harriet the Spy* notebook, though she found their unwillingness to add up to anything a perennial disappointment. She tried to run away, emulating a million children in a million books, but she and her suitcase, printed with the image of a little old-fashioned girl in a bonnet, never made it past the rhododendrons before she lost her nerve.

She never managed to find herself in these books no matter how she tried, exhuming traits from between the pages and donning them for an hour, a day, a week. We think, in some ways, we have all done this our whole lives, searching for the book that will give us the keys to ourselves, let us into a wholly formed personality as though it were a furnished room to let. As though we could walk in and look around and say to the gray-haired landlady behind us, 'We'll take it.'

The idea of the magic set came from a novel about a boy whose magic set turned out to be really magic, and led him on adventure after adventure into strange worlds, guided by his tiny plastic wand and rescued from peril with a multicolored scarf, or a Gordian knot of string.

Our family was not big on store-bought things. This was part of our parents' somewhat indeliberate effort to opt out of consumer culture, symbolized by their anti-television stance. Our toys were hand-me-downs, too, puzzles with missing pieces, blocks that never fit together quite right, our dolls not name-brand, their clothes made by our mother on her sewing machine. Our parents

272

greeted Cordy's request for the magic set with skepticism and the surety that she would cast it aside quickly in favor of the next internal fad.

Except she didn't. She begged and begged and begged for it, until finally, on her birthday, she was rewarded with one of those rarest of all gifts in our house: something shrink-wrapped.

Mastering the tricks didn't take long; the set had been made, like the book from whence the fascination had come, for a younger child. She trailed us around the house, knocking on Rose's closed door, begging for admittance, digging a skirt she used as a cape out of the dress-up box and putting on a show for us in the basement. And then, a few days later, it was forgotten. In Cordy's defense, the tricks had been somewhat flimsy; the beads slipped off the string and rolled away under one of the couches (where, we assume, they remain to this day), the wand lost its lovely white tip. But soon she had moved on to another fascination: a doll with hair that grew so she could learn how to braid.

Abracadabra.

This was it, of course. To this day, when she expressed interest in something, someone in the family would invoke the cursed magic set, with a roll of the eyes as if to say, 'Oh, there she goes again.' So to us, the baby was another magic set, another afternoon eating chocolate-chip cookies in the closet, reading by the light of the flashlight.

But it wasn't.

Was it?

A pair of students working on campus for the summer came by and ordered iced coffee. As they moved away from the counter, Cordy went to put the money in the till, her fingers pausing on the bills. She'd never stolen like Bean had stolen, but if her boss was particularly awful,

273

she wasn't above mis-ringing a few orders and pocketing the difference, especially if it meant the difference between a bus ticket and hitchhiking her way out of town.

Why had she defended this place? It was a trap. Our father was tying silken cords around her ankles, tying her to Barnwell with his impenetrable messages. Our mother held her hands with her sickness. And we tripped each other up with our pasts, made mincemeat of the future with our thousand failures. Cordy felt stifled by her anger, felt an urge, an itch, a burn to get out, to be anywhere but here.

Oxford, in summer, was not as Rose had expected. The City of Dreaming Spires, where she imagined students rushing to class clad in robes, professors discussing earnestly the teleology of Plato's *Republic*, yards of ale, and serene campuses bedecked with gargoyles and stern English gardens, was busy and well-touristed and more modern than she had hoped. Through the film of jet lag, she found the motion exhausting, overwhelming, and it made her understand, for the first time, the wisdom in a quiet cup of tea or a mid-morning pint.

When she arrived, she threw herself into Jonathan's arms, the stress of the flight, the absent months, her own heartbeat, collapsing in a pile of sticks when she saw him. Her body, confused by the lack of sleep, by the bright sun when there should be darkness (and where was the rain? wasn't it supposed to always be raining in England?), moved on its own.

They took the train to Oxford, her eyes bouncing from Jonathan to the blur of pastoral land out the window. At home, she had watched the suburbs grow farther and farther from the city, the gap between their tiny tracts and the wide fields of Barney growing less and less, and something in her lurched and prayed at the green space she saw here, the stone houses left free from progress, the simplicity of a flock of sheep.

How like a winter hath my absence been from thee! Rose thought as she felt the warmth of his body beside hers, his warm, dry palm in her cold one. They arrived at his rooms, fell into bed, and rediscovered each other. After, she lay with her head on his chest, allowing herself to feel small, feminine, protected, the splay of her hand on his beating heart. She dozed, he woke her with gentle reminders of the dangers of sleeping through her first day, she dozed again.

They went to dinner embarrassingly early, Rose still dizzy from exhaustion and newness. Jonathan led her into a pub, its beamed ceilings so low she had to bend when she crossed from one room to another, the staircase to the second floor more like a crawl space than a passage. 'The oldest pub in England!' Jonathan announced, or maybe it was the oldest pub in Oxford. It was not fair to test her comprehension at that moment. He ordered a couple of pints at the bar, and they climbed upstairs. They sat down across a table, battered and scarred, burned dark between the scrapes, and held hands. She had not forgotten what he looked like, but seeing him in person, she realized what she had lost in memory was the intensity, the precise deep of his eyes, the geometric angle at which his perpetual cowlick rose, the burn of his skin on hers.

'I'm so glad to have you here,' he said. 'You don't know how I've missed you.'

Her smile matched his, a quiet blush in her cheeks. 'I've missed you more,' she said. 'Going through all this without you has been so hard.'

'How is your mom?' he asked, his brows pulling together.

'She was better, but the radiation has made her so tired. She just seems miserable.'

Jonathan exhaled. 'I'm so sorry.'

'You'd think by now they'd be able to come up with a better solution than poison.' She looked up at him, smiled. 'You're a scientist. You fix it.'

He lifted their hands and slipped his fingers through hers so they pressed palm to palm. 'You know full well that's not my area. But I can assure you they're working on it.'

'Not in time for her,' Rose said.

In time for us?

'How's she feeling, you know, mentally?'

'She rests a lot, and we read to her, and that's what she needs most of all. If Bean and Cordy . . .' She stopped herself.

'Bean and Cordy what?'

'Well, I was going to say if Bean and Cordy would help more, but that's not fair. They've actually been tremendously helpful, both of them. Surprisingly.'

'Mmm.'

'I'm still with her more, but they're working. So I guess I understand.' Rose felt a stab of guilt at this assessment, but she was so used to criticizing us she could not stop herself.

'And how's Cordy . . . progressing?'

Rose pulled her hands from his and took a sip of her drink. In some ways she hated talking about us with Jonathan. He was so damn level-headed.

He saw her hesitation. 'Be fair, now.'

'Physically, she's fine. I took her to the doctor and she's healthy and everything's as it should be. She's actually managed to keep the job. But . . .' She took another sip. Jonathan curled his hands around his own glass, and she marveled at the beauty of his fingers, loved him anew. 'But I worry about her. She asked so few questions at the doctor's, she doesn't know who the father is, and doesn't

276

really seem to care, and the job at the coffee shop is fine for now, but she can't live on that with a baby, and it's totally unfair to ask our parents to support her when they've got their own problems.'

Jonathan nodded, said nothing.

'She's not ready to have a baby,' Rose said.

'She's not ready to have the baby the way you would,' he said.

'Ouch.'

'No, I mean it. You know one of the things I love the most about you is your ability to marshal everything – tangible and intangible – into some semblance of order. But that's the Rose way. That's not the Cordy way.'

'I'm afraid the Cordy way won't be enough.'

'Cordy's survived this long, in circumstances that would have had you running for the hills long ago. Obviously she's figured out some kind of way to take care of herself.'

'But we're not talking about taking care of herself. We're talking about taking care of the baby. I'm scared for her. I don't want it to be hard for her.'

'Exactly,' he said, smiling. She found him maddening that way, serene in the face of the storm. His peace made it impossible for her to have anything to rail against. She shook her head. 'And what of fair Bianca?'

When Bean had confessed her sins to us, she had begged for our secrecy, but Rose had been unable not to tell Jonathan. So he knew the whole sordid story, or as much as Bean had told us, at least. 'She's better. She's gotten quite involved at Saint Mark's. Going to do service projects, hanging out with Father Aidan. It's like a conversion.'

'There are no atheists in foxholes,' Jonathan said.

Rose considered that, looking around. 'I'd like to think that's all it is. But Father Aidan is handsome . . .'

'Bean?' He clutched his heart in mock horror. 'Getting

involved with something for a man? I'm shocked you would suggest such a thing.'

'Believe it,' she said. 'Though I have the feeling she's going to be tremendously disappointed when she discovers he probably adheres to that whole no-sex-outside-of-marriage thing.'

'Ah, it'll be good for her,' Jonathan said.

'She's working on paying it back, too. I don't know – I thought she might just go into hiding, but she's really working to make amends.'

'So maybe she is genuinely repentant,' Jonathan said.

'Maybe. I hope so.'

He reached out, covered her hand with his own, smiled at her in that way she never could resist. Oh, she knew he was not the most handsome man in the world, not the one whom women would pause on the street to watch walking by, but to her, he was the only light in the sky. 'See, I told you people can change. It's not so hard.'

If Rose had not been so busy leaning in to kiss him, to taste the ale on his lips, to luxuriate in the fact of being able to touch him rather than holding herself as his voice whispered across the ocean, she might have questioned that idea. Change was the hardest thing of all.

EIGHTEEN

It was all Bean's idea. We were fifteen, twelve, nine. None of us, obviously, had a driver's license. Occasionally, if it was a clear day and we were in no hurry, our father would pull over by the side of the road and let Rose drive on one of the wide country roads surrounding Barney, spreading out in ropes of black licorice away from the town. On all sides lay pastures, cows looking balefully at us as we sped by. Though 'sped' would be the wrong term, as Rose never wanted to take the car above twenty-five miles per hour. Boys in sports cars with T-tops would whiz by, screaming, music exploding from the windows, making her hands jerk on the wheel, ten and two.

But Bean had barely been given this chance – maybe twice, three times. Our parents were out of town, our father speaking at a conference where serious professors would assiduously take notes on each pearl he cast before them, and then go drinking in the hotel bar, stumbling to their rooms full of wine and paled purpose. Our grandparents were with us, but Nana and Pop-Pop had long ago reached the age where their bedtimes aligned with ours, and the excitement of the change in the house had made us too wired to sleep.

Rose was in bed, lost in the world of *Treasure Island,* when she heard Bean and Cordy giggling in the next room. Their growing friendship frightened her, made her freeze, terrified of being left behind. Throwing back the sheet, clean and white in the cast of the reading lamp, she placed her toes on the floor and padded over to Bean's room. The door stood open, a wedge of light pooling on the hall floor, and she hesitated, hand on the knob, before she opened it and slipped in, the squeak of the hinges announcing her arrival.

Bean and Cordy were changing, bodies still flat and futile, slipping on jeans and T-shirts and sneakers.

'Come on,' Bean said to Rose, for if we made her our ally, she would not stop us. 'We're going to the Deee-Lite.'

'Now?' Rose asked. Whatever she had pictured us getting up to, certainly it had not been this. 'It'll take an hour to walk there.' The Deee-Lite was at the other end of town, where the houses turned to cornfields, all dark and empty at that time of year.

Bean and Cordy turned to each other and giggled. Cordy slipped on her shoes. 'We're taking the car,' she said, and for some reason, this struck us as hilarious again, and we laughed so hard we thought for sure Nana and Pop-Pop would wake up.

Of course Rose tried to talk us out of it, but there was something about that night, about the snap of fall in the air – the Deee-Lite would close for the winter the next week (a regular occurrence, not our fault) – about the freedom we felt with our parents far away and our grandparents innocently asleep down the hall. And we think it had something to do with the three of us alone together, so rare and beautiful that it made our insides hum like the strings of a guitar.

But when she saw we were going with or without her, she decided to come. To keep us safe, she said.

And now that we think about it, how stupid were we? How foolish was it for three girls, only one of whom had any real driving experience to speak of, none of it at night, all far too young to be going out into the darkness where there were boys in fast cars and girls in short skirts dragging the strip, in search of a little danger to break the monotony? We have now done a million things more foolish than that night, but it still makes us shake our heads.

But we didn't know that then. All we knew was that we were wild and venturesome, and the night was ours, and there was power in the three of us, the Weird Sisters, hand in hand.

Rose made a big deal out of everyone taking her jacket, as though it were some sort of talisman, a charm against the sheer idiocy of our action. And she knew it was crazy and stupid, and completely unlike her, and conceivably that is why she agreed to go along with it.

When we had all dressed, we went out the front door, holding our breath as we walked on the boards that were sure to creak and betray us, opening the heavy door and hearing the aching squeal of the screen door, not yet taken down from summer. Rose carried the keys, because we had bargained that she would drive. She had never actually started the car before, and she let the engine grind hard for a moment before she took her hand off the key and found the headlights and we pulled out into the darkness.

Bean had called shotgun and was flipping through the radio stations, something that, typically, was absolutely Not Allowed, until she found a pop song she liked, and we rolled down the windows and we crept out of town with the music swirling around us, and we felt like we were in a movie, and this was the soundtrack for our great escape. All around us, the houses were dark and still, but as we drove by the dorms, we heard lights and music, and that energized us and made us feel part of a world where things happened and three girls could sneak out of the house to hit the open road and everything would be okay, and we could be anyone – Rose especially; we did not have to be ourselves anymore, but someone thrilling and fearless.

Every time we hear that song we think of that night, and how happy we were. Bean looked over at Rose, her hands gripping the wheel, forehead tight with concentration as the streetlights flipped across her face, light and dark, light and dark. In the back, Cordy leaned against the seat, singing along and staring out the window.

When we passed out of the town limits, Bean suddenly pushed her head out the window, threw herself into the night down to her shoulders, and howled wildly at the moon. Scared the crap out of Rose, too. Then Cordy clambered over to the side and held her hand as we raged against the dying of the light, and behind us, Rose's nattering criticisms turned to laughter, and then we joined her in laughing in the face of the darkness. A half a mile of quiet pasture lay between the end of town and the Deee-Lite, but it felt like the world spread wide before us, our futures and our open lives.

It felt unnatural and pedestrian to come down from our giddy high and find ourselves in the parking lot of the Deee-Lite, where the families had long since gone home and the pavement had become a place where romances kindled and extinguished, where rumors spread and friendships were destroyed or cemented, where this all-American life outside Barney and the Coop and our no-television world spun its thread. And though we each in our way wanted to be part of that world and all its shiny idealism – Bean with her teen magazines, Rose with her romances, Cordy with her curious dreams – we

282

realized we could be so much more than that, the way we were that night.

The ice cream was only important to Cordy, we think. She got sprinkles on a twist cone, and Bean had a banana split, and Rose, assuredly, had vanilla, and paid for all three with her allowance money. She spent more money than anyone else, but she always seemed to have the most, too. Rose, parsimonious, would count the coins carefully out of her hand as though she were allotting parts of herself to the disinterested cashier, but she had never denied us anything we asked for, either.

We let Cordy get a large cone, something our parents always refused on the grounds that it would give her a stomachache (and may we just point out that they were absolutely correct). But she ate the whole damn thing anyway, leaving her mouth covered with sprinkles and dried soft serve, and her hands sticky and smelling of milk. Rose and Bean were talking and laughing, while Cordy ran circles around one of the tables outside, the plastic ones with the cockeyed umbrellas, making herself sicker by the second.

There might have been a full moon. Certainly when we think back, we remember it as so tremendously bright; images coming in sharp relief, museum-perfect, display-lit. And that, too, might have had something to do with the mood, the way even Rose, perfect as a petal, came with us, and laughed when we were about to kill ourselves hanging out the window, and whispered and joked with Bean about the boys who skulked past, loose hips and curled lips. Cordy lay back on one of the tables, her head hanging upside down over the edge, and watched as Bean sauntered over to a trash can, pebble and plastic, coming scandalously close to a couple of boys who were smoking, watching the parade. Rose covered her mouth, laughing silently as Bean swished her nonexistent hips, and of

283

course you know the boys' silent eyes followed her, the way they would for years to come.

We were so happy when we got back in the car to come back. It seemed the danger had been in the leaving, and the going home was simply a task to be performed. So maybe that was why Rose gave Bean the keys. Or maybe because we felt so close at that moment, full and sleepy and sweet-sick on ice cream, our baby sister running like a released Ariel around us, her hair flying in the darkness, while we played at being girls other than us. And maybe because we had gone there a million times, driven that road a million more, we knew every inch of fence and pavement, every straggle of grass, and Barney had always made us feel safe and contained.

But whatever the reason, she did it, and Rose sat back in the passenger seat and told her what to do, and watched her do it, and we didn't feel unsafe, even then. Cordy lay in the back, her hands on her bloated belly, moaning softly to herself, and Rose turned the radio down.

At first Bean pressed too hard on the accelerator, and we bucked and shook out of the parking space and then screeched to a halt at the edge of the lot as she looked right and left. Wild in the wind, a motorcyclist came in beside us, the shriek of rubber on the pavement, the flatulent rev of the engine, and she started, taking her foot off the brake and allowing the car to drift into the road. Rose inhaled sharply, gripping the edge of the seat, but Bean placed her foot firmly on the pedal, and then accelerated.

The pleasure in driving is lost the more you do it, but that night it was fresh and cold independence, and we sped down the road, faster than technically prudent, and Bean hardly saw the shape of the deer leaping over the pasture fencing and into the headlights.

Rose saw it. She swears she did, she saw it an instant

284

before Bean did, but she couldn't even open her mouth to scream, it was that fast, and then the heavy thud of the impact, and the squeal of the brakes and the way the car fishtailed crazy into a fencepost. In the back, Cordy slid off the seat and ended up arched over the tiny hump on the floor, bumping her head on the door handle as she went. She cried, of course, but when Bean and Rose opened the doors and went shrieking out into the night, she pulled herself up and came out behind us, one tiny slick tear trail cutting through the ice cream on the side of her cheek, looking pitiful and confused. It struck us as we stood there that the amount of trouble we were going to be in was immeasurably large. This was the worst thing we had ever done. Even our parents, who were incapable of consistently applying groundings or time-outs or any punishment more severe than a stern talking-to, were going to have to do something.

'I was driving,' Rose said. Oh, Rose – sensible even in the face of disaster, and don't think we don't love her for it. But Bean didn't even hear; she was standing in the middle of the road, her hands pinned to her mouth in horror. The deer lay just to the side of the thick yellow lines down the middle of the road, as if obeying the signs: this is a NO PASSING zone. A doe, still a rich butter-chocolate brown from the summer, a patch of white at the base of her neck. Every time she lifted her head, trying vainly to move her body, the white fur flashed like a star in the headlights.

Rose tried to keep Cordy from seeing it, but she struggled out from under Rose's firm hands and stepped into the road. She reached for Bean, who stood, still silent, panting under her cupped hands, staring at the deer, watching its death throes, hearing its quiet groan, a plea for assistance. Bean refused Cordy's touch, turned away from her, but her eyes were still locked with the doe's.

285

One of its legs was broken and there was blood on the pavement.

Who knows how long we stood in the road, shell-shocked, sugar-shocked, until the police cruiser came by. We knew the deputy, Officer Franklin; he had breakfast at the diner next to the bookstore, and when he walked by us on the street, he'd pull a quarter from one of our ears and make us laugh. He was young, and we would ask if we could try on his hat, partly to laugh at the way the wide brim slipped down over our foreheads, and partly to see the vulnerable pink of his scalp under his crew cut.

The spinning lights of his cruiser turned the silent road into a carnival ride, spinning blue and red and whirling us around. He looked at us, at the car, at the empty spaces where our parents should be, and then he looked at the deer, the patch of white fur going red – from blood or from the cruiser's lights, we can't say. Without saying a word, he walked back to his car, his heels a heavy *click-clack* on the road, and he returned with a shotgun. There was the heavy metal slap of the barrel as he pumped it. We all watched, the three of us, as he raised the gun, looking at us over the stock, and his voice was gravelly when he said, 'You girls need to look away now.' And we did.

He must have been a good shot, because for a moment there was just the scrabble of the doe's hooves on the road, and then sharp thunder, echoing again and again into the night and making our ears ring, and then nothing. Cordy ran to the side of the road, gripping the sharp edge of the wire fence in her hands, and she vomited her ice cream into the pasture.

We never did anything like that again. Any of it.

We think about that night often, but what comes back to us isn't the terrible ending but how free and happy we were together, and how we felt like together we could do anything, rule the world and damn the consequences.

We remember the open windows, the breeze pushing hard against our skin, howling into the night, the sound of that song fighting the scream of the wind and the tires on the pavement, the way Rose stood strong and steady, protecting us from harm, and we remember the promise we made never to hurt anything ever again, and we wonder where those girls went, if they died with the doe that night on the road, or if they would have disappeared anyway.

NINETEEN

I know,' our father said, wiping corn kernels from his
beard, turning birds out of the nest, 'illegitimacy does
not carry the stigma it once did. But it seems to me a
capitally bad idea to bring a child into the world without
a father.'

'My baby has a father,' Cordy said. 'It's not going to
spring fully grown from my head.' They were alone at the
table, our mother having struggled vainly through some
soup and a fresh tomato, and excused herself to rest, and
Bean off for the evening.

'What kind of father? You haven't even been able to
name him.'

*'I am a bastard, too; I love bastards: I am a bastard begot,
bastard instructed, bastard in mind, bastard in valour, in every
thing illegitimate,'* Cordy said. Which was mostly patently
untrue, but we had always loved that line.

'And the father has responsibilities,' our father said as
though she had not spoken. 'You may feel you can give
the child what it needs emotionally, but what about finan-
cially? He should be held accountable for that, at least.'

'I don't want his money,' Cordy said.

'Wanting and needing are two different things, Cordelia.

288

I am a fool, and full of poverty.' He moved his silverware, setting his fork and knife across the plate, handles at four o'clock. Cordy, waitstaff instincts kicking in, wondered if this was a signal for her to clear. She stayed put.

'I'm not a baby anymore, Daddy,' she said, thereby managing both to support and undercut her point with just one sentence.

Our father only harrumphed. 'Do you even know who the father is?'

Cordy thought of the painter. He had spoken little to her, asked her for less, and in the end, she had gone to him, one of the few times that, in sharing her body, she had still felt she possessed it. Why did the thought of naming him feel like a betrayal? 'It doesn't matter,' Cordy said.

Our father slammed his hand on the table. The silverware jumped, chattered against china. 'Goddammit, Cordy, stop being so irresponsible.'

Cordy looked up at him, mirror to mirror. *'Why speaks my father so ungently?'* she asked. Oh, Miranda, our father's undoing. Shakespeare is full of fathers who will not let their daughters go, who desire to protect them, to keep them young, virginal, owned. But none melts our father's heart so as Prospero and Miranda, the release from the prison of Eden. He looked at her, waiting, and Cordy's heart leaped. It was the first time since she'd told us of her pregnancy that she felt like he might actually hear her.

'I have made a million mistakes,' Cordy said, staring down at the table. 'I've been a child. I've allowed you – I've begged you to support me.' She paused, looking up at him, searching his dark eyes for a sign to allow her to go on. He nodded, and Cordy nodded back and continued.

'I've been running for seven years, trying to make myself into someone special, someone important. I've fallen for men just so they would hurt me, and shied away from the ones who would help me.' She clenched her fingers into fists, loosened them again, spreading her palms flat against the table. 'But I came home because I was done. Not because you asked me to. Because I was tired of spinning in circles. So the baby isn't a new leaf. It's part of the leaf I already turned over.' She looked up at him again, her speech finished. He was sitting, his arms folded across his chest, his glasses slipping down his nose so he looked at her over the rims as though he were teaching one of his classes.

Our father sat silent for a long time. In class, he often did the same thing, listening to a student's comment and then staying silent, holding it in his mind like a crystal, watching the light hit it from different angles before replying. The habit took some students time to get used to, those seemingly awkward pauses, but they grew to appreciate it, taking it as the compliment it was that he would so carefully consider their words, this Great Man who could have felled their ideas with one verbal blow. 'You cannot support a child on what you make at the Beanery,' he said. 'And you don't have insurance.'

Bean nodded. 'I know. I'm working on that.'

'And you'll live here?'

'I don't have to. There's the apartment above the Beanery. Dan usually rents it to college kids, but he said I can have it if I want.'

'Your mother wants you to live here. I think she wants to have a baby around, but I don't know if it will be good for her. Babies . . . You get so little sleep.'

'She'll be finished with the treatments by then,' Cordy said. 'And it might make her feel better. I think it makes her feel like she has something to look forward to. But I haven't decided yet.'

He stood, clearing his dishes, rinsing them slowly, deliberately, setting them in the dishwasher. He held his hands along the rim of the sink and stared out the window, the palest breath of light allowing him to see out before the glass became a mirror in the darkness. 'Why do you make it so hard for yourself, Cordelia? Why can you girls never choose the easy way?'

'I don't know,' Cordelia said sadly.

When Cordy turned the conversation – the argument, really – over in her mind that night, her cheeks flushed with chagrin. Rubbing angrily at the red stains of embarrassment, she tried to stop herself from saying aloud the words that sounded so childish to her now. An apartment above the Beanery. A leaf she had already turned over.

How did he have this power to make her sound so young, so silly? Those words that sounded so strong in her mind and her heart fell from her lips like jump-rope rhymes. Staring out into the garden, she blew sharply against the glass. He was right. She wasn't prepared. She couldn't do this – couldn't take care of a baby when she was such a baby herself.

It hardly seemed like a surprise when she heard a car in the driveway and then a soft knock at the door, a muffled tap in the sleeping house. She pulled herself from the window seat and opened the front door to find Max, the friend who had dropped her off in the middle of the night when she'd first come home. His hair fell over his forehead in greasy strings, and he wore a T-shirt studded with holes over a long-sleeved shirt and a pair of threadbare cargo shorts. It seemed to her that it had been years since the last time they'd seen each other, and Cordy felt inexplicably relieved at the sight of him.

'Cordy,' he said with a quick jerk of his head. 'I could use a place to stay.'

She hesitated, standing there in the doorway, the night's heat wrapping itself around her. Max needed a shower – she could smell the road on him: unwashed clothes and gasoline spilled on his shoes from the last time he'd filled up, the remnants of coffee and cigarettes on his breath. A rush of memories came at her so hard she had to wrap her hand around the door handle to keep from stepping backward. That was where she should be. On the road. Free. Where no one judged and no one questioned and no one ever thought about tomorrow.

'I could use a ride,' she replied.

Bean was grateful for the instinct that had told her to keep a couple of good outfits back from the consignment shop, even if it meant that many more hours of Story Time in the children's room to pay off her debts. She had something important to do that day and she wasn't doing it without the armor of good clothes.

She dressed carefully, the way she always had in New York, and had done less and less of since she was here, letting the layers of artifice she'd shellacked over herself peel away each day. She straightened her hair until it lay smooth, used every brush in her makeup kit, and finally nodded at herself in the mirror, satisfied.

It was sad how eagerly Edward leaped from his chair in the living room when she knocked on the front door, watching him through the front window. She felt suddenly, magnanimously, sorry for him, how horribly lonely it must have been to have Lila and the kids away for so long, how hard it was to watch youth and your looks drifting into the realm of memory, how he worked to hold himself up to standards he'd adopted long ago – which books to read, which wine to drink, which music to listen to – when he could have thrown it all aside and been who he wanted to be.

'I was hoping you'd come by tonight,' he said, reaching for her. 'It's been too long.' He went to kiss her, but she stepped aside and his mouth only brushed against her hair, thick with perfume.

'I can't stay, Edward. I just came by to say I'm sorry.'

'Nothing to be sorry for,' he said. He went to kiss her again, his breath heavy with wine, and she let him get close, let herself feel his warmth one more time before she stepped away again.

'What's going on?' he asked.

Bean clasped her hands in front of her waist. 'I can't do this anymore, Edward. We have to end it.'

He looked surprised, then shocked. He reached out for her hand, took it in his. 'Don't be silly. We don't have to end it. We'll have to be a little more careful, of course . . .' His smile turned into a leer, and her mood soured. The very thought of being with him revolted her now, and the idea of sneaking around behind Lila's back, sending him home to his children with the taste of her on his lips, made her want to cry.

'No, Edward. It's over. We should never have done this in the first place. God, I think about Lila and I just . . .' She thought of the picture of Lila on the refrigerator and felt sick and angry. She turned away, looking at the blankness of the wall behind the door.

'I don't want to talk about Lila.'

'You don't want to talk about her?' Bean nearly shouted, turning back to him. She paused, composed herself. 'We have to talk about her. You are married to her. And she loves you. I can't imagine why, but she does. And you should be on your knees every night thanking God that she puts up with you, that you have anyone who loves you enough to promise to put up with your bullshit 'til death do you part. We should all be so lucky.'

Edward was wide-eyed and speechless. Bean's palms were sweating, and she could feel herself breathing as though she'd run a lap.

293

'Goodbye, Edward,' she said, and turned on her (couture) heels and walked out the door, feeling like, for maybe the first time in her life, she'd done something completely right.

While Cordy had packed her bags, Max had showered and eaten approximately half of the contents of the refrigerator, and then they had left, Cordy behind the wheel, her belly brushing its fake fur cover.

They spent the night in an empty, anonymous house, Cordy sleeping on a racked-out couch that pressed its frame urgently into her back. When she awoke coffee-shop early, she wandered the house, no different from a hundred others she'd slept in before. At some point it would have been inherited upon the death of a parent, and taken over by some slacker with only the mildest of intentions to update the tired décor. But then the furniture began to swell with the bodies of friends just passing through, and the refrigerator filled with beer instead of food, and the screened porch was speckled with the tiny ends of hand-rolled cigarettes, and it became a way station instead of a home, and it just wasn't worth fighting anymore. And though Cordy had certainly been grateful for houses like this time and time again, they always left her feeling bleak and a little empty, as though she were walking away from a mewling stray kitten.

And then they drove to a festival in a park miles from anywhere she knew, another of a million attempts to re-create Woodstock with a cast too self-conscious to stage an effective revival. Cordy was sitting in a tent with Max and some of his friends, and trying hard to remember what it was she had hated enough about Barnwell to have forced her here. She should be at her shift at the Beanery right now, she thought, and the idea of that place made her ache with longing – the smell of the

294

coffee, the clatter of silverware, the way the sound rose and fell during the day from sleepy early risers to the bubble of the lunch crowd to the purr of afternoon lingerers. Had she really fallen madly in love . . . with a coffee shop?

Cordy sighed and leaned back against a pile of backpacks in the corner, resting her hand on her belly, stroking it slowly. No matter how much she loved the Beanery, it wasn't hers anymore. She'd blown that by taking off. She looked over at Max, who was staring at her stomach intently.

'You're pregnant,' Max observed.

This brilliant thought had taken him over a day to assemble.

'It happens,' Cordy said.

'Not to me,' Max said vaguely. Cordy wondered whether he meant that literally, that he was somehow surprised that he had never been pregnant or just that he had never had the pleasure of knocking someone up.

'So are you on the kick again?' he asked. A boy – he was a boy, really, lanky and red-eyed, with patchy stubble on his cheeks – stumbled into the tent and collapsed on one of the sleeping bags in the back, promptly falling asleep with his leg draped unceremoniously over Cordelia's thighs like a disobedient lapdog.

She hadn't heard that phrase in a while. People had all sorts of names for that world, where you rolled from town to town like tumbleweeds, following bands, following dreams, following lovers, following stars. But Max had always called it being 'on the kick', given his penchant for getting kicked out of places for minor issues like refusing to pay his hotel bill.

'I don't know,' Cordy said. Suddenly the tent felt close and hot, the sunshine through the red nylon making Max's hollow cheeks glow in an eerie trace of veins and blood.

'I need . . .' She pushed the boy's leg roughly off her own, stood up and opened the tent flap to emerge into the air.

The stage was far away, beyond a small copse of trees that hid the campsite's restrooms and showers, and the music was only a dull blur of thumps and shouting. A group of people played hacky sack by a cluster of tents and camp chairs. A young woman near a battered RV was rinsing laundry under a spigot. Her blond dreadlocked hair tangled down her back, looking thick and dirty in the fading afternoon light. Behind her, a toddler wobbled unsteadily around a broken camp chair. Cordy's fist opened and closed.

The woman looked up at Cordy, her face wearing the mask of a woman twenty years older. Cordy's hand went to her own throat, stroking the bones gently. She could do it. She could raise a child on the kick, bring it up on the open road and bands and starlight campfires in the desert. It would grow up open-minded and free, a leaf on the wind.

And she would look like that woman, untethered and exhausted. And the baby would never know the map of a bedroom ceiling the way she knew hers. And her milk would dry up on the thin and inconsistent food of the road. And Cordy would not feel Dan's warm and grounding arms around her, and we would not know our niece or nephew, and our father would not murmur sonnets to his grandchild, and the baby would never know what it meant to hate Barnwell so deeply that she couldn't help but return to it.

The band finished a song, the crowd cheered. The hacky sack players gave up and wandered back toward the stage and Cordy drifted after them, pulled in their wake. The field was massive, hemmed in on each side by tidy municipal fencing, and inside its boundaries a teeming rush of people, so many bodies in motion. *Witness this army of such mass and charge.*

In that field was her past, a blur of sight and sound, a flood of experiences all designed to keep out the world, not to embrace it. Inside her body was her future, her family, all that would hold her in. Her stomach twisted slightly in guilt as she thought of us back home, wondering where she was, assuming the worst, assuming the truth.

But if she went back right now – if she could find someone to drive her all night – maybe we'd forgive. Maybe we'd forget. Maybe we'd understand.

Maybe we'd believe that this time the change was for real.

Cordy rushed back to the tent to get her things.

She couldn't have known that at that moment we were hardly thinking of her at all.

TWENTY

When Bean got home after work, our father was standing at the front door like a dog begging to be let out. He and our mother had long ago begun a tradition of pre-prandial walks, the most our mother could ever be expected to adhere to a schedule. He might come home from the office late in the afternoon and she would leave her dinner preparations (and us, once we were old enough), and the two of them would wander the sidewalks of the town. And despite the fact that our mother could no longer participate, he persisted in this tradition.

'Your mother's resting,' he said, by way of greeting, and walked out of the door into the cooling evening.

But when Bean walked upstairs to change, she heard a strange gasping sound coming from our parents' room. Her heels spun gunshots as she ran to their door and opened it. Our mother was definitely not resting. She was bent strangely, as though she had been interrupted while getting off the bed, her back arched, one leg stretched out, hovering above the floor. She lay on one bent arm that was shaking with the effort, and her eyes were wild as her other hand reached for Bean.

'Mom!' Bean shouted, rushing toward her. 'What the hell is going on?' She was looking for blood, for vomit, for anything, but all she could hear was the dangerous rasp of our mother's breathing, and all she could see was the jerking, flailing motions of her limbs. Bean pushed her back against the pillows, tugging the bent arm out from under her. Our mother gasped for breath and tried to sit up again.

'Jesus,' Bean said. 'Rose!' she screamed. Her voice echoed in the empty house. She opened her mouth to call for Rose again, and then realized her error. Rose wasn't here. Rose wasn't going to rescue her. Not this time.

She grabbed the phone off the table and dialed. Our mother's breathing had slowed, but was still rough and wheezing, her eyes wide, the circles beneath them dark against her shockingly white skin.

'I need an ambulance!' Bean shouted into the phone when someone answered. She ran to the window and shoved it open. 'Daddy!' she shouted. He couldn't have walked that far. And then she shouted again, half into the phone and half into the night, as our mother shook behind her, 'I need an ambulance!'

Bean was completely furious.

How was it possible that Rose was not here right now? This was absolutely 100 percent Rose's kind of emergency. This was completely the place where Rose would shine. Where she could climb right up on her martyr's cross and talk about how she'd saved our mother's life and wasn't it so lucky that she had been there?

And where the hell had Cordy gone? No one had seen her since a few nights before, when our father had run into a slovenly refugee helping himself to leftover chicken, which he was eating directly from a plate in the refrigerator. Had she finally decided that we were right, that she had no business raising a child, and taken off on the winds that had blown her here?

Here is a measure of how upset Bean was: she didn't even notice how handsome the doctor sitting beside her on the waiting room chair was. She didn't even glance at his perfectly tousled hair, didn't even purse her lips temptingly at the gleam of his white teeth, didn't even watch his broad hands smoothing his white coat as he sat down.

Or maybe this was a measure of how much she had changed, after all, somehow, and finally.

There had been a clot, in our mother's arm, or maybe her leg, and worsened by the enforced disuse of her bed rest, by the chemotherapy, by the radiation, it had broken off and traveled into her lungs. Perhaps the doctors had told our parents that it was something to guard against, but between our father's mind being eternally on the book in his hand and our mother's mind being perpetually . . . well, elsewhere . . . they hadn't told us. And while they swore it was nearly impossible to predict, shouldn't we have known?

But we wouldn't have heard it anyway, would we? With all of us wrapped up in our own private traumas, we weren't any good to anyone. Not even our mother.

So it had crept through her veins and into her lungs, which is what had left her wheezing so desperately. And she was going to be okay, she was going to be okay, the handsome doctor said this many times, and Bean nodded agreeably each time he said this, but they were going to keep her for a little while. And we could go home and come back for visiting hours tomorrow.

But our father, of course, set up shop in an uncomfortable chair in our mother's room, so Bean went home alone.

Where Cordy was waiting.

300

'Holy crap, Bean, what's going on?' she asked, when Bean came in, slamming the door behind her. 'Where is everyone?'

'Where the hell were you?' Bean asked. She stalked to the refrigerator and flung open the door. Cordy had been curled up on the sofa, but she padded after Bean into the kitchen.

Cordy hesitated. 'I just went . . . out. With some friends.'

'Going out lasts for a few hours, Cordy. Not days. What'd you do, hit the road and then chicken out?'

Cordy's back stiffened. 'I didn't . . .' she said, but she couldn't finish the sentence.

'Well, you picked a hell of a time to disappear. Mom's in the hospital.' Bean fluttered her fingers impotently at the food in front of her and then closed the door.

'What's wrong?' Cordy asked, and her voice cracked a little. This was the time she had chosen to leave. Excellent work, as usual.

'A blood clot ended up in her lungs. Crack nursing staff that we are, we somehow completely failed to notice this until she nearly asphyxiated tonight. So good on us, right? How was your trip?' Bean picked a pitcher of iced tea off the windowsill and poured herself a glass.

'Is she going to be okay?'

'No, I left her at the morgue. She's going to be fine, you moron. Dad's staying with her, and I'll go back to visit her tomorrow.'

'I'll come, too,' Cordy said.

'Don't put yourself out,' Bean said, slamming the glass down, the tea leaping dangerously close to the edges and then receding like a tide.

'I'm glad you were here.'

'Oh, me too. Thrilled. Lucky me.' Bean turned toward the cabinets for a moment and took a drink and then turned back to Cordy so quickly the liquid splashed on

301

the bodice of her dress, leaving a dark stain across a bright red poppy. 'Cordy, where the hell have you been? You can't just take off like that and not tell anyone. What if I hadn't been home?'

'Someone would have been there,' Cordy said, pulling the sleeves of her sweatshirt down over her hands.

'Who? Dad was out for his walk, Rose is in England! We can't just keep covering for you, Cordy. There's not going to be someone to pick up after you for the rest of your life!'

Cordy, who was pulling into the fabric that covered her like a turtle, shot back sharply, 'You're giving me advice, Bean? If you hadn't been home, where would you have been? In bed with your married lover? Like I'm supposed to give you a medal that you weren't fucking him right at the time that Mom needed help?'

'I broke it off with him,' Bean spat, steely.

'Then it just would have been someone else,' Cordy said quietly, and they froze for a moment, Bean because it was so true, and Cordy because she had never said anything quite so cruel before.

'You're in no condition to go casting moral aspersions on anyone,' Bean said, and placed her glass in the sink. 'Now I have the infinite pleasure of calling Rose and telling her the news. Unless you'd like to do the honors.'

Cordy worried the sleeves of her sweatshirt against her fingers. 'If you want me to.'

'Don't be an idiot. You weren't even here,' Bean said, and flounced off to phone Rose.

When the phone rang in that strange, double-toned way Rose was sure she would never get used to, she sprang into wakefulness with a gasp. Jonathan rolled over sleepily and answered it. 'Hello?' he asked, and Rose could hear the mumbled pitch of Bean's voice. 'No, it's okay. Is everything okay?' A pause. 'She's right here. Hang on.'

302

'What's wrong?' Rose asked, clutching the phone in her hand.

'Charming to speak to you, too,' Bean said dryly. Her voice echoed tinnily in Rose's ear. 'I see England hasn't improved your manners any.'

'Shut up, Bean. It's five in the morning here – you wouldn't be calling if there weren't something wrong. What's going on? Is it Mom?' Rose was already standing, fumbling for her clothes, which she had uncharacteristically left scattered on the floor. The phone cord scraped across Jonathan's nose and he pulled on it, forcing Rose back onto the bed.

Bean sighed loudly, as though it were Rose who had interrupted her sleep. 'Yeah, Mom's in the hospital.'

'What?' Rose shrieked. Jonathan leaned over and put his hand on her bare thigh, the warmth of his skin shocking. 'I'm gone for a few days and she's in the hospital? What happened?'

Bean explained quietly, patiently. Rose was nearly panting, her teeth gritted hard, scraping against each other as she wrapped her fingers in the sheets. Why was this happening when she was over here? She should be the one taking care of a crisis. She would have known what to do, whom to call for help, how to talk to the doctors. There was no way Bean and Cordy could be managing things half as well as she would have.

'What's the number of the hospital?' she asked. She snapped her fingers at Jonathan, who rolled over and then back, producing a pad and pen where she jotted down the number. 'Okay. Call me if anything changes.' She walked over to Jonathan's side of the bed to hang up and then began to dial again, but Jonathan put his hand on her wrist.

'She's okay, right?'

'That's what Bean says, but I want to hear it from the doctor. Would you let me dial?'

'No,' Jonathan said. He kept his hand on hers and reached out with the other to take the receiver, putting it back in the cradle. He pulled her down so she was sitting on the edge of the bed beside him. 'It's the middle of the night there. Let them sleep. You can talk to the doctor in the morning.'

Rose looked at him, his hair sleep-rumpled, his eyes tired. 'But what if . . .'

Jonathan smiled, slipped his hands over her palms and then lifted them to his lips and kissed each one in turn. 'You can't control everything from three thousand miles away, Rose. Let them take care of things.'

'I won't be able to sleep if I don't talk to someone there.'

'Then we'll stay awake together,' he said, and pulled her down beside him, tucking her body under his arm and kissing her forehead softly as the dawn broke around them and the old city stirred.

When Cordy and Bean awoke in the morning, the house was like an empty pea pod, and they rattled around inside, always seeming to be in each other's way, despite the unaccustomed space.

Bean had to go open the library, so Cordy was left to go to the hospital herself. She dropped Bean off at work and drove alone, the windows open, the radio blaring futilely into the rush of air. Her trip with Max seemed a lifetime ago, and the motion of the wheels over the pavement stirred no wanderlust inside her.

You might think that it was Rose who had the strongest moral compass of all of us, but we believe that this is actually Cordy's gift. Rose's beliefs are cold and hard, and suffer no sympathy for humanity. But Cordy both knows right from wrong and understands that they are not inflex-ible ideals, that people compromise for the sake of war, and love, and pain, and that they are simply doing what they must.

'I'm here to see my mother,' Cordy said at the front desk, and showed her ID and signed her name.

'Third floor west,' the receptionist said, and Cordy clipped the proffered badge to her shirt and stepped into the elevator.

It was precisely because of her sympathetic scruples that Cordy felt so guilty for having left when she did. Oh, she had made a brave show of it to Bean, and while she knew that it was all a coincidence, a terrible, horrible coincidence, that her run and our mother's fall would come so close together, she could not shake her sadness.

The light of day on her flight of fancy dulled the romance and pulled away the glitter to reveal the irresponsibility at its core. And this more than our father's letters made her resolute – that she would stay, grow roots, be still. Not because there was anything wrong with the life she had lived, but because it was time to face the reasons she had been living it.

'Good morning,' she said, dropping a kiss on our mother's hairline. 'How are you feeling?'

'Better,' she said, though her voice was rough and her eyes tired. 'Where's Bean?'

'Work,' Cordy said.

'The doctor should be by soon. I was hoping she'd be here to talk to him, since Rose isn't here,' our mother said. She glanced over at our father, but he was reading, stroking his beard thoughtfully, pushing his fingers through the bristles of salt-and-pepper.

'I can do it,' Cordy said. She reached into her bag and produced, after only a moment of rummaging, a tiny bound book and a pen. She held them up and smiled. 'See? All ready for class.'

Our father humphed from behind his book.

'Where'd you go, Cordy?' our mother asked, holding out her hand. Cordy walked over and took it.

'I had to go away for a while,' she said. 'But I came back. I'm better off here.'

Waiting, after Jonathan left for work, was torture. Rose puttered around his tiny flat, organizing, picking up her book and then putting it down again after staring, uncomprehending, at the pages. She called the airline to find out how she could change her ticket, and shuddered slightly when the agent quoted her a price for a new one leaving that night.

She looked at the clock over and over again, calculating the time difference, waiting until it was late enough to call. When she did, our father answered.

'Rosalind!' he said, and there was that same surprise in his tone, as though he had forgotten her existence completely. *'What news from Oxford? Hold those justs and triumphs?'*

'It's fine, Dad. Bean called me. How's Mom? I called the airline and I can come back tonight.'

'Don't be silly. Your mother is fine. We just met with the doctor and she'll be going home tomorrow. Gave us a great raft of information, but Cordelia's got that well in hand.'

'Cordy?' Rose asked, the shock in her tone unchecked.

'Nay, stare not, masters: it is true, indeed. Bianca is working, but she'll be home tonight, and Cordelia will take care of us quite well. How is Jonathan?'

'Fine,' Rose said. This was insane. Was he really saying that Bean – and *Cordy,* of all people? – were going to keep things running smoothly at home? 'It's not a problem for me to come, Dad. I haven't really even unpacked.'

'Rosalind, calm yourself. We are fine. *Nought shall go ill; The man shall have his mare again, and all shall be well.*

Your mother and I appreciate your concern, but she is not in danger – we have Bianca to thank for that – and we will be happier if we know you are with Jonathan.'

Rose wanted to object again, opened her mouth even, but then just nodded. 'Okay,' she said, her determined drive cooling. 'Let me talk to Cordy.'

'Hel-*lo*,' Cordy answered the phone. 'We're fine. Stop worrying.'

'How do you know I'm worrying?'

'Because this isn't the first time I've met you,' Cordy said. 'I talked to the doctor. I wrote everything down. You can obsess over it when you come back.'

'Are you sure you don't need me?' Rose asked, and though she tried to sound determined and responsible, her voice was pitched and keening. She cleared her throat.

'We are going to be just fine. I have to hang up – the phone's attached to the bed and the nurse is trying to get in here. Okay? Have fun! Send us a postcard!' There was a series of clatters and some murmuring as Cordy fumbled to hang up the phone, and then the line went dead.

On her end, Rose slammed down the receiver but kept her hand on it, as though she were expecting – hoping – it would ring again. It stayed frustratingly silent.

So this was it, then. She'd been replaced. Bean and Cordy were going to be the ones to put everything right. She thought of herself sweeping around the living room at home, putting bookmarks in the books to save their spines, dusting the lampshade, pushing everyone out the door to get to church on time. Apparently we could have done it without her all along.

She threw her things into a backpack and left the confines of the small rooms without a plan. It was nearly noon and the streets were swollen with tourists. A tour group passed in front of her, the tour guide holding a closed umbrella high like a lantern. At the back of the crowd, two women in kitten heels struggled along the stone street, the tiny points of their shoes slipping into the worn cracks between the stones. Rose looked down at her sensible, heavy walking shoes and pushed ahead.

So she was useless, then. We only wanted her if we were feeling too lazy to do what we were apparently perfectly capable of.

If only we'd been there to talk to her, to soothe those fears, to tell her that no, we could not have done it without her all those years, it was only now, only after all we had been through, only because we had seen her managing things that we could step in and take up the reins, do our part. That what Jonathan had said was right – people could change.

That maybe the time was ripe for her to change, too.

Or maybe she would figure that out for herself.

Rose strode down street after street, twisting into backways, residential corners hidden behind the colleges, stomping angrily along the sidewalks. People passed in a blur. She ignored the newsstands, the headlines written in thick marker on sheets of paper, always the same mysteriously tidy handwriting, screeching at her.

A tiny alley spit her out onto the High Street, flooded with people. She struggled through the traffic. The sidewalks clogged with a collision of nations who drove, and therefore walked, on different sides of the pavement. Her feet beat a tattoo as she turned things over in her mind. If she'd been home, if Jonathan hadn't been offered this job, if . . . if . . . if . . .

In front of Carfax Tower, ninety-nine steps to the top, she paused. A school group scampered ahead of her, following a tiny National Trust guide inside. She paid the fee and then stepped into the darkness. It wasn't until she had started the climb that she could feel her heart flickering inside her chest, and went immediately into the measured breathing that kept the pounding in her head quiet. Far above her, the children emerged onto the rooftop; above the traffic and the chatter of a thousand languages she could hear them calling to each other, teasing as they leaned dizzily over the edge.

What if she couldn't make it to the top? What if she passed out? She didn't even have Jonathan's office number with her, and then they wouldn't be able to get ahold of him until he got home. . . .

At that moment, she hated herself. A couple of backpackers, scruffy and road-weary, edged by her. She hated her body for its vulnerability, for the way it exposed her fears and her anxiety in the vivid tattoo of her heart. She hated herself for not pushing harder, not fighting against our genetics to become strong and taut, like Bean. She hated herself for standing in this city of beauty, with the world swirling around her, shivers of energy running through her veins, and allowing her legs to stand locked beneath her. Her conversation with our mother came back to her, the gentle wistful nostalgia in our mother's eyes for what might have been, oh, if only she had chosen differently. Rose could see a million of those moments in her own life, a million turns she could have taken, a million moments when she could have stepped on the accelerator instead of the brake.

And why couldn't this be a moment, Rose? Why couldn't this be your moment, like Cordy taking the road home instead of the one that led away, or Bean closing the door on Edward?

Why can't you let it go?

What if there was no what if?

In the darkness, she climbed, the stone walls cool and damp around her, shutting out the bright heat of the day. Her heart pounded, her feet echoed against the emptiness – the students had spilled out, shrieking and joyous, before

309

she had summoned the courage to enter – and her thighs shook with the effort. She pressed on, breathing deeply, counting the steps in sets of three as she breathed in and out.

And then, joyful, elated, exhausted, she burst out into the open air, the sounds of the street below filtering up to her, the breeze blowing stronger, and she spun around, the door laid open behind her. She climbed up the wide steps to the highest riser and looked out on her domain. Below, cars and buses hummed on the same busy streets, pedestrians strode, meandered, bicyclists spun by. In the distance, the spires of the colleges, the peaked stone roofs, the gentle slope of faraway hills, green as memory. She caught her breath, her throat rubbed raw, and laughed.

Oh, if we had only been there with her, only been able to see the smile on her face, watch her look out over what she had conquered, see the pure pleasure gracing her body, her arms sprinkled with sweat. But had we been with her, it would have spoiled the moment. She would have gone only because we had made her. Or to look out for us. Or she might have stayed behind while we ran off and did something foolish, our tether to the ground. We had not realized, until that moment, how much Rose gave up for us, and it was up to her to reach down to the ground and untie herself in order to float free into the sky.

The afternoon spilled blue and cloudless over the city. Rose came down from the tower, slightly misted with sweat, and darted into a pub, where she ordered a Coronation Chicken sandwich and a half-pint of hard cider and watched the people going by. When she finished, she admired the tiny half-pint glass, its perfect miniature proportions. She couldn't have explained why she was so charmed by, why she was so drawn to it, and she certainly couldn't have explained what she did. Lifting the glass to her lips, Rose drained the last drops and then slipped the tiny thing into her bag. As she left the pub, her backpack cradled in her arms like a baby, protecting her booty, her heart pounded madly. But this was not the same wild heartbeat of fear – this was a strange feeling of exaltation, the thrill of a roller coaster, and as she hustled away from the pub, the glass shaking gently in her bag, she couldn't help but laugh out loud, sending her unexpected happiness out into the wild air.

Crunching down a path of gravel, she saw a collection of people standing on the impossibly green grass, moving slowly, pulling their limbs as if through honey. Rose recognized it as a tai chi class, and it brought back the delicate feelings of peace she had felt when she had first started yoga. The instructor was dressed in white, the loose legs of her pants fluttering in the breeze as she stepped wide with a calculated movement, bringing her arms up and over in a delicate arc, and held for just a moment.

It was the most beautiful thing Rose had ever seen.

As though her body were no longer her own, she felt herself drawn toward the group, and when she stood in the back, at the end of their ranks, she dropped her backpack and slipped off her sandals and stepped into the motion flawlessly. Far away, the gentle hum of cars, of people. Here, only the wind and the sun on her bare arms and the quiet sound of her own breathing. They moved together, the movements of the students barely discernible from that of the teacher. Rose could feel the muscles in her legs stretching, the gentle quake of her shoulder muscles as she held out her arms, and she looked up into the wide expanse of sky and felt, for the first time in a long, long time, like she could fly.

TWENTY-ONE

In *All's Well That Ends Well,* Helena, by curing the king with one of her deceased father's potions, shows she is the heir to his talent. Or at least to his stock of potions. Did it bother our father that none of us was the heir to his? That after all those bedtime stories, plots thinly disguised, actual plays when we grew older, the amateur dramatics, the Pilgrimage, the notes left, the required recitations, the naming, for pity's sake, none of us had fallen for the Bard as he had?

We are, in fact, grateful for it, not only because to follow in his footsteps, bearing his name, would have been both foolish and repeatedly painful, but because we do not want that kind of mania. And yet we have inherited it anyway, in tiny drops, his one obsession spread thin over the three of us. Rose's passion for order. Bean's for notice. Cordy's for meaning. Are we not, in our own ways, just as tied to our quests as he to his? And are we not the fools in the situation, as at least his quest has the promise of some small remuneration?

Bean clicked up the pebbled stepping-stones toward Mrs Landrige's door. At the end of the day she could smell the must of the books on her clothes, and her hands had gone dry from touching paper, no matter how much lotion she used. At first the quiet had seemed claustrophobic. Upon her move to New York, she had been constantly aware of the sound. Even with the windows closed, the city hummed outside. Conversations, cars, sirens and crashes, horns, construction. She slept poorly for months until it became part of her, until she had to listen consciously to hear the cacophony. And now, back in the middle of nowhere, the stillness seemed alien.

The silence surrounding her forced her to confront things, to page through the history she had written for herself. It had changed nothing for her except to calm the rush of pain that followed when she remembered.

'Come in!' Mrs Landrige called when she rang the bell. Bean smiled to herself. This was the safety of a small town; the open invitation to all, no locks, no barred windows, no alarm systems.

Bean entered. We had never visited her house when we were little. Like schoolchildren think of their teachers, we presumed that when we left the library, she winked out of existence, flickering back like an image on a television set when we saw her at church, or went back for more books.

Inside, it was dim and warm. Mrs Landrige sat on an overstuffed sofa, plump and full as she was delicate and slender. Her feet were raised on a hassock, and a walker stood by the arm. A wicker bike basket festooned with plastic flowers hung over the front of the metal bars, and inside Bean could see a neatly folded newspaper.

'Bianca,' Mrs Landrige said. 'I'm so glad you could come. You'll pardon me if I don't get up.' She gave a small smile, her cheeks like withered apples.

'How are you?' Bean asked. Mrs Landrige wore a dress, as always, but had forgone the panty hose for slippers.

313

Her hair was done and she wore lipstick, creasing in the wrinkles on her lips.

The old woman waved a hand. 'Old,' she said. 'Go into the kitchen and get us some lemonade. There are some cookies in there, too. Dr Crandall brought them by, so I don't guarantee they're not poisoned, but we'll give them a try.'

Doing as directed, Bean walked back into the hallway and turned into the kitchen. The sink was empty of dishes, but clean glasses and plates and a few groceries lined the counter. Above the door, a cuckoo clock ticked anxiously, waiting for its big moment. Bean pulled a glass pitcher from the door of the refrigerator and poured two glasses, unwrapped the plate of cookies and carried everything back into the living room.

'Thank you. I'll tell you one thing, this hip replacement is a pain in the ass,' Mrs Landrige said.

Bean, shocked by her language, laughed in surprise. 'Or a pain in the hip,' she said.

'That too. Here, put these down so I can reach them.' She leaned forward, wincing slightly, and took a cookie and the glass Bean handed her. 'Thank you. Coaster, please,' she said as Bean put her glass down on the table, and Bean's hand shot out instantly and rescued it before the beads of water could drip onto the wood. 'Now,' Mrs Landrige said when they were settled, Bean perched on the edge of an armchair that threatened to swallow her. 'I suppose you're wondering why I called you here today.' She said this without a trace of irony, as though she were the President, calling an audience with a member of her Cabinet.

'Okay,' Bean said. She took a bite of the cookie, and genteelly put it down. Poisoned it was not. Unfortunately, neither was it tasty.

'I'm not coming back to the library,' Mrs Landrige said.

314

She put up her hand, palm out, though Bean hadn't objected. 'I've decided it's time for me to retire. Recovering from this surgery is going to take months, and I'm no longer interested in spending whatever diminishing time I have left behind a desk.'

'I'm sorry to hear that,' Bean said, unsure of the proper response. 'Or I'm happy for you. I'm not entirely sure which I should be.'

'A little bit of both, probably. But that's not why you're here. You're here because I want you to take over. You're going to be Barnwell's new permanent librarian.'

Bean nearly choked on her lemonade. This was a stopgap. A temporary thing. She wasn't going to, forgive her for saying it, become Mrs Landrige, whose only love did not seem to be her long-deceased husband but that aging little building and all the wonders inside it. After all, Bean was going to San Francisco. Or somewhere. Wasn't she? 'I can't do that,' she said.

'Nonsense,' Mrs Landrige said. She sipped at her lemonade, pinky up, leaving a faint lipstick mark on the glass. 'You've been doing a wonderful job, everyone says so.'

Ah, the spies of Barnwell. Among the locals, at least, you never could keep anything secret for longer than it took the cashiers at the Barnwell Market to bag your groceries. 'But I don't have the right degree. They'll never hire me.'

Leaning forward, Mrs Landrige deposited her glass, still half full, neatly in the exact center of a coaster. 'These cookies are dreadful,' she said evenly, taking another bite. 'Don't worry about the board. You'll have to get your master's eventually, of course, but they'll hire who I tell them to hire. And it's going to be you.'

'But I wasn't going to stay,' Bean said weakly.

Mrs Landrige narrowed her eyes, looked at Bean long

315

and hard. Bean felt uncomfortable, shifted her eyes around the room. On the mantel, there was a picture of a couple emerging from St Mark's after their wedding. The picture was old and faded, the bride's face going as white as her gown. Was it Mrs Landrige and the mysterious Mr? She wanted to get up and look, but Mrs Landrige's gaze held her in the chair, pinned like a bug on the cardboard display she had made for Coop's science fair one year. 'Back to New York?' Mrs Landrige asked finally.

'Maybe. Maybe California. But not Barnwell – the plan wasn't to stay in Barnwell.'

There was another long pause. 'You're not going back to New York,' Mrs Landrige said finally. 'You might have needed to go to begin with, but you're not going back. I saw it the minute you came back into the library. You weren't happy there, and something there bit you bad enough to make you need to come home. You want to go back and get bitten again?' Her voice had a hard edge we had never heard before, used to the quiet library voice of our youth. It slid across Bean's skin, sharp and hard as a blade.

'I was happy there,' Bean said, and she felt herself wanting to cry. The truth stared her down, cruel and cold.

'If you had been happy there, you wouldn't have come back,' Mrs Landrige said. Bean looked back at her and saw, though her voice was still stony, her eyes were soft.

A tear slipped out and plopped, fat and translucent, onto Bean's hand.

'So what's it going to be, Bianca? Are you going to go back somewhere that hurt you? Or are you going to stay in the place that loves you and make a life for yourself?'

There is nothing that is not beautiful about bread. The way it grows, from tiny grains, from bowls on the counter, from yeast blooming in a measuring cup like swampy islands. The way it fills a room, a house, a building, with its inimitable smells at every stage of the process. The way it swells, submits to a firmly applied fist and contracts, swells again; the way it stretches and expands upon kneading, the warm, supple feel of it against skin. The sight of a warm roll on a table, the taste – sweet, sour, yeasty on the tongue.

At night, when she could not sleep, Cordy rose, paced the halls in her nightgown (*Nor heaven nor earth have been at peace to-night*) and slipped into the kitchen, sylph-like, where she drew out bowls, the flour sifter, ingredients, left the butter softening on the windowsill as she flitted around. She made the dough, kneading it in rhythm with the ticking clock, the only sound in the oppressive still of the night. Retreating into the living room, she read on the sofa until she fell asleep, waking in the dark, as if summoned by the bread itself, to punch it down and then doze again. We woke that summer, nearly every morning it seemed, to the smell of dough drifting through the house like visible smoke.

She made bread out of anything, any recipe, and the miracle of our mother's kitchen, where cabinets opened and disgorged everything she needed – currants, almonds, wheat bran, brandy – kept her well supplied. After dinner, we would find her in the living room, poring over one of the cookbooks from the shelves in the pantry, their pages bearing stains like birthmarks, crusts of flour and splashes of sauce.

That morning, Cordy showed up at the Beanery with a basket of bread covered in kitchen towels. Still warm, so Continental. Three loaves: all braided. She had become more and more fascinated with the look of bread: learning the skill of painting on the egg wash to add color, experimenting with placement in the pan to allow for just the

317

right shape, using cookie cutters to add patterns to the tops. But braided breads drew her the most; learning to make the strips even, to tie them together so they would merge as one and yet remain distinct when baked. That day she had made Santa Lucia, glazed and sticky in its crown; chocolate in long loaves, dark as pumpernickel; and Hawaiian, light and sweet, the secrets the potato flakes in the dough and crushed macadamia nuts coating each strand.

Inside, the Beanery already smelled of rich coffee, and when she peeled back the towel, she inhaled the combined scents, twisting into the air, twining together like the dough. 'Damn, that smells good,' Dan said, emerging from the office.

Cordy started. 'You scared me. I thought Ian was opening today.'

'Ian,' Dan said, waving his hand. 'He's not so reliable in the morning. Did you make those?'

'I did. Would you like some?'

'Are you kidding? Fire it up.' He brought out two mugs, wide as soup bowls, and poured coffee into his, set a tea bag to steep for her. 'What are these?'

Cordy pulled out a cutting board, plates, a serrated knife, and gestured with the blade to each loaf, naming it. 'I've been baking a lot lately,' she said. 'Nesting, maybe.'

Dan nodded. They had spoken so little since that afternoon in the kitchen, their conversations heavy in their emptiness. She set a plate in front of him, three slender slices, and he broke a piece off of each in turn, letting the flavors settle on his tongue.

'These are incredible.' Dan patted his stomach. 'This used to be a beer belly,' he said sadly. 'Now it's just a belly.'

'Dan?'

He looked up, and their eyes locked. He said nothing.

'I'm sorry if I was cruel to you. I was so . . .'

'Cordy,' he said, his voice soft, balmy. 'It's okay.'

'No. It's not. I was just scared and I snapped at you, and I'm sorry. You were right. I have no plan. I was just trying to . . . Well, I knew what my father would say, and I guess I thought it would hurt less if I said it first.'

'So you've told him.'

Cordy nodded. 'Reaction as expected. He's coming around, I guess. Because of Mom, mostly. I think it's kind of important to her in an odd way — because she's sick, you know.'

'Yeah, I ran into Bean at the library the other day. We talked about it a little.' If Cordy saw this as a betrayal, she said nothing. 'Bean, man. Did you ever think Bean would be a librarian?'

'Not in a million billion years,' Cordy said, and they grinned at each other, and Bean would have completely forgiven this joke at her expense, for the way it retied the bond between them.

'You know it doesn't matter to me, right?' Dan said. He reached out, put his hand on hers, warm. Stilling.

'What doesn't?'

'The baby. I mean, here's the way I see it. I'd have no problem dating a woman who had a kid, you know? So what's the difference in dating a woman who's pregnant?'

Cordy could think of about a million and nine differences, actually. Hormones, sex, breastfeeding, the constant visible reminder of another man's presence inside her body . . . but on the other hand, no. No, there was no difference at all.

'I had a crush on Bean, you know? Back in school?' He shook his head, a lock of hair fell into his eyes. He pushed it back. 'For about five minutes. I think it was because she could drink me under the table. But she – Bean's just raw, you know? Sheer force of will. Sharp edges, like she'll cut you if you get too close.' He paused.

'But you're different, Cordy. I mean, after you came to Barney, I totally saw why Bean had such a complex about you.'

'About me?'

His eyebrows shot up. 'Totally. Like everything she could do, you could do better. She hated it. And people love Bean, you know that. But not like they love you. Bean's like a whirlwind, she bowls you over because there's just so much of her. But you, you're like this silent meteor. You come in, and you make a crater, and you don't even try. I used to watch you walking around campus and you were like a fairy princess. Like your feet never touched the ground.'

The bell on the front door tinkled. Dan jumped up off the stool. His cheekbones stood high and red, his ears burning. Cordy could hardly move.

'Mrs O!' Dan said, as though the intimacy of the conversation between them had never been. It had, though, Cordy could feel it in the air, wrapped around them like a spiderweb, glossy, but substantial.

'Good morning, Daniel. Hello, Cordelia. Oooh, are these macadamia nuts?' She pointed at the bread.

'Cordy made it. Try some,' Daniel said, looking over his shoulder as he flicked down the tab on one of the urns, pouring coffee into a cardboard cup for her.

'I decidedly should not,' Mrs O said, but Cordy had already whisked out a tiny plastic container and was putting slices in it for her to take away. 'So are you going to be a baker now?' she asked.

'No,' Cordy said. 'Well, maybe. Why don't you tell me how you like those and then we'll decide?'

Mrs O'Connell nodded, as though she had known her

opinion would be the key, paid, and headed out the door. She was always early, but her arrival meant there would be more customers soon. Even in summer, there was a slow drift in the morning as employees headed in to work, or some of the retired farmers came in to drink coffee and read the paper to each other, lost without the rhythm of their chores.

'I never knew,' Cordy said, turning back to Dan as though they had not been interrupted. She reached toward him, their hands connecting, fingers interlacing, and he pulled her to him, kissed her, the gentle scratch of stubble against her chin, one hand in her hair, the other at her waist, and the swell of her belly between them, soft and yielding against everything about him. And if her back pressed up against one of the urns, if the hot steel burned a tiny line into her back, well. She didn't notice at all.

Jonathan came home from the lab to find Rose cooking happily over the tiny stove in his rooms, the scent of spices thick in the air. 'Did you know they call zucchini something different here? Courgettes.' She lifted her head for his kiss, and smiled at the thrill his mouth still brought to hers. How many times had they kissed now? Hundreds? Thousands? Rose knew that no relationship can sustain the passion of newness, the energy coursing through a million cells at the same time at the touch of a new lover, but it brought her great satisfaction that she still anticipated his touch, did not take it for granted in the fade of comfort.

'Those wacky English people,' he said. He wound a finger around a loose tendril of hair that had curled in the steam rising from a pot on the stove and let it spring back. 'Why can't they learn to speak American?'

Rose lifted a wooden spoon, mock threatening. 'How

was your day? Any breakthroughs bound to win the Nobel Prize?'

'Sadly, not yet. We'll have to keep hoping to win the lottery instead. You're cheerful. How was your day?' He sat on the arm of a faded, heavy armchair and pulled off his shoes, wiggling his toes inside dark socks.

'Glorious,' Rose said. 'I climbed Carfax Tower.'

'Quite a view, isn't it? I told you this city was beautiful.'

'It was completely worth it. I nearly didn't go – I thought the stairs would kill me, but I made it just fine.'

'You don't have enough faith in yourself,' Jonathan said. He padded up behind her, slipped his arms around her waist and kissed the back of her neck. 'What else did you do?'

'I crashed a tai chi class at Magdalen College. And I stole one of those little pint glasses from a pub. And I don't feel guilty.'

Jonathan laughed and squeezed her against him. 'Don't bother. People do it all the time. I always knew there was a rebel hiding inside you.'

'I want to stay, Jonathan,' she said. She turned a burner down on the stove and then slipped out of his arms so she could face him. 'I can see myself loving it here.'

He went back to the arm of the chair and perched there, his arms crossed over his chest. His face was serious, thoughtful. Like our father, he was prone to quiet consideration, and he let Rose speak.

'I feel . . . different here. Like, not myself. Freer.'

Jonathan nodded. 'It might not stay that way forever. The new becomes commonplace.'

Rose wrinkled her eyebrows and thrust out her bottom lip for a moment. 'I don't think it's like that, really. I mean, maybe it is, somewhat. But I was thinking today, maybe it all happens for a reason. Maybe the reason Cordy and Bean came home was to send me a message.'

'What do you think the message is?'

'That it was okay to leave. It's like for years I've drawn this mental circle with Barnwell at the center of it. I never felt I could go beyond the edges, that someone had to be there – oh, it's silly.'

'No, finish.'

'Like I was the thing holding the family together, and if I left it would all fall apart. And with Cordy and Bean gone, it was like my parents were mine again, like my sisters didn't exist and I was an only child, so they needed me. But now that they've come back, and they handled this thing with Mom – it's like they didn't even need me and . . .'

'You're free to go,' Jonathan finished for her.

'And maybe I should. Maybe all these things that have been holding me there weren't the problem. Maybe they were a symptom of staying too long. A signal that I should have broken free years ago.'

She turned back to the stove and lifted a lid of a pot and then, satisfied, removed it from the burner and fished out a vegetable steamer, tiny perfect rounds of zucchini going translucent in the heat. When she turned back, Jonathan was sitting in the chair, his feet up on the coffee table.

'I suppose the only nagging question is what you would do while you're here. I don't know that you're cut out to do nothing.'

Rose joined him, sitting across from him in an equally battered armchair. 'No, I don't think I am either. But I've never let myself do nothing, either. When I used to look at my mother and wonder how she filled her days, maybe I was being too judgmental. Because if she . . .' Rose caught herself before she said the words that, however unlikely, we had not dared speak aloud for fear of tempting fate. 'Because if she doesn't make it, I don't think she'll be wishing she'd spent more days at work. I think she'll be wishing she'd spent more days in the garden, or reading, or taking walks with our father.'

Jonathan nodded. 'Are you still worried about the wedding?'

'Not worried, no. Neither of us really wants anything big anyway, do we?' She tilted her head at him.

'I can't think of anything that would give me less pleasure,' Jonathan said, smiling. Funny, she thought, that this man who delivered such excellent papers to audiences at conferences, who spoke with such ease in front of his classroom, would be so unwilling to be the center of attention.

'And I wouldn't have to wear one of those awful dresses,' she laughed, holding the back of her hand to her forehead, mock drama. 'We don't have to do a big thing at Barnwell. At the end of the day, we'll be married anyway, and that's all that matters, right?'

'See? Blessings abound,' he said. 'Now come over here, little hen, and give us a kiss.'

Rose climbed out of her chair and delicately sat in Jonathan's lap, but then he threw his arms around her and pulled her close, and her tension dissolved into laughter. Were we wondering what it was that she so loved about him and he about her? Perhaps this: he had the singular ability to knock down her carefully bricked defenses, which was a compliment to them both, and the secret of their love.

That night, as they lay in bed side by side, she contemplated the shadow of the moon as it washed slowly across the duvet. It was, as the poets say, the same moon that shone over us back home.

Well, here she was. And she could continue to exist in

the darkness of her fear, or she could tend and coax the seed of hope inside her. And Rose, with all the determined ferocity that had made us so proud as she had axed and hacked her way through the battles of academia, chose hope. She had changed the wide Midwestern sky for the blue and gray of England, but the place did not matter. It mattered only that she took the step from safety and trusted she would soar.

The letter seemed heavy in Bean's hands. She turned it over, checked the seal on the envelope, turned it back. She had enclosed a check and a note – how she had agonized over the wording of that brief missive.

Too little payment for so great a debt, both literally and figuratively. A check had arrived from the consignment shop, more than she had expected, but less than she needed. And a cheery note from the owner, letting her know that if she had anything else to sell, she should feel free to bring it by! As if. She had taken nearly everything she owned, the pound of flesh for her sins. Looking in the closet now was dispiriting, the way the hangers moved easily out of the way as she flipped through the now-meager possibilities. She had quit smoking, not because she had any fear for her own mortality, but because it saved her money she could send in the next check. But she would not complain.

Bean checked herself in the mirror over the hall table, flipped her hair over her shoulders. We did not know what secret she used to keep it so sweetly straight in the curling humidity. Animal sacrifices, perhaps. She gauged her appearance critically, slipped her bag over her shoulder. She had nearly emptied her bank account with this check. Not that she needed the money; it had been ages since she had spent anything. The secret to a wealthy life: living with your parents at the age of thirty. The thought left a bitter, metallic taste in her mouth.

'Well then, to work?' our father asked, emerging from the kitchen. He was in uniform – short-sleeved shirt, tie, shapeless gray slacks. This is what he had worn for time immemorial, whether he was going to the office or not, and this is what he would wear until the end of days.

'I'm going by the post office first,' Bean said.

'I'll walk with you,' our father said. 'Just a moment.'

Bean sighed, the letter weighing even heavier in her purse. Just a letter to some friends in the city. Just a note to say hello, don't sue me, here's some money, I'll get the rest to you as soon as I can. You know, the usual.

She heard his footsteps on the stairs and they headed out the door together, the squeak of the spring on the screen door announcing their departure. Outside, sprinklers hissed in the grass of a neighbor's yard. She could hear some kids playing baseball, the crack of a bat and the shouts as they ran. Woven through it all, the hum of the insects and the peaceful morning greetings of the birds. The sounds of home.

'I hear you're considering taking over for Mrs Landrige,' our father said, without preamble. He slipped his hands in his pockets, his steps slow and measured beside hers. Had he always moved so slowly, or was this the evolution of age? *The sixth age shifts into the lean and slippered pantaloon, with spectacles on nose and pouch on side . . .*

'Considering it,' Bean said. 'I'd have to go back to school.'

He nodded. 'Not so difficult.' Though the streets were silent, Bean looked left, right, checking for traffic before they crossed the street. She could feel the burgeoning heat of the pavement through the thin soles of her shoes.

'Do you think I should?'

Surprised, our father looked over at her, pulling his gaze away from the ground. 'You were always so determined to get out of here,' he said. 'I'll admit to wondering why you came back.' He raised a hand, greeting Mrs Wallace, who was out front gardening. She nodded back, dug her trowel into the ground, loosened a clump of wide-mouthed petunias.

'I don't really want to talk about it,' she said. 'I just . . . It wasn't right for me anymore.'

'The lottery of my destiny bars me the right of voluntary choosing,' he said. 'Portia.'

Sometimes we had the overwhelming urge to grab our father by the shoulders and shake him until the meaning of his obtuse quotations fell from his mouth like loosened teeth.

'Mmm,' she said instead.

'Having you home would be nice,' he said. 'Not that you need to stay with us permanently, though it has been tremendously helpful having you girls here right now. And to become a librarian! Not what we might have expected, but that may be better. A good, steady occupation. *Knowing I loved my books, he furnish'd me from mine own library with volumes . . .'*

'*. . . that I prize above my dukedom,'* Bean finished with him.

He smiled at that. '*Tempest* was always one of your favorites.'

'The lost island. Like *Swiss Family Robinson.'*

'You've always been so good with people, Bianca. This might be an opportunity for you. Though I fear you will find the social life of Barnwell . . . lacking.'

'I suppose I'm too old to date those handsome college boys,' she mused. They turned onto Main, strolled past the Beanery. Inside, Bean could see Cordy's braid bouncing as she worked behind the counter. Something inside her withered. Is this what we'd become? We'd inherited our father's genius to squander it on food service and academic peripateticism and librarianship? Life wasn't supposed to

327

be like this. Life was supposed to be martinis and slick advertising campaigns in slick offices with slick men by her side. Not stupid, frumpy Barnwell and its narrow alley of possibilities.

'Have you talked to Father Aidan?' he asked. She clenched her teeth. Had he heard? Aidan wouldn't have said anything, would he?

'Sure,' she said, coolly. 'We've hung out a few times.'

'No, I mean as a priest.'

Bean paused to look in the window of the hardware store. Long ago, before we can remember, really, it had been a dress shop, with windows designed to display the finest couture Barnwell had to offer. Deliciously, however, the couple who had bought the store had taken it upon themselves to outfit the windows as though their wares were as fine as any Paris fashions. Here they had created a garden, with tools and supplies standing in for the greenery: a bouquet of hammers in a vase, work gloves blooming in neat rows, labeled with seed packets.

'I asked him to look out for you,' he said.

Bean turned, the postmodern garden forgotten. 'You what?' Her voice bounced across the empty street, fluttering against the plate glass windows. 'What am I, five?' She felt her mouth pulling down as her mind worked a thousand hours overtime, recasting every moment with Aidan in the light of this new information. So he hadn't . . . he'd never . . .

'Holy shit,' she said. She had never misjudged anything as egregiously as she'd misjudged his interest in her. There hadn't been any interest at all. None. Only textbook psychological transference and the pity of a man who didn't actually care about her at all, who was just doing his job. She burned at the thought of how he must think of her. 'What did you tell him?' Her voice cracked, hysterical.

'It's not like that, Bianca. Just that you had come back

suddenly and seemed hurt somehow, and you might need someone to talk to. Someone who wasn't us.' This last bit sounded melancholy, a sadly accepting smile directed at the ground. Bean turned and walked away, ahead, shame pressing her shoulders forward until they ached.

In front of the post office, she pulled the envelope out of her purse and opened the slot, dropping it in, listening to the whisper of paper against paper as it fell down. The collected earnings of the library, the sale of that awful car, and all the glittering artifice of her life in the city. Thinking she could go back now was foolish. She hadn't the wardrobe for it anymore.

Our father came up beside her and they stared into the empty darkness of the mailbox's maw for a moment. 'Barnwell's not such a bad life. I know you always wanted more, but I wonder what you believe you need so badly that you cannot find here.' She let the door of the mailbox clang shut and they walked on. 'You were the youngest to start walking, you know that? Rose crawled so well it took her ages to decide she wanted to walk, and Cordy was content when we carried her. But you, you went straight from lying down to running at full tilt. I think of that every time I read *Midsummer. My legs can keep no pace with my desires.'*

They were nearing the library. Our father, walking on the outside of the sidewalk, ducked under the branch of an elm tree that swept its leafy arm across the sidewalk as though taking a bow. 'If you felt lonely in the midst of all those people, Bianca, there is nothing to be lost by letting the crowd go. The question to ask is what will satisfy you? What will bring you peace? And perhaps the answer to those is in asking yourself when you were last happy.

'The city, that burning desire you had for freedom, what has it brought you? *Sound and fury, signifying nothing.*

You may think I'm a foolish old man, gone to seed already, but we chose this life, your mother and I, and we have never regretted it. *I earn what I eat, get what I wear, owe no man hate, envy no man's happiness, glad of other men's good.* We won't hold you back, Bianca, but we want you to find happiness.'

His St Crispin's Day speech ended, they came to a stop in front of the library's wide stone steps. Bean turned to our father, put her hand on his arm, and gave him a kiss on the cheek, the tickle of his beard so familiar on her lips. 'Thank you, Dad,' she said. He nodded, stood with his hands still in his pockets, his shoulders hunched forward, and watched her until she got inside. Then he walked away, staring up at the sky, and Bean watched him go. She wanted to hate him for asking Aidan to look after her, for making her an object of misfortune instead of beauty. But hard as it was to admit, she knew he had done it out of love.

The knowledge hit her then, hard: someday he would be gone. His inscrutable quoting, his missives by mail, his old-fashioned fashions, the protective web he and our mother had spun around themselves, would evaporate, and leaving us only with the memories of his thoughtful smile, his distance, and a lifetime of work that would have mattered most to a man dead four centuries ago. She let the door shut, placed her head against the cool glass, and prayed.

TWENTY-TWO

There had been no response from New York, but they had cashed the check. Bean didn't know what she had expected. A thank-you for the return of something that had been theirs to begin with? A reprimand for the money still owed?

She had thought an installment would make it easier, but it had only intensified the disgust she felt with herself. At night, she ran. She waited until the heat of the day had cooled, until it was dark and she could weave in and out between the streetlights, running for blocks beside darkened houses. Occasionally she would pass children playing on a lawn, chasing fireflies, playing hide-and-go-seek, aided by the shadows of trees, and she would cut to the other side of the street. People passed by, walking their dogs, and Bean nodded, breathing hard as though she were a force of nature, constantly propelled forward, incapable of stopping to chat. She ran until she was drenched with sweat, until squeezing her braid released a trickle of cold liquid down her back, until her legs screamed with every step, and only then would she turn around and go home.

Running was the only place she could forget. New York

had always held distractions. Other people, new places. It was the best place to hide whatever was dark inside her. But here there was no escape. She ran and she ran, desperate to put distance between her heart and her head, memories of Edward, of Lila, of the thousand ways she'd been ready to make a fool of herself for Aidan, when he hadn't cared for her, when she hadn't known him at all.

Tears mingled with the sweat on her face. Every pounding beat was a recrimination, a tom-tom reminding her of what she had lost – her life in New York, her self-respect, her job, her ability to see her future. Now she saw nothing. Before it had seemed like there were a million possibilities in front of her, a thousand paths not taken stretching out into the years ahead, and now one path led straight ahead, and she was terrified to take it because it meant she could no longer hide from the fact that she was terrifyingly, completely normal.

One night, pounding her way back home, feet crying out for relief, she ran smack into Aidan. Of all the people to see at that moment, he would have been her last choice.

They were only a few blocks from the church, and he was heading in that direction, hands in his pockets, strolling slowly along the darkened streets. Her head hit his chest, her ankle twisted, and he grabbed her shoulders to steady himself as much as her.

'Bianca?' he asked. 'Are you okay?'

She looked up at him. They stood, as the great movie director of our lives would have it, in the pool of a streetlight, and she knew her face was swollen from crying and beaded with sweat. She was soaked; her shirt clung to her back, her shorts plastered to her thighs with sweat. Her breathing was quick and raspy.

332

'Bianca?' he said again, and she noticed that he always seemed to use her full name. It sounded so strange coming from his mouth, hearing it in this town, where everyone knew who she was, everyone knew she was just Bean Andreas, trouble with a capital T. 'What's wrong?'

She looked up at him, at the gold in his hair and the light in his eyes, and she said, 'I need to make a confession.' And then she burst into tears, and he pulled her close and held her as her tears and her sweat soaked his shirt and it didn't even occur to her that after all this time, she was in his arms.

Confession in our faith is not like the cinematic Catholic version, with tiny boxes and screens. It is not even required, as the weekly service contains a penance in a tidy, practical, terribly English way. But we know that when she was ready, confession was the only word that seemed right. Maybe it was a slow accretion of change over time, maybe it was simple desperation, but something inside her was shifting, and the thousand ways she'd violated things she cared about felt not just amoral but like a cruel middle finger to everything good she had been given in the world.

They went into the rectory, which looked like the house of an old man – apparently Father Cooke had not taken much with him when he went to Arizona, and Aidan hadn't bothered with redecorating. Aidan disappeared into the kitchen, and emerged with a glass of ice water and a bag of frozen peas for her foot – she wondered if he actually intended to eat them ever or if these vegetables were designated for sports injuries only – and they sat in the living room.

'What's going on, Bianca?' he asked, when she had downed the glass of water and was holding the bag awkwardly against her ankle, which was already swelling nicely.

Bean started crying again. He reached out and took her hand, and when she quieted, he stood. 'I'll be right back,' he said, taking her empty glass. He returned with it filled, a box of tissues in his other hand. He put both down beside her, and she plucked a tissue from the box and blew her nose inelegantly.

'Take your time,' he said. 'I'm in no hurry.' He moved his chair closer to Bean's, so they sat face-to-face, and nodded at her.

She took a moment, struggling to breathe through the aftermath of the tears, trying to compose herself. 'I'm a thief,' Bean blurted out finally. 'I'm a thief and a liar and a whore and I don't deserve anything good.'

'Bean,' he said. She was crying hard now, she couldn't look at him. 'Bean,' he said again. He rested his hand on her arm. 'You're none of those things. You're human. You're fallible. You make mistakes. And when we make mistakes, we repent. And when we repent, we can be forgiven anything.'

'Anything,' she whispered, and it was an echo, not a question. Her voice caught, she breathed as though she were laughing, four long, shuddering breaths. 'I got fired,' she said. 'I got fired because I stole money from my job.'

She told him the whole story. She cried, she looked away, she cried again. She held the glass of water in her lap, drinking from it when her mouth went dry from talking. He said nothing, listened, leaning forward, elbows resting on his thighs, not pulling his eyes from her. She couldn't meet his gaze for longer than a few seconds. She told more than she had told us, she talked about the men she had seduced, the lies she had told, to herself and to others, and how she saw the lights of her future winking out in front of her like candles being extinguished at the end of the service. She told him about Dr Manning, about the way she had fallen into his arms because it made the pain of remembering so much duller, and the ways in which she had so conveniently forgotten his wife and his children and ignored the fact that what should have been pleasurable felt more and more like pain each time. She even told him that she'd wanted Aidan to fall in love with her, certain that the good in him would cancel out the darkness in her, and he did not judge her for any of this. She did not care anymore about impressing him; she only wanted to be free of the weight aching in her chest.

'And what now?' he asked. She had finished, leaned back in her chair. The bag of peas lay sweating on the table, and her voice had grown hoarse from talking.

Bean stared off into the middle distance, barely watching the ticking arms of a clock on the mantel. 'Now, I don't know. Now, I'm just trying to keep from dragging myself down into this swamp.'

'The financial debt?'

'I'm paying it back. Little by little, sure, but I don't think they cared about the money. I just think they wanted me gone.' She picked up a tissue and blew her nose hard.

'And the men?'

'What men? I've slept with one man since I've been home, and that's over. It was over before it began. I can't take it back, but the only person I hurt there would be hurt even more if she knew. And it's not likely to happen again, anyway. You're the only available man I know in Barnwell who's not sleeping with my little sister, and, well . . .' She didn't have to finish the sentence.

'I'm not asking about potential. I'm asking what you'll do when you're faced with that temptation again.'

Bean looked up at him boldly. 'I'm not becoming a born-again virgin.'

Aidan laughed, leaning back in his chair to match her posture. 'That's not what I mean. I'm supposed to tell you premarital sex is strictly forbidden, but I can operate on the level of the prescriptive and the probable at the same time. But what I'm worried about is what all these things mean. The stealing, the promiscuity, the lying' – and oh, how it hurt to hear him say those words, to apply them to her – 'they're all part of a bigger pattern. What's the pattern, Bean?'

'That I'm an idiot?'

He said nothing. She looked at him, looked away. Her eyes were red and raw, and she felt bone-achingly tired. Her ankle throbbed, her stomach hurt. 'Can I have another glass of water?'

He nodded, took the glass, and walked through the archway leading to the dining room. Bean leaned her head against the back of the chair and exhaled, long and slow. When he came back, she sipped carefully at the glass of water he put in front of her. He still said nothing, waiting for her.

'Rose was always the smartest. She can do anything. She can be a total bitch, and everything always has to be perfect, but she can make it that way, so it doesn't matter. She's got a PhD. She's got this perfect fiancé. She can speak in public and talk about all these things I couldn't understand in a million years, and she makes me feel stupid all the time. And Cordy . . . everyone loves her. You know, she flits around and drops out of college and goes and lives like a backpacker for years, and everyone's like, "Wow, that's so adventurous." She comes home pregnant, and she doesn't even know who the father is, and Dan falls in love with her and everyone's lining up to throw her a baby shower. She's everyone's favorite.'

Aidan looked puzzled for a minute. 'But we're talking about you, Bean. We're not talking about Rose and Cordy.'

'But don't you get it?' Bean threw her hands up in the air and leaned forward. 'There is no me. There's only Rose and Cordy. I'm just like this speed bump in the middle, slowing everyone down because I keep fucking up. And I'm not smart like Rose or cute like Cordy, so I don't get that free pass. No one's throwing me a parade.'

Aidan mulled this for a moment. 'So if Rose is the smart one, and Cordy is the cute one, what are you?'

'I'm nothing.'

Aidan frowned at her. Bean met his gaze, belligerent. He leaned back in his chair and looked out the window, where the barest edge showed the dark of the night beside their reflections. When he spoke again, he did not turn his head, but continued staring into the window as if reading a crystal ball.

'We all have stories we tell ourselves. We tell ourselves we are too fat, or too ugly, or too old, or too foolish. We tell ourselves these stories because they allow us to excuse our actions, and they allow us to pass off the responsibility for things we have done – maybe to something within our control, but anything other than the decisions we have made.'

He leaned forward, and Bean, who had turned away, felt pulled back into his eyes. 'Your story, Bean, is the story of your sisters. And it is past time, I think, for you to stop telling that particular story, and tell the story of yourself. Stop defining yourself in terms of them. You don't just have to exist in the empty spaces they leave. There are times in our lives when we have to realize our past is precisely what it is, and we cannot change it. But we can change the story we tell ourselves about it, and by doing that, we can change the future.'

On the sofa, Bean knotted her hands in her lap and began to cry again.

'You wouldn't have asked to talk to me tonight if you hadn't wanted to change your story, Bean. So what's it going to be?' He held out his hands, palms up.

A very long time passed before she took them.

When our mother came home from the hospital, we put her to bed immediately. We changed her compression bandages, massaged her arms and legs, led her through the exercises they had given us. The radiation was done, the medications were tapering off, but we could not do enough to try to make up for how we had been so wrapped up in ourselves that we had nearly lost her.

After a week or two of our exhaustive caretaking, our mother had had enough. She got out of bed one day, did her physical therapy exercises herself, demanded that Cordy help her shower, and then stalked down to the kitchen, where she and Cordy began to bake bread as though it were an Olympic event.

Cordy and our mother had transformed the kitchen into their workspace. On every available surface, and some unavailable, were bowls of rising dough, cooling breads. The air-conditioning was no match for the heat of the oven, and the still air held the scents of yeast and bitter chocolate in a thick sweat on our skin, unstirred by movement. Our mother had finally recovered her taste buds and her stomach, and Cordy was always hungry. They were in an ecstasy of creation, testing, sampling, trying combinations and recipes and taking pleasure in the rush of discovery.

Bean wandered in and out, complaining they were determined to make her fat, but accepting eagerly the rich, steaming slices they handed her to try. The living room was cooler, so she retreated there, letting the smells tempt her back in mid-chapter, when her mind wandered.

Hands sticky with dough, Cordy was hand-kneading a loaf of heavy gingerbread when she paused, putting her hand to her stomach, where it left a floury handprint on her shirt. 'Mom,' she said.

Our mother was whisking icing, her good wrist spinning expertly inside the bowl, churning the sugar into a sweet froth. 'What?' she asked, not looking up.

'Do you think I'm going to be a good mother?' Cordy asked. She pressed the gingerbread into a pan and then checked the oven. Her hands fluttered to her stomach again.

'I believe you will be an excellent mother.' She poured the icing over a Bundt cake resting on tinfoil, watching it drip and streak its way artistically down the sides.

'You don't think I'm too irresponsible?' Her mouth pulled down, her eyes shaded.

Our mother put down the bowl again and rested her hands on her hips. 'Oh, Cordy, it's so hard for us, you know? You're our baby – all of us. Your father and I – we look at you girls and we don't see the adults. We see the children, the nights awake with you with colic, lost teeth, skinned knees, all those handmade cards. And with you I suppose it's even harder, because you were Rose and Bean's baby, too.' She shook her head, carried the bowl over to the sink where it clattered, the dirty dishes resettling like silt shifting to the bottom of a pond.

'But they're right, aren't they?' Cordy looked around the kitchen, her hands held wide, helpless. 'I've pissed away my whole life.'

'That's Rose talking.'

'Don't be ridiculous. Rose would never say "pissed"',

Bean said, coming in and poking a finger into the icing that had pooled on the tinfoil. Our mother idly smacked her hand away.

'What do you think all those years were for if not for this?' our mother asked. 'We don't just come from the womb bearing our talents. They grow from all the things we learn. And if you hadn't worked at restaurants, or you hadn't learned to throw together meals from whatever you had, you'd never be the kind of cook you are now.'

'Some are born great, some achieve greatness, and some have greatness thrust upon them,' Bean said. 'And some of us couldn't find it with both hands. But we survive.'

'I don't want to be great,' Cordy said. 'You were the one who always wanted to be famous. I just want to be happy.'

Our mother had not heard either of us; she was sitting sidesaddle in one of the chairs by the kitchen table, having moved a loaf of dark wheat from the seat and put it to cool on top of the refrigerator. Her forefinger rested on her chin, Classical. Though the exhaustion had passed, she was still weak, and her skin was both pale and bright, as though she burned a constant fever. 'I've always admired both of you for your resourcefulness,' she said. 'You're fearless. Bean's moving to New York and making her way in what I've always found to be a completely inhospitable city.'

'And you,' Bean said, nodding at Cordy, 'surviving all those years without anything, really, but your hands and your brain. I never could have done it.'

'I couldn't have, either,' our mother said, shaking her head.

Cordy had never considered those years as an achievement. She had, in the days when it was still heady and romantic to her, believed she was a sort of anthropological

340

pioneer, that she was breaking trail and broadening her horizons with each new person she met, each story she heard, but she had never thought of that time as a success. And to hear it from Bean was even more of a surprise.

'That's why you're going to be a good mother,' Bean said, nodding as though she knew whereof she spake. 'Because you're a survivor, Cordy. You'll do what you need to do to get it done.'

'Daddy doesn't think so,' Cordy said sadly.

Our mother cast this thought aside as she brushed a lock of hair from her forehead. 'It's not about you, Cordy, really. Not about your capabilities. Your father is just concerned. He doesn't want it to be difficult for you.'

'That's what he said to me,' Bean said. 'He said he didn't understand why we made it so difficult for ourselves. Why we always chose the hard way.'

'And end up doing nothing,' Cordy said. 'Except Rose.'

Our mother shook her head. 'By whose calculations? You girls are all the same like that. I don't know what we did to give you the idea that you had to be some master in your field by the time you were thirty.'

She might not have known, but we surely did. The idea had come from living in the shadow of our father, in this tiny community where nothing mattered but the life of the mind, when the greatest celebrity came not on the movie screen or the world stage but behind the lectern, in the footnotes of journals.

'I don't really want to be a master in my field,' Bean said. 'But I'd like not to be a complete and total fuckup.'

Here we expected our mother to rebuke Bean for her language, but she didn't. She just smiled indulgently and said, 'Oh, honey, we're all fuckups in our own special ways,' which made Cordy laugh so hard she sat down

341

on the floor in a pile of flour, which caused Bean to laugh so hard she started to cry, and the only thing we wished was that Rose had been there to see the whole thing.

TWENTY-THREE

In the library, Bean hoisted a heavy monitor up onto the circulation desk. She had pushed all of the tools of Mrs Landrige's trade to the side: stamp pads, stamp with tiny rolling digits, tiny pencils shaved to within an inch of their lives, and oh the paper, paper, paper.

Her first order of business as officially knighted, coronated, and installed Barnwell Public Library Librarian (Head of All Matters Library, Cordy called her) had been computerizing the system. Surprisingly, the great town fathers were not only willing, they had set aside money years ago, waiting for the rather Luddite Mrs Landrige to see the technological light. Which had, of course, never happened. So there the funds had sat, and all Bean had to do was ask for them, and lo, she received.

She had just finished aligning the wires, crawling out from under the desk, brushing the dust and burn from her knees, when the door opened and Aidan came in. 'Madam Librarian,' he greeted her with a nod.

'Father Aidan,' she returned with an achingly poor Irish accent. He winced, winked. 'What can we do for you today?'

'Just need a quiet place to work,' he said.

'Saturday procrastination?'

'No, standard-issue weeklong procrastination leading to emergence of Saturday work ethic. Speaking of which, are you on for service next Saturday?'

'I'm in. What are we doing?'

'Driving into Columbus to work at a food bank. Stacking cans, handing out rations. Glamorous and sure to be attended by all the finest paparazzi.'

'Then how could I say no?' Bean tossed her hair and struck a pose.

'I'll call you to set things up. Will Rose be back? We could always use extra people.'

'She might be. But I'm pretty sure most of what she'll be doing when she comes back is packing.' Bean bent down and pressed a button, and the computer whirred to life.

'So she's going, then?'

'Ayup. Odd, isn't it? That she's off to the jet-setting life and I'm consigned to indentured servitude to Barnwell?'

'England will be good for her,' Aidan said. He leaned against the counter, holding his books and papers beside his hip, long fingers curled around the edges. 'She's been long overdue to get the heck out of Dodge. And Barney will be good for you. You'll see.'

'Sure,' Bean said, with a sharp little nod.

'I'll see you in services tomorrow, then?' Aidan asked. He pushed himself back, stood, stepping away.

'Wouldn't miss it for the world,' Bean said. He smiled and sauntered off to the carrels in the back, where he settled down to work. She watched him walk, the easy swing of his gait, his T-shirt hanging from thin shoulders.

She did not want him. Had she ever? It is so easy to look at love when it is over and think it was never real. But there was no dismal residue of disaster to cast a once grand affair into gray, dirty light. There was only the world

344

Bean had come back to, the world of truth and facts and consequences, and if there was less excitement in it, there was also no lingering threat, no fear of discovery and exposure. And with that calm came Bean's solemn accounting of what she had dreamed, and what was.

Aidan was nothing magical. Burned by her own sin, unable to seek absolution anywhere, she had made of his attention the only thing she knew how to understand. And she knew now that despite our father's request to him, Aidan considered her a friend, was happy to have her in his flock, and, perhaps most incredibly, never treated her as though she were less because of what she had told him. He had known at some level, possibly, what she had really needed, and she loved him more for that than she ever could have loved him as a partner.

Besides, she would have died in a relationship without sex.

Shuffling a deck of due date cards absently, she looked out the front doors, to the spread of the tree over the sidewalk, where her father had quoted *As You Like It* to her. Rose's play, really, but no matter. *I earn what I eat, get what I wear, owe no man hate, envy no man's happiness, glad of other men's good.* The words of a poor shepherd, mocked for his simplicity. This was Barney to her, and she had played the clown, finding sin where there was none. Living here had so affected us all, Rose endlessly seeking its comfort, an infant suckling at the breast. Cordy and Bean fighting its inertia, sure the secret to life lay just over the next hill, past the next taxi rank idling smog into the air. But where had it gotten us, this tattoo of our birthplace? We were still the same people, and Cordy and Bean, who had wanted it least of all, come home to roost in the nest.

Bean sat down at the desk and pulled a long drawer of the card catalog over to her. She could do nothing to

345

change Barney, she knew. Turning the blond wood of the card catalog into the binary code of a computer catalog was only cosmetic, would alter nothing at the heart of the town, which would still creep *in this petty pace from day to day to the last syllable of recorded time*, but she could change her place in it. She could leave her mark, pay her debts to man and to God, and someday, anchored in it instead of weighed by it, she would take the part of her that was Barney and spin it out into the world, and this time she would not fail.

As Bean had foreseen, Rose came home with her only thought leaving again. Spare months ago, when she had moved her belongings back into this house, she had knelt on the floor and rolled each of her belongings through her fingers as she unpacked. They seemed different now, heavier, each piece less important. She needed little: clothes, notes for the articles she wanted to research. Good walking shoes (but Rose hadn't, of course, any other kind). Strange how little it all mattered to her now. Rose had always been the worst of us in terms of possessions, though we thanked her for it when we wanted to look at the scrapbooks she had made of our family trips, our shoe boxes full of old papers and notes and art projects. Now she was like Cordy, wanting nothing more to weigh her down than a backpack. When she had sent her letter of resignation, artfully written to convey in the most genteel manner possible that Columbus University could take its job and shove it, a sudden weight had lifted off her shoulders. She would never have to go back to her dingy office and the gray classrooms and the exhausted students. That the lethargy plaguing her since she had set foot on the campus would never wrap its tentacles around her again, that she might even, dare she say it, be happier without that place.

Cordy herself was lying on Rose's bed, covered slightly with the discarded clothes Rose had tossed over her when she refused to move. She was always like this, our Cordy, wanting to be near the action, watching us dress to go out, or following behind us when we did. As teenagers, we had found it grating, but now it was comforting, though Rose did complain about Cordy's inertia, and that she was wrinkling the clothes spread around and over her.

'The clothes going into storage, you mean?' Cordy asked, deliberately rolling back onto a shirt that had fallen off her hip and crushing it under her ever-expanding bottom. Oh, the joys of our metabolism and of pregnancy.

Rose snatched the shirt out from under Cordy and shook it out. 'Yes, those. Unless you're offering to iron them all for me when I get back.'

'You're never coming back,' Cordy said, and then blinked, as if she had not intended to speak.

'Don't be ridiculous. I'll be back at Christmas, and then in August, and anytime Mom needs me.' With a practiced snap of her wrist, she flicked a pair of pants into submission and then rolled them into a tight cylinder, pressing it among the clothes inside her suitcase. She picked up a winter coat, contemplated its length, and then discarded it in favor of another.

'Not here, though. Not Barney.'

Rose stopped and stared at Cordy, who spoke with such cool certainty it made her shiver a little. 'How do you know?'

'I just do,' Cordy said, and then giggled. *'Beware the Ides of March!'*

'That's a possibility,' Rose said, sitting on the edge of the bed to push in a pair of shoes. 'But I imagine I'll get pretty homesick after a while.'

347

'Maybe,' Cordy said. She reached out to Rose's bedside table and picked up a bottle of lotion, squeezed some into her palm and rubbed it in. 'I never was, not really.'

'You're not like me,' Rose said.

Cordy looked at her like a curious squirrel. 'Don't be ridiculous. I'm exactly like you. We're all exactly alike, you know.'

'Sure. In the way that we're completely different. Move,' Rose said, nudging Cordy's leg. Cordy, ever obliging, moved off a neatly rolled row of underwear. Rose picked up the bundles and edged the gaps at the sides of her suitcase with them.

'No, in the way that we're all the same. We all want what Mom and Dad have. We all want to be the favorite, the best-loved, the star of our own movie. And we all want to become something better than Barney, but we won't.' She paused for a moment and then stared at the ceiling, thinking. 'Not that it's a bad thing, you know. Barney's not so bad.'

'I've been telling you that for years,' Rose said.

'You've been telling us that for years because you were scared to leave because you thought we'd forget about you, or that we'd survive without you, and then where would you be? You'd lose the only role you ever had.' Cordy put the bottle of lotion back on the table and turned her head to look at Rose.

Rose stared at our youngest sister. *'My oracle, my prophet,'* she said finally. When in the hell had Cordy ever become so wise?

'My years on the road have taught me much, grass-hopper,' Cordy said, as though Rose had spoken her thought aloud.

Such are the minds of sisters.

EPILOGUE

On Christmas Eve it snowed, a light fall starting in the morning and continuing through the day, the whisper of flakes promising magic and coating the trees with silent beauty. We stayed inside for as long as we could, until the tracing of frost on the windows and the promise of cold snow against our skin drew us out. Enough snow had fallen for the children to go out to Wilson's Hill; we could hear the shouts and shrieks as they sledded down the gentle slope that had seemed so high to us years ago.

'Let's go into the woods,' Cordy said, and headed off, so we were bound to follow. The baby had come early, or the doctors had just been off (our mother assured us this was possible, as Cordy herself had arrived almost a month later than expected), and she was enjoying the new pleasure of her own mobility. She walked, light and quick, along the gathering snow, and we placed our feet in her steps, widening them with our own imprints.

Rose and Jonathan would be married in a week's time, a small ceremony and a small reception, the service at St Mark's, the reception in a restaurant. Celebrating her marriage at Barnwell College had seemed wrong now, an unnecessary return to the past. Bean had chosen the dress, a deep midnight blue that made Rose's eyes glow, her creamy, delicate skin set off by its richness. When Rose had tried it on, she turned and turned in front of the mirror, partly amazed by her own beauty, partly to listen to the delicious rustle it gave with each twirl. Everyone else would be celebrating the end of an old year, the dawn of a new, and we would be celebrating our sister and the man who had captured her heart in the forest of Arden.

'Are you nervous?' Bean asked. She stepped over a fallen log; the moss still showed, burned and brown, through the cover of the snow.

'Not at all,' Rose said. She smiled, her teeth white against the cold apples of her cheeks. 'Isn't that silly? I should be, shouldn't I?'

'Not necessarily. Not if you're sure of what you're doing.'

'I'm sure,' Rose said. And we felt that spoke of more than her relationship with Jonathan. She had come back from England taller, prouder, scented with strength like perfumed oil. An article had been accepted for publication. After the wedding, they would honeymoon out west, where the mountains gave way to the sea, and visit universities or colleges that might want them both after they returned from England. But they held nothing certain but each other, and we saw that for our Rose, this was now enough.

'Ooh, look. They're setting up the Nativity,' Cordy said, pointing toward the church. On the lawn in front, bales of hay and a tiny shed had risen from the white, and figures, wrapped in heavy clothes, moved with crates and boards in their arms. 'Remember when that cow died during the Nativity and no one knew?'

'Ugh. That's so depressing. Do you have to bring it up?' Rose asked.

'Yes,' Cordy said, and trotted off toward the church.

We walked past Father Aidan on the front steps, knocking snow off his boots before he headed back inside, and he raised his arm, waved. 'See you all tonight?' he called. We had always, for as long as even Rose could remember, gone to the candlelight service on Christmas Eve at St Mark's. When we thought of the church, we pictured it like that, bright with holly, the lights down, all rich reds and the waxy cream of candlelight as we – yes, even we – sang hymns to the winter, to the Christ child, to the darkness and the light.

'You know it!' Cordy said. She pointed at him, clicked her fingers. Pow.

'God, Cordy,' Bean said. 'You're so embarrassing.'

'That's my job,' Cordy said, swinging her arms by her side.

We walked back toward home through town, shuttered shops dark behind the swirl of snow. The old-fashioned streetlights had come on in honor of the darkened sky, and they shone twice as bright with the strings of holiday lights wrapped down their posts.

'This is the prettiest time in Barney,' Rose sighed.

'Isn't Oxford pretty at Christmas?' Bean asked. The streets were empty, only a few light footprints rapidly being covered by new snow showed that anyone had passed here at all. In the distance, the central campus quad lay pure and undisturbed.

'Not like this,' Rose said. 'It's wet. And there are these horrible neon lights that totally spoil the image.'

'The Baby Jesus would totally hate that,' Cordy said, straight-faced.

'Rude!' Bean laughed.

'I'm glad you're here,' Cordy told Bean. 'Are you going over to Matthew's later?' Bean had begun dating a single father who lived a few towns over. He was older, his children nearing adolescence, but that was probably best

351

for Bean, who was a great deal happier exchanging makeup tips than changing diapers.

'No,' Bean said. 'He's coming to the service tonight after he drops the kids off at their mom's.'

'Oh, goody!' Cordy said, and thumped her gloved hands together as we turned onto our street. 'It'll be like the whole family's here. Dan's coming over after church. He's a godless heathen, but I think he's up for hot cider and Christmas bread.'

We turned into the wide patch of white covering our driveway, our lawn, our walk. The house looked beautiful, lit up and glowing, the Christmas tree in the front window glittering, warm lights in every window, our parents and Jonathan moving shadows behind the glass.

Inside, Ariel would be waiting for a feeding. Her every feature was the image of Cordy, of us. She was wholly our own. We thrilled at the sight of her tiny, helpless hands grasping at air as Cordy held her to her breast, and with each tiny breath taken, we felt the wonder in the world increase by a thousandfold. Perhaps the only person more infatuated with her was our father, who refused to let her out of his sight, or even his arms, unless she was feeding. If we had thought he preferred Cordy, that predilection paled beside the love he had for Ariel, and her birth had laid to rest any conflict between them.

Inside, our mother, healed and happy, would be turning the kitchen into a hearth, warm and sweet with the scent of dinner, bringing us the promise of her presence, this year and always.

Inside, our father would be rereading the Christmas speech from *Hamlet*, preparing for the toast he would give over dinner.

Some say that ever 'gainst that season comes
Wherein our Saviour's birth is celebrated,

The bird of dawning singeth all night long:
And then, they say, no spirit dares stir abroad;
The nights are wholesome; then no planets strike,
No fairy takes, nor witch hath power to charm,
So hallow'd and so gracious is the time.

Inside, the tree, surrounded with presents, the people we love. Inside, our beds, our memories, our history, our fates, our destinies. Inside, we three. The Weird Sisters. Hand in hand.

EXEUNT.

ACKNOWLEDGMENTS

Enormous thanks . . .

To Amy Einhorn (the BEE, and my BFF), for taking on *The Weird Sisters,* and for the jaw-dropping insights and thought-provoking questions that turned a manuscript into a novel. To Halli Melnitsky, for answering every question I could think up and making me laugh in the process.

To Ivan Held, Leigh Butler, Lance Fitzgerald, Marilyn Ducksworth, Mih-Ho Cha, Katie Grinch, Michelle Malonzo, Kate Stark, Lydia Hirt, Chris Nelson, and the rest of the incredible staff at Amy Einhorn Books/Putnam. Your boundless encouragement and expertise have been invaluable.

To Elizabeth Winick Rubinstein, a tenacious agent, an elegant, funny, and bright woman, a calm and patient presence in the midst of the hurricane – and one heck of an NYC tour guide. I am forever grateful that you said yes. To Rebecca Strauss, Alecia Douglas, and the team at McIntosh & Otis, for your enthusiastic support.

To my early readers: Dyani Galligan, Rebecca Kuhn, Lauren Wilde, Lily McGinley, Jennifer Eckstein Coon, Denice Turner, and Francesca H. Redshaw. Thank you for believing in me.

To the cancer survivors, oncology specialists, and OB/ GYNs who took the time to answer my questions: Darlene McGinley, Susan Westgate, Linda Ross, Cara Leuchtenberger, and Nana Tchabo. Your input was absolutely invaluable. Any remaining errors are completely my own.

To my parents, Bill and Cathy Brown, for making me a reader. It's a gift I can never thank you enough for.

To the teachers who taught and encouraged me to write: Terri Rubin, Ann Scott, Cheryl Wanko, and Steve Almond. And in loving memory of James Andreas, John Kelly, and Don Belton, three professors whose passion and humor inspired me and countless others. We miss you and are blessed to have known you.

To the friends not mentioned elsewhere who have supported me and my writing without fail: Michele Delaney, Amanda Holender, Amy and Rob Schoen, Lissette Diez, Tammy Doll, Alan Newton, Nicole Gellar, Jennifer Chaffin, Wayne Alan Brenner, Holly Fults, Jonathan Segura, Marcela Valdes, and Hanne Blank. I am lucky to have all of you in my life.

ABOUT THE AUTHOR

Eleanor Brown is the youngest of three sisters. She lives in Colorado with her partner, the writer J. C. Hutchins. You can find her online at www.eleanor-brown.com and twitter.com/eleanorwrites